Millionaires' Row

With best wishes –

Kathy Keller

A. J. Baltman

Millionaires' Row

Kathy Keller and A.J. Billman

Authors Choice Press
San Jose New York Lincoln Shanghai

Millionaires' Row

Authors Choice Press
an imprint of iUniverse.com, Inc.

For information address:
iUniverse.com, Inc.
5220 S 16th, Ste. 200
Lincoln, NE 68512
www.iuniverse.com

This is in part a work of fiction. Although inspired by actual events, the names, persons, places, and characters are inventions of the authors. Any resemblance to people living or deceased is purely coincidental.

ISBN: 0-595-18882-6

Printed in the United States of America

INTRODUCTION

In the years following the Civil War, expansion of the industrial revolution in the North and reconstruction efforts in the South created a greater demand for lumber. The invention of new machinery enabled mills to increase production capacity. Thus, the stage was set for a town situated in a valley in North Central Pennsylvania, surrounded by woods abundant in virgin timber, to become the lumber capital of the world. Millionaires were made overnight and, in a relatively short time, the community emerged from a small transportation depot to become an important commercial center.

Central to the community's wealth and success was the creation of the "boom". The boom was a series of piers or stones piled in the middle of the river, set approximately 175 feet apart. On top of the piers sat cribs. Cribs were built from heavy timbers and filled with stones to hold them in place. Big timber or boom sticks, held by cable or heavy iron chains, connected the piers and floated in the water, rising and falling with the level of the water. Logs, each carrying a sawmillís brand, were, then, driven in between the piers and held there by the boom sticks until they could be sorted and sent to the proper mills.

Before the boom, only a few logs at a time could be floated down the river from the lumber camps. The only way to capture the logs was for men in boats to grab hold of them and drag them to shore. The creation of the boom enabled hundreds of logs to be captured at once. This more than doubled the capacity of the mills. At its height, the boom could hold 300 million feet of lumber.

The lumber industry also gave rise to other industries related to lumber that, in turn, led to an enormous expansion of the retail business. By the mid 1880's, the city was the commercial center of North Central Pennsylvania. This city was Williamsport.

While our book draws heavily upon the rich history of this community and of the leaders of the time, the story is fictitious and the characters are not intended to represent real people. Dates and detail were manipulated to suit our story. Thus, we did not use the name Williamsport, but chose, instead, to call the town Rossburg after Michael Ross, the founder of Williamsport.

—-*Kathy Keller & A .J. Billman*

North Central Pennsylvania, 1868

PROLOGUE

Thirty of the town's most prominent businessmen met in secrecy in the back room of the Union Hotel. They included the owner and president of the local bank, the owner of the locally operated railroad, the owners of the larger sawmills, and several lumber-related manufacturers. A cloud of cigar smoke hung heavy over the newly rich of Rossburg.

Cyrus Morgan sat at the head of the table, the recognized leader of the group.

"We are all agreed then," he said. "We must protect our interests against outsiders. It was our vision that brought Rossburg from the backwater transport depot it was to the thriving town that it is today. It is only right that we be the ones to steer its course. What is good for us is good for Rossburg."

"Gentry built the Susquehanna boom. Shouldn't he be a part of this?" asked one of the mill owners. "If it weren't for the boom, we would know only a portion of the wealth we have come to realize."

As a chorus of agreement went around the room, Cyrus Morgan brought the gavel down sharply on the table.

"Gentry isn't one of us," he said curtly. "He lacks our vision. Any other comments?" Morgan looked around the room, his narrowed gaze, discouraging any further debate. "Then, I hereby declare the creation of the Board of Trade, formed on this day, the twenty-first of February in the year Eighteen hundred and sixty-eight. New members may be nominated to the Board only in the event of vacancies and must be admitted by unanimous consent. All in agreement…all opposed…"

There was no opposition. One by one the declared members of Rossburg's newly formed inner circle came forward to sign the charter.

As the last person placed his signature upon the document, Morgan again struck the table with the gavel. "Gentlemen, the iron gate is closed."

March 1877

CHAPTER I

The sun dipped in and out of the clouds throughout much of the morning, so no one took particular notice as the moon stole slowly across the noonday sun to suddenly plunge the cemetery into darkness. Father McKinney paused in the midst of the service and looked up at the sky. The light breeze gathered momentum, turning the air sharply colder, and an uneasiness swept through the mourners.

Mrs. O'Hara shivered and crossed herself. "'Tis an ill wind that blows," she said darkly. "I can feel it in me bones."

Mrs. McInnis scoffed at her friend's superstitious nature. "'Tis only an eclipse. See, 'tis passin' already."

"'Tis an ill omen, I be tellin' ye. Mark me words," said Mrs. O'Hara with the firm set of her chin.

Almost as quickly as it had begun the wind stopped, and a gray light began to filter through the clouds. Calm returned, and the priest quickly concluded the service.

Seventeen-year-old Ian Douglas watched stone-faced as his mother and sister Katherine were laid to rest, oblivious to all that had passed around him. Every nerve ending was drenched in pain, creating a numbing coldness inside of him that he didn't think could ever be warmed. His crippled father sat hunched on a chair, staring vacantly at a spot beyond the grave sites.

It had been a terrible winter…one of the coldest that Ian could remember and reportedly the worst influenza epidemic on record. The image of his mother and sister lying shivering on cots beside the coal stove, fever burning bright in their pale faces, their thin bodies wracked with coughing spasms was an image he knew would never leave him.

As the caskets were lowered into the ground, and the diggers began to fill in the graves, Ian's dazed father was led away. Ian didn't move, seemingly unaware that the service had ended.

Tommy O'Brien and Maven McInnis stood beside him. Since childhood, the three of them and Katherine had been inseparable. They were the "Pine Street Warriors," invincible and strong. No force was great enough to break their bond. They hadn't counted on death.

Tommy put a hand on Ian's shoulder. "Come along, lad. 'Tis time to go home."

"I promised to take care of them," said Ian.

The guilt and pain, so naked in his ragged voice, tore at Maven's heart, and her eyes brimmed with tears.

"Ye did all ye could," she said softly. "'Twas God's will."

Ian looked down at the fresh mounds of dirt. "'Tell that to Mum and Katherine. Tell them it was God's will that the doctors did na come because they were too busy seein' to patients who could pay them. God's will be damned! 'Tis about money an' nothin' else."

"Hush, Ian. 'Tis blasphemy ye speak," said Maven, gently chastising him.

"Tis the truth—blasphemous or not."

Maven looked at Tommy in silent appeal.

"Ian," he said, "this does ye no good. Influenza knows no boundaries rich or poor. Many died. There was nothin' more ye could have done, money or no."

Ian turned and spread his arms wide, his eyes flashing with anger. "Look about ye, Tommy. God lays a gentler hand on them that has."

"Have ye forgotten yer lessons, man?" asked Maven. "Money be the root of all evil."

"If money can provide a better life for them on the Row, how can it be evil for us? Answer me that."

Maven shook her head. "I can na, Ian. I just know 'tis wrong to want too much. 'Tis best to accept one's place in life, to be grateful for the good things and strengthened by the trials. That's the way of it."

"'Tis not my way. 'Twill ne'er be my way."

Maven sighed wearily. "Our lot in life has been cast. Why must ye always fight against it?"

Ian turned a gaze hard and unyielding on her that sent a shiver up her spine. "Hear me well, Maven. I'll not let my past become my future. I will control my lot and none other. I bow to no man, high or low."

"Then I fear 'tis a hard life ye'll be knowin' for sure, Ian Douglas."

The sky darkened again and the wind picked up, this time by nature's hand, and a cold rain began to fall on the remaining three warriors.

CHAPTER 2

If the sun shone over Rossburg, there were those who swore that it shone a little brighter over a wide, tree-shaded street, affectionately and not so affectionately, dubbed Millionaires' Row. The only paved residential road, Fourth Street stretched four blocks in tribute to the eclectic collection of Italian-style villas, Romanesque stone manors, and Victorian mansions.

Cyrus Morgan paced the grounds of his grand estate. Several times he stopped to look off in the direction of the river, his heavy, dark brows drawn together in a deep frown. Each time he took out his gold watch and marked the time, but the hour would be of no consequence today. He turned at the calling of his name. A tall, thin man waved from the veranda, and Morgan quickly crossed the manicured lawn to meet him, moving with an amazing agility for a man of his size and stature.

Arthur Waring smiled pleasantly. "Good morning, Cyrus. I have those papers for you to sign." He pulled out a fine, linen handkerchief and patted his brow. "Going to be another hot one today, though I trust not too uncomfortable for the day's festivities." Waring suddenly noticed that his wealthiest and most powerful client did not look pleased. "Is something wrong, Cyrus? You appear rather upset."

"Of course there is something wrong! Look over there." Morgan jabbed at the horizon with his fist. "What do you see?"

Waring looked in the appointed direction. "Why, I see a clear, blue sky," he said, his brow wrinkled in confusion.

"Exactly! The mills are not in operation today."

Waring breathed a sigh of relief that he was not the source of Morgan's ire. "Independence Day and Christmas are the only two paid holidays of the year, Cyrus. Surely you don't begrudge the mill hands that. The poor bastards work from dawn to dusk six days a week."

"With the freezing of the river and millponds in the winter, we're lucky to be in operation seven months out of the year. Let the workers find another holiday when the mills aren't operating."

"You're a powerful man, Cyrus, but not even you would dare to make such a suggestion. Especially not with labor unrest stirring again in the coal mines and on the railroads."

"Damned agitators. Give 'em an inch and they'll take a foot. They want a shorter work day. Next they'll be wanting a shorter work week."

Arthur Waring shrugged. "Careful, Cyrus, you know how fast uprisings can spread. As your attorney, I would advise you to throw your mill hands a few bones before they decide to go after the meat as well."

Morgan gazed out over the topiary garden. "Someday, these grounds, this house, the lumbermill will all belong to my grandchildren. There will be a Cyrus Morgan the Second sitting at my desk, leading Morgan Mill Yards to greater prominence." His eyes narrowed and his voice turned low with determination. "This is my legacy, Arthur. As God is my witness, I'll crush anyone who dares to threaten it."

*   *   *   *   *   *   *   *

Maven pulled back her thick, auburn hair and caught it loosely in a ribbon at the nape of her neck, then firmly set a straw hat atop her head. She took one last look in the mirror, patted some color into her cheeks and nodded, finally satisfied with her efforts. She knew the boys waited for her at the end of the lane, but she couldn't help that.

She wasn't about to arrive at the town's biggest celebration of the year half put together.

When she stepped onto the porch, she saw Ian wave impatiently to her. As fast as she could, she picked her way to them, lifting her skirts above the drying mud with one hand and juggling a picnic basket with the other. Tommy quickly came forward to take the cumbersome basket from her.

"'Tis a bonny lass ye are today, Maven," he said shyly.

Maven's cheeks, already flushed from the heat, turned a brighter pink. Nobody had ever told her she was pretty, except her mother and father and that didn't count. Parents always thought their daughters were pretty. She considered herself unremarkable, neither homely nor beautiful. A tad this, a tad that but nothing in full measure. She thought her green eyes too large for her face and a fraction wideset, her pink lips too full, and while her nose was straight and well formed, she disliked the way it tipped up at the end. It was beginning to bother her more and more that she was so tall and thin with none of the discernible curves that most girls her age seemed to enjoy.

"A bonnie lass indeed, ay, Ian?"

Maven eagerly sought Ian's eye for some confirmation.

Ian responded with a quick, ineffectual glance and a tone of indifference. "Aye, that ye are, Maven."

The light in Maven's eyes dimmed, and her smile faded. Her nose burned from the tears she was determined to force back.

Tommy nudged her shoulder playfully. "Pay him no mind. He be havin' one of his moods."

Maven managed a weak smile and nodded. She shot Ian a worried glance. Ever since his father's accident at the mill, his manner had sobered, but since the deaths of his sister and mother, the lighter side of him seemed to have disappeared altogether.

Tommy nudged her again. "'Tis a handsome dress ye be wearin.'"

"I made it special for this day," said Maven.

Again, she glanced over at Ian, hoping that he might have noticed that she had spent long hours designing the dress to fit the small measurement of her cloth and sewing on it with tiny, perfect stitches. But Ian continued to walk ahead, indifferent to her efforts, his hands jammed into his pockets, his thoughts private.

He gave an impatient wave of his arm. "Hurry up, or we'll be missin' the streetcar to the park."

As Tommy and Maven fell in behind, she leaned over to Tommy and whispered, "How goes Mr. Douglas?"

Tommy shook his head. "Not well. He hardly eats or sleeps."

They had just reached the corner when they heard the clang of the bell of the horse-drawn streetcar. When it came to a stop in front of them, a dozen men, women, and children dressed in their Sunday best, crowded onto the car.

It wasn't yet noon, but the temperature had climbed to an uncomfortable mark. Pressed between perspiring bodies, Maven dismally felt herself beginning to wilt. Sweat trickled down her back and between her small breasts; wispy strands of hair clung damply to her forehead and neck. She tried to smooth out the wrinkles forming in her green, plaid skirt but soon gave up the cause as more and more passengers crammed onto the airless car at the next stops. Maven breathed a sigh of relief when they finally arrived at the park.

Tommy and Ian jumped off the streetcar before her, and each took one of her hands. Ian's hand was large, his grip strong and firm; Tommy's was wide, warm, and comfortable. She eyed the boys closely for a moment. They were opposites in every way. Where Ian was fair-haired, tall, and lean, Tommy was ruddy, average in height and stocky in build. While Ian was self-controlled, cool, and stubborn, Tommy was easy-going, fun-loving, and tractable. Both were very dear to her in a different way.

The park was cool and shady beneath the canopy of maple and elm trees. Already a large number of people had gathered and laughter and excitement filled the air. Carnival games and ice cream stands were scattered throughout the park. Children played games and rolled hoops in front of the gazebo festooned with red, white and blue bunting. A brass band played stirring marches that lifted spirits higher. Even Ian was not immune to the gaiety. His mood was becoming less distant, and an unguarded smile escaped him. Maven led the way to a spot beneath a shade tree. She took a cloth from the hamper and began to lay out a picnic of fried chicken, biscuits, beans, and apple pie, her hopes for the day rising.

If Maven had any doubts about her ability as a cook, they were dispelled as she watched the boys gorge themselves.

"'Tis a fine lunch ye've made," said Tommy, patting his stomach in defeat.

"Aye," joined in Ian. "A fine picnic indeed."

Maven beamed. The day seemed only to get better as they moved arm-in-arm from the ring toss booth to darts and horseshoes. Ian particularly thrived on the challenge of competition, and the cold gray of his eyes softened to a more congenial blue as his manner became lighter with each win.

They were making their way to the river, when Ian's gait slowed to a stop, his attention riveted on the young girl alighting from a black, shiny carriage. She was the most exquisite creature he had ever seen. Her fashionable, pearl gray suit complimented a fashionably curved figure that emphasized full breasts and a tiny waist. She wore her hair up, dressed close to her head, but honey blonde tendrils escaped alluringly from the pink, rose-trimmed hat. He thought her to be about his age and was surprised that she didn't blush or flinch when she looked over to find him staring at her. Instead, she returned his bold appraisal and graced him with a smile before turning back to her escort. Ian felt his heart flip.

"Easy lad," said Tommy. "She be beyond yer reach. 'Tis Cyrus Morgan's daughter. She just returned from a boardin' school in Philadelphia. I hear that men pay just to look at her—men with more money to burn than ye'll ever see in a lifetime."

"And how might ye be knowin' so much?"

"Me aunt helps out at the Morgan place sometimes. Ye best pull yer eyes away before ye lose yer job. Mr. Morgan be mighty particular about the lass."

"And who might the dandy be?"

"Peter Jeffries. His da owns the Pennsylvania and Erie Railroad line."

As Ian reluctantly pulled his gaze away from the pretty, young woman, Maven became conscious of her plain appearance, and the hope that she had held for the day faded. She wondered if Ian could ever look at her in the way that he looked at Eleanor Morgan.

October, 1877

CHAPTER 3

"Catch me here, catch me there, catch me catch me if you dare." Katherine's laughter filled the air as she raced to a distant point. "I won, I won," she shouted, her blue eyes shining.... "Ian, up with ye, lad or 'tis late for school ye'll be."

His mother's lilting voice brought a smile to his lips. The dream was always the same and so real that for a moment Ian felt warm inside. He reached out a hand to touch them as images of the mischievous, smiling Katherine and his sweet, loving mother floated before him.

This was the time he treasured most, when fantasies still remained woven around his slumbering consciousness. In such a state, everything was as it had been, as it should still be. But despite his struggle to hold onto it, the illusion always vanished with the awakening. Such dreams were a double-edged sword, he concluded, for while they gave solace in sleep, they were a source of much pain in consciousness.

Ian reluctantly opened his eyes and gazed up at the ceiling. The brown water stains and peeling paint remained the only constants in his life…those, and the knot in his stomach. It was there when he fell asleep each night. It was there when he awoke each morning.

He threw aside the quilt and rose from the cot, stealing himself against the wintry drafts that whistled through the old house. The water had frozen in the basin; a thin sheeting of ice coated the inside of the window. He shivered in spite of the woolen underwear and groped for his clothes, quickly dressing in the graying light.

Ian lit the lamp and carried it into the kitchen. He came to an abrupt halt as the light fell across a crumpled figure hunched over the kitchen table; a half empty bottle of whiskey lay within easy grasp. He stared hard at his father. James Douglas looked years older than his forty-two years, and Ian found it difficult to reconcile the image of the strong, muscular man he had known with the broken, old man who sat before him now, unkempt, uncaring.

"Ye been here all night?" he asked unable to conceal his anger.

James Douglas looked up at his son through bloodshot eyes. "Do nae be judgin' me, lad. I judge meself harsh enough."

Ian set the lamp on the table. "That stuff will kill ye, or is that what ye want?"

His father swung his useless arm across the stump of a severed leg. "'Tis dead I be already, lad," he said with quiet finality. "Half of me died when that log crushed me in the mill pond, and the rest of me was buried with yer mum and sister Katie. It just remains for the flesh to go the way of the spirit."

He reached for the whiskey bottle, but Ian angrily knocked it away.

"Does nae a part of ye yet live for me, Da?"

A knife twisted inside the elder Douglas at the hurt in his son's eyes, and he had to look away. "I'm sorry, lad. When a man can na do for his family, he no longer be a man but a burden…. 'Twould be better that I cease to exist."

"I'll nae hear ye speak such rubbish!"

"'Tis truth, lad. If I were a whole man, I could have put more food on the table, more coal in the stove. My family would na had to depend on the half wages of me son, and the few coins of my wife from takin' in rich people's laundry." James Douglas let out a bitter laugh. "A few cents…'twas all her life and the life of yer sister were worth in the end…a few cents. I brought us to this country to find a better life, instead I—"

"Da, stop!"

"If yer mum and Katie hadna been at that house collectin' laundry that day…"

Ian abruptly turned away and reached for his coat. It was an argument he could never win, and he was tired of trying. The mill accident had cost his father more than an arm and a leg. It had cost him the pride that was the mark of a man. It was too hard to respect a man who didn't respect himself, even if he was his father…most especially because he was his father. Ian wrapped up some bread and cheese and angrily jammed it into his pocket.

"I'm off to the mill," he said. "Try to keep the fire in the stove alight, if ye've a mind to do more than lift that bottle. Mrs. McInnis will look in on ye later."

James Douglas winced at the scorn in his son's voice. As Ian yanked open the door, he called out to him. "Ian…I love ye, lad."

His father's words were not slurred by whiskey as they had been throughout their conversation. They were clear, his voice low, gentle and strong, and Ian shut his eyes for a moment seeing the father he once knew. But anger still burned deep inside him, and his only response was the slamming of the door behind him as he left the house.

James Douglas' face was twisted with anguish, and a sob caught in his throat. "May God forgive me."

The blast of cold air that immediately greeted Ian as he stepped outside took his breath away. The sun peeked over the horizon, but a blanket of fog enshrouded the morn. Lamps in the windows of early risers made little more than a ghostly blur in the mist as it rose up from the Susquehanna River. Ian was so preoccupied with his thoughts, it was a few minutes before he heard Tommy calling to him.

"Ian, wait up." Tommy hurried alongside him, breathless from running. "Why did ye na stop for me?"

"Sorry, I forgot. Had a row with Da before leavin'."

"Yer da's a proud man. 'Tis a lot not settin' right with him."

"'Tis a lot nae settin' right with me."

"He'll come around. He just needs more time."

Ian shook his head. "The man has given up, Tommy. He has just given up."

The boys trudged on in silence through the mud-frozen streets, turning down Front Street to Mill Street. As they crossed the footbridge to the mill they could see the logs amassed in the millpond, lying in wait for them like prehistoric serpents.

Tommy pulled the collar of his coat higher against his neck. "The river'll be freezin' over soon, an' 'tis all scramblin' for work we'll be to carry us through."

A faint sliver of light broke through the fog to cap the eastern horizon as mill hands filed into Morgan Mill Yards. The yard was filled with neatly stacked lumber waiting to be delivered to builders and craftsmen. Off to the side stood a huge incinerator that burned scraps of wood and excess sawdust. The mill, itself, was a long, barn-like building positioned over flowing water. At one end, double doors opened onto three ramps and the millpond. Inside, flatbeds with levers moved between the ramps and saws. Behind the saws, near the freight wagon entrance, stood sorting tables.

Hawkins, the foreman, greeted workers at the entrance. "Along with you now…no time for laggards here. Kreitzer and Donovan ramp number one…Carey and Smith, carriage number two…Hemmings and Delaney, saw number two…Douglas and O'Brien ramp number two…"

Ian shot Tommy a wry smile. "Ferret-face gave us light duty today, ay."

"Could be worse," said Tommy. "He could have put us off-bearing on the green chain."

Both boys grimaced at the thought. Carrying the heavy, green planks of newly cut lumber from the saw to the sorting tables was work at its most back breaking and Hawkins' favorite punishment. One had to possess strength, agility and stamina as well as the right timing to keep up with the steady outpouring of planks for hours at a stretch. It was a job that mill hands disliked most.

Morgan Mill Yards was the only mill that rotated jobs. Aside from alleviating the boredom factor, Cyrus Morgan had learned the value in having all hands proficient in all jobs at the mill. When the flu epidemic had hit, the mill was brought to a grinding halt with many of the off-loaders and saw carriage operators stricken.

When the foreman had finished meting out assignments, the workers took up their positions. At the sound of the six o'clock whistle, the saws were started up, the deafening roar putting a jarring end to conversation.

Tommy threw open the ramp door and waved to one of a dozen pikemen on the pond. The pikeman waved back and began to maneuver a timber one hundred feet long and six feet in diameter toward ramp number two. Ian shed his coat and rolled up his sleeves, in spite of the cold, and picked up a peavey, a pole with a hook and pike on the end of it. Minutes later, the chains groaned as the bark caught and the log was slowly pulled up the ramp.

When it reached them, Ian and Tommy speared the log and wrestled it to the saw carriage, careful to keep the heavy pine straight with their peavies, while another team of men rolled it onto the carriage. Other workers on the dolly-like carriage manipulated levers that moved the timber to the waiting band saw. Everyone inwardly braced himself for that first violent collision of the day when metal blades met wood. With the harsh jolt of impact, a blizzard of sawdust filled the air, nearly choking the men on the saw carriage and the off-loaders as they rushed forward to gather the cut planks falling to the floor. Four young boys, ranging in age from ten to twelve, scurried around sweeping up the sawdust to prevent the saws from sparking a fire.

Ian's ears rang with the discordant shrieks of the saws. Sweat soon soaked his woolen underclothes and ran down his face, stinging his eyes, as he and Tommy continued to coax and prod stubborn, cumbersome logs off the ramp.

When the six o'clock whistle finally blew, the blare of it scarcely penetrated the din, but instinctively the men knew that it had sounded and began to shut down the saws. The silence that followed was as deafening as the roar had been.

Darkness was fast overtaking them as the workers streamed from the mill, dirty and tired. Several of the men turned off at Cozey's Saloon to lift a few pints before heading home.

As Tommy and Ian turned down Pine Street, Tommy squinted through the last rays of light. "Looks like ye have company, Ian. Isn't that Father McKinney's carriage out front of yer house? And there's Maven sittin' on the porch." He raised an arm and waved. "Ay, Maven…"

When Maven raised a tear-stained face to them, an icy hand gripped Ian by the throat, and he broke into a run. He leaped onto the porch and pulled Maven from the swing.

"What's wrong! Why is Father McKinney here!"

Tears slowly ran down her face. "'Tis your da, Ian," she said breaking into a sob. "Mum went to check on him and…"

Ian abruptly released her and tore into the house. The front room and kitchen stood empty, and he quickly retraced his steps through the hall to his father's bedroom. He staggered to a halt at the sight of the dark, red stains splattered across the wall. His horrified gaze travelled to the still form of his father lying on the bed. Mrs. O'Hara and Mrs. McInnis quietly stepped aside as he slowly crossed the room. Ian was struck by how peaceful his father looked. What eluded him in life he seemed to have found in death.

"My son," said Father McKinney, stepping forward, "'tis an unfortunate judgment yer father has exacted upon himself…"

Ian, his eyes still riveted on the lifeless form, impatiently waved aside the priest and knelt beside the bed. He choked back a sob and buried his face in his hands.

"Ah, Da, why did ye nae live for me?"

Father McKinney approached him again. "Ian, I must speak with ye, lad."

Ian slowly stood and allowed the priest to guide him into the hallway.

"Ye realize, of course, that yer father can na be buried in the cemetery next to yer mum and sister."

The quiet words echoed hollowly in Ian's ears. When they exploded in his brain, steel-blue eyes locked on the priest. "Why not?"

Father McKinney recoiled from the chilling intensity of Ian's gaze. "B-because suicide is a mortal sin. Ye be knowin' that a man who takes his own life can na be buried in hallowed ground."

"Who says Da took his own life? Be there a note about?"

"Well, no, but…"

"Then 'twas an accident. He was cleanin' his gun, and it went off. Isn't that right, Father?"

"Ian, I can na be party to such a sin. May God forgive ye…"

"Don't ye be speakin' to me about God, Father. I'm findin' God intolerable these days. I think ye'll find it to yer reward to agree that Da was cleanin' his gun when it accidentally discharged."

Father McKinney bristled. "My blessings are not for sale."

"Aren't they, Father? I believe that Franklin Jeffries found otherwise."

Father McKinney took out a handkerchief and mopped his brow. "What do ye know of that?"

"The servant's grapevine is well in place. I should think ye'd be knowin' that by now."

"'Tis gossip…all gossip."

"Gossip begins with a certain amount of truth, Father."

The priest took a deep breath and, after a lengthy pause, crossed himself. "I prefer to err on the side of doubt on such matters. In the absence of any note, perhaps a case of accidental shooting might be made fer yer da."

"Ye see to the arrangements, Father. I'll see to yer pockets."

The priest flinched and quickly left the house.

The ladies set aside their preparations and quietly left the room when Ian returned.

Mrs. O'Hara leaned over and whispered to Mrs. McInnis. "The lad has the evil eye upon him. Ye'd best be keepin' yer lass away from that one."

November, 1877

CHAPTER 4

Ian and Tommy took out their lunches and waded through a fine mist of sawdust to one of the half-cut logs. Tommy sat down on the makeshift bench, massaging sore muscles in his shoulders and neck.

"Mary Mother of Jesus! Workin' the ramp makes fer a long day."

Ian straddled the log and unwrapped the cheese and slice of bread. "Every day be a long day in the mill." Hunger gnawed at his insides, but he forced himself to eat slowly. He had learned that the longer he drew out a meal, the less hungry he was when he was finished.

Tommy tasted his sandwich, consuming half in one bite. "Now that ye took that room in town, 'tis little we've seen of ye since yer da's funeral," he said offhandedly. "Maven's been worried about ye."

"Been busy."

"Doin' what?"

"If ye must know, I've been workin' in Cozey's Saloon."

"Why? 'Tis eighteen ye'll soon be an' makin' full wages."

"A man can na have enough money, Tommy. Besides, the ponds will be freezin' over and the mills will be closin' for the winter."

"Come on men, step lively now," shouted Hawkins. "Back to work with ye. Time is money."

"Yeah, my time is Morgan's money," said a disgruntled worker as the mill hands started back to their positions. Other workers within earshot murmured in agreement.

Ian and Tommy took up their places at the ramp.

"Ye will na forget Maven's birthday, ay, Ian? She'd skin ye alive."

Ian cracked a half smile. The most he'd done in weeks. "Aye, I'll be there."

The day was well into the afternoon when Ian saw the men struggling on the carriage next to him. The log was slipping. He quickly motioned to Tommy, but before either could react, the log hit the saw at an angle, breaking it and sending pieces of blade and severed fingers into the air. Even above the roar of the saws, they could hear the screams of the sawyer. Blood spurted from his mangled hand, staining the sawdust on the floor. Ian leaped over the carriage and grabbed a rag to wrap the man's hand, while Tommy shut down the machine. As workers shut down the other saws and gathered round, Hawkins came running.

"Douglas, O'Brien, get back to the ramp! The rest of you, go back to your jobs. Go on, get those saws up and running." He gestured to one of the boys. "You there, throw some sawdust over that blood. Delaney take the man home. He's upsetting the others. Ye'd think ye never saw an accident before."

The injured sawyer reeled, and Delaney quickly stepped forward to catch him, half carrying him to the door.

"The man lost three fingers, Hawkins. He's in shock. He be needin' a doctor," said Ian.

"That's not my concern. All of ye get back to work now. It's just a little accident."

"Just a little accident ye say! Tell that to the man's wife and four children. He'll most likely lose that hand an' with it his livelihood, or is that of no concern to ye either?"

"When you work in a sawmill you take those risks. Production is my only concern, Douglas. Yours should be your job."

Ian's jaw and hands were clenched in tightly controlled anger. "'Tis the third accident this month, Hawkins. Yer quotas be too high. The men play out. They can na keep up without bein' a danger to themselves and to others."

There was an agitated stirring among the workers. "He's right," several of them chorused.

Hawkins turned to the gathering, the vein in his forehead beginning to pulsate. "You don't like it, you can go elsewhere. I've no shortage of laborers itching to take your places."

Disgruntlement increased, and emotions were high as everyone tried to talk and shout at once.

Tommy tugged at Ian's arm. "We'll all be losin' our jobs for sure. Worse yet, we'll be blacklisted in all the mills for rabble-rousing. Settle the men down. They listen to ye."

Ian stepped atop a timber, and raised his arms. "Lads, settle yerselves. Hawkins can na hear yer words for all the shoutin'."

"There ain't no words to hear," said Hawkins. "Get back to work, or I'll replace the lot of ye."

Ian stood his ground. "Hawkins, if ye were to grant an afternoon break, accidents would decrease."

"Breaks!" exclaimed Hawkins incredulously. "Mr. Morgan already pays a nickel more than the other mill owners. Now you want him to pay you for resting?" He burst into laughter. "Next you'll be wantin' Saturday off, too."

Tommy gestured wildly to Ian to hold his tongue, but Ian ignored him.

"Ye say production is yer concern," he continued addressing Hawkins. "What if I guarantee ye an increase in production if ye allow the break?"

"YOU'LL guarantee…" Hawkins' laugh was derisive. "And just how do ye mean to do that? You ain't producin' if ye ain't workin', Douglas."

"I'll pledge my job on it," said Ian.

At this, a murmur swept through the workers, and Tommy groaned, rolling his eyes heavenward.

Ian remained undaunted and continued to press his case. "A rested man works twice the pace of a tired one and makes less mistakes. Look around ye. The saws have been down nearly a half hour. Every accident not only costs ye production time, but an experienced worker as well."

"The saws are down because of yer jaw flappin'. Mr. Morgan don't bargain with workers. If you want to work here, ye agree to Mr. Morgan's terms." Hawkins turned to address the millhands. "Now all of you get back to work. Any lost production you don't make up will come out of your pay."

The air was tense as the men looked from Hawkins to Ian, uncertain of where they stood and what they should do next. The situation was not lost on either Hawkins or Ian. It was a defining moment for both men, though neither was quite sure in what way. At Ian's signal, the men returned to their positions. From the catwalk, Cyrus Morgan observed the scene unnoticed.

*   *   *   *   *   *   *   *

Hawkins lost no time reporting the incident.

"I'm telling you, Mr. Morgan, Douglas is trouble. He nearly excited the men to riot today. Ye'd best heed my advice and get rid of him...and that friend of his, O'Brien, too."

Cyrus Morgan was a stout man and amply filled his chair. It creaked as he leaned back in it and laced his hands behind his head.

"Tell me more about this Ian Douglas."

Hawkins shrugged. "Ain't much to tell. He's one of my best hands, but he's got a chip on his shoulder. His father was crippled in an accident on the millpond a while back. The kid quit school, and I hired him on at half wages, him being under eighteen an' all. Lost his mother and sister in the influenza epidemic. The old man died some weeks ago. Story has it that a gun went off while he was cleaning it. Rumor has it, it weren't no accident. It's the usual story with these immigrants. I'm telling you, sir, the kid is trouble."

"He's a natural born leader, Hawkins. They're always trouble if you can't bend them to your advantage. Send him to the lumber camp for the winter. Hank could use a few more choppers. Let's see how tough Douglas really is."

"What if he refuses? I can't make him go."

Morgan heaved his bulk out of the chair and went to stand at the window overlooking the millpond. "The mills will be shutting down soon...jobs will be scarce. He'll go."

"Yes sir."

"Oh, and Hawkins, give the millhands their afternoon break."

Hawkins looked at Morgan, stunned. "Mr. Morgan, you ain't gonna give into them. The other mill owners will raise holy hell."

"Leave the mill owners to me. Let's give Douglas enough rope to hang himself. If production doesn't increase, take away the break...and fire him."

A crafty smile spread across Hawkins' face. "Yeah, that's right. Douglas pledged his job, didn't he now. The mill hands can't quarrel with a bet made and lost, and we'll be rid of the troublemaker." The smile suddenly faded with an uneasy thought. "Douglas is awful sure of himself. What if he's right?"

Morgan turned and smiled at his foreman. "Then I may give him your job."

Hawkins' responded with a half-hearted laugh, not quite certain if Morgan was joking or not.

CHAPTER 5

The McInnis house was cramped and dull. The flowered wallpaper was faded and water-stained; the paint blistered inside and out. It was like all the other houses in the Basin, a section of poor immigrants. But today, music and laughter lifted the dwelling from its dreary existence if only for a few hours.

The parlor was jammed with O'Haras, O'Reillys, McInnises, O'Briens and McClearys all come to celebrate Maven's sixteenth birthday. Furniture had been moved aside to make room for dancing. The aroma of corned beef and cabbage filled the air, and Patrick McInnis saw to a steady supply of ale and whiskey.

Maven was dancing with Tommy when she saw Ian walk in, and her eyes lit up. He stood a sturdy six feet now, and his years at the mill had put muscle on his lanky body. His dark, brooding nature seemed to lend intrigue and maturity to his youthful, good looks, so that now he wore more the mark of a man than a mischievous boy. She had heard the other girls in the Basin talk about the change and had thought them silly at first. But now she was quite conscious of the change as well, and it annoyed her when the girls plied her with questions about him and asked for her advice in catching his eye. Her heart thudded hard against her chest when he looked her way and waved.

When the dance finally ended, she hurried over to rescue Ian from the young ladies who began to encircle him.

"'Tis glad I am ye've come, Ian," she said, pulling him from their midst. She didn't miss the looks of disappointment and the tinge of envy on their faces. "'Tis little enough we see of ye. I was afraid ye would na show yerself."

"I would na miss yer birthday, Maven," said Ian, the old twinkle momentarily back in his eye. "Can nae risk havin' the wrath of every saint called down upon my head now, can I?"

"An' she would, too," said Tommy, joining them.

"Would not...well, perhaps one or two," Maven admitted with a laugh.

"When her ire is up, the rats run fer cover. What chance has a mere mortal?" asked Tommy with a melodramatic flair.

Ian winked at Tommy. "Da always said ye can na argue with an Irishman. An Irish lass is twice as deaf."

"O-o-oh, the two of ye are impossible. The next time Officer McCarty picks ye up for mischief, 'twill not be me silver tongue what saves ye."

Tommy chortled. "Saves us! 'Twas yer silver tongue what nearly landed us in the jail when we were caught sneakin' into the music hall."

Ian scratched his head in feigned confusion. "I seem to remember it a bit different, meself."

"Well," sputtered Maven, "we dinna land in the gaol now, did we?"

Tommy laughed. "Only because of Ian's quick thinkin'."

"Humph," said Maven with a sniff, "some people have no sense of gratitude. Come join me in a dance, Ian, and let's put our minds to more pleasant tasks.... I see Tommy already has," she added dryly as Tommy moved off to flirt and tease with some of the lasses.

Ian's lighter mood took a more somber turn. "I can na stay, Maven. I just come to say good-bye. I'm off to the lumber camp in the morn."

A worried frown crossed Maven's face. "Aye, Tommy told me the two of ye had signed up for the winter. Have a care, Ian. Lumberin' be a hard life."

'Tis a hard life here at half the wages."

"Ian, come join the fun," broke in Tommy. "The lasses have an eye on ye for a dance."

Maven cast a look of annoyance over the buxom, young ladies standing giggling behind Tommy. For a brief moment, she felt an impulse to throw herself in front of Ian like a protective shield.

"Ye take my place, Tommy. I've no doubt ye're up to the task," said Ian. "I'm off now. 'Tis a long walk back to my room, and I've much to do before the morrow. I'll see ye at the train station, ay." He bent down and kissed Maven lightly on the cheek. "There now, ye can na say ye ne'er been kissed."

"She could na say it before neither," said Tommy, a mischievous glint in his eye. "I beat you by an hour."

Maven's heart was still pounding from Ian's kiss, and she struggled to make light of the matter, fearful of betraying her feelings. "Oh, ye two are impossible. If this is how men gossip, 'tis small wonder mothers be always warnin' their daughters against the likes of ye."

Tommy threw back his head in laugher. "How about a dance to cool your temper, Maven, me love?"

"Ah, perhaps later, Tommy. I'm goin' to walk Ian out."

Maven grabbed a heavy shawl off the hook and threw it around her shoulders. They walked out onto the porch and a damp chill enveloped them, but Maven scarcely felt the cold.

"Will ye be comin' back to us?" she asked.

Ian looked at her perplexed. "Of course I will. Where else would I go?"

"I mean with yer heart and yer soul, or have ye left us already?"

"If ye be talkin' about the room in town, 'tis something I had to do." The dreams had ceased to give him solace anymore. With the death of his father, the pain was too great asleep or awake.

"Ye can na run away, Ian."

"Maven, ye do nae understand..."

"I miss them, too, Ian. I see Katherine everywhere I go. There's nary a day that I not be thinkin' of her, yer mum, and yer da. Ye should be here in the Basin with people who care about ye."

"I have to make my own way now, Maven."

"Ye do na have to do it alone."

"'Tis not alone I go. I have ye and Tommy." He forced a lightness into his tone and chucked her under the chin. "Remember, we're the Pine Street Warriors…thick as thieves the four of us be…"

Maven laughed and finished the ditty. "Where there's one, ye'll find the other three." Her tone became wistful. "We had such wonderful times together."

"Aye, 'twas long ago," said Ian abruptly, staring off into the distance. "Those times are gone…forever."

An awkward silence fell between them.

"Mrs. Drury agreed to take me on as an assistant dressmaker," said Maven, searching for something to say. "She said in due time I might try me hand at some designin'."

"I'm glad for ye. 'Tis what ye've wanted to do. Mum always said ye was clever with a needle…. Well, ye're cold, and I must be leavin' now." He leaned over and kissed her on the cheek again. "Happy Birthday, Maven. I'll see ye come February."

As she watched him step off the porch and walk away, Maven's heart fell. She put a hand to the cheek he had kissed, and a smile at once hesitant and shy touched her lips as she dared to hope.

CHAPTER 6

The train steamed steadily up the mountainside. Ian and Tommy shared the rail coach with six veteran loggers who had hired on at other lumber camps in the area. They slouched in various degrees of boredom and resignation, collars turned up and coats pulled tighter against the cold as the temperature took a noticeable dip. Tommy sank deep into the bench, his chin pressed tight against his chest, considering that this might possibly be one of his biggest mistakes. Only Ian sat erect in excited anticipation, his eyes glued to the window. He had never been this high in the mountains before, and he was awe-struck by the pristine beauty that surrounded him.

Fresh snow blanketed the still virginal forest, transforming trees into stately, white sentinels. Gushing rivulets, now captured in winter's grip, hugged the mountain cliffs, resembling giant stalactites. By now the new fallen snow in Rossburg would be dirty slush, thought Ian.

A shrill whistle shattered the crystalline silence, announcing the arrival of fresh recruits and supplies. Ian snapped out of his musings and threw his pack over his shoulder as the train ground to a screeching halt in front of a make-shift station. He was the first to jump off.

The cold, crisp air cut like a knife, but Ian felt invigorated, unshackled, free for the first time in a very long while. In spite of the heavy pack, he bounded through the deep snow cavorting and laughing, kicking up spouts of powdery dust. Behind him, Tommy followed a good deal less enthusiastic, irritably sidestepping Ian's playful snowballs. The other loggers looked at each other knowingly and shook their heads at the naiveté of the youth as they struck off on crudely marked paths to their lumber camps.

Tommy's breath hung on the frosty air. "Mary Mother of Jesus, 'tis cold up here!"

"Cheer up. Once ye start workin', ye will na notice the cold."

Tommy snorted, his mouth curved down in a grumpy frown. "I doubt it. What makes ye so bloody happy about being exiled to this God forsaken place for the winter! Hawkins dinna do this out of the kindness of his heart ye know. He means this to be a punishment, not a reward."

"Then we should na give him the satisfaction, ay. Are ye nae always tellin' me to make the best of a bad situation? Maybe Hawkins done us a favor."

"A favor! Just how do ye be figurin' that?"

"When the river freezes and the mill closes down, we'll still have a job makin' over two dollars a day. We'll have all the food we can eat—free of charge—and fresh air to breathe instead of sawdust. What more can a man ask for?"

Tommy blew on his gloved hands and stamped his feet. Somehow it didn't feel as good to him as it sounded. "Better not let Hawkins hear ye talkin', or he'll assign us to off-bearing on the green chain—permanently. Ian," broached Tommy on a more serious note, "ye've got to mind Hawkins less with your tongue. If ye continue to bait him, 'tis fired ye'll be. 'Tis luck ye still have a job after that last stunt."

"A break will decrease accidents and increase productivity. Every man at the mill knows I'm right. If Hawkins weren't so stupid, he'd be knowin' it, too."

"No matter what he knows or doesn't know, Hawkins *is* the foreman. Ye'd best keep that in mind if ye be wantin' to hold on to yer job. Look, I know it ain't easy. I do na like Hawkins any more than ye do, but the sawmill is all we know. An' Morgan pays a nickel more than the other mills. Nobody wants a rabble-rouser, Ian. If ye do na watch yourself, ye'll be findin' yerself out altogether. Hawkins could have ye blacklisted at every mill in town if he had a mind to, and me along with ye. If ye don't be needin' yer job, I need mine."

"I never ask ye to back me up. I do na expect ye to lose yer job on my account."

Hurt flickered across Tommy's face. "I'm yer friend, Ian. A friend stands up fer a friend through thick or thin. We're a team, remember? A bloody good team. Hawkins would soon as fire ye as look at ye. He'd a done it a long time ago if together we weren't the best team he has. We be the only hands who regularly meet his quotas. But ye can push him only so far. Supposin' he does fire ye. What good will it do ye?"

Ian had no ready answer. Tommy was right. What good would it do him to get fired and be blacklisted, to be out of the only work he knew how to do? At the very least, he couldn't endanger his friend's position at the mill.

"All right, all right," he said begrudgingly, "from here on I'll keep the fact that Hawkins is a horse's ass to meself."

Somehow the promise lacked sincerity to Tommy, and he let out a sigh of exasperation. Ian could be stubborn and proud to an annoying degree.

The boys trudged along in silence. A half mile later, the logging camp rose up before them. A large, log shanty stood in the center of a clearing, surrounded by smaller outbuildings. The camp was quiet, forbidding, desolate. Not even the smoke curling around the top of the shanty roof seemed a welcoming host.

Tommy's step faltered. "They say loggin' is the toughest job there is," he murmured with an uncertain gulp.

Ian carelessly waved aside his friend's fears. "Can na be any worse than the jobs Hawkins has thrown at us at the mill. Loggers are nothin' more than a bunch of farmers waitin' out the winter. How tough can it be?"

Tommy threw Ian a doubtful look and reluctantly followed him into camp. They entered the first building they came to. A man sat beside a potbelly stove reading a newspaper. Shelves loaded with woolen socks, gloves, Mackinaw coats and blankets lined the small, square cabin. It was obviously the company store. The storekeeper, a tall, thin man with a beard and wire-rim glasses stood up and went behind the counter.

"What can I do ye boys for?" He was a friendly man, eager for company.

"We be lookin' for the foreman," said Ian.

"Travelers, ay?"

The boys exchanged questioning looks. "Travelers?" asked Tommy.

"Yeah, you know. That's what we call loggers who travel from camp to camp. How long ye stayin'?"

"We're not—"

Ian jabbed Tommy in the ribs. "Long as it takes."

The man extended his hand. "The name's Bailey. Hank is the man ye wanna see. He's the bull of the woods. This is a good camp. The cook is fair and the pay is regular."

"Where might we find this Hank?" asked Ian.

"Yer in luck. He just come in from the woods. Yer likely to find him in his office over yonder."

The boys thanked the storekeeper and struck off for the office. It was a cabin of equal size to the store. Inside, a man sat behind a desk, flanked by file cabinets. A small stove was set in the corner of the room.

With one glance at the "bull of the woods," Ian thought him aptly titled. He was a large man with sharp brown eyes, a mustache and coarse, weathered features.

The man in turn sized up the boys as Ian explained their business.

"So you're the two Hawkins sent." The foreman stood, taller than they had expected, and came from around his desk. His gaze settled on Ian. "You must be Douglas."

Ian started to answer when he suddenly felt a stab of pain in his jaw and found himself lying on the dirt floor. Dazedly, he looked up to see the foreman standing over him and Tommy staring down at him, his friend's mouth hanging open in astonishment.

Ian scrambled to his feet as quickly as he could, his features taut with anger. "What did ye do that for!" he demanded, gingerly working his jaw,

The foreman crossed trunklike arms across his barrel chest. "Jest settin' ya straight on who's boss around here. Hawkins said you was a hottempered smart ass, no respect for authority. That true?"

"Depends."

"On what?"

Ian returned the foreman's narrowed gaze. "The authority."

As the foreman silently took stock of Ian again, Tommy mentally crossed himself and sent up a prayer on Ian's behalf, fully expecting to see his friend go flying through the air once more.

Instead the foreman gave him a warning. "Keep your mouth shut and do as your told, Douglas, and you may survive. You too, O'Brien. Report to the large shanty. The cook will settle you in. You'll be paid by the day. Board and bunk is included. You'll start tomorrow as choppers. If you fail to make quota you'll be docked until the quota is made. If you more'n make quota, you'll be given extra credit. Any questions?" The boys shook their heads.

As they left the foreman's office, Tommy expelled his breath in a long sigh of relief. "Geez, Ian, ye'd best watch yer step with that one. He looks like he could break a man in two with little effort or conscience. Ye all right?"

Ian angrily shook off Tommy's concern and headed toward the log shanty. As they made their way across the clearing, in the distance they could hear saws at work and feel the vibration of felled trees.

The shanty was crude with just two windows and a large bunkroom that connected to a smaller dining area. The dining area contained six long tables and benches that seated ten people each. A cambuse fire or open fire was set in the center of the bunkroom, and top and bottom bunks lined the walls. A bunk consisted of a board nailed along a frame about forty inches wide; the bottom was slatted or poled and lined with straw. A large hole in the ceiling let out smoke and let in freezing air.

The cook, a small, wiry man, pointed out two lower bunks and recited the rules. "Sleep in yer clothes and keep yer hats on if you value yer parts. Hang yer wet socks on the nail there at the end of yer bunk. Wash yer hands and face before you sit down to eat. Wait yer turn. And no talkin' durin' meals. Avoids arguments that way. You got a complaint about my cookin', take it up with the foreman." At this, he threw the boys a look which dared them to actually do so.

The boys had just settled in when they heard the blare of a long trumpet calling the loggers in for supper. It was a half hour before the men began straggling into camp and over an hour before the horses were cared for and the loggers washed up. Ian and Tommy shifted uneasily beneath their scrutiny as the motley bunch assembled around the table.

"Men," said the foremen, "the newcomers are Douglas and O'Brien. They're freshies. They were sent here to learn a few things. Let's see to it that they learn them."

The men grunted and a few put out their hands, but they were more in the mood for food than introductions at the moment. Ian and Tommy found two spots, side by side. They started to sit when a meaty fist grabbed each of them by the scruff of the neck, hauled them backwards over the bench and deposited them, none too gently, on the floor. The room rocked with laughter.

The boys gathered their wits and scrambled to their feet, coming face to face with the largest man they had ever seen. They had thought the foreman was a mountain of a man; this one dwarfed them all. Ian, himself six feet tall, barely came to the giant's chin. Weighing pride against certain destruction, he decided on survival and relaxed his pugilistic stance.

"You're in Tiny's place," explained the foreman when the laughter subsided. "Newcomers don't sit until they're given a place. Take a seat over there."

The boys gave Tiny a wide berth as they moved to take seats at the end of the table.

"Hello, I'm Parker Stanton. But everyone calls me Lawyer Stanton."

Ian shot the young man beside him a skeptical look. He figured him to be a few years older than himself, attractive, friendly with a rakish smile, and speech which smacked of education.

"If ye're a lawyer, what are ye doin' here workin' as a logger?"

"I'm the latter working toward the former." At the look of confusion on Ian's face, the man laughed. "I do some logging in the winter to get money to continue my law studies."

At the clang of the supper bell, silence descended, and the cook set the food on the table. The men hungrily consumed salt pork, potatoes, dried peas and barley soup, careful to observe the no-talking rule. Afterwards sugar pie and molasses cookies were served with tea. The meal was surprisingly tasty, but then Ian and Tommy would have found it so if it had tasted like shoe leather. The cook's warning about complaints still rang loudly in their ears.

With their stomachs full, some of the loggers retired to their bunks to read while others sat on log benches around the fire, swapping stories and enjoying a pipe. Tommy joined those at the fire; Ian took to his bunk. His hands laced behind his head, he stared moodily up at the rafters until sleep overtook him.

CHAPTER 7

Just before dawn, the loggers were rudely aroused from their sleep by the cook beating on a pan. After a breakfast of oatmeal, prunes, pork and beans on toast, raisin pie, bread and cheese and hot, strong tea, Ian and Tommy were given axes and placed with an experienced chopper. By the end of the day, they were numb with cold and swayed with exhaustion as they waited their turn in the wash line.

"Hey, Douglas, I seen women hold up better'n you two," shouted one of the wood hicks.

Ian strongly resented being the butt of their humor, and at the sound of chuckles and sniggers, he started toward the logger. Tommy quickly yanked him back.

"Be ye daft, lad! There ain't a man here who can na mop the floor with ye. As it is ye can barely stand."

Ian canvassed the loggers. While most of the men were not large in size, he knew them to be seasoned and tough. He had watched many of them work. Tommy was right. Even the smallest man in the camp could most likely take him, especially in his present state, and then he'd be the butt of even more jokes.

He spent the balance of the mealtime glaring down at his plate. At the end of the meal, the men began to drift into the bunkroom and gather around the fire. Ian, again, went straight to his bunk.

The next morning the boys were sore in places they didn't think possible and were the subject of more jests and laughter when they had to roll out of their bunks on all fours to get up. It occurred to them then that they had been given lower bunks for good reason. It would seem that all of the lifting and hoisting of logs they had done at the sawmill hadn't seasoned them as well as they had thought. Clearly, this wasn't going to be the picnic Ian had envisioned for them.

Tommy glared over at Ian when he was able to pull himself to a standing position. "'Bunch of farmers,' ay…'How tough can it be,' ay…"

Ian winced as he drew himself up as well, his mood snappish. "Okay! So 'tis a little tougher than I expected. I'm hurtin' just as much as ye are. Another couple of days, an' we will na feel a thing."

"Aye, we'll most likely be dead!" Throwing Ian another dark look, Tommy hobbled off to breakfast.

When the loggers struck off for the woods, their step seemed more brisk than usual to the boys. Ian and Tommy had to struggle to keep up, their gait stiff and awkward, and Ian was certain the quick pace was deliberate. One more joke on the "freshies."

When they came to the area being forested, the foreman bawled out, "O'Brien and Douglas, you team up with Jones for the day. Pick your tree and get to work."

Jones surveyed the trees. "This one'll do."

Ian and Tommy exchanged doubtful glances. Even to their inexperienced eye, it was an inferior choice.

"'Tis full of knots and lacks diameter," said Ian in a low voice to Tommy.

Tommy nodded. "Aye, but remember what the foreman told us. Stay to our business and keep our mouths shut."

"C'mon, boys, let's get choppin'," said Jones. "I'll jest stand over here and supervise."

The boys set to work on the tree, eyeing Jones from time to time as he lounged against a neighboring tree.

Ian muttered to Tommy. "Supervisin' does he call it now? Another word comes to mind for it."

"A little faster boys. We ain't gonna make our quota choppin' at that rate," Jones admonished them.

As the foreman approached, Jones picked up his ax and took a few swings, then resumed his resting position when the foreman had disappeared from sight. Jones proceeded, then, to offer his critical assessment of the camp, which he found less than satisfactory. The boys exchanged looks of annoyance, felled the tree, and moved onto another. They were positioning themselves, when an ax suddenly came whipping past them to bury itself in the trunk of the tree where Jones lazed, just missing his head by inches.

"Mary mother of Jesus, what the bloody hell was that!" exclaimed a shaken Tommy.

Ian shook his head. They looked to Jones for an explanation and were stunned to see him streaking out of the woods. Just as astonishing to them, no one seemed to take any undue notice of the incident. As Ian and Tommy looked about them in confusion, the foreman came along, retrieved the ax, and ordered them to keep working.

At the lunch break, Lawyer Stanton approached the boys.

"Heard old Jones was given the card this morning."

Tommy looked at Stanton blankly. "The card? Someone nearly split his skull with an ax if that's what ye mean. Could a taken me ear with it, and not so much as a word from anyone. I know lumberin' to be a dangerous bit of work, but I ne'er figured on axes flyin' through the air."

Stanton chuckled. "If Morrissey had wanted to take off your ear or split Jones's head he would have done so. I've seen him throw an ax at thirty paces and be true to the mark on a tree a half dozen times straight."

Tommy's eyes widened. "Ye mean to say it wasn't an accident?"

"It's called giving the card. If a man is found to be a sluggard or disagreeable to work alongside, he's given a subtle hint that he's no longer welcome in camp."

"By nearly splittin' his skull? I would na be callin' that subtle now," said Ian dryly.

"Perhaps not, but it's effective."

"What if Jones hadn't left?" asked Tommy.

Stanton shrugged. "There's never been a man foolhardy enough to stay around afterwards."

*   *   *   *   *   *   *   *

Ian lay in his bunk after supper that night, still mulling over the "card" incident. It had affected him more than he wanted to admit. A shadow blocked the light, and he turned his head to find Stanton standing alongside his bunk.

The logger lit a pipe and took a few puffs, draping his arm casually over the crossbar of the upper bunk. "The boys have been pretty rough on you and your friend. They're just testing your mettle. They'll let up when you prove your worth. You might take a lesson from your friend though."

Ian sullenly returned his attention to the straw ticking hanging down from the bunk above.

"What's that?"

"Get yourself a better attitude." Stanton inclined his head toward the fire where Tommy sat exchanging jokes with several loggers. "Like your friend there. It'll go easier for you."

"I do my work."

"There's more to being a wood hick than just doing your job. You have to be part of the team. Getting out the timber is dangerous work. Men have to be able to depend on one other. They have to know you to trust you."

"I know Tommy. Tommy knows me. He's all the team I need."

"There's more to a team than the two of you. You work in a sawmill. You should know that. These fellows aren't a bad lot. Some are farmers who have been lumbering in the winter for years to make ends meet.

Others are experienced woodsmen. Right now, we're all loggers. If one person isn't part of the team, another risks serious injury or loss of his life. Jones wasn't part of the team."

Stanton took a puff on his pipe, a cloud of aromatic smoke wreathing his head. "One more word of warning, Douglas. The wood hick can be a vindictive son-of-a-bitch. If he isn't happy with the camp, he has been known to bury an ax high up in the trunk of a prime tree just before quitting."

"So?"

"If the chopper doesn't spot it, the vibrations from the chopping of the tree can knock it lose. I saw a man's head split once from a falling ax. Only thing you can do is forfeit the tree or get someone crazy enough to climb up and get the ax."

"Ye're tellin' me ye think Jones…"

"Jones was lazy and a pain in the ass, but he wasn't vindictive. My bet is on the German. The others' bets are on you."

As Stanton moved off to join the other loggers around the fire, Ian stared after him. He had gotten the message, loud and clear. Furthermore, he had the feeling that it wasn't by accident that he and Tommy had been placed with the hapless Jones this morning.

Over the days, Ian found loggers to be a strange breed. They had a funny way of getting their points across, but get them across they did. They were a rough lot, ready to fight at the drop of a hat over any real or perceived insult, yet they held themselves to an exacting code of conduct and a curious sense of honor.

In this remote area of little law, Ian was amazed to find that the logging camp had more rules and regulations than a municipal government and all were strictly enforced. Few were given a second chance. No man was permitted to touch another man's ax or saw, and God help the man who helped himself from a dish before passing it to the person who asked for it. No man was considered worthy to remain in camp if he refused to aid the sick or injured. If a chopper failed to shout the warning "timber" in sufficient time to allow safe retreat, he was labeled a killer and run out of the woods. In a "legal fight," anything was fair until a party yelled defeat. If the party did not call defeat and was seriously injured, he was the one held at fault. Ian found this strange society intriguing and curious. He was at once repelled by the brutality and attracted by the simple honesty of the system. It may have seemed savage, but there was order. Every man was judged by the same scale and always knew where he stood. Ian liked that.

*   *   *   *   *   *   *   *

The sweat ran down Ian's face as he and Tommy chopped away at a stubborn white pine. He paused to swipe his arm across his brow when a red blur caught his eye.

"Why ye stoppin'?" asked Tommy.

"Look over there. 'Tis the German, Franz Mueller. He's leavin' the woods in a big hurry."

"Good riddance I say. He's a sullen son-of-a-bitch," said Tommy with a hard swing of the ax.

"Where was he workin'?"

"How should I know?"

Ian was insistent. "We have to find the tree he was choppin'."

"Why? We have our own to finish. We can na leave a half felled timber."

Tommy was right. Wood chips flew as Ian set to work at a furious pace. "Come on, hurry up, Tommy!"

Tommy shot his friend a curious eye. "What's gotten into ye?"

"I'll explain later," said Ian.

It seemed an eternity to Ian until the boys finally yelled, "Timber!" and the one hundred foot tree fell with earth-shaking precision. Quickly, Ian recounted what Parker Stanton had told him about Mueller and vindictive wood hicks, and they ran to the area they had seen the German leaving.

"Stanton!" shouted Ian. "Was Mueller working here?"

Stanton pulled up on his ax and wiped his forehead. "Yeah. He started on this hemlock when he got the runs. He went back to camp." Stanton drew back to deliver another cut when Ian caught his arm. "What the…"

"Stanton, I do na think Mueller is sick."

Stanton paled as his eyes followed Ian's. About thirty feet above the ground, nearly obscured by a tree limb, was an ax embedded in the trunk.

He drew a long, deep breath. "That bastard."

"I don't remember calling a break," barked the foreman. "What's so all-fired interesting?"

Stanton pointed to the ax. "It was Mueller. Claimed he was sick and headed back to camp. If Douglas hadn't gotten suspicious…" He shook his head, still shaken by the close call.

"The dirty, no good bastard!" exploded the foreman. "Had a bad feeling 'bout him from the start." He spat out a wad of chewing tobacco in the snow. "If we abandon the tree, we'll have to abandon the whole area. A good wind could knock that tree over without any warning. Son-of-a-bitch! This area has the most prime trees."

"We could try to knock down the ax," said Stanton.

"I can't send a man thirty feet up a half-cut tree. Dangerous enough under normal conditions." The foreman fell silent for a long moment, his experienced eye canvassing the trees around him. He let out another expletive. "Stanton get me a damned rope."

Stanton looked at the large, bulky foreman. "Hank, I don't think it's a good idea."

"What choice do I have?"

Ian stepped forward. "Me, sir. I stand a better chance than ye."

"I appreciate the offer, Douglas, but I can't let you do that. It's my responsibility."

"'Tis your responsibility to do what's best for the camp, sir."

The foreman sized up the tall, lean youth. "You sure you know what yer doin', Douglas?"

Ian nodded.

Word was spread among the choppers to cease felling trees to limit vibrations. Ian took off his coat and fastened a rope around his waist and around the tree trunk.

Tommy tested the knots. "Jesus, Ian, ye're crazy to do this."

"I've climbed many a tree, Tommy."

"Not thirty feet and half-cut. What'll I tell Maven?"

"Nothin'. There will na be nothin' to tell. Geez, your faith is overwhelmin'."

"Ian, ye do na have to do this."

Ian looked over at Parker Stanton, recalling their earlier conversation. "Yes, I do, Tommy."

Stanton gave him the high sign. "Good luck, Douglas. Easy does it."

News of the event had reached the entire camp and everyone gathered round as Ian slowly inched his way up the tree. Despite the twenty degree temperature, sweat trickled down his face and chest, burning his eyes and dampening his shirt. It hurt to breathe. Higher up, he encountered ice on the trunk. He was about twenty feet off the ground when his foot slipped, and he slid several feet tearing the leg of his pants and skinning his shins. The tree swayed and cracked, and a hush fell over the loggers. No one spoke or breathed.

Slowly, Ian began his ascent again, finally, coming within arm's reach of the ax. It came free in his hands with just one tug. It crossed his mind that Parker Stanton would not have been long for this world with a few more strikes to the tree. Watching from the ground, Stanton knew it, too.

There was another loud crack, and Ian felt the tree sway with greater freedom. He threw the ax into a clearing and started his descent. He had about twenty feet to go when he noticed that the rope was beginning to fray, caused by the friction from his earlier slip. The diameter of the trunk was too big for him to discard the rope. Ian descended again as quickly as he dared. Twelve feet up, he shouted for everyone to clear the area below him of any debris. As the men scrambled to make a safe area for him to land, Ian took out his knife and cut the rope around his waist.

The lumbermen stood back and watched as Ian dangled above the ground. He kicked himself away from the tree and jumped just as the rope around the trunk broke. He landed hard and rolled, the wind momentarily knocked out of him. Stanton and Tommy gave him a minute to catch his breath before helping him up.

"You all right, Douglas?" asked the foreman.

"Anythin' broken?" asked Tommy anxiously surveying him.

"I'm fit," Ian assured them.

"Blanding, Carleton, cut that damned tree down," yelled the foreman. "Nice work, Douglas. You best return to camp and have that leg looked at."

Ian shook his head. "Not yet. Tommy and I have a quota to fill."

The foreman nodded and ordered everyone back to work. The loggers offered their hands and slapped Ian on the back as they returned to their positions.

Chopping was hard work, the hardest Ian had ever experienced. He was exhausted at the end of each day and, like the others, fell into bed with clothes and shoes on, which were more often wet than dry. Belts were loosened and shirts opened to allow for the circulation of air. The harsh, Spartan life agreed with Ian. For the first time in a long while, he felt a sense of accomplishment and worth. He and Tommy always made their quota or better. And as the time wore on, he found it easier to join in. He looked forward to Sundays, a day of ax throwing, wrestling, chopping and log spinning contests. They spoke to Ian's sense of competition, and he readily rose to any challenge. He rarely won, but acquitted himself creditably enough to earn trust and respect. He had never realized how important this was to him until now.

*   *   *   *   *   *   *   *

Ian awoke with a feeling of dread, the source of which he couldn't put his finger on. Then he remembered. It was mid February, time to go home.

For the next few days, the wood hicks readied themselves and the camp to leave. Their job was over for the winter. The skidders and teamsters would be arriving any day to haul the timber out of the woods to the river.

Ian sighed and pulled himself away from the door. Here, he felt a sense of belonging, a fraternity that he was reluctant to leave. Here a man's worth wasn't measured by which side of town he came from.

Feeling no such bond, Tommy eagerly gathered his belongings. "C'mon, Ian, get yer belongin's together. I do na aim to be missin' this train now."

Ian was noticeably moody. "'Tis almost time for the spring thaw. I wish we could stay for the log drive."

"Been long enough for me. After this, even off-bearing on the green chain will be a piece of cake."

"It hasn't been that bad here."

"Not if ye find frozen socks, chilblain, and bugs to yer likin'. First thing, I'm goin' to make me a hot bath. Just to see a face without whiskers. I'll even be glad to see me sister again…and Maven," he added with a smile.

When the boys were ready to leave, they said goodbye to the cook and stopped by the foreman's office to pick up their pay.

"I had my doubts when I first saw you boys," the foreman confided gruffly. "But you did all right. Be glad to have you in my camp any time you want to come back." They shook hands, an honor that was earned as well.

As the boys struck off for the station, this time it was Tommy who eagerly led the way while Ian lagged. They were almost there when Ian stopped.

"Tommy, wait. I'll nae be leavin' with ye."

Tommy turned and laughed. "For a minute I thought ye said…"

"Ye heard me right. I'm goin' back and hire on as a skidder."

Tommy stared at Ian incredulously. "Ye can na be that daft, man!"

"Tommy, I-I'm just not ready to leave yet."

"What about yer job at the mill? We're a team, remember?"

"We'll be a team again. As long as Hawkins remains foreman, there will always be accidents happenin' and positions to be filled."

"Yer mind be made up then?"

Ian nodded.

Tommy let out a long sigh. He didn't understand at all, but then he rarely understood Ian these days. "I guess I'll be seein' ye in the spring then. Take care of yerself, lad."

The two boys clasped each other by the shoulder, bid farewell, and went their separate ways for the first time in their friendship.

March 1878

CHAPTER 8

"Maven, why don't ye and Tommy take yerselves out on the porch fer a spell."

Maven groaned inwardly at her mother's transparent attempt at matchmaking. "I should help ye with the dishes, Mum."

"Yer sister and brother can do that."

As the younger McInnis siblings loudly protested, their mother sent them a quelling look.

"Mum...," said Maven, a warning note in her tone. The glint in her eyes sent an even stronger message, but her mother was either blissfully obtuse or intentionally ignorant.

"Shoo, off with ye now."

"Why should they be wantin' to go out on the porch? It be forty degrees out there."

Mrs. McInnis glared at her husband. "'Tis a fine March day. It clears the head."

Mr. McInnis shot Maven a conspiratorial wink. "Well, then, perhaps I should join Maven and Tommy on the porch meself."

"I think, Mr. McInnis, that ye'll be joinin' me in the kitchen if ye do na have a care."

As her father burst into laughter, Maven grabbed their coats from the hall rack and hustled Tommy out the door before she was completely mortified.

"Thank ye for Sunday dinner, Mrs. McInnis," Tommy called over his shoulder.

"'Tis welcome you are at any time, lad. Isn't that so, Maven?"

Maven rolled her eyes heavenward and shoved Tommy the rest of the way out the door, pulling it shut behind her.

"'Tis especially fair ye look today, Maven," said Tommy.

Maven blushed. "Thank ye, Tommy…. When do ye think Ian will be comin' home?"

Ian…her thoughts went back to him as they had done so often over the winter. She wondered what he was doing, how he was surviving. Had he missed her at all?

Tommy steadied the porch swing for her and sat down beside her. "Ian will be comin' soon I expect. Ye know, the mill will be back in full production soon, and I'll be gettin' me full wages again…. 'Tis nineteen I am now and time to be thinkin' of takin' a wife."

"That's nice, Tommy. Maureen O'Donnell has always spoken of a great fondness for ye."

Tommy shifted uneasily. "Well, Maureen, be not who I had in mind…exactly. I was thinkin' more of the likes of…"

Maven jumped up from the swing. "Tommy, I have a terrible chill. I think I'm comin' down with an illness. Do ye mind if we say good-bye now?"

"Yes…I mean no…Maven I need to talk with ye, lass," sputtered a flustered Tommy. "'Tis important."

"I'm sorry, Tommy. I do na feel meself today. I feel a fever comin' on. Can we not speak of this another time?""

"Aye, if ye not be feelin' well."

He reluctantly escorted her to the door, at great pains to hide his disappointment. He moved to kiss her, but she quickly ducked inside the house. She breathed a sigh of relief when she heard his footsteps trail off the porch. When she turned around, she inwardly groaned as she met the hopeful smiles of her parents.

*   *   *   *   *   *   *   *

It was Sunday in mid April.

Ian awoke to a steady, dripping sound. At first he thought it was rain, but then he realized that the water trickling off the shanty's roof was melting snow. At that moment, a skidder came running back from the outhouse shouting. Annoyed, semi-conscious loggers threw boots or whatever came to hand at him, but he was undeterred.

"The ice is breaking up on the river!" he yelled, dodging various articles of dress. "We're going home!"

Heads popped up, and a loud, collective cheer went up. After long, hard months in the woods, the farmers were heartsick for their families and anxious to get back to their farms. The professional woodsmen, most of whom were unattached, were just heartily sick of logging and yearned to see the inside of a tavern and feel the warmth of a good woman.

Ian leaped from his bunk, crossing the room in long, impatient strides, and swung open the door. A wild sweetness rose up to greet him, setting his pulse to throbbing. The spring thaw had begun at last! At the edge of the woods, where the snow had begun to melt, he could see delicate pink and white arbutus blooms peeking out at the new world. Still curled in their fuzzy white sheaths, ferns poked through wet leaves, ready to unfold into lacy fronds. In the distance, he could hear the ice breaking on the river. Ian threw back his head and drank in the sounds and smells of spring.

Over time, the rage in his heart had lessened and although an ache would always remain, the emptiness inside of him was not quite the void it had been. Now he was ready to go home, too.

First, there was much work to be done before anyone would be going home. The Morgan timber mark had to be hammered into the ends of hundreds of logs and the squared, more select timber saved for ship building, had to be lashed together into cribs and the cribs into large rafts. Then the headlong race would be on to rush Morgan logs downstream to the boom before the other mills had filled its limited capacity.

It was well into the third week before the rafts were ready to go. The high, rushing waters of the river were already carrying the loose logs, guided by log drivers, to the boom. Those wishing to travel overland had left the camp the previous day, leaving behind those brave or foolish enough to ride down river with the rafters. Ian had opted for the latter. With the railroad track washed out in sections from the mudslide, the river was the quickest mode of transportation.

For four days, the men lived on the rafts as they floated down the river, sleeping in a tent, cooking on a cambuse fire and amusing themselves by singing and dancing. After months of isolation, the air was filled with their high spirits and ribaldry. With a speculative eye, Ian surveyed the passing mountain of timber. One day, he promised himself, he would own a tract of it.

"Rapids ahead!" shouted the raftsmen aft.

Immediately the men jumped to attention.

"Christ! Look at that!" exclaimed another man.

Ian felt a trickle of fear as turbulent white water rose up before them like a boiling cauldron. Normally, it was a manageable rapid, but the fast moving river, engorged with the melting snows from higher up in the mountains, made it a dangerous, whirlpool.

"Hold tight!" yelled the pilot.

Everyone ran to grab onto a place on the aft or stern oar. As the raft pitched over the falls, it did a dizzying dance and for a long, agonizing moment, Ian thought it was going to flip over. Everything not nailed down took flight. Ice cold water spewed over them, threatening to rip them from their sanctuary. At the sound of a loud crack and shouts of alarm, Ian saw that a crib had broken loose of the raft, and he watched helplessly as two men were spilled into the icy river. At one point, he had lost his footing and was nearly pitched into the water with them.

The terrifying ride lasted only a few minutes, but to Ian it had seemed an eternity. If he had thought he had been close to death before as a skidder, he figured he had looked the grim reaper full in the face this time.

Panting from exhaustion and chilled to the bone, the men took stock of the damage. The two rafters who had gone overboard were not sighted and did not answer to any calls. There was always the hope that they had grabbed onto some flotsam or an ice floe and been carried down river to a spot where they would be either picked up or could make it to shore. But secretly, everyone knew it was a slim chance that the men had survived. A stark sobriety settled over the crew.

As they continued to survey the debris along the way, a new horror seized them—this wreckage wasn't from their raft. One man pointed to a fiddle caught in a low hanging tree; another recognized the hat bobbing in the current as belonging to a teamster who had been on the first raft. A sick feeling struck them in the pit of their stomachs and several of the rafters crossed themselves. Further down river, a more grisly sight awaited them. Two bodies were caught in the brush along the bank. Judging from the mass of logs floating up ahead, there was little doubt now that the raft that had preceded them had broken up going over the rapids.

They picked up bodies along the way and put into shore to erect the customary crosses to mark the deaths. It unnerved Ian to see how many markers there were along this stretch.

The next day, the raft put into Rossburg to pick up supplies and drop off loggers and the dead before continuing onto Harrisburg. Their mood greatly subdued, the woodsmen were eager to see the inside of a tavern for a different reason now than when they had started out. They had all lost friends on that raft, and everyone knew that but for the luck of the draw, he was lucky to be alive. Ian joined them for a drink before heading off to his own business.

CHAPTER 9

Tommy soundly clapped his friend on the back in an enthusiastic greeting. "Ian! Mary mother of Jesus, 'tis good to see ye! When did ye get back? Geez, ye look like hell."

Ian smiled. Good old Tommy. "Thanks, I missed ye, too."

"Come in, come in. Mum's visitin' down the street and Da's liftin' a few pints down at the saloon. What happened? Ye look as though ye've been pulled through a knothole backwards."

As Ian followed Tommy into the kitchen of the O'Brien house, he told him about the near escape on the rapids and the rafting accident.

Tommy shook his head. "'Tis sorry I am to hear it. I remember a couple of the lads. Have a seat." He reached for the teapot, then changed his mind. He rummaged in the back of the cupboard and pulled out a bottle of Irish whiskey instead. "Strictly fer what ails ye or fer special occasions. I figure this to be special enough." He splashed a hefty shot in two glasses and handed one to Ian. "To friends, here and gone," he said, lifting his glass in salute.

"To friends," said Ian.

They threw back their drinks in a single gulp, and Tommy refilled the glasses. He took a chair across the table, critically assessing his friend as Ian relaxed and stretched out his long frame. His face was lined with fatigue, but Tommy could see that the tension was gone from his eyes and the dark intensity from his manner.

"The woods have agreed with ye, Ian."

"I think ye can better say 'twas me that agreed with the woods. How is Maven?"

"The same. Stubborn as always."

Ian laughed. He could just see the indignant set of her chin and the flash in those big, green eyes. He hadn't realized how much he had missed her.

"Where might ye be stayin' now? We've a spare room here fer ye."

"Thanks for the offer, Tommy, but I got my room back at the boardin' house."

Tommy's brow furrowed as he swirled the liquor in his glass. "Maven said ye'd say no. Why? This be yer place here."

"I can na come back to the Basin, Tommy. Let's leave it at that."

"She said ye'd say that, too. Sometimes I can na figure either one of ye."

"How did ye fare the winter?" asked Ian, changing the subject.

Tommy slumped in his chair. "Same old story. The mill has been down longer than usual this winter."

"The river?"

"Mostly. But it would na made much difference if the river had flowed all winter. The mill used up all the logs that were left in the boom two months ago. And this late thaw dinna help matters. We were all scramblin' for what odd jobs there was just to keep body and soul together."

"The mill is open now, isn't it?"

"Aye, but no tellin' for how long."

"Why? The boom should be full of timber by now."

"It is, but mostly with Thompson's and Brown's timber. Their tract is closer, and the lumber was shipped most of the way by rail. The boom can hold only so much."

"Morgan can contract to buy some of Thompson's or Brown's timber until he can get his own in the boom."

Tommy shook his head. "There be bad blood there, especially between him and Thompson. It seems Morgan tried to shut 'em out a few year's back to reduce the competition. The mills could stay open in the winter when the millpond isn't frozen over if the boom could hold more timber."

Ian fell silent for a moment. "I have an idea that will solve that problem with the boom, but I need more time to work on it."

"Better work fast," said Tommy soberly. "At this rate, I'll ne'er be able to afford to marry."

Ian laughed. "Ye…marry. Go on with ye. What lass are ye thinkin' to marry?"

Tommy threw Ian a bashful grin. "Maven. I've been keen on her for a long time now."

"Maven?" The amusement on Ian's face disappeared. "Ye can na do that, Tommy. Nae Maven. She's one of us. It would na be right."

"C'mon, Ian, we're not kids anymore. Maven be a woman now. She'll be seventeen. She'll soon finish her schoolin' and is learnin' the trade at Mrs. Drury's dress shop."

Ian bolted down the rest of his drink, hard-pressed to hide his distress. Maven…a woman. He had never considered the possibility of her marrying anyone. He couldn't think of her as a wife to any man—certainly not Tommy. Maven was the one constant in his life.

"Ian, be ye ill, man?" asked Tommy. "Ye look a wee bit pale."

Ian mustered up a tight smile. "Ye took me by surprise is all. How does Maven feel about yer plans?"

"I tried to ask her last month, but she was na feelin' well, and then the mill dinna open. I thought it best to wait 'til I was makin' a steady wage. Maybe ye could put in a good word fer me, bein' that you two always had a special kinship. I have to tell ye, I used to be a bit put out by it at times."

"I'd like to help ye, Tommy, but ye know how Maven is about makin' up her own mind to things."

Tommy laughed. "Do I now! She read me out good the other day when I tried to hurry her decision on a piece of cloth at the dry goods store."

"Ye been spendin' a lot of time together, have ye?"

"As much as I can find."

"Maybe ye should give Maven a chance to miss ye," suggested Ian. "Ye know the old saying: 'Absence makes the heart grow fonder.'"

"Aye, but there be another: 'Out of sight, out of mind,'" said Tommy.

*   *   *   *   *   *   *   *

Maven was hunched over a table in the dress shop, preoccupied with the task of cutting out cloth for a customer's gown.

"Yer pardon, lass, might I have yer attention?"

Her head shot up at the sound of the low-timbred voice, and she thought her heart was going to leap to her throat. She whirled about shock, disbelief and pleasure melding in her face.

"Ian!"

Ian grinned. "Is that the best ye can do now?"

Maven dropped the shears and threw herself into his arms. She didn't stop to consider the impropriety of such behavior. She didn't care.

Laughing, Ian caught her and swung her around, lifting her easily off the floor. When he set her on her feet again, she could only stare at him. His distant, tightly coiled manner had eased, and there was now a maturity about him to support the physical changes. Ian Douglas was a man.

"Have I grown two heads?" he teased

Maven blushed and quickly lowered her gaze. "I-I can na believe ye're here. 'Tis been such a long time."

"Only five months. Did ye miss me now?"

"Aye, about as much as ye missed me," she said in a bantering tone.

Ian put a hand beneath her chin and raised her eyes to his. "Then, ye must have missed me sorely," he said soberly.

Maven gave him a wobbly smile and stepped out of his embrace. Her heart was beating so hard, she thought it likely to burst.

"Will...will ye be goin' back to work at the mill?"

"Aye, provided Morgan has a position open."

Maven hadn't realized that she had been holding her breath, fearing the answer, until she expelled it in a rush of relief.

Ian looked around the dress shop at the bolts of material neatly stacked on the shelves, at the various bric-a-brac and spools of thread strewn haphazardly across the work table. In the corner, a dressmaker's dummy was draped with the skeleton of a dress.

"Tommy told me ye are boardin' here now."

Maven nodded. "I have a room at the back of the shop. Mrs. Drury has been most kind. She has even made use of a few of me designs."

"I'm glad ye're away from the Basin. Ye do nae belong there."

"We can na deny who we are, Ian. I'm not ashamed of me roots."

He saw her back stiffen and her green eyes spark. "'Twas not what I meant, Maven. I can na watch ye breakin' your back for naught, doin' other people's cleanin' and washin'. Ye deserve more."

"When did ye return?" she asked, changing the subject. She hadn't waited all this time to see him only to bicker.

"Yesterday late afternoon. By the time I settled in at the boardin' house, 'twas too late to see ye." His voice deepened, and it held a mixture of awe and regret. "Ye've changed, Maven. Ye be wearin' yer hair up like a lady now. Tommy said ye were grown. I guess he was right."

Maven put her hands on her hips. "Now might ye be thinkin' that ye and Tommy are the only ones who are allowed to grow up, Ian Douglas?" Her tone was light and bantering, but he could see a serious glint in her eyes. "Things change, Ian," she said on a more somber note.

Ian shook his head. He didn't want things to change. He didn't want to come home to find that Tommy was waiting for an opportunity to ask Maven to marry him. That the intimacy he and Maven had shared as children was replaced by a self-conscious awkwardness between a man and a woman meeting for the first time. He was gone for only five months. How could everything have changed so quickly?

Chapter 10

The noon whistle blew, and the mill shut down. Tommy pulled out a sandwich and cast Ian a sidelong glance.

"We haven't seen much of you since ye come back from the woods. Ye ne'er come by the neighborhood. Maven's been wonderin' about ye."

Ian shrugged. "Been busy."

"Doin' what?"

"I've been workin' on a plan to expand the boom, if ye must know."

"Hey, you…Douglas," the foreman yelled. "Mr. Morgan wants to see you in his office." Hawkins jerked his thumb in the direction and spat a stream of tobacco juice in the layer of sawdust on the floor.

Tommy looked at Ian. "Why would Morgan want to see ye?"

Ian gathered the remains of his lunch and stood up. "I'll let ye know when he tells me."

The two-story structure stood a safe distance from the sawmill as a precaution against fire. Lumber lay stacked for curing in the exposed lower level. It was quieter here away from the mill, and Ian's boots made a loud, clumping noise as he climbed the wooden stairs to Morgan's second floor office.

Why had Morgan sent for him? he wondered. A complaint couldn't have come from Hawkins. Ian was marking time now and being careful to keep his nose clean while he was doing it. He had a plan to see through that he wasn't about to let Hawkins spoil. His weeks at the logging camp had taught him that he could achieve far more in a much shorter time by going from the inside out rather than from the outside in.

He knocked firmly on the door displaying *C.P. Morgan* in gilt letters.

"Come in," a voice gruffly commanded.

Ian opened the door and entered the office. A heavy-set man with a thick thatch of gray hair neatly parted in the center was hunched over his desk.

"Mr. Hawkins said ye wanted to see me, sir."

Cyrus Morgan looked up from his papers. Light gray eyes, sharp and assessing, gave Ian more than a cursory glance. "Have a seat, Douglas."

"Yessir."

Ian settled himself in the simple, wooden chair and took a quick look about the room. The sparse, crudely furnished office was not what he would have expected of one of the richest, most powerful men in Rossburg.

Instead of a great mahogany desk, finely detailed and polished, Morgan's desk looked like something rescued from a scrap mill, scarred and nondescript. In the absence of any carpeting, the pine floor was bare and pocked from the spiked boots of the workers who had preceded him. A few wood planks supported by bricks provided a makeshift bookcase for a dozen or so books. Behind Morgan, a window, thinly coated with sawdust and soot from the huge incinerator outside, kept watch over the yards like an omniscient eye.

Even Morgan's dress was in keeping with the room. He wore no suit coat, just a vest over a crisp, white shirt, the sleeves rolled up to his elbows. All that he saw belied everything Ian had ever heard about the man. His prodigious wealth and love for the ostentatious was well documented by his grand estate and legendary parties. Unless...unless Cyrus Morgan was shrewder than he thought.

Morgan watched Ian closely. "I take it my office is not what you expected."

Ian smiled. "Actually, sir, I was thinkin' that the reputation ye have for shrewdness is well-deserved and perhaps a bit underrated."

"Oh? How so?"

"In times of labor unrest, it is advisable to capitalize on a man's humbler beginnin's."

"You're smart, Douglas, but perhaps you overlooked the fact that I find more comfort here in my humble beginnings."

Ian didn't look or sound convinced. "Perhaps."

The worn leather creaked as Cyrus settled back in his chair to take his own measure of the young man before him. He already had Hawkins' assessment. The boy was respectful but not reverent. Ian Douglas would never hold anyone in awe, he determined. He could see it in the youth's rigid manner, in his unflinching gaze beneath Morgan's frank appraisal. Even so, Douglas did not strike him as being the fire-breathing anarchist his foreman would have him believe.

"I understand that you and my foreman have differences."

Ian's face reflected surprise. "I've given Hawkins no cause for complaint."

"Not since you've returned. That's what has him so worried. He thinks you're up to something. I can't afford rabble-rousers on the premises, stirring up trouble, interrupting production, Douglas, just when we're reopening after the winter."

Ian wanted to laugh aloud. He was damned if he did and damned if he didn't. "Are ye firin' me, sir?"

"No, unless you give me good reason. What have you got against Hawkins anyway?"

Ian's reply was succinct. "Ye give respect, ye get respect."

"He gets the job done."

"By endangerin' the workers."

"How's that again?"

"The idea of job rotation is good to a point. But it gives Hawkins leave to place men in positions they aren't always suited to. He also sets near impossible quotas."

"A good foreman gets more out of his men than they think they have to give."

"It depends on the cost to the mill and to the worker."

Morgan's gut instinct told him to get rid of Douglas as Hawkins strongly advised, but there was merit in what the boy had to say. Since the afternoon break was instituted, accidents had decreased and production was slightly higher.

"How old are you, Douglas?"

"Eighteen, sir."

Cyrus Morgan pulled on his chin with a well-manicured thumb and forefinger. If the boy was kept separated from the mill and the hands, how much trouble could he cause?

"I need a good pike man on the millpond. It would mean a twenty-five cent per day increase in your pay. Are you interested?"

"Tommy O'Brien and I are a team."

"I believe that can be arranged. Report to the millpond tomorrow."

Ian had no sooner left than Hawkins appeared.

"Well, what's Douglas up to?"

"Nothing that I can see," said Morgan. I've assigned him to the millpond. If he's separated from the mill, he can't cause much trouble."

"I say you should get rid of him."

"I can't, Hawkins."

"Why not?"

"He wagered his job on that afternoon break. He won." Morgan folded his hands across his chest, his manner contemplative. "Ian Douglas has a purpose. Until I know what that is, he bears watching. A man with a purpose has to be reckoned with sooner or later."

CHAPTER II

Stars like a thousand flickering fireflies dotted the darkening sky, playing tag with the clouds. A soft breeze drifted off the river to lend the spring evening a certain balminess in spite of a gathering dampness.

A set of rolled up plans tucked under his arm, Ian jumped off the streetcar and walked down the street known as "Millionaires' Row". Once again, he rehearsed in his mind what he was going to say. It was a bold move to enter the sanctuary of the rich, and he had to wonder now what idiocy had possessed him to come here. One by one, he passed the great shadowy monuments to wealth and vanity, protected by ornate wrought iron fences and illumed by street lamps. There were no street lamps in the Basin, he noted with cynical amusement, nor were the streets paved liked this one. He wondered what it must be like to be free from choking dust in the summer and mud in the winter.

In the middle of the block, Ian stopped before the grandest house of all, a massive three-story, stone house with high, vaulted arches. It was said that the house had cost nearly a million dollars to build. Ian couldn't begin to comprehend a figure like that. He hesitated for a moment, somewhat awed and a bit intimidated. With a renewed sense of purpose, he willed himself to open the iron gate and pass through the stone arch. Once inside the circle of privacy hedges, he saw that statues and fountains graced a brick piazza-like patio. His legs felt like lead as he walked up the steps to the front door. Like everything else about the house, the thick, mahogany door with leaded windows, too, was solid and intimidating.

Ian ran a finger around his stiff collar, squared his shoulders, and took a deep breath. He raised the heavy knocker and let it fall with a dull thud. As he waited, he tapped the plans nervously against his leg. When there was no response, he put more authority into his knock. After a few minutes and no response, he reached out to lift the knocker again, then decided against it. It wouldn't do him any good to beard the lion in his own den.

As he started down the steps, the door opened and a woman answered, "Yes, what is it?"

Ian quickly turned back, swallowing hard. "Is Mr. Morgan at home?"

"All deliveries are made at the rear of the house."

"I'm not makin' a delivery."

"Well, then, who are you?"

"Ian Douglas. I work for Mr. Morgan at his mill."

"Mr. Morgan sees his employees at the mill during the day. I suggest you wait 'til Monday."

"I need to talk to him now. 'Tis a matter concerning the mill."

"Mr. Morgan is expecting guests soon."

"I won't be long," Ian said resolutely. What he had to present to Morgan could very well wait until Monday, but the stubborn Scotsman in him refused to let it do so. He wasn't going to be turned away like a lowly vendor by a woman of no better circumstance than he.

The housekeeper's irritation was apparent. "Wait here." She closed the door on Ian in a telling gesture. It seemed an eternity before she opened it again. "Mr. Morgan will see you in his study. Follow me and be quick about it."

Ian had never been inside a fine house before, and it was all he could do to keep from gawking. It was evident that the lumber baron had spent as freely on the interior as he did on the exterior—both being a far cry from his office. The entrance alone, with its rich wood paneling and fine millwork, was five times the size of his room at the boarding house. He had never seen nor imagined anything so grand.

"This way," said the housekeeper, casting him a look of disapproval. She briskly ushered him through double doors into a room equally as impressive. "Mr. Morgan will join you shortly."

Heavy drapes were drawn against the night and a low fire blazed in the Italian marble fireplace to ward off a gathering chill. Ian wondered if Morgan had ever read any of the hundreds of books that lined the walls in bookshelves. He sat down on a green leather sofa. When he heard the echo of approaching footsteps on the marble-tiled foyer, he jumped to attention.

Morgan entered the room and drew the doors shut before seating himself behind a magnificent mahogany desk, its patina polished to glossy perfection. "Well, Douglas, what's so important that it can't wait until Monday?" he demanded, rummaging around in a drawer until he came up with a cigar.

Ian's voice rose with his excitement. "I've been doin' some checking, sir...about the boom."

Morgan cocked a brow as he struck a match and lit the cigar, puffing on it a few times to get it started. "What about the boom?"

"The owner of the Susquehanna Boom Company is willin' to sell with favorable terms. As it would most certainly benefit ye to buy it, I thought that—" Ian stopped short as Morgan burst into laughter.

"Sorry, Douglas, but Gentry has been trying to unload that white elephant for three years. Looks like he sure pulled the wool over your eyes," said Morgan still chuckling. "The company barely turns a profit. Don't know why. Gentry finds enough strays. He gets to keep any lumber that comes into the boom lacking a mill brand. Some of us have wondered how Gentry seems to find so many. I've decided to plant a man there to see if the scoundrel is cutting the jobbers stamp off the timber. Rustling is becoming a problem. I think I shall bring the matter up before the

Lumbermen's Exchange." Morgan puffed on his cigar, lost in thought for a moment.

"Mr. Morgan, about the boom," said Ian. "If it could be made larger, it could store more lumber over the winter and the mills would na have to close for lack of timber."

"And it would be an even easier target for the spring floods."

"No, sir. If ye'll just look at my drawin's." Ian unrolled the plans and laid them across the desk. "We can sink the cribs and make them taller, strengthen the boom by attaching cables to a string of logs like so. The boom should easily withstand a flood. I got the idea from beaver trappers when I was loggin' in the mountains. They use a similar method to keep their traps from floatin' away in the spring thaw."

"Very interesting, Douglas. When did you become an engineer?"

Ian's brow rippled with confusion. "I'm not, sir."

"Exactly. Sorry, boy. Better men than you have looked to improve the boom. There's nothing to be done about it, or else someone would have done it."

"This new construction will work, Mr. Morgan. I would stake my life on it."

"First your job, then your life...you like to wager high, don't you, Douglas?"

"No wager is too high when I believe in somethin'."

"That's admirable, I suppose, but you don't understand about business. Assuming your plan does work, do you think for one minute mill owners will stand for one of their kind to own the boom? It would be unfair competition." Morgan leaned forward for greater emphasis. "Douglas, the short of it is, while they could be better, we like things just the way they are."

"All of ye can buy the boom with equal partnerships."

"I haven't gotten where I am today by investing in foolish ventures."

Morgan stood, stubbed out his cigar, and came from around his desk. Ian clearly read the dismissal in his manner. He could see that all arguments on the subject would be futile. There was nothing left for him to do but leave. He felt like a little boy being patted on the head and sent off to reconsider his silly notions. Choking back his frustration, he rolled up the plans and turned to leave when the doors slid open.

"Father, I…oh, I'm sorry. I didn't mean to interrupt. Our guests have arrived."

"That's quite all right, my dear. The young man is just leaving."

Ian stood rooted to the spot, unable to do anything more than stare at the young woman. She was even more beautiful than he had remembered. Her honey blonde hair was dressed high on top of her head, curls fluffed and frizzed bewitchingly over her forehead and around tiny shell-like ears. The blue satin evening gown, cut low in the neck, set off her alabaster skin to perfection. She stood three inches over five feet if she stood an inch, he figured, and her waist was so tiny, he would have bet that he could span it with his hands.

As he continued to stare at her, Morgan gave a snort of amusement and introduced him. "Mr. Douglas, my daughter, Eleanor."

"Enchante, Monsieur Douglas," she said sweetly, holding out a small, manicured hand.

Ian, aware that he was making a fool out of himself, quickly pulled himself together, but his face remained a study of befuddlement at her strange words and gesture. Caught off balance and not knowing what else to do, he took her hand and shook it.

He was immediately aware that he had blundered when Eleanor let out a soft laugh. He could feel the heat of humiliation travel up his neck and flood his face. Clearly, he was out of his element here, and he felt more than ever the country bumpkin. She thought him so, too. He could see it in her eyes, and he inwardly cursed his awkwardness. After worshipping her from afar, this was not the way he had fantasized their introduction.

Eleanor turned to her father. "Don't be long, Father. You know how Mr. Jeffries hates to be kept waiting. Bon soir, Monsieur Douglas." With that she regally swept out of the room, taking Ian's heart with her.

"She's boning up on her French for the European Grand Tour. Can't understand half of what she says anymore," said Morgan with a grumble. "Well now, I'm afraid that I must see to my guests. The housekeeper will show you out."

Ian was a churning mass of emotions. He was totally smitten with Eleanor Morgan. But even in his insanity, he knew how impossible the odds were that she would ever spare him so much as the time of day. They came from two different worlds with his being the inferior, a fact that was brought home to him for a second time when the housekeeper arrived to escort him out through the back door.

As Ian made his way home, his desires solidified into a driving determination that would accept no detours, no roadblocks. One day he would be one of them.

CHAPTER 12

Maven stared out the window of the dress shop with increasing anxiety. It had been raining in a steady downpour for three days and still showed no signs of easing. The swollen river had already crested at thirty feet and, aided by strong winds from the southwest, was spilling over the banks. So far only the lower end of town was flooded with two to four feet of water, and everyone was holding his breath. All work had ceased, the mills had shut down, stores had closed as the more cautious scurried to move what goods they could to attics or warehouses on higher ground and to fill sandbags. She had just finished helping Mrs. Drury move bolts of cloth to higher shelves.

Maven was particularly worried about her family. The low lying Basin was the most vulnerable part of the city. The last report she had from Tommy was that the water there was up to the top step of the porch. She wanted to return home, but her parents sent word for her to remain where she was.

All through the afternoon, Maven listened to the pounding of the rain. The intensity seemed to increase with each hour. The water was nearly up to the door of the shop, when Ian arrived with sandbags.

"Where's Mrs. Drury?" he asked.

"She went home to check on her cats. Have ye any word of the Basin?"

Ian placed sandbags outside the door. "The houses are beginnin' to flood."

Maven's voice cracked with tension. "I must go home. I must be with me family."

"No, ye're safer here. Tommy is seein' to yer family. We've been workin' to get everyone out, but few will leave. They think the rain is goin' to stop soon."

"Mrs. Drury said the river hasn't been this high in twenty years."

"Aye, 'tis what the old-timers say. Keep the door closed, Maven. I'll be back as soon as I can."

As Ian disappeared into the night, she had never felt so alone.

A torrent of rain continued into the night. Maven tried to keep her mind occupied with sewing, but after pricking herself several times, she finally set aside the gown and retired to her room. The hour was late. The clock on the dresser chimed midnight. She set the lamp on the table, turned down the wick to a low glow, and fell on top the bed fully clothed.

It seemed just minutes later when Maven was awakened to a gloomy dawn by an urgent pounding on the door. She had enjoyed only a fitful sleep, and she groggily swung her legs over the side of the bed. She came fully awake with a start as her feet sank into a foot of water. Maven looked around her in disbelief. Water was everywhere. She was spurred into action by Ian's shouts and pounding on the door, and sloshed through the shop as fast as she could, weighted down by her sodden skirts.

Quickly, Maven unlocked the door, but found that she was unable to open it. The pressure of the water made it immovable. Ian put his full weight against the door, but it refused to budge. A chair from the general store floated past, and he reached out and grabbed hold of it.

"Get your Mackintosh and stand back," he said.

As Maven snatched her coat from the stand, Ian rammed the chair through the shop window.

"Hurry, we have to get out of here," he said, reaching for her hand and helping her out. "The river is at thirty-three feet. The boom has broken, and there are a hundred million feet of lumber headin' for town. The bridge up stream has already washed out."

The blood drained from Maven's face. "Ian, me family…"

"They're all right. They're waitin' for ye. Tommy is helpin' to get the rest out by boat."

"By boat?"

"The Basin is eight feet under water now."

"Oh, dear God!" cried Maven. "What of Mrs. Drury?"

"She is safe."

"Where are we going?"

"To the park. 'Tis the highest point in town."

Ian took her by the hand and pulled her into the street. Water swirled around her knees, and the current was strong. Her skirts were like heavy weights around her ankles, clinging and entangling her legs. Debris slammed into them, throwing her off balance, and she would have slipped under the water had it not been for Ian's strong grip on her. Nausea seized her as garbage and dead animals floated past. Cries and mournful wails carried through the air. In the gray light, Maven found the scene unnerving.

When they arrived at the park, she saw that most of the townspeople were there, including residents of Millionaires' Row. Rich or poor everyone was in the same predicament. Tents had been erected and more were arriving. Dogs barked; babies cried. People moved about in shock, calling out names of loved ones, their faces either blank or etched with horror. Maven had a tearful reunion with her family, and now that Ian was sure that she was safe, he left to help with other rescues.

From the hilltop, Maven and her family watched as houses were lifted from their foundations like playing pieces on a game board and floated down the swift-flowing river. Farm animals, cats, and dogs swirled about them, struggling to find sanctuary on a passing roof. There came a more deafening noise, and people wept and cried out for God's mercy as a sea of timber roared through the center of town, crashing against buildings, shattering shop windows, tearing away store fronts, snapping street lights in two like match sticks. There was a resounding crack as more timber slammed against the Canal Street Bridge supports. And all watched in further horror as the bridge broke up, sweeping away several children and adults clinging to it.

It was nearly noon before the rain slacked off to a drizzle. Ian had returned once to tell the McInnises that their house was still on its foundation. In spite of her relief, Maven felt numb as she looked down upon the destruction and considered the loss of life. Someone had draped a blanket around her shoulders and had thrust a tin cup of coffee into her hands. In the background, the mournful cries continued.

*   *   *   *   *   *   *   *

The clean-up was slow and arduous, hampered by the hundreds of copperhead snakes that had been washed into the debris. It was three days before the water receded and tracks could be repaired so that trains could bring in food, clothes, and supplies from neighboring towns. It was a week more before mill owners could retrieve their runaway lumber from around town. Over half a million board feet had been lost down river. Twenty-three people had drowned, mostly children, from the Basin. A foot of mud had been deposited in houses left standing along the canal. Store goods were soaked and ruined. Gas pipes had broken, sparking fears of fires, and paved roads had crumbled. The destruction was beyond anyone's imagination. The city reeled with shock. Some parts of town had no sanitation, and there was widespread fear of a typhus epidemic.

The owner of the Susquehanna Boom Company sat at a makeshift desk in his office, a half empty bottle of whiskey before him. The wood shack smelled musty. Papers were laid out on every available surface to dry, the ink on most having run to the point of illegibility. He was ruined. Gentry held his head and groaned.

"Mr. Gentry?"

The owner lifted a bleary eye to a nattily dressed young man in his mid twenties, standing in the doorway.

"Yeah. Who wants to know?"

The man came forward and offered his card.

"Parker Lewis Stanton, Attorney at Law," Gentry read aloud. "Why should I care?"

"I have an offer here to buy the Susquehanna Boom Company and all of its appointments from you."

Gentry's gristly jaw dropped, and he stared at the young man in astonishment. "I couldn't sell the damned thing before the flood and now that it's ruined, you want to buy it!"

"Not I. I represent someone who does."

"Who?"

"My client prefers to remain anonymous." The lawyer dropped a small leather sack onto the desk. "There is the sum of two hundred and fifty dollars in there—"

"Two hundred and fifty dollars! The boom is worth a helluva lot more than that!"

"That may have been the case before, Mr. Gentry." Parker jerked his thumb toward the papers. "The ink is run on all your ledgers. You can't tell which mill owes you what. How do you expect to collect on the spring harvest? At its best, the boom was barely making a profit. It'll take some time to recover the cost of rebuilding it, if, in fact, you can afford to rebuild it. I think any percentage of nothing is generous, don't you?"

The owner hesitated for a long moment before scooping up the bag. "All right. You gotta deal."

"Good, now if you will sign these papers." Stanton produced legal documents from his case and pointed to the signature lines.

Gentry scowled as he reluctantly signed the papers. "What now? How long do I have here?"

"As long as you like."

"How's that?"

"My client is willing to pay you a fair wage to oversee the boom after it is rebuilt. I should say that you'll both be in operation in a month. You and your crew will be notified.... Oh, and one other thing, Mr. Gentry, my client prefers that no one know of this change in ownership. It is to be our little secret. Should you think of breaking the confidence, sir, your employment will be immediately terminated.

CHAPTER 13

Most of the mills were rebuilt and, subsisting on the lumber which had been rounded up in town and downstream, were in full operation by the following month. Mill owners were hopeful that their supply would last until the summer harvest of timber hit the boom. After that, it would be hand-to-mouth until the winter harvest came through. There was the unspoken acknowledgment and resignation that lean times lay ahead.

The boom was nearly rebuilt. A few hundred wooden structures or cribs, resembling small log cabins sitting on top of the water, dotted the south side of the river for a stretch of nearly two miles. The partially submerged cribs were actually thirty-three feet in height this time and would be anchored with heavier cables and linked by a chain of floating logs. Silhouetted against the horizon, the boom seemed to stand in defiance of any act of nature.

Cyrus Morgan climbed the stairs to his office in the mill yard with a slow, heavy foot. He wasn't as young as he used to be, he thought, as he paused midway to catch his breath. The flood had taken a great toll on him. His residence had suffered less than most and the mill had withstood only the damage of some saws, but the loss of the timber was another matter. The fact that his losses were no worse than any other businessmen of Rossburg was of little consolation to him. He had borrowed heavily on margin against the profits of that crop of lumber.

Morgan wheezed as he entered the office and lowered his bulk into his chair. The summer harvest wasn't going to begin to cover his deficit. Year after year, there had been little more than some surface flooding from the melting snows in the mountains. Who would have guessed that after twenty-four years...

The flood had ruined everything. His mood wasn't improved either by the knowledge that Rossburg's Basin population had feasted for days on a very expensive cargo of oysters meant for his table. The delicacy had been shipped all the way from Baltimore.

Rising water had completely covered the piers at the railroad crossing at West Third Street. When the train had tried to cross the bridge, the rails had sagged under the weight, and the timbers broke, plunging the "oyster train" into Lycoming Creek. Floodwaters had washed several kegs of oysters downstream into the Susquehanna River.

"Damned fools should have known they couldn't cross the river then," he mumbled. He still didn't see the humor in the event that the newspapers had seemed to find. It would appear that his string of bad luck ran to oysters as well.

Morgan groaned and passed a hand wearily across his face. At least he hadn't been fool enough to buy the boom company.

Gentry...now there was a curiosity, Morgan thought to himself. After years of hearing the man complain that he could scarcely eke out a living with the low boomage fee, it was a surprise to find him rebuilding so quickly. They had all expected Gentry to cut his losses and turn to something else. Not that the mill owners and boomrats weren't happy to see him rebuild, but they all had to wonder where he had gotten the money. Gentry wasn't talking, and after awhile mill owners decided it didn't matter so long as the chore was accomplished without their pockets being touched.

"Ye wanted to see me, sir?"

Morgan looked up, startled for a moment to find Ian standing in the doorway.

"What? Oh, yes, Douglas, come in…. How would you like to be foreman of the mill?"

Ian blinked in astonishment and wondered if he had heard correctly. "Foreman?"

"Yes, foreman."

"What about Hawkins?"

"You have ideas that work. Hawkins doesn't. Right now I need ideas that work. It's as simple as that. You're young, but I think you can handle the job. The men respect you. You seem to have a way with them that Hawkins never did."

"I know nae what to say, sir."

"No need to say anything. I'm not doing you a favor, boy. There are bad times ahead. There's only timber enough in the boom to keep the mill open until September, maybe October if we're lucky enough to buy out one of the smaller mills. The men are likely to get ugly when they can't feed their families. That flood was a major setback. It's gonna take a long time to recover from it."

"Mr. Morgan, what if we start our own planing mill and sell finished lumber directly to furniture and cabinetmakers instead of rough-cut timber to a middle man? Ye could keep the men on through the winter. Finished lumber fetches a higher price than rough-cut timber. 'Twould more than pay the wages and turn a tidy profit besides."

Morgan contemplated the proposal, tapping his fingers on the desk. Ian shifted uncomfortably, wondering if this idea was going to be met with laughter, too.

"By God, I knew you were the man for the job!" Morgan suddenly exclaimed, startling Ian. "I like you, Douglas. You're a thinking man. Some mill owners consider that a liability. I don't."

"I do nae intend to spend the rest of my life as a mill hand, sir. Someday, I expect to be ownin' my own mill," declared Ian with a quiet confidence that almost bordered on defiance.

Morgan studied the youth with keen interest. Now he knew of whom the lad reminded him.

"I wasn't much older than you when I said the same thing," he told Ian. "I saved every dime I could get my hands on and bought a thousand-acre tract of land that no one else wanted. The trees were too small, but I had the time to wait. Ten years later, that tract was in much demand. I sold off a few acres and used the money to build my own sawmill. A piece of advice, Douglas. Live frugally. Don't spend your wages. Loan them out at a satisfactory interest instead. You can find other, smaller jobs to give you spending money."

"Aye, sir."

May 1879

CHAPTER 14

"How about it, Ian? Just this once talk to Maven fer me."

Ian looked up from the manifest in annoyance. "What am I supposed to say to her, Tommy?"

Tommy grinned. "Just tell her what a great lad I am. How difficult can that be?"

"We've been through this before. I thought we had agreed to let her make up her own mind."

"I keep askin' her to marry me, and she keeps puttin' me off."

"Sounds like she has more sense than ye do."

"What's that suppose to mean?"

"Look, Tommy, 'tis been almost a year since the flood, and the mill is just gettin' on its feet. How are ye to support a wife and family now, answer me that?"

"C'mon, Ian. Ever since ye convinced Morgan to build that planing mill, we haven't been out of work a day. In a few weeks, the boom'll be filled to overflowin' with the winter harvest. If Gentry keeps addin' to the boom the way he's been doin', we'll ne'er be out of work. What be ye gettin' so sore about anyway?" Tommy eyed Ian speculatively. "Ye not be thinkin' I'm not good enough for Maven, are ye now?"

"No, that isn't it." But even as he said it, Ian knew it was a lie. He hated to think of Maven living the type of life that women in the Basin led, living hand-to-mouth, one babe hanging on her skirts with another in her arms, drudgery aging her beyond her years, despair beating down her spirit. He had hopes that somehow she would find a way to cheat this destiny.

"What is it then?"

"Nothin'. Look, I'll talk to her, okay? But just this once," said Ian curtly.

"When?"

"I can na say."

"Hey, Ian," shouted a worker running in from the yard, "Mr. Morgan hollered down that he wants to see you, an' he ain't happy."

Thankful for the interruption whatever Morgan's mood, Ian quickly set off for the yard.

"Sunday, Ian," Tommy called after him. "Talk to Maven on Sunday."

When Ian entered Morgan's office, he found him pacing the floor in a furious state.

"Do you know what this is!" Morgan roared, waving a sheaf of papers at Ian.

"Nae, sir."

"It's a notice. The Susquehanna Boom Company petitioned the state legislature and received permission to raise the boomage fee from fifty cents to a dollar twenty-five per thousand feet! Gentry went sneaking behind our backs!"

"What if Gentry had told ye of his intentions?" asked Ian.

"The petition would have been voted down like every other time he tried to raise the fee."

"In other words, the Lumbermen's Exchange did nae have time to make arrangements with certain legislators."

Morgan swung a sharp eye on Ian. "I told you before, Douglas, you don't understand business. Gentry didn't pull this off by himself. My man would have heard something. I would have been notified of it. Bring my carriage around, Douglas. We're going to get to the bottom of this!"

As Ian drove the carriage upstream along the river bank to the Susquehanna Boom Company, he let out a long, low whistle. The boom stretched as far as the eye could see.

"I hear tell it goes for seven miles," said Ian. "That's double what it used to be. It must be able to hold over three hundred million board feet of lumber now. At a dollar twenty-five a foot, Gentry is going to be a very rich man."

Morgan glared at Ian. He hadn't missed the innuendo. He could very well have made one of the biggest and most costly mistakes of his life not buying the boom. "Bah, a small flood will knock most of it out anyway," he said on a note of dismissal.

The rest of the trip was made in stony silence with Morgan sporting his darkest scowl. By the time he burst into the Susquehanna Boom Company's office, he presented a formidable appearance.

"Gentry!" he shouted. "Show yourself, man!"

Gentry, himself a burly man, emerged from an inner office with cool confidence.

"Well if it ain't Mr. Morgan himself. Had a feeling I might be hearin' from you."

"What's the meaning of this!" Morgan demanded, waving the notice in front of the other man's face.

Gentry smiled. "Looks like a notice of an increase in the boomage fee to me."

"I know what it is!" snapped Morgan. "How dare you go behind our backs to the legislature without so much as a warning."

"You mean before you had a chance to feather a few nests?"

"Look here, Gentry, I can't help it if you can't handle your finances. We've been generous with you."

Gentry let out a boom of laughter. "A nickel increase to smooth my ruffled feathers each time you and the others manage to get my requests voted down for a fee increase. You're generous to a fault, Morgan. All I know is that I barely made ends meet while you and the others grew rich. You may rule this town, Morgan, but you're not going to rule the boom anymore. This time somebody has outsmarted you."

Though close to apoplexy, Morgan's sharp ears caught the slip. "What do you mean somebody? There *is* someone else in this with you! I knew it. You're not smart enough to pull this off by yourself. We all wondered where you suddenly came up with the money to rebuild. Who is it? Who's your partner?"

Gentry folded his arms across his chest and his tobacco-stained lips turned up in a smug smile. "Talk to my attorney, Morgan."

"Your attorney! Since when do you have an attorney?"

"Since now. His name is Parker Lewis Stanton II...up on Market Street."

Morgan emerged from Gentry's office in full-blown fury. A visit to Parker Stanton yielded no more satisfaction. Indeed, a good deal less. The young man was new to Rossburg, and if he was ignorant of Morgan's position in town, it held little sway once the older man informed him of it. Ian watched through the window, as Stanton deftly turned aside Morgan's furious demands. When Morgan emerged, he was breathing heavier, and it was with some difficulty that he pulled himself into the carriage. Ian returned his employer to the mill in a greater temper than when he had left.

"Is there anything else, sir?" asked Ian.

"No!...Wait. Rally the members of the Lumbermen's Exchange. I'm calling an emergency meeting in an hour. Then pick up my daughter at the Pennsy passenger train station at four o'clock. She's arriving from New York from her Grand Tour. Tell her...tell her I'll see her at dinner."

Ian's heart did a flip, and he struggled to conceal his excitement. "Aye, sir."

He tore around town, delivering Morgan's message to all the members. It left him with just enough time to stop by his room and change into his Sunday clothes. When Morgan had ordered him to pick up his daughter at the station, Ian couldn't believe his good fortune. Here was his chance to show her that he wasn't the awkward, tongue-tied bumpkin he had first appeared. This meeting would go differently, he determined, straightening his tie and looking himself over in the mirror.

Twenty minutes later, Ian stood nervously on the station platform, pacing back and forth, readjusting his tie and jacket sleeves that were too short for his arms. Finally, he heard it, the distant scream of the train whistle. He snatched up the bouquet of spring flowers from the bench and walked to the end of the platform.

The train came to a screeching halt, and Ian's eyes scanned the coach windows, trying to catch a glimpse of Eleanor Morgan. A cloud of steam enveloped the tracks, momentarily obscuring his vision. When it cleared, he saw a beautiful, young woman alighting from the train with all the grace of good breeding and all the poise of class. He hadn't seen her in over a year, not since that humiliating encounter in her father's study, but he could never forget her. Tommy was wrong. Absence does make the heart grow fonder, thought Ian, his eyes taking in every curve of her petite figure. He wondered if she remembered him. When he summoned the courage to approach her, her smile was cool and reserved, and his confidence dipped lower. She was obviously disappointed to see him.

Ian snatched the cap from his head. "Mr. Morgan is in an emergency meetin', Miss Morgan. He asked me to escort ye home."

"Yes, I gathered as much," she said in a dull, flat tone. "There is always an emergency meeting, isn't there? I would think that after being away for all of this time, Father could…well, never mind. Why should today be any different? Are those flowers for me…Mr. Douglas, isn't it?"

Ian nodded and thrust the bouquet at her, surprised that she remembered his name. Ordinarily, he would have been thrilled, but given her lackluster welcome, he was beginning to wonder if it was such a good omen after all.

"The flowers are lovely. Thank you," said Eleanor, her manner warming a bit.

"The carriage be over here, Miss Morgan. I'll get yer bags."

"I sent several trunks ahead. I have only those two bags and that trunk over there." Her gloved hand pointed out the luggage being set out on the station platform by a porter.

Ian strode over to the bags, hefted the trunk on one shoulder and picked up both bags with the other hand. His agility and strength didn't go unnoticed by Eleanor.

After securing the trunk and the bags in the boot he helped her into the carriage. Her hand was small, her touch light as a feather. God had never created a more exquisite creature, Ian concluded as he climbed onto the driver's seat and took up the reins. The carriage was open on all sides, but the covered top provided some degree of privacy and intimacy.

"I'm sorry if I appeared less than happy to see you, Mr. Douglas. The disappointment wasn't in seeing you, but in not seeing my father," said Eleanor. She didn't know why but she felt the need to explain.

Ian's hopes soared. "I understand, Miss Morgan."

"Perhaps we can start anew. Tell me about yourself, Mr. Douglas. What do you do at the mill?"

"I'm foreman, miss."

"Foreman and so young. My father must think highly of you. What of your family?"

"My mum and sister died in the influenza epidemic. My da died some months after."

"I'm sorry. You must miss them very much." Her voice was soft with genuine sympathy. "My mother died when I was ten-years-old, and my father has little time for…at home. I daresay you and I have something in common. Many times I've felt orphaned as well," she said in a choked whisper.

Ian twisted around in his seat. "Are ye all right, Miss Morgan?"

She forced a smile that shot straight to his heart. "How silly of me to become so emotional. It's much too pretty a day to dwell on the unpleasant. Mr. Douglas, please drive through the park. I should like to see the flowers."

They started down the circuitous path through the arboretum when Eleanor waved and called out. "Peter! Peter! Stop the carriage, Mr. Douglas."

Ian pulled up on the reins, and an attractive young man sporting a boater and blue blazer ran up to the conveyance.

"Eleanor, my dear, you look smashing, absolutely smashing. I heard you were returning this week."

"I just came in on the train as a matter of fact."

"If I had known I would have met you."

"No need, Peter. Mr. Douglas was waiting for me."

Peter Jeffries regarded Ian closely. Taking in the cheap, unstylish suit of clothes, he immediately dismissed him as a threat. The man was obviously a servant of some sort.

"When did you return from the Grand Tour, Peter?" Eleanor asked.

"Three weeks ago. I'm afraid I had just missed you in England. Dreary weather that country. Small wonder the Brits are so humorless. Robert, James and Caroline are also home."

"How wonderful. I shall have to have a soiree. I will speak to Father about it immediately. Can I drop you somewhere?"

"I say, that would be lovely," said Peter, affecting an Oxford accent.

As he climbed into the carriage, Ian rolled his eyes. He'd like to meet this guy in a log rolling contest. He listened to their chatter as they compared notes on their tours around Europe, the things they had seen and done. He was so far removed from them. Theirs was a world so frivolous, free of responsibility and care. Their biggest worry seemed to be how to fit in all the "soirees"—whatever the hell they were. Ian suddenly felt a flash of anger. It was people like him, his father, and Tommy who enabled the Peter Jeffries to live so grand, yet they dared to look down upon him and his kind. Ian clenched the reins tighter. One day, he vowed, that would all change. One day he would live on Millionaires' Row and the Peter Jeffries would no longer turn a disdainful eye to him.

"Driver! If you don't slow down, we'll be spilled at the next corner," said Peter in a scolding tone.

"Just tryin' to get ye home sooner than later, sir," said Ian.

"I may not get there at all, if you don't temper your speed." He turned to complain to Eleanor. "Honestly, one can't find decent help in the states. Now take the Brits, they're a people who know their place."

Ian threw Peter a scornful glare. Young Jeffries was so busy talking, he took no notice of it. But Eleanor did. Her brow arched and her lips curved up in playful admonishment when she caught Ian's eye.

His self-confidence surged, and a great sense of well-being and warmth exploded inside of him. He was sitting a little straighter as he rounded the corner to Fourth Street and jerked to a stop in front of Peter's house.

"You really must talk to your father, Eleanor, about replacing this domestic. He is most insolent and incompetent," Ian heard Peter say as he took her hand and kissed it. "Thank you for the lift, my dear."

Young Jeffries barely had both feet on the ground when Ian snapped the reins, nearly unbalancing him. Forgetting his gentlemanly demeanor, an outraged Peter shouted and shook his fist at the speedily departing carriage.

Indignant herself, Eleanor straightened her hat and regained her seating. "Mr. Douglas, this really is too much. What have you to say for yourself?" she demanded.

"Nothin', Miss Morgan, nothin' at all."

Eleanor blinked at his audacity. "Aren't you even going to defend your actions or offer up an apology?"

"Nae," said Ian flatly.

She thought about it for a moment, then burst into light, musical laughter. "Peter can be a bit insufferable at times," she confessed with a giggle. "I dare say I didn't know that he was acquainted with such words."

As they drove the remainder of the block, she took a closer look at Ian. There was no denying it. He was a very attractive, young man though unpolished...a curious man...a forbidden man. Perhaps that was what made him so interesting.

CHAPTER 15

Ian looked over the quota for the day and nodded with satisfaction. As was his habit, he passed among the men to congratulate them for work well done. When he came to Tommy, he sensed dissatisfaction. Now that he thought about it, his best friend had been distant all day.

When the length of timber had finally passed through the saw, he signalled for Tommy to shut it down and drew him off to the side.

"Somethin' wrong, Tommy? Ye haven't been yerself today."

"Where were ye on Sunday, Ian?"

"Sunday?"

"Ye were supposed to talk to Maven…put in a good word for me, remember? I kept her home all afternoon waitin' for ye. Now she's angry with me for makin' her miss her day off at the park."

Ian grimaced as he suddenly remembered. "I'm sorry, Tommy. I was so busy I forgot."

"Aye, I heard how busy ye were Sunday squirin' Morgan's daughter about town."

"The regular driver took sick. I was just fillin' in is all."

"Be careful ye do na get too close to the fire, Ian, or 'tis burned ye'll be. She ain't our kind, an' we ain't hers."

"It isn't like that…she isn't like that."

Tommy nodded toward the door. "Just remember what I said."

Ian turned and saw that Eleanor Morgan had walked into the mill. The saws went still one by one, and work stopped as the men, signalling each other down the line, turned to stare. The six o'clock whistle blew.

"All right, that's it for the day," said Ian in sharp dismissal.

Usually, there was a mad stampede for the exit, but this evening the men seemed content to take their time leaving.

She appeared to be lost.

"Can I help ye, Miss Morgan?" asked Ian, quickly coming to her rescue.

She flashed him a bright smile, relieved to see a familiar face. "Oh, Mr. Douglas, yes you may. I haven't visited the mill in a very long time. I'm afraid much has changed. Would you kindly direct me to my father's office?"

"'Tis upstairs in another buildin' across the yard. But yer father is nae here. He left for a Board of Trade meetin' an hour ago."

"Oh, dear, I hadn't expected to miss him. I was shopping in town and thought the two of us might take supper at the Carleton House. Now I have neither a dinner partner nor a ride home. I had friends drop me off you see."

"I would be happy to escort ye home," said Ian. "A lady should na go about the city alone in the evenin', especially down here."

"Thank you, Mr. Douglas, I would appreciate your company."

"I have to close up first."

"Of course."

Eleanor watched Ian from under properly lowered lashes as he quickly went about closing up the mill. Again, she was amazed by his agility for his height and impressed by his strength as he leaped over the log carriages to secure the chute doors and the hatch. When he disappeared into his office, she looked about the large barn-like building. The ceiling was high, open to the rafters, and a row of fire buckets on hooks lined one beam. Several windows admitted light. The scent of pine from freshly cut timber mingled with the sweat of the departed workers, and, in the twilight, she could see particles of sawdust still drifting through the air. Such a different world this was here. There was a rough edge to it that she didn't find totally unattractive...rather like Ian Douglas.

When Ian joined her, she noticed that he had put on a jacket and had combed through his sandy brown hair. He was so handsome, she thought. What a pity he was just a mill hand.

As they walked across the canal bridge to the streetcar stop, Ian was conscious of every man's head turning to glance at Eleanor in admiration and at him in envy, and his chest swelled with pride. Usually impatient for the arrival of a streetcar, he didn't care if he had to wait all evening for this one. After smelling sweat and sawdust all day, her light, fragrant perfume was heady to his senses. How he wished he could stretch this hour into two.

"There'll be a streetcar by soon," he said.

Eleanor smiled up at him. "I don't mind waiting. It's a lovely evening."

At the clang of the bell of the approaching streetcar, he slipped a hand into his pocket to fish around for the extra nickel fare. He was two cents short, and panic set in. Heeding Cyrus Morgan's advice, Ian never carried more coin than he absolutely needed. The temptation was too great to spend it. As for emergencies, his planning was always such that they were never allowed to happen. When he had left for the mill this morning, it was a day like any other. He had certainly never expected to be escorting the girl of his dreams home.

When the horse-drawn car stopped before them, Ian boarded with a good deal less self-assurance than he had when he left the mill. He would rather die than ask Eleanor to pay for her own fare or to have to admit to her that he was short of coin. As she seated herself in the middle of the half-filled car, Ian quickly whispered his plight to the conductor, placing himself at the man's mercy.

The crusty, old man glanced at Eleanor. "Steppin' pretty high, ain't you, son?"

Ian reddened, and he turned away in embarrassment. He was debating whether or not to throw himself under the wheels of the next train when the conductor said, "Take your seat, son. You can pay me tomorrow."

Relief flooded Ian's face. He hated having to ask anybody for anything. Ian Douglas took no charity. He prayed that Eleanor hadn't overheard the exchange. When she smiled at him as he seated himself beside her, he decided that she hadn't. He relaxed and settled back to enjoy his remaining time with her.

"Father says that you are the best foreman he has ever had," she said.

"I do an honest job for honest wages," said Ian.

"Father says that you aren't like the other workers."

"I do nae intend to spend the rest of my life as a mill hand, if that be his meanin'."

"Unless you have a service to offer, the mills are the only real means of livelihood. What do you intend to do, Mr. Douglas, if not work in the mill?"

"Own several, Miss Morgan."

Eleanor thought it a joke and was about to laugh, when she saw the clear resolve in his silver-blue eyes. He was serious. He actually believed it, she thought in astonishment. Ian Douglas was a most unusual man. She didn't know what else to say and fell silent. Ian was never one for idle conversation himself and was content to just be with her.

At the clang of the bell, she looked out the window. "I think this is my stop."

They stepped off the streetcar, and Ian walked her to the door. When she turned and extended her hand, he remembered how Peter Jeffries had brought it to his lips and lightly kissed it. But such affectations were not for Ian, and at the risk of again appearing gauche, he took her hand and shook it.

Eleanor gave him that half smile of amused forbearance. In a way she admired his independent nature. "Thank you for seeing me home, Mr. Douglas. Shall I expect to see you at the park on Sunday?"

Ian nodded, not trusting himself to speak, as that little ball of happiness exploded inside of him.

Eleanor was thoughtful as she watched him walk down the street. He was so different from all the other young men she knew.

CHAPTER 16

"You wear a suit of clothes well, sir. The breadth of your shoulders lends itself quite nicely to this coat."

Ian stared at himself in the mirror of the clothier shop. He yanked at the knotted tie and looked doubtfully at the gray-striped trousers, the waistcoat and short, loose hanging jacket.

The tailor quickly assured him. "I guarantee you, sir, it is the height of fashion. You'll find a suit like this in every gentleman's wardrobe. Perfect for that Sunday afternoon stroll in the park."

As Ian picked up his old cap, the tailor made a clicking sound with his tongue and shook his head.

"This is what every well-dressed gentleman wears," said the tailor holding out a black felt bowler.

Again Ian had his doubts, but he set aside the worn cap and tried the bowler. He looked even more of a stranger to himself.

"Ye're certain?" he asked with the hint of a threat in his voice.

"Quite."

"I'll be takin' it then. How much for everythin'?"

When the tailor presented him with the total, an invisible hand clutched at Ian's throat. Taking a deep breath, he slowly and reluctantly counted out twelve dollars and fifty cents.

* * * * * * * *

It was a glorious summer day. A gentle breeze off the river kept the temperature at a comfortable level.

Ian arrived at the park late, just after two o'clock, cursing Mrs. Simpson's runaway dog. It had taken him an hour to chase down the mutt. He canvassed the arboretum, the beach area, and most of the park, but could find no sign of Eleanor Morgan. He was about to resign himself to the fact that he had missed her when he saw a familiar pink parasol bobbing in a crowd around the art exhibit. Of course that's where she would be. As relief flooded him, a broad smile banished the ill-tempered frown. Quickly, he crossed the grounds and was about to approach her when she turned and saw him.

His smile wavered. She showed no sign of recognition. "Miss Morgan, 'tis me…Ian Douglas."

Her vivid, blue eyes widened in surprise. "Why, Mr. Douglas! How silly of me not to have known you. You've cut your hair, and your clothes…How very grand and handsome you look. Girls, look here," she called to her friends. "I want you to meet someone."

To Ian's dismay, four young ladies immediately surrounded him. He felt like a hog on display at the fair.

"This is Mr. Ian Douglas," said Eleanor.

"Oh, are you of the Philadelphia Douglases?" inquired one girl with an openly admiring eye.

Ian looked at the attractive brunette blankly for a few seconds before Eleanor replied, "No, Caroline, Mr. Douglas is a native of Rossburg."

"How odd that we've never seen you at any of the social events," commented another.

"Well, obviously, Mr. Douglas has been studying in Europe for the past several years, isn't that right?" said another young woman, confident in her assessment. "Where did you study, Mr. Douglas, Cambridge?"

"Come, ladies, Mr. Douglas must think you have no manners at all, bombarding him with such questions when he has only just arrived."

Eleanor laced her arm in his and smiled up at him. "Come along, sir, perhaps we can find some privacy on the lake in a canoe."

As she led him off, one of the girls called out to her. "Eleanor, what shall we tell Peter when he arrives?"

"Tell Peter, he's too late," Eleanor called back.

The afternoon was magical for Ian as he rowed Eleanor about the lake, bought her ice cream, and walked arm in arm with her through the arboretum. He had spent two week's wages over the past few days, but it was worth it to see Eleanor smile up at him, to be able to stand close enough to her to smell the fragrance of her hair. But as it must do, the day came to an end.

"I'm afraid that I must return to my friends now," she said, "or I shall soon find myself without transportation."

"I've rented a carriage," said Ian. "Perhaps ye'll allow me to see ye home." After the near fiasco with the streetcar, he wasn't about to let anything to chance.

"Perhaps," said Eleanor coyly. She glanced up at him demurely from under lowered lashes. It was an action that never failed to send a ripple of excitement through a man. And Ian was not immune.

He had managed to drag out the journey home, but still the carriage drew up in front of the stately stone mansion sooner than he would have preferred. Reluctantly, he jumped off and helped Eleanor down. His hands lingered around her waist as they became lost in each other's gaze. He had been right. His hands did span her waist. Eleanor quickly lowered her eyes.

"I had better go in."

Ian pulled himself together and escorted her to the door.

"Thank you," she said. "I had a perfectly wonderful time."

Ian didn't want to let it end there. "Perhaps next Sunday—" He was interrupted when the door suddenly opened and the house-keeper appeared.

"Good afternoon, Miss Eleanor," she greeted warmly. She looked at Ian, and employing her haughtiest tone said, "Mr. Morgan wishes to have a word with you."

Eleanor sighed. "I shall say goodbye to you, then, Mr. Douglas. You mustn't keep Father waiting."

As Eleanor disappeared up the stairs, Ian followed the housekeeper across the marble foyer to the study. Cyrus Morgan stood staring out the window that faced the street. He didn't look at all happy, and Ian wondered if it had something to do with Gentry and the boom.

"Is there somethin' wrong at the mill, sir?"

Morgan slowly turned to face Ian, his hands locked behind his back. "You know I like you, Douglas. You're a good a worker, hell of a foreman. You're a thinking man with a good head on your shoulders. Starting that planing mill was a stroke of genius, and you've earned my respect. But that's as far as it goes."

Ian looked at him in confusion. "I do nae understand, sir."

"To get to the point, Douglas, I know that you and my daughter have been spending some time together lately."

"Ye asked me to act as her driver."

"I didn't ask you today, and gauging by your suit of clothes, it was more social than business."

"We met in the park, and I offered to see her home."

"I don't want you to see Eleanor again. Is that clear?"

Ian stared at Morgan thunderstruck. "Ye're sayin' that I not be good enough to know yer daughter?"

"I'm saying that you and Eleanor come from two different worlds. You will never be accepted in hers, and she certainly will never be happy in yours."

Ian struggled to control his temper. "I believe yer roots are in my world, sir," he said evenly.

"That's true, however, when I was your age, society in Rossburg was just evolving. Now it is formed and set, and Eleanor is a product of it.

You're not. It's as simple as that. Avoid a lot of trouble, Douglas. Stay away from Eleanor and remain with your own kind."

"Or what?" demanded Ian.

"I will be forced to hire another foreman. Do I make myself clear?"

Ian reeled from the ultimatum. He had thought this was America where everyone had the same opportunities. Hard, steel-blue eyes held Morgan's unyielding gaze for a moment, then Ian gathered his dignity and left the room.

In the foyer, girlish chatter and laughter on the stairs caught his attention. Eleanor was leading her friends up to her room. He was debating whether to defy Morgan's edict and call out to her when he heard his name.

"Your Mr. Douglas is simply gorgeous!" exclaimed one of the girls melodramatically swooning.

"Okay, fess up," demanded another. "Where did he come from? How come we haven't seen him before this? Have you been hiding him somewhere?"

As they all bombarded her with questions, Eleanor laughed. "You silly geese. He is my father's foreman at the mill."

"A foreman!" they echoed in shocked unison. Eleanor might as well have told them he had leprosy.

"A common mill hand." One of the girls groaned mournfully. "What a shame…a fine looking man like him."

"Eleanor, what must you be thinking?" asked another in admonishment. "What's Peter to say? He was absolutely livid when he arrived to find you had gone off with someone else. He'll be simply apoplectic when he hears it was a mill hand."

"I don't care. Peter hasn't been properly attentive lately," said Eleanor petulantly.

"Eleanor, you're not seriously considering taking up with this…this laborer, are you?" asked another.

"Would that be so bad? He is handsome and rather intriguing."

The girl gasped. "It would be positively scandalous! Think of your reputation. You'll be labeled an outcast."

"Sarah, you're such a ninny. Of course I'm not considering taking up with him," said Eleanor. "But Peter doesn't have to know that Ian Douglas is a mill hand now, does he? Perhaps it will light a fire beneath him. Peter is growing entirely too complacent about our relationship."

"Eleanor Morgan, you are positively wicked." The girls dissolved into conspiratorial laughter that crescendoed up the stairs.

A searing heat rose up Ian's neck and exploded in his face. He felt as though a knife had been plunged into his chest, and his breath came in short, ragged gasps. Such humiliation at the hands of a woman, a woman he worshipped, was almost more than he could bear.

He strode furiously across the foyer and out the door, leaving it open behind him. Abandoning the carriage, he walked the two miles home, fury echoing in every footstep as the words "common mill hand" reverberated in his brain. Along the way, he contemptuously threw the felt bowler into a nearby trash barrel.

By the time he reached his hotel, he was hot, tired and dusty, and his white-hot rage had simmered into an anger that would drive him for years to come.

Ian burst through the door of his hotel room, discarded his coat carelessly on the chair, and yanked loose his tie. He took out a bottle of whiskey and tossed down a few shots, pacing angrily about the cramped room. He tossed back a few more shots and flopped onto the bed, only to shoot up again. Tommy! He had promised to speak to Maven for him. Ian cursed loudly and dragged himself off the bed. He let out a bitter laugh. Who was he to say that Tommy wasn't right for Maven?

Night had fallen, the streets were deserted when Ian arrived at the dress shop, disheveled and a bit unsteady on his feet.

"Maven," he called out, knocking loudly on the door, "'tis Ian. Are ye there, lass? I have to talk with ye…" His voice trailed off, and he leaned wearily against the door. "I promised Tommy…"

Maven flung open the door, a startled cry escaping her as Ian nearly fell on the floor at her feet.

"Ian, what has happened to ye! Be ye hurt?" She anxiously scanned him for injury. Finding none, she put his arm around her neck and helped him into the back room. "Have ye been set upon?"

Ian laughed bitterly. "Aye, I've been set upon all right."

Maven struggled beneath his weight as she guided him to a chair.

"But I thought I was too bloody smart to be played," he said, stopping to expound. "Well, they'll not get away with it. By God I'll make them pay."

"Who? What…ye're not makin' any sense. Ye've been drinkin'."

"Aye, not near enough."

Maven coaxed him to the chair. "Sit down. I'll get ye some tea, and ye can tell me what has happened to upset ye so."

She continued to talk to him, telling him the news of the old neighborhood, in that way she had of soothing a child in distress. She had a passionate temper to be sure, but there was a warmth and grace and serenity about her that enfolded one in a protective cocoon, and Ian soon felt the anger in him subside. She could always make him feel better no matter the circumstance.

As she prepared the tea, his attention suddenly focused on her in a different way. He noticed that she was in her nightgown, the outline of her tall, willowy body silhouetted against muslin and lace in the soft glow of the lamp. Her hair hung loose down her back in a cascade of curls, a few tendrils escaping the ribbon to sweetly frame her oval face.

Maven poured him a cup of tea and turned, startled to find Ian standing behind her intently regarding her. He took the cup out of her hands and set it aside. Maven held her breath as he reached out a hand, then, to caress her cheek. Ian could feel her whole body tremble when he drew her into his arms and kissed her. Maven's response, tentative at first, became more certain, and the moment took on an urgency both were powerless to control. In one sweeping motion, he lifted her easily into his arms and carried her to the bed.

*   *   *   *   *   *   *   *

Tommy nervously massaged his knuckles, barely able to contain himself, until Ian had finished checking in the mill workers and assigning positions. When the last man had been dispatched, he pounced impatiently. "Well, did ye see her?"

"Who?" asked Ian, his attention deliberately trained on the production board.

"Who! Who do ye think!" Tommy exploded in exasperation. "Maven, of course! Did ye not talk to her as ye promised?"

Ian reluctantly raised his eyes, certain that Tommy would be able to see the guilt written all over his face. "Aye...I saw her."

"What did she say?"

"She said...she said she wasn't without feelin's for ye..." Just then the whistle blew.

"What else...Ian, what else did she say?"

"Time to get to work. We'll talk about this later," said Ian. Hastily, he strode to the yard before Tommy could question him further. What the hell could he tell his best friend...that he had just bedded the girl Tommy hoped to marry? Waves of disgust swept over him, and his stomach heaved at the deceit he was practicing.

Later that night, Ian stole across town to the dress shop with the intention of telling Maven that last night had been a mistake. The guilt was tearing him apart. The look of disappointment and hope on Tommy's face when he told him that Maven wasn't ready to settle down yet was more than Ian's conscience could bear.

Maven answered his soft rap on the door and quickly drew him inside. Since nightfall she had been waiting, flushed, impatient, and fearful.

"I-I was afraid ye might not come again," she said, haltingly. She had set aside her sewing duties for the day to finish the soft, pink nightdress she wore, hoping, praying that he would come. Beneath its sheer bodice, her creamy shoulders glowed like polished ivory. Auburn ringlets, still damp from her toilette, glinted like a thousand fireflies in the lamplight.

Ian's breath caught in his throat as he gazed down at her. Her naked vulnerability, her willingness to entrust herself to him, body and soul, touched him in a way he had never been touched before, and all resolve and reason abandoned him.

"Sweet Maven, 'twould be easier to stop breathin' than to nae see ye again." He pulled her into his arms and kissed her deeply.

Here with Maven, he didn't have to answer to the world, to his conscience…or to Tommy. In the fiery passion that soon overtook them, the demons that drove him were temporarily laid to rest. The tormenting image of a fair-haired goddess faded; visions of grandeur and golden idols were no longer an obsession. And in the end there was peace.

Maven lay cuddled against Ian's chest, a slim leg entwined with his as they lay quietly in the hazy aftermath of shared pleasure.

"What might ye be thinkin' now, Ian?" she asked softly, her finger tracing the muscular lines of his chest.

"That is the beauty of ye, Maven, my love. With ye, I think not at all," he said, drifting off to sleep.

February, 1880

CHAPTER 17

Parker Lewis Stanton had fallen upon good times. His success was evident in the tastefully decorated office, in the elegant cut of his dark suit, and in the diamond stickpin he wore in his silk cravat. Gone was the heavy beard of his days as a woodsman. Instead, the glossy black hair was neatly trimmed with fashionable sideburns.

The strong, whip-thin body, seasoned by years of lumbering, seemed poised in a constant state of alertness as piercing dark eyes looked out at the world with a keen vigilance. An aquiline nose, given to tingling at the hint of interesting possibilities, seemed able to ferret out the best and most lucrative transactions in a town suddenly caught up in the throes of growing pains. It tingled now as Parker, with wary curiosity, watched his visitor settle his considerable bulk into a chair.

"What can I do for you today, Mr. Morgan?"

Morgan twirled his cigar between his lips. "More's the case of what I'm going to do for you, Mr. Stanton," he said expansively.

"And what is that, sir?"

"I'm here to make an offer for the boom."

The attorney quickly framed his surprise in cool indifference. "I see. I wasn't aware that Mr. Gentry was still looking for a buyer."

"Everything has its price. However, it doesn't matter if he is or isn't looking to sell. My business is with you."

"I beg your pardon?"

"Come off it, Stanton, I know you're the power behind this whole boom deal."

"Oh? What makes you think that?"

"A little investigation and common sense. For instance, I know that you use to lumber in the winters around here to put yourself through law school."

"And?"

"I doubt that Gentry would have thought to use lumbermen just out of the woods from the winter harvest to rebuild the boom. Large work force, knowledgeable in the task with their own tools of the trade…that was smart. Gentry didn't have the money to bankroll the project either. You did."

"How do you know that?"

"George Steiner, the bank president is an old friend of mine. Also, you are the only one who could have gotten that raise in the boomage fee past the legislature. The way I see it, Gentry is a front for you."

"Why should I need a front?"

"You're a smart man, Stanton. You know how people feel about outsiders messing in their business."

Stanton leaned back in his chair, tapping the tips of his fingers together. "What is your offer, Mr. Morgan?"

"Three prime lumber tracts totaling one thousand acres in Logan Township, one hundred thousand dollars in cash, and a one hundred thousand dollar note redeemable from the first proceeds of the boom's winter harvest.

Stanton's brow rose in surprise, but he managed to suppress a whistle. "Given the value of the land, it will take you two years to regain your initial investment."

"That's my business. What do you say?"

"Given the current size and boomage fee, that boom will be worth millions over the next several years. I'll have to think about it."

"I'll give you twenty-four hours. One other thing, Stanton. The transaction is to be done in complete secrecy. In no way can the sale be traced to me."

Stanton smiled. "It is true then what they say."

"What's that?"

"There is no honor among thieves."

In a dark corner of Cozey's Saloon, Parker Stanton presented Morgan's offer to an even more interested party.

The man took a sip of beer and leaned back thoughtfully in his chair, Morgan's plan as transparent to him as it had been to Stanton. By silently buying the boom, not only would Morgan save the boomage fee, but by virtue of his anonymity, he could also move to increase the fee each year without fearing repercussions from the other mill owners. Morgan had found a way to break the delicate balance of power the mills had established, and to enrich himself at the expense of fellow members of the Lumbermen's Exchange.

"Three timber tracts, one hundred thousand dollars in cash and a hundred thousand dollar note," said the man, digesting the offer.

"You aren't thinking of actually taking it, are you?" asked Stanton. "That boom will make you millions. You've already realized nearly a quarter of a million dollars. Of course, a portion of it has gone to rebuild and expand the boom, but—"

"Where is Morgan getting his cash? The flood all but wiped him out, and last year's harvests didn't cover his debt."

"The president of Rossburg Trust has extended him a line of credit until this winter's harvest. I checked it out."

"Take the offer."

"Are you crazy! As your attorney, I have to advise against it."

"So noted. Now draw up the papers. I have my reasons."

CHAPTER 18

The summer of 1880 was particularly long, hot and dry, stretching well into September. Tempers were short. Ian walked a tightrope between men getting poorer and *a* man getting richer.

Even in the haven of Maven's arms he found little refuge. He rose from her bed, restless and distracted, and prepared to leave in the pre-dawn hour.

"Ye've not been yerself these days, Ian. Be there trouble at the mill?" asked Maven anxiously.

"The men are of an angry mood, tempers are short. Morgan has turned back demands for a nickel more in wages." Ian laughed. "The man is a millionaire, and he begrudges a nickel increase."

Maven bit her lip in a nervous gesture, reluctant to broach another subject. "Tommy came by the shop after work yesterday. He asked me to the social. I told him I had to work to finish a gown. We must tell him about us, Ian. We can na continue on like this, deceivin' Tommy, deceivin' my family…. It isn't right."

"We can na tell anyone, not yet. Tommy is my right hand at the mill. I need him to help me keep the men in line. The tensions will soon ease with the weather. We'll find a way to tell him then."

Maven's voice held a note of uncertainty. "Ian, ye do love me…?"

Ian bent down and kissed her on the cheek. "Ye be special to me, Maven. Ye always have been, ye always will be. Ne'er doubt that."

The troubled crease in her brow deepened as she heard the door close behind him. He omitted saying the one thing she needed to hear.

*　　*　　*　　*　　*　　*　　*　　*

The sun beat down hot and uncompromising. The boom stood nearly empty of Morgan's mill reserves, and operations had switched to the planing of lumber. It was close and dusty inside the small outbuilding, worse than in the sawmill.

Ian was inspecting a finished piece of wood when a worker came running in from the yard. The noise of the mill drowned out his words, but his wild gestures boded ill. Ian dropped the lumber and quickly collared the man before he could raise a panic.

"What is it!" he demanded.

"Fire," the man puffed breathlessly…"in the far eastern ridge."

Ian paled. He thrust the man aside and ran out into the yard. Behind him the mill had gone silent, and the men followed him out, their murmurs of shock and fear reverberating through the yard as they focused upon the distant billow of smoke. Everyone knew this to be the general vicinity of many of the logging camps.

"What's going on down there!" shouted Morgan from his office window. "Douglas, why aren't these men working!"

Ian detached himself from the group and hurried upstairs to Morgan's office, taking the steps two at a time.

"The eastern ridge is on fire," he said as he walked into the room.

The cigar dropped out of Morgan's mouth, as his face registered horror. He rushed back to the window, craning his neck in the direction.

"Dear God! Put O'Brien in charge and get to the telegraph office. Find out what you can from the towns up river."

News trickled in slowly over the next few days. By the time the fire had burned itself out, over a hundred thousand acres of prime timberland were gone and twenty lumbermen had lost their lives. There followed a mad scramble for alternative lands before the season was further lost.

Morgan's distress was evident from the way he chewed on his cigar. He had lost nearly a third of his harvest. He regretted bargaining away those Northern tracts now. But the real joke was that most of what was left in the boom of the summer harvest was *his* timber. He would be his own best damned customer. Morgan yanked the cigar out of his mouth and threw it across his office in a fit of pique.

Most of the other mill owners had lost fifty to seventy-five percent of their timber. With no further capital to buy other tracts, some of the smaller mills had already announced their closing. At least, there was one silver lining, thought Morgan with a cynical laugh. His workers would cease their unrest now. As mills closed, they would be damned grateful to have a job.

The winter was less harsh than most, as though to give the town a respite from its troubles. But Morgan felt no such reprieve.

"The larger mills have turned to planing their lumber as well. They're driving down the prices on finished pieces. What's to be done, Douglas?" he demanded.

Ian shrugged. "I would say that Morgan Mill Yards needs an edge."

"Yes, but what!" snapped Morgan. He looked at Ian. He was well aware that theirs had become an adversarial relationship. Still, he trusted him. He had to. He needed him. He was acutely aware that the larger success of the mill was owing to Ian. Not for the first time did he wish that the boy had been born on the right side of town. "Have you any ideas at all?"

"Perhaps," said Ian, refusing to be rushed. "We already finish the lumber. Why not do some of the easier millwork as well? Doors, railin's, banisters, for instance, and sell them directly to the builders."

Morgan turned to stare out the window, absently stroking his chin. His mind quickly sifted through the pros and cons of such an undertaking. It would mean extending his credit again for additional machinery and another building.

After a long moment of deliberation, he ordered, "Do it."

Over the next few months, the mill was expanded and part of its operations switched over to millwork. Ian hired four master carpenters with four mill hands apprenticed to each one of them.

Morgan anxiously watched as the winter harvest of logs began to arrive at the boom with the spring thaw. By the end of the week, the boom, which should have been filled to capacity, was only half full. Unfortunately, the largest customer was Morgan Mill Yards. He had no choice now. He ordered his carriage to be brought around.

When Morgan arrived at Rossburg Trust, he was quickly ushered into the richly appointed office of the president, a fact he noted with satisfaction. Everyone knew better than to keep Cyrus Morgan waiting.

George Steiner immediately rose from his chair, always happy to see his most important customer. "Cyrus, what a pleasant surprise. How about a cigar? Fresh out of Cuba."

Morgan impatiently waved aside the offer and fell heavily into a leather wing chair. "I need a favor, George."

"Oh? What sort of favor?"

"I need an extended line of credit."

A frown settled over the bank president's features. "You have one hundred and twenty thousand dollars on margin now soon due, Cyrus. In all these years, I've known you to make loans, never to take them. You always used to say—"

"I know what I used to say, George, but there are extenuating circumstances. I need the money to close a business deal. You know me, George. You know I'm good for it. Between the summer harvest and next year's winter harvest, I'll have that and a whole lot more. The fire caught me short is all."

"How much do you need?"

"Another hundred thousand."

The bank president shook his head. "I can't do it, Cyrus. The fire brought in mill owners requesting loans. The bank is dangerously overextended. I've been selling off some of the loans to a secondary market as it is. The most I can give you is twenty thousand."

"George, I've got to cover a one hundred thousand dollar note within the next few weeks or lose my investment. We've been friends a long time, served on The Board of Trade for many years. Whenever your bank needed capital, I saw to it you got it."

The banker detected a note of desperation in Cyrus' voice and a slight tremor in his hands as they grasped the edge of the desk.

"Believe me, Cyrus," he said regretfully, "if I could help you I would. Not even if you were my own father could I extend you that much money right now."

"Then at least extend the due date of the bank's note. Can you do that much?"

"I could if I still owned your note. Yours was the largest one on the books. It's unusual for anyone to want such a large note."

"You sold my note? George, how the hell could you sell my note!" exploded Morgan.

The bank president lost some of his aplomb in the face of Morgan's hostile glare. "The bank needed the reserves, Cyrus. It was nothing personal, just business. You, more than anyone, should understand that."

"Who has the note?"

"Can't tell you for sure. That new fellow in town, Parker Stanton, arranged everything." As Morgan continued to glower at him, George Steiner cast about for a change of subject. "Say, the missus and I are looking forward to the Lumber Baron's Ball at your home. You always do it up right. That may account for why you keep getting elected president of the association," he said with a forced laugh.

Morgan's stomach churned. He didn't find anything amusing. He didn't find one damned thing funny about any of this. As he left the bank and lumbered to his carriage, he considered what to do next.

"Where to, sir?" inquired the driver.

"Waring and Cross Law Offices on Third Street, and be quick about it!"

"Yessir."

Morgan didn't wait to be announced, but marched straight into the principal's office with the clerk in worried pursuit.

Arthur Waring, flustered as well by the impromptu visit, waved the clerk off and shut the door. "Cyrus, what brings you here?" he inquired anxiously. "You look a bit disturbed. I hope it has nothing to do with the services of this firm."

"What do you know about Parker Stanton? He's an attorney in town."

"Yes, I've met him. He's a bright, personable young man. Charming, charismatic. He received his law degree from the University of Pennsylvania. I tried to get him to join the firm, but he said he preferred to have his own practice."

"Do you know any of his clients?"

"Can't say as I do. Waring and Cross handles the business of everyone of note in Rossburg. I'm afraid he is going to find slim pickings here."

"Apparently he has found one client wealthy enough to buy up notes from the Rossburg Trust," Morgan said with a snarl.

"That so. Whoever it is can't be from around here. I would have heard something."

"Find out who it is, dammit! We don't want any outsiders interfering in our business."

"I'll get my man on it right away, Cyrus."

Slightly mollified, Morgan wearily made his way to his carriage. The throbbing in his head kept perfect tempo with the beat of the horses' hooves against the pavement.

*   *   *   *   *   *   *   *

The grand house was ablaze with lights and abuzz with activity. Guests wearing the latest fashions from Philadelphia and New York alighted from glossy black carriages that lined the circular piazza. Through the open windows of the second floor ballroom, strains of a waltz floated out upon the warm June night.

In his study, Morgan tensely puffed on a cigar. "I pay you a small fortune and all you can tell me is nothing?"

Arthur Waring shrugged apologetically. "Stanton shields his client well. I had my best man on it. No one arrived at or left his office. He met with no one of note outside the office, nor was there anything in his records or in his rooms to suggest this client's identity.

"The best I can tell you is that Stanton is an industrious young man with quite an eye for the ladies—usually married. He comes from a fine Philadelphia family, but had some kind of a falling out with his father. Put himself through school lumbering in the winter." Waring helped himself to a generous shot of Cyrus' best brandy. "He still drinks with loggers in Cozey's Saloon when he's not sweet-talking some pretty little thing into bed," he added with a chuckle.

Morgan waved his hand impatiently. "How the hell is this supposed to tell me who he's working for!"

"I'm afraid only Stanton can tell you that, Cyrus."

"Has anyone invested large sums of money in the bank?"

"No. I personally talked with George on the matter. Could be that Stanton is the principal, and he's drawing from an outside bank. That would also account for why we can't find a name."

"Or could be Stanton is a front for a prounion movement."

Waring laughed. "Come now, Cyrus. Getting a bit paranoid, aren't you?" He downed his drink and reached for another.

Morgan swung hard eyes on the lawyer. "Don't underestimate Gompers and his people. They're clever, Arthur. The only thing that makes them more dangerous is that they're zealots. They wait for us to let our guard down, and then they strike. The flood and the fire left the town vulnerable, just right for a takeover."

Waring glanced at Morgan dubiously, but decided it was wiser to placate his wealthiest client. "I-ah-I'll check on Stanton further," he said.

He clapped Morgan jovially on the back. "Well, now, Cyrus, what say we join the party and try out some of that delicious food your cook is famous for. By the way, I understand you're going to announce Eleanor's engagement to young Jeffries tonight. Excellent match, excellent match. Had to settle for Floyd Cross, myself…brought him into my practice so he could support my daughter properly. But you'll have no need to worry about that."

Morgan's dark mood lightened, and he actually managed a smile. This was a subject dear to his heart. The alliance between Peter Jeffries and his daughter was an alliance between Franklin Jeffries' trains and Morgan's lumber.

"You're right, Arthur. We'll talk of this later."

CHAPTER 19

"What's this all about, Cyrus?" grumbled Franklin Jeffries, nursing a headache from the ball the night before.

"Yeah, Morgan. What's so all-fired urgent you couldn't wait until Monday?" demanded another bleary-eyed attendee.

Morgan raised his hands to command silence. "Gentlemen, if you will all take your seats, I'll explain."

Rossburg's power elite continued to grumble, though more quietly, as they seated themselves around a long, rectangular table in the exclusive Rossburg Men's Club. A black attendant in a starched white uniform passed out cigars while another poured coffee fortified with brandy.

"The Board of Trade Meeting is hereby called to order," announced Morgan. "On the agenda, gentlemen, is a matter of grave concern to the business community."

"What could be any worse than the flood or the fire?" quizzed one of the men dryly.

"The union," said Morgan.

An uneasy murmur swept the room, especially among the mill owners.

"What makes you think we are being threatened by the union?" asked Ed Brown, Morgan's largest competitor. Though there was doubt in his tone, a look of concern had crept into his eyes.

Morgan took a puff of his cigar and eyed each man around the table. The effect was dead silence and absolute attention. "Deduction, gentlemen."

There was nervous laughter with a measure of irritation and relief all around.

"You call a Saturday morning meeting and scare the bejesus out of us because of deduction!" exclaimed Brown. "Present your case, Cyrus, and it had better be a damned good one."

"I think we are all agreed that it wasn't Gentry's money that rebuilt the boom."

"Couldn't have been. Gentry barely had two nickels to rub together," interjected another lumber baron.

"Exactly, and if none of us gave it to him, who do you suppose did...no doubt for a percentage of the profits? How else could Gentry have slipped that increase past us right under our very noses? Now someone is buying up our notes. And in all cases, this man Parker Stanton is standing squarely in the middle of the whole business. I thought at first that he was Gentry's partner, but now I'd be willing to bet my last cigar that the person who is buying up our notes and the person who rebuilt the boom are one and the same.

"Who is it?"

"We don't know," said Arthur Waring. "I've had my best man on Stanton, and we haven't been able turn up anything. George, here, can tell you that no one in town has made a sizable deposit in his bank in the last several months. Has to be an outsider."

"How do you know it's union connected?"

"We don't," admitted Morgan reluctantly, "but who else would have the most to gain by investing such funds in Rossburg? Whatever the case, we don't want an outsider in our business, either. The fire on the heels of the flood has left us and the town easy pickings. If the union is going to make a move, now is the time."

At this, all eyes turned accusingly on the bank president.

George Steiner swallowed hard. "The bank needed capital," he said defensively. "How was I supposed to know there might be some grand scheme to buy up the notes? Any other banker in my position would have done the same thing. Besides, I'm not convinced that Cyrus isn't overstepping himself. Everything could be perfectly innocent and aboveboard."

Morgan's voice was heavy with unveiled criticism. "Yes, no doubt you'd like to think so, George. No one likes to think he is responsible for selling out his town."

The bank president angrily pushed back his chair. "Now wait just a damned minute…"

"Gentlemen, gentlemen," said Waring. "George does have a point. We weren't able to turn up any evidence to suggest a conspiracy." Somewhat mollified, the bank president retook his seat.

"But we can't take the chance," said Franklin Jeffries.

"I'm with Cyrus," chimed in Ed Brown. He was immediately joined by several of the larger mill owners.

"What do you propose we do?" asked Jim Conover.

Morgan thought for a moment, a light coming into his shrewd, gray eyes. "If Stanton is taken out of the picture, his client would have to come forward and collect his own debt. Then we'll see who and what we're dealing with."

"Now hold on, Cyrus. I won't stand for any violence," said Waring.

Morgan leaned back in his chair, his mouth stretching into a wide smile. "Relax, Arthur, I'll see to this personally."

* * * * * * * *

Parker Stanton sat at his usual table in the back far corner of Cozey's Saloon, one eye trained nervously on the door. He bolted down two drinks in quick succession and ordered another. He jumped as someone noiselessly slipped into the chair beside him.

"Geez, I wish you wouldn't do that!" he exclaimed irritably.

"What?"

"Slink around. Give me some warning or something."

The man raised a questioning brow, his eye taking in the empty whiskey glasses and the attorney's disheveled appearance. "Ye seem a bit jumpy this evenin', Parker. Something wrong?"

Stanton licked his lips. "I-ah-have a little trouble. I haven't been able to go back to my rooms or the office."

"What kind of trouble?"

"I was with a woman last night."

"Married no doubt."

As the attorney nodded, the man groaned. "Dammit, Stanton! I told ye to keep away from women until this thing was over. Let me guess, her husband came home unexpectedly and caught ye."

"She told me he was out of town for a few days. I barely escaped with my life. I hear he's still looking for me…have to get out of town for a few weeks…leaving on the 10:15 tonight." Stanton, usually elegant and verbose in the nature of a lawyer, gasped out short, ragged sentences in his desperation.

His companion was clearly annoyed and offered no sympathy. "Ye play with fire, ye get burned."

Stanton winced. "No platitudes, please." He paled as he spied a large, brutish man entering the saloon. "I'll be in touch," he whispered, jumping up from his seat and beating a hasty retreat out the back door.

Stanton's client signaled the waiter to his table.

"Joe, who is that man makin' his way to the bar?"

"Don't know his name," said the waiter. "He was in here a couple of times. Said he works for the railroad and was in town for a special job."

Stanton's client thought for a moment, and a smile suddenly tipped the corners of his mouth. "Morgan…," he murmured to himself. Parker was going to feel very foolish indeed.

CHAPTER 20

The plush, leather chair groaned in protest as Cyrus Morgan settled behind his desk to await his visitor. He looked at the clock and impatiently tapped his fingers on the desktop.

He loosened his tie and collar. He hadn't been feeling well since the morning and had left the mill early. Neither had he consumed his supper with the usual vigor. Mentally shutting out his physical discomfort, he tried to quell the nervous excitement building in his stomach.

"Tonight, you bastard, I'll know your identity."

Morgan smiled, pleased with himself. Thanks to his cleverness, "Mr. X" was obliged to collect personally on his notes. Then all the cards would be out on the table. He fingered the deeds he had removed earlier from the wall safe. Hopefully, they would satisfy enough of the debt to win him a stay of execution. He had already determined that he was going to hold onto the boom and the veritable gold mine it promised to be at any cost.

A discreet tap sounded as the mantel clock struck the ninth hour, and the butler slid the study door partially open.

"A Mr. Douglas to see you, sir," he announced, smoothly withdrawing and closing the door behind Ian.

"Douglas!" exclaimed Morgan vastly annoyed. "What the blue blazes are you doing here! I don't have time to discuss problems at the mill. I'm expecting an important business associate. We'll talk tomorrow."

Ian strolled forward, undaunted by the rude welcome. "I'm not here about the mill, sir. I'm here to collect on the notes."

Morgan's jaw dropped. First Stanton, now his own foreman had been recruited to run interference. He had been outsmarted again and in a most insulting manner.

"Who sent you?" demanded Morgan. When Ian didn't answer, his tone turned threatening. "Douglas, need I remind you just who it is you owe your allegiance to?"

"No, sir."

"I'll ask you one more time, who sent you?"

"No one sent me. After ye set about seein' to my attorney's departure, I found it necessary to come on my own behalf…just as ye had planned it."

Morgan shot out of his chair in utter disbelief. "On *your* behalf…it's been you all along? Where in the hell would *you* get the funds to buy up notes?"

Ian bristled but held his temper, savoring his sweet victory. "From the boom," he said.

"My God," Morgan whispered raggedly, "I bought the boom from you?"

"I believe payment is also due on that note as well, sir."

"What skullduggery are you up to?"

"Just takin' yer advice, sir…lendin' money at a fair rate of interest."

Morgan's face became mottled, the purple vein in his temple throbbing dangerously.

"How dare you! I made you foreman, and you repay me with a knife in my back!"

"My position has benefited us both."

"You deliberately maneuvered me to expand the mill to increase my debt."

"Poor judgment and greed were yer undoin', sir, not me. Ye should keep to yer own advice. Now, if ye'll redeem yer notes, I'll be on my way."

"I should have listened to Hawkins. He said you were trouble." Morgan threw the deeds at Ian.

"What's this?" asked Ian, bending to pick up the documents.

"Property...five properties."

"The notes call for cash."

"These properties will be worth three times that."

Ian quickly scanned the papers. "Someday...maybe. Most of these deeds are for low lands. They flood, Mr. Morgan." He started to refuse them, then took a second look and changed his mind. "All right, sign over the deeds. I'll take the properties and fifty thousand dollars in cash for the notes."

"Fifty thousand...do you think I'm crazy!"

"No, I think ye're a man who does nae have a choice. What do ye think the other mill owners might do if they found out that ye, the largest mill owner in Rossburg, now owns the boom?"

Morgan went deathly pale. "You bastard!" he sputtered, gasping for breath. He sank into the chair, his legs no longer able to support his weight. Shakily, he signed over the deeds. "I'll need a week to get that much money together. Now get out! And if you come within one hundred yards of the mill or this house, I'll kill you where you stand."

"I'll just keep the notes until I see my money," said Ian. "Nothin' personal, ye understand. Perhaps we'll meet again at the Men's Club for a Board of Trade Meeting."

"As God is my witness, Douglas, you'll never sit on that Board."

"I would nae take any wagers on that. I'm sure other mill owners will be grateful enough for an extension of their notes in exchange for their votes. And I expect that the president of Rossburg Trust would be most appreciative of a sizable deposit. Since ye can na afford to have certain information get out, I shall count on yer vote as well. The Board of Trade...not bad for a lad from the wrong side of town, ay?"

In that moment, Morgan was acutely aware of a shifting of fate in Ian's favor, but he took solace in one fact that he knew would never change. "You could be the richest man in town, Douglas, and you will never be allowed to cross that line," he said with a sneer. "It's a matter of birth."

Ian's features hardened and his silver-blue eyes turned cold as steel. "Or perhaps of marriage."

Morgan jumped to his feet so enraged, he was speechless for a moment. "It'll be over my dead body!" he shrieked when he found his voice again. "Get out! Get out of my house!"

Smiling victoriously, Ian turned and casually sauntered out of the room as Morgan continued to hurl threats and epithets at his back.

The front door had just closed on Ian when a stab of pain suddenly shot up Morgan's right arm. Clutching at his chest, he gasped and collapsed across the desk.

CHAPTER 21

The sun took refuge behind a bank of clouds, and a warm breeze wafted through the trees, stirring veils and taffeta skirts with a languid finger. The fragrance of wild roses mingled with the sweet scent of the hybrids that blanketed the ebony casket.

Standing apart from the crowd of local dignitaries and Rossburg elite, the mill hands watched with indifference and anxiety, bonded by the uncertainty of their futures, as Cyrus Morgan was laid to rest.

Ian stared hard at the small figure in the front row. Eleanor leaned on Peter Jeffries' arm and dabbed at her eyes, an occasional sob shaking her body. Jeffries, suave and debonair in his European suit, stiffly patted her hand in sympathy.

Beneath the wispy, black veil, Eleanor's pale features seemed cast in delicate porcelain. Even garbed in a stark, black dress, she looked so regal, so achingly vulnerable that he was finding it difficult to despise her. As though to give him cause, the humiliating conversation he had chanced to overhear between her and her friends that day suddenly leaped to mind. The words "common mill hand" and Eleanor's mocking laughter reverberated in his brain with renewed intensity. His eyes narrowed and his rugged features hardened with greater resolve.

At last the service ended and the crowd began to disperse.

"What do ye think will happen with the mill?" asked Tommy anxiously.

Ian shrugged. "Can na say as yet."

"The burial be over now. What say we go lift us a pint?"

"Ye go on ahead. I have somethin' to do first. I'll meet ye later," said Ian, spying Morgan's attorney.

* * * * * * * *

A late afternoon thunderstorm capped the gloomy mood of the day. A chill permeated the parlor in spite of the summer season and a low fire burned in the marble fireplace. Light from the lamps reflected in the imported glass chandelier, painting multi-colored rainbows on the ceiling and walls.

Eleanor sat in a small, red velvet chair. She twisted a handkerchief in her hands, lifting it every now and then to dab at her eyes. Peter Jeffries stood behind her, a hand on her shoulder, looking very stoic. His father occupied the rosewood sofa, while the domestic staff of eight hung discreetly to one side of the room. Their eyes were all turned expectantly on Arthur Waring, who sat at the French desk fiddling with papers as he prepared to read Cyrus Morgan's last will and testament.

Waring ran a finger along the inside of his collar. It suddenly felt very tight. And his gaze continually went to the doorway.

"Arthur, can't we get on with this?" asked Franklin Jeffries brusquely. "I'm sure Eleanor could do with a rest. I dare say we all could."

"In a minute, Franklin. We're waiting for another party to arrive."

Just then, Ian appeared in the doorway, and everybody turned to look at him in curious surprise, wondering who he was and what he had to with this very private matter. His black suit was of a very good cloth and cut and hung well on his tall, broad-shouldered frame. The thick, sandy-colored hair and the mustache he now sported were neatly trimmed.

Ian's lips curled up in a half smile of smug satisfaction when he saw a stunned look of recognition flicker across Eleanor's face. Peter spared him a scant glance before haughtily turning his attention back to Waring, obviously ignorant of Ian's identity. Neither had the housekeeper placed him as the "common mill hand" she had patronized more than once, but continued to gawk at him in unabashed interest.

"Whoever this young man is, he has arrived. Now can we proceed, Arthur?" demanded Franklin Jeffries impatiently.

"Yes, of course." Waring cleared his throat and began. "I, Cyrus Morgan, being of sound mind and body, do hereby bequeath my possessions in the manner as follows: a gift of one thousand dollars to be given to each member of my staff with more than ten years of loyal service; a gift of five hundred dollars to be given to each member of my staff with five to ten years of loyal service; and a gift of two hundred and fifty dollars to be given to each member of my staff with less than five years of service. To my daughter…"

Ian saw Peter's hand tighten on Eleanor's shoulder and Franklin Jeffries lean forward with greater interest.

"To my daughter…" repeated Waring, once again nervously tugging on his collar, "I leave the balance of my estate which shall include the mill yards, lands, the house, the art and all monies not heretofore encumbered." At this, Waring looked up and excused the staff.

Peter's hand relaxed and Franklin Jeffries leaned back in his seat, his stern features wreathed in a rare smile. "Miss Eleanor," he said, "permit me to say that Peter is a lucky, young man."

Arthur Waring glanced over at Ian, who stood observing the proceedings with a slight smile, at once smug and amused. The attorney took a deep breath. "I-ah-I'm afraid that things are not quite as they seem. Miss Morgan, your father appears to have accrued substantial debts, the notes of which were never redeemed."

Eleanor looked confused. "Debts? What kind of debts? I don't understand, Mr. Waring."

"What are you trying to say, Arthur!" demanded the elder Jeffries sharply.

The attorney hastened to explain. "Now, Franklin, I knew nothing of any of this until Mr. Douglas approached me at the cemetery yesterday. Cyrus acted completely without my counsel."

"Explain yourself, man. What are you blubbering about?"

"This young man," said Waring pointing to Ian, "holds notes from Cyrus totalling some two hundred and twenty thousand dollars. In addition, Cyrus had signed over several pieces of property to Mr. Douglas."

All eyes turned on Ian.

Franklin Jeffries jumped up from the couch. "The devil you say!"

"I'm afraid the papers are quite in order," said Waring.

Eleanor's eyes were wide with disbelief. "Are you trying to tell me, Mr. Waring, that I have nothing?"

"Well, not exactly. You do have the house, the furnishings and a few pieces of property."

"No money?"

Waring shook his head regretfully. "A few thousand perhaps. You have the option, of course, of selling anything you like. However, in today's market I'm afraid nothing will fetch anywhere near its worth."

Eleanor nearly swooned, but only Ian seemed to take any notice.

"What of the mill?" croaked Peter.

"It was used as collateral for one of the notes. I'm afraid it belongs to Mr. Douglas now. Even if Eleanor could come up with the money to redeem the notes, the due date has passed, and Mr. Douglas is exercising his option."

"This is outrageous!" Franklin Jeffries turned on Ian. "I don't know who you are or how you managed to get the best of Cyrus Morgan, young man, but mark my words, we'll be keeping a close watch on you. Come along, Peter." He angrily strode from the room.

As Eleanor looked up at him for reassurance, Peter returned a tight smile and hurried after his father.

Waring quickly gathered together his papers, eager to be away from here as well. Somehow, he felt accountable for Cyrus's lapse of sanity and offended at the same time. He had handled the man's affairs for years. Why hadn't Cyrus seen fit to consult him on this matter as well? In any case, he couldn't bear to look Eleanor in the eye. She sat very still, staring blindly into space, obviously in shock. He tried to think of something comforting to say, but nothing came to mind.

"I'm…sorry, Miss Morgan," he finally murmured and hastily departed.

When they were alone, Ian walked over to Eleanor. If she knew he was there, she gave no sign of it. He had held so much anger for her but now seeing her this way, he felt only pity for her.

It was an awkward moment. He didn't know what to say or do anymore than Waring had, and he turned to leave when she spoke.

"My father always said you were different from the others. Knowing that, it would appear he still underestimated you."

"I'm sorry," said Ian.

Eleanor slowly turned her head. "Are you, Mr. Douglas? I think not. I think this is exactly as you planned it."

"Perhaps…in the beginning," Ian admitted. "But now I must confess to feelin' a certain amount of regret and pity on yer account."

"Pity? I am engaged to wed the son of one of the wealthiest, most powerful families in Rossburg. Pity not me, sir, but yourself. Franklin Jeffries will not let this stand. You will see that your new-found wealth has gained you little." She rose from the chair and stood defiantly before him. "To this town," she said, clearly enunciating every word, "once a mill hand, always a mill hand."

As she swept past him, Ian caught her arm. "I would nae bother to set a weddin' date if I were ye, Miss Morgan. Money marries only money."

Eleanor gasped as Ian cast her off and strode out of the room. Eleanor slowly sank onto the sofa stunned…and worried. He had spoken a terrifying truth.

CHAPTER 22

It rained for three days. The flood of 1878 was an all too vivid memory, and while everyone kept an anxious eye on the river, Tommy kept a worried eye on Ian. He had never seen his friend in such a state. Ian hadn't shaved in days. He ate little and slept less. As the river rose higher and higher, threatening the boom, he feverishly paced the bank and canal night and day, watching for any break in the cable. For Ian, it was the ultimate test of Nature, the ultimate challenge of a dead man.

"Ian, come in out of the rain," pleaded Tommy. "The weather is na fit for dogs. Ye'll catch yer death, man."

"He's watchin', Tommy. He's watchin' and waitin'."

"Who? Waitin' for what?"

Ian didn't answer, momentarily caught up in a different reality. He saw Morgan's face in every cloud, heard the man's whispered taunts in every gust of wind.

Tommy was certain his friend had snapped when Ian raised a fist to the storm and yelled, "Ye'll not beat me, Morgan! I'll meet ye in hell first!"

Icy fingers tracked up Tommy's spine when the challenge was immediately met with a clap of thunder and a bolt of lightning. He crossed himself and murmured, "Mary, mother of Jesus, he's lost his bloody mind."

Everyone breathed a sigh of relief when the downpour dwindled to a light rain, finally ending altogether on the fifth day. The next morning, the river was found to have crested at twenty-eight feet with some surface flooding at the lower end of town. More importantly, the boom had held, as defiant to the end as its creator.

The next afternoon, newsboys stood on the corner shouting the day's headlines: FOREMAN NEW OWNER OF SUSQUEHANNA BOOM COMPANY AND MORGAN MILL YARDS...MEMBERS OF LUMBERMEN'S EXCHANGE CHARGE TRICKERY...BOARD OF TRADE CALLS FOR INQUIRY AND A BOYCOTT OF DOUGLAS MILL PRODUCTS.

* * * * * * * *

Tommy strode angrily down the walk, clutching the newspaper in his hand, heedless of the greetings of the shopkeepers as they closed up for the night. Now he knew why Ian had been in such a frenzy throughout the storm. The bloke not only owned the bloody boom, but the mill as well and had never said a word about it to him—his best friend. The mill had been open a week since Morgan's death, but he had to hear of Ian's new ownership from Franklin Jeffries' driver down at the saloon. He still wouldn't have believed it if he hadn't seen it for himself in the newspaper. Tommy cursed under his breath. He'd get some answers out of Ian if he had to beat them out of him.

As he neared Ian's boarding house, he heard sounds of a scuffle and stopped to peer down the dimly lit alley. He could see two men holding someone while another thug delivered punches to the hapless victim's midsection and jaw. There was something vaguely familiar to him about the victim, and Tommy suddenly tore down the narrow street when he realized that it was Ian beneath the blood and bruises,

In a mad fury, he pulled one of the thugs off Ian. He managed to get in a few punishing blows of his own, before he was jumped from behind by the third man. Ian found enough strength to throw off his other attacker and come to Tommy's defense. A few more punches were exchanged before the thugs scattered and ran.

Tommy picked himself up off the ground. "Are ye all right?"

Ian gasped. "Aye. Just help me to my room."

He let out a pain-filled moan, then, and Tommy took a closer look. Blood streamed from his nose and a cut about his eye, and he gingerly held his side.

"Mary mother of Jesus, Ian, ye're really hurt! I've got to get ye to the doc's."

"I'll be all right. Few cuts and bruises is all. Take more'n a few thugs to do me damage." Ian tried to grin, but it came out lopsided and the effort made him wince. "Just help me to the boardin' house."

Tommy caught Ian as he stumbled and nearly fell to the ground. "Here, lean on me."

As they entered the boarding house to the curious stares of the other boarders, Tommy shouted to one to fetch the doctor.

It was an hour before Ian was cleaned up and more comfortably settled in his bed, his ribs taped, and the gash on his forehead stitched.

"Nasty beating you got there. Stay in bed and have this prescription filled. I'll check on you in a few days, young man," said the doctor sternly.

When the door had closed behind the doctor, Ian looked out of a swollen eye to find Tommy glowering at him.

"Lucky for me ye happened by," said Ian.

"I dinna just happen by," said Tommy curtly. "I come lookin' for ye to beat the truth out of ye meself. Why did ye na tell me 'twas ye what bought the boom and rebuilt it after the big flood? I thought ye had lost yer mind pacin' along the river durin' the storm and shoutin' craziness at a dead man. How the deuce did ye end up with the mill and some of Morgan's property anyway?"

Ian groaned as he shifted his weight. "Can we nae talk about this later? 'Tis a long story."

"I know it isn't easy fer ye to talk now, but I'll not be leavin' here without an explanation. Ye be owin' me that much. Maybe if ye'd been straight with me from the start, ye would na be lyin' here all busted up."

"All right, all right. Sit down, and I'll tell ye everythin'."

With difficulty, due to a stiffening jaw, Ian explained what he had done and how he had accomplished it. When he was finished, Tommy jumped up from the chair and paced about the small room, still trying to understand.

"Geez, Ian, why could ye na tell me all this before! Why did ye na ask me to help ye? I thought we was best friends."

"That's why I did nae tell ye, Tommy. 'Twas risky what I was doin'. If somethin' went wrong, I did nae want ye to be losin' yer job—or worse."

"Did Maven know?"

Ian shook his head, and Tommy was somewhat mollified that he wasn't the only one left in the dark.

"'Twas better nobody knew 'til everythin' was settled. After tonight, looks like things may get a whole lot worse."

"It isn't just tonight, Ian. Those broken saws and that fire yesterday were no accident. This time yer gonna let me help ye, or we not be friends anymore."

✳　　✳　　✳　　✳　　✳　　✳　　✳　　✳

Maven stared at Mrs. Drury incredulously. "No, I can na believe it."

"It's true, it's true," said Mrs. Drury breathless with excitement. "It's all here in the newspaper. Ian Douglas owns Morgan Mill Yards and the boom. Why, he's quite possibly a millionaire."

Maven grabbed the newspaper and read the account for herself. Even then she could scarcely believe it. She sank heavily into a chair. All those nights he had come to her, the passion they had shared…Ian wouldn't have kept something like this from her. If he was dishonest about this, what else had he been dishonest about?

She jumped up and reached for her shawl. "I must go out for a little while. I won't be long," she said.

She covered the distance to the boarding house quickly before she could change her mind. Luckily the downstairs was empty. Mrs. Brockton knew her, and she wasn't in the mood to face a raised eyebrow. Only one type of lady went unescorted up to a gentleman's room. But then, she thought with a bitter laugh, perhaps she qualified after all. She ran up the stairs to the third floor and found Ian's room. She wanted to burst through the door, but settled for two firm raps.

A weak, muffled voice called for her to come in. It didn't sound like Ian, and she hesitated, wondering now if she had the right room. She cautiously opened the door and peeked inside the room.

A man lay on the bed. A cover was pulled up to his midsection, and his chest was bandaged.

"Ian?" Maven let out a strangled cry when Ian turned his head to her, his face barely recognizable. "Ian! Oh, dear, God. What has happened to ye?" She flew into the room and knelt beside the bed. "Why did ye na send for me?"

Ian reached out a hand to touch her face. "Maven, dear sweet, Maven," he said in a hoarse voice. "Ye should nae have come, lass. I told Tommy not to tell ye."

"He dinna tell me. I came to ask ye about…the stories in the papers."

"I could nae tell ye, Maven. 'Twas too dangerous."

"Who did this to ye?"

"Some thugs who were nae happy about a few changes in ownership." Ian winced. It still hurt to talk. "They surprised me last night in the alley. Tommy came along and helped me fight them off."

Maven took off her shawl and rolled up her sleeves. For the next two days, she nursed Ian, allowing Tommy to relieve her at night. Her own hurt and uncertainties were forgotten in her concern for Ian.

*   *   *   *   *   *   *   *

"Maven, ye've hardly said two words this evenin'," said Tommy. "Come to think of it, ye hardly say much at all anymore. And look at ye. Ye're as glum as an undertaker and as peaked as last year's rose."

Maven managed a wan smile. "Sorry, Tommy. I guess I'm still worried about Ian. He insisted on goin' back to the mill too soon. He should have been another week in bed."

"Ye know Ian. Another week in bed would have killed him. Besides, he had to take over management of the mill yards right away."

"How go things at the mill?"

"Ian has his hands full to be sure," said Tommy. "What with the vandalism and threats, he can na leave. We organized a militia of loyal workers to patrol the grounds night and day, and Ian has taken to sleepin' there. Do na worry, Maven. 'Tisn't anythin' he can na handle. Ye more'n anybody knows he always lands on his feet."

Tommy stood up and pulled her out of her chair. "Go fetch a wrap. We're goin' fer a walk."

"Oh, Tommy, I can na do that. I have this gown to finish and—"

"I will na take 'no' fer an answer, Maven. Ye need to get away from the shop for a spell. Fresh air'll do ye good…put some color back into yer cheeks. C'mon, 'tis Saturday night."

Maven laughed and set aside the satin trim, no match for his light-hearted persistence. "All right, you win."

A blanket of stars twinkling in the darkening sky and a light autumn breeze greeted them as they stepped out into the twilight.

"Ah, 'tis a fine evenin' indeed," said Maven, throwing back her head and breathing deeply of the cool night air.

Tommy smiled and tucked her hand into the crook of his arm. "That it is, Maven, me luv. That it is."

Their footsteps echoed hollowly on the narrow boardwalk as they silently strolled along, Tommy blissfully content, Maven pensive.

Tommy fingered the ring in his pocket, but something told him this wasn't the right moment.

*   *   *   *   *   *   *   *

Mrs. Drury laid aside the delicate French lace, and cast a worried glance over her spectacles at Maven.

"Land sakes, girl, you comin' down with something? You haven't been yourself for days now."

Deep in thought about Ian, Maven started at the sound of her mentor's voice. For several minutes she had been staring unseeingly out the window, her work laying forgotten on her lap. She turned to Mrs. Drury, forcing a weak smile. "'Tis nothin'…a headache is all."

"I heard down at the market yesterday that the grippe is making its rounds. Perhaps you should go home for a few days and take some of your mama's chicken soup and boneset tea."

Maven shook her head. "I can na leave. The Caulder trousseau is na finished."

"I can see to the rest of the details myself. Truth is, I'm going to need you in fine form by the end of the week. Eleanor Morgan will be coming in to be measured and to select material for three walking dresses. I promised them to her by the end of the month."

Maven looked at Mrs. Drury in surprise. "Eleanor Morgan? But she goes to New York for all of her clothes."

"Indeed she did. As I hear it, her father didn't leave her as well off as she had expected, though she would rather die than admit it. Anyway here is our chance to show her and her high society friends that we're just as good as them fancy dressmakers in New York and Philadelphia." Mrs. Drury's brow furrowed with a worrisome thought. "Oh, dear. I do hope she can pay for them."

Maven felt a stab of envy as she recalled how easily Eleanor had always drawn Ian's interest. Clearly, she didn't share Mrs. Drury's excitement at the prospect of serving the young woman.

"Yes, a few days off is just what you need, I think," continued Mrs. Drury. "Give that young O'Brien fellow a chance to court you," she added with a wink.

A bright, red blush started up Maven's slender throat, spilling across her pale features. "Mrs. Drury, I think you misunderstand. 'Tis good friends we be, an' nothin' more."

"Pshaw, I'm not that old that I don't know a young man in love when I see one. He'd be a good man for you, too. Steady. Not like that Ian Douglas. That one courts trouble. If ye ask me—"

"Mrs. Drury, perhaps I will go home for a few days, if ye can manage. I am feelin' a bit poorly," said Maven.

She was weary of the debate, the conversation, the high emotions that the mere mention of Ian's name seemed to provoke in town. Maybe back in her old neighborhood, she could find some respite from it all.

CHAPTER 23

Eleanor Morgan paced back and forth across the Aubusson rug in the cherry-panelled drawing room, the discordant rustle of her underskirts emphasizing her agitated state. Suddenly thrust into the position as head of the household, she was faced with a multitude of duties which confused and infuriated her, the latest and most humiliating being the heretofore patient staff demanding their wages. She had visited the bank that day to obtain another draft when the president warned her again of her precarious financial status.

"Damn Peter Jeffries! Damn Ian Douglas! And damn Father's stupidity!" With total exasperation, Eleanor spat out the impieties that only a few months ago would have been unthinkable to her.

Twin spots of color flamed against her pale cheeks, and a scowl marred the perfect features. She suddenly felt suffocated and swept through the open French doors onto the terrace to breathe in the late afternoon coolness. Her thoughts tumbled willy-nilly, refusing any sort of order. She bit her lower lip as tears of frustration brimmed in the violet-blue eyes.

In the rapidly approaching dusk, a chorus of insects began their frenetic serenading. Ornamental shrubs sculpted in the forms of animals cast misshapen images in the lengthening shadows. Cyrus Morgan had spent a fortune on topiary landscaping, effecting yet another degree of endless wealth.

Eleanor gazed out over the vast expanse of the manicured grounds. At the thought of what she might be forced to give up, her anger gave way to a moan of self-pity. How could her father be so careless in his business transactions as to render her vulnerable to such humiliating circumstances? If only Peter would marry her.

Her face flamed anew at the thought of the gossip that had reached her ears. Peter had been seen promenading around the park on Sunday, arm in arm with her good friend Caroline, hanging on her every word when he used to think her such a dolt. Eleanor dug her nails into her palms. Had Ian Douglas been right? Was Peter's devotion only as solid as her bank account? She wasn't so naive as to not realize that her societal acceptance certainly was. Already invitations were beginning to fall off. But Peter...Peter loved her, worshipped the ground she walked on. He had told her so often enough. Then what was he doing in the park with Caroline?

Eleanor drew in a deep breath and slowly expelled it in a sigh of resignation. She knew what she must do. With renewed purpose and determination, she returned to the drawing room and sat down at her mother's writing desk. She took out fine, cream-colored linen paper with the Morgan crest embossed in gold at the top, and meticulously formed the words in proper, boarding-school script:

Dear Mr. Douglas,

It is my express wish that you call upon me the day after tomorrow, Friday, between the hours of one and two in the afternoon to discuss a matter of utmost importance. I believe it will prove beneficial to us both.

She paused, tapping the pen contemplatively against her fingertips, then added:

Please be prompt as I have a three o'clock tea. I trust we can forthwith resolve this matter quickly and to the satisfaction of all concerned.

Sincerely,
Eleanor A. Morgan

Eleanor smiled, pleased with her efforts. It was a most business-like request, firm but polite enough without betraying any of her desperation. She hadn't been her father's daughter for nothing, she thought smugly.

Her eyes narrowed in speculation. Given his arrogance at the reading of the will, she felt quite certain that Ian Douglas would be flattered to receive an invitation to the mansion. She reread the note, rather pleased at the subtlety with which she had managed to disclose her social obligation. It would never do for him to discover her waning popularity. He would know that Eleanor Morgan yet commanded a prominent position within Rossburg's elite inner circle, despite whatever gossip he might have heard to the contrary.

Friday came and went. Eleanor lounged dismally on the chaise in her bedroom with a cool cloth across her forehead. It had been a dreadful day. Ian Douglas, damn his arrogance, hadn't responded to her invitation. Nor had the tea gone well. She had been treated with courtesy on the surface, but she hadn't missed the patronizing note in the ladies' tones, the pity in their eyes when they looked her way, or the whispered gossip. Already, she felt a certain ostracism among her peers.

"I hate them! I hate them all!" she exclaimed, flinging the cloth across the room.

"Miss Morgan," said a maid timidly from the doorway, "a messenger just arrived with this note for you."

Eleanor bolted upright. "Is it from Peter…no doubt begging my forgiveness for so sorely neglecting me. Well, he won't get off that easily."

"No, miss. 'Tis from your solicitor, Mr. Waring."

The rush of energy immediately turned to a crush of disappointment and a dull luster replaced the momentary sparkle in her eyes as Eleanor slumped back against the chaise.

"Throw it away."

"Beg your pardon, miss?"

"I said throw the note away," said Eleanor impatiently.

"Are ye not goin' to read it?"

"What for? It's like all the others he sends, reminding me of how little funds I have, and that I must curtail my spending." Eleanor began to sob. "How could Father do this to me?"

"Now, miss, me da always used to tell me to look for the pot of gold at the end of the rainbow."

Eleanor wiped away the tears and flounced off the chaise. "Well, I don't see any rainbow, but I know where there's a pot of gold. Margaret, get out my best walking dress."

*   *   *   *   *   *   *   *

Tommy poked his head in the door. "Ian, Miss Morgan be here to see ye."

A smile slowly wreathed Ian's mouth. So, the mountain had come to Mohammed. "Show her up, by all means."

He walked over to the window and watched as she gracefully stepped out of the carriage. Eleanor Morgan had filled his head like an intoxicating wine for too long, his clouded emotions running the gamut from admiration to hatred; from pity to vengeful desire. It had pleased him considerably to imagine her great show of temper when he refused to heed her summons.

As Tommy escorted her across the yard, Eleanor looked about her in surprise. The mill had expanded a good deal since her last visit. Four large buildings now flanked the original slant-roofed building, and there was a bustle of activity as men hurriedly loaded wagons with lumber. Through the open door of the saw mill, she could hear steel saws rip through huge logs, sending flurries of sawdust flying through the air, as perspiring mill hands continually fed the insatiable monsters. Her jaw tightened, and a wave of anger swept over her when she spied the sign *DOUGLAS MILL YARDS.*

A weathered, slightly tilted sign indicated that the office was up the stairs. At least that hadn't changed since her last visit, she thought scornfully. Eleanor followed Tommy up the steps with a determined glint in her eye. But when Tommy opened the door for her, she suddenly felt less certain of herself. In her own element, she could be formidable. In this very foreign environment, she felt a measure of intimidation.

Ian sat on the edge of his desk, favoring no particular emotion. He seemed neither surprised nor pleased to see her and seemingly much less interested when she entered the room. She debated for a moment whether to turn and run while she still had some dignity, but it was too late. The door had closed behind her.

Eleanor looked about the office. "Well, I see that much has changed and nothing has changed," she said off-handedly, trying to match his manner of indifference.

"What can I do for ye, Miss Morgan?"

She took a deep breath. "Why did you ignore my invitation?"

"There must be some mistake. I received no invitation."

Eleanor blinked in surprise. "You must have. Ben told me he delivered it straight to your hand."

"I received no invitation, Miss Morgan. What I did receive was a summons, and I do nae answer summonses."

Completely taken aback, it was a moment before she could react. A stinging retort jumped to her lips, but she bit it back. She didn't dare antagonize him further.

"I'm sorry that you mistook the tone. I meant only to convey an urgency. May I sit down?"

"Of course. Forgive my manners. I'm afraid I am lackin' in the social graces. I'm just a 'common mill hand' ye see." He stood and seated himself behind the desk.

A crimson tide started at the edge of Eleanor's lacy bodice and spread to her face. The meeting was not going as she had planned. She had dressed with exceptional care this morning, very much aware that she had once commanded his interest. And it had been her intentions to call upon all the grace, charm and feminine wiles of her education and breeding toward rekindling that interest now. But his curt indifference had thrown her completely off balance, and she was at a loss as to how to proceed.

Eleanor perched stiffly on the edge of a crude wooden chair, took a deep breath and tried again. "I came here hoping to persuade you to forgive a portion of my father's debt. At the least, to settle a substantial dowry in exchange for some of the art and furnishings of the house."

Ian locked his fingers behind his head and leaned back in his chair, a faint smile playing upon his lips as he considered the offer. "I'm not in the market for art and fancy furnishin's, Miss Morgan."

"Property then. I still have some choice pieces of land," she said, her voice rising with her desperation. "Mr. Douglas. I've nowhere else to turn. I have no other way to live if I cannot raise a decent dowry to attract a suitable husband."

"I take it Peter Jeffries hasn't been the knight in shinin' armor ye expected."

Eleanor's eyes flashed violet. "Peter loves me. It's his father who keeps us apart. If I can raise a substantial dowry, I'm sure the matter will be resolved."

The cock of Ian's brow and the smug smile hovering about his mouth reflected his doubt. He had forced her to come to him, had succeeded in stripping away her cool sophistication at the expense of her dignity. He stopped short of bringing her to her knees. He found he couldn't stand to see even her, perhaps most of all her, beg.

"I believe we can work out something that will enable ye to continue in comfortable circumstances…and give me what I want."

As Ian outlined his proposition, the relief and hope on Eleanor's face faded, and her eyes widened in degrees with shock, disbelief, anger and ultimately dismay. At the meeting's end, she blindly stumbled down the stairs and across the yard to the carriage. When the driver handed her in, she collapsed onto the tooled leather seat. Ian Douglas' offer was generous…generous beyond her wildest expectations. But the price he demanded went far beyond what she had been prepared to pay.

Chapter 24

Even in the Basin, Maven found she couldn't escape the running commentary on Ian's tour de force. But at least here she found some solace in a differing attitude. Ian was regarded as something of a hero rather than the villain portrayed in the newspapers. Still, a nagging fear and uncertainty tormented her as day after day passed without word from him. He had promised her that they would resolve their situation as soon as he had everything under control at the mill. She had thought she would have heard something from him by now.

Mrs. McInnis watched her daughter with a worried eye as they prepared the evening meal. Maven still wasn't herself to a mother's satisfaction. She was too quiet, too pale, too distracted. She seemed to have withdrawn into a world of her own.

"Mother Superior says yer sister will make a fine school teacher next year," she said, trying to draw Maven into conversation.

Maven smiled. "I'm glad. 'Tis something Meghan has always dreamed of."

"Course, Sister Margaret Mary be despairin' of your poor, dear brother. The lad be given more to shenanigans than to book learnin'....My, my that Tommy O'Brien has become an important lad. Foreman of the mill, imagine that." She eyed Maven pointedly but got no response. "And who'd a thought that Ian Douglas, of all people, would end up in control of the mill...there be some in the Basin who be thinkin' he's overstepped himself. Course there are others who cheer him for givin' them people on the hill their comeuppance…"

"Mum, can we na talk of somethin' else?" interrupted Maven curtly. "'Tis all I hear about in town. 'Tis becomin' wearisome."

Mrs. McInnis glanced at her daughter curiously. "Aye, if it be pleasin' ye…I've invited Tommy to take his supper with us this evenin'."

Maven sighed. "Why?"

"I thought you might enjoy his company. Ye've been so glum, and he always makes ye laugh."

"Mum, I do na feel up to seein' anyone tonight! I wish ye would ask me before ye be makin' decisions fer me."

Her mother drew back in astonishment. "Maven, lass, what's got into ye? Tommy has had an eye fer ye ever so long. And now with his new position at the mill, he can do ye proud. He won't be waitin' on ye to make up yer mind forever. Ye'll be sorry, ye will, if he looks to another."

Maven threw down the paring knife and turned to storm out of the kitchen when she collided with Tommy.

"Maven, did ye na hear the news, " he said, his face flushed with excitement. He snatched off his cap, suddenly remembering his manners. "Good evenin', Mrs. McInnis."

"What news?" asked Maven impatiently.

"Ian is set to wed Eleanor Morgan day after the morrow. 'Tis a private affair owin' to the fact that Miss Morgan be still in mournin'. They'll be leavin' for New York fer a ship bound fer Europe."

Maven's face turned ashen. "It can na be…ye must be mistaken."

"'Tis truth. Ian told me himself at the mill today."

"Our Ian Douglas set to marry the likes of Eleanor Morgan," said a wide-eyed Mrs. McInnis. "Imagine that…Maven, where are ye goin', lass? Supper will be ready soon."

Maven bolted out of the house and tore through the streets to the mill. The work day was over and the mill was deserted except for six mill hands who patrolled the grounds. She flagged one of them.

"Is Mr. Douglas around?"

"Upstairs in the office." He jerked his thumb at the building behind him.

When Maven burst into his office, Ian wasn't surprised to see her. He had been expecting her.

"Is it true?" she demanded. "Are ye marryin' Eleanor Morgan?" He didn't answer her. He didn't need to. She could read the truth of it in his face. She pressed her back against the door and closed her eyes, fighting back tears. "Why, Ian, why?"

Ian walked over to her and tried to take her in his arms, the pain in her eyes, in her voice too much for him to bear. But she angrily pushed him away.

His arms dropped helplessly to his side. "I'm sorry, Maven. I did nae want ye to find out this way."

"When was I supposed to find out? After ye had left on yer honeymoon?"

"It all happened so quickly. I-I did nae know how to tell ye."

"Ye mean ye dinna have the courage to tell me, so ye left it up to Tommy. Ye're a coward, Ian Douglas...a deceitful coward. I...I thought ye loved me."

"Maven, let me explain. 'Tis nae the way ye think."

"Stay away from me, Ian. I do na ever want to see ye again."

She flung open the door, and fled the office. He didn't try to stop her. He knew Maven well enough to know that it would be useless to try to reason with her now. When he returned he would make things right between them, he decided.

CHAPTER 25

In the parlor of the Morgan mansion, September 30, 1880, Ian and Eleanor stood before a Justice of the Peace. The only people in attendance were the servants. It was raining outside. Inside the mood was somber. It was a far cry from the society wedding Eleanor had always envisioned for herself. As the Justice pronounced the couple man and wife, Eleanor looked dismal. When Ian kissed his bride, he found her cold and unresponsive. There was no celebratory reception following the ceremony, no joyful send off. Instead, the servants quietly offered perfunctory best wishes beneath the portico as Ian handed Eleanor into the carriage bound for the train station.

The train ride to New York was quiet and uneventful. Eleanor spoke not a word and stared out of the window. The frown on her face and the intensity of her gaze left Ian in no doubt as to her state of mind. He was not in the mood to draw fire and passed most of the trip in the club car, trying to forget the hurt in Maven's eyes. Bending Eleanor to his will, winning the game, was all that had mattered to him in the heat of the moment. He hadn't considered the pain he would cause Maven until it was too late. She was the last person in the world he had wanted to hurt, and he was determined to make amends. Somehow, he would make her understand.

* * * * * * * *

In the honeymoon suite at the Waldorf-Astoria, Eleanor lay beneath satin sheets and willed herself invisible. Beyond countless flirtations, there had been little to prepare her for what she had often heard whispered as the dreaded "wedding night".

Her eyes widened in fear when Ian's tall, muscular form appeared in the doorway. She shrank deeper into the mattress as he approached the bed and slowly pulled back the sheet, his hot gaze seeming to devour every inch of her.

He threw off his robe, lay down beside her, and pulled her to him, his hunger to possess the lovely Eleanor driving his passion. She gasped as his mouth covered hers in a deep searching kiss, and she struggled to push away his hand as it moved over her buttocks and down her satiny thigh to slowly explore the rest of her body.

When Eleanor managed to break free of him, her chest heaved with indignation, and she clutched the sheet tightly to her. "What unspeakable things do you practice!"

Ian looked at her in surprise. "'Tis a natural act between a man and a woman."

He reached out to fondle a lock of honey blonde hair, and she instantly recoiled from his touch. When he tried to gather her to him again, he could feel her resistance.

"Peter would never have stooped to such base behavior," she said accusingly.

The puzzled frown on Ian's handsome face deepened into a scowl. "But a common mill hand would?"

Eleanor said nothing. She didn't have to. With a savage grunt, he pulled her against him and shocked her sensibilities further.

Eleanor closed her eyes against the humiliation, shutting out the workings of his hands and mouth upon her body, unable to rise above the shame of it to accept any pleasure. She had never dreamed that such things could go on and thought she surely must be experiencing more than just those acts that were supposed to occur in the marriage bed. He made no allowance whatsoever for her sensibilities. He hadn't even extinguished the light. Peter never would have treated her like this, and she felt an even greater contempt for Ian's low birth.

As she remained cold and unresponsive, in spite of his skill, Ian became angry. He pinned her roughly beneath him, with no further attempt at gentleness. Eleanor erupted into hysterics, the wrenching sobs washing over him like waves of cold water, barely enabling him to consummate the marriage. When he had finished, he rolled away from her, drained, confused, and angry. It hadn't been like this with Maven.

"Oh, dear God! You've ruptured me. I'm going to die!"

Ian jumped at Eleanor's horrified shrieks and turned to see her stabbing a finger at a crimson stain on the sheet. Telltale blood trickled down the inside of her thighs. He stared at her, astounded by her outburst, then quickly pulled her to his chest to muffle her cries. Any minute, he expected to hear a pounding on the door from the clerk and hotel security.

"For godsake, Eleanor, be quiet. Ye're not going to die. 'Tis natural for a virgin to bleed the first time. Someone must have explained things to ye."

No one had explained anything to her, and Ian frantically tried to calm her before she woke up the entire hotel. But he was awkward and ill-prepared for the task, at times exciting her to greater hysteria. When she finally quieted, he slipped on his robe and walked across the room to the washstand. He poured water into the bowl, wet a cloth and took it to her.

Glaring up at him through a veil of tears, she snatched the cloth from his hand. "Turn around."

With a weary sigh, he did as ordered. When she was finished washing, he stripped the bottom sheet off the bed and replaced it with the top sheet. She stood there shaking, wrapped in a blanket, sniffing back sobs, and he was suddenly consumed by conscience. Gently, he coaxed her back into bed.

When he touched her shoulder, he could feel her wince. "I did nae mean to hurt ye, Eleanor. 'Twill nae be like this again." He wanted to take her in his arms, but fearing her reaction, he fell back against his pillow. He felt so damned helpless.

Despite his efforts to overcome Eleanor's fears and revulsion, the next few nights were much the same as the first. On the fourth night at sea bound for England, Ian was encouraged that she hadn't burst into tears when he approached her. Instead she lay stiffly on the bed, much like a martyr accepting her fate, and Ian's desire withered.

"In time, Eleanor, ye'll find an empty bed a cold and lonely one," he said.

*   *   *   *   *   *   *   *

Shame sliced through Maven every waking moment, causing her greater pain than any actual knife could. Now she knew the true meaning of "hell on earth". She could find no relief, no refuge from the hurtful memories. Work proved to be not much of a panacea. It merely chased away the days faster, forcing her closer to the ever sharpening horns of a dilemma.

Dawn was painting the horizon with bright pink and purple hues when Maven shakily emerged from Granny O'Neill's cottage, vial in hand that had cost her one week's wages. Oil of tansy...she had only to mix it with tea and wait. Granny O'Neill guaranteed it. Maven stared at the little bottle. The contents at once offered her protection from scandal and promise of damnation. She had no more of a choice now than she did before. With a strangled cry, she threw the vial into the bushes.

Tears pelted her shawl like raindrops as she stumbled down the walk and onto the road, blind to any traffic. She half walked, half ran across the canal, her instincts of self-preservation subordinated to a more powerful need to escape the pain. Her mind was a blank, the sights a blur, and it came of no particular surprise to her that she found herself at the river's edge.

The river was running high and swift from recent rains; the bank was slick from the morning dew. She felt her heel slip. It would be a sin to take her life, but how easy it would be to lose her footing, to slide into the water and be carried away by the current. Drowning could be no worse than the suffering she had endured these past weeks.

She closed her eyes, crossed herself and moved closer to the slippery edge. As the pebbles beneath her foot shifted, a hand clamped firmly over her arm to pull her back from the brink.

"Mary, mother of Jesus! What the hell do ye think ye're doin', lass!"

Maven opened her eyes and stared up at a white-faced Tommy.

He saw that he had frightened her badly. He took a deep breath and softened his tone.

"What are ye doin' here, Maven? Ye know how dangerous the river is here."

"I…I was just watchin' the sunrise," she stammered.

"Maven—"

"I must go, Tommy."

She broke away from him and ran back to the road. Anger at his interference turned to embarrassment and more shame, and tears streamed down her face unchecked. What in heaven's name *was* she doing? She didn't know anymore. Her life was spinning out of control, and she didn't like where it was going. But she felt powerless to change course.

It was a long day, longer than usual. In spite of her busy schedule, Maven couldn't get her mind off of the look on Tommy's face when he pulled her back from the river's edge. She knew she owed him an explanation, but what could she tell him?

The shop bell tinkled, startling her and she upset the tin of threads on her lap.

"Goodness, child, you're as skittish as a colt today." Mrs. Drury chided her as multi-colored spools rolled across the floor. "It's just your young man come to visit. A good evening to you, Mr. O'Brien. I haven't seen you around for some time. Busy at the mill no doubt with Mr. Douglas away on his honeymoon."

At this, an anguished groan escaped Maven's lips, drawing a curious gaze from Mrs. Drury, and she quickly bent down to gather up the spools of thread from the floor.

"Aye, 'tis that I am, Mrs. Drury," said Tommy.

A worried eye still on Maven, Mrs. Drury approached Tommy and drew him aside. "I'm glad you're here, Mr. O'Brien," she said in a whispered tone. "The poor child simply isn't well. I don't mean in body, mind you, but here." She put a hand to her chest. "In the soul."

Tommy nodded, his normally jocular manner solemn. "Aye, she's not the same lass to be sure. Mrs. Drury, could ye be leavin' Maven and me alone for a bit. I'd like to speak with her."

"Well, I do have a church meeting in a half hour. I suppose I could be a mite early." Mrs. Drury turned to Maven. "I'll be off to my meeting now. I'll leave you to close up, dear."

When Mrs. Drury left the shop, Maven wished she hadn't. She didn't know what to say to Tommy, and if Ian's name came up, she knew she didn't have the strength to disguise her emotions.

She set the tin of threads on the work table and began winding bolts of cloth. "What brings ye here? The mill must be in sore need of ye," she said, trying to keep her voice even.

"Ye bring me here, Maven. I've something to say to ye. I've had something to say to ye for a long time now."

"Tommy, I—"

"Maven, hear me out, lass." He hesitated for a moment and cleared his throat, his manner determined. "I can na offer ye the things what Ian can," he said, "but ye always be sayin' I make ye laugh, an' if the love I feel for ye counts for anythin', well then ye'll be the richest woman in Rossburg. Maven McInnis, will ye marry me?"

Tears filled Maven's eyes, and, unable to help herself, she broke into heart-wrenching sobs.

Tommy drew her into a tender embrace, his callused hand gently stroking her hair.

He forced a light laugh. "Be that a 'yea' or a 'nay'?"

Maven lifted a tear-stained face to him. " Ye're a good, kind man, Tommy O'Brien. But ye do na understand."

Tommy looked deep into her eyes. "Aye, I understand. I understand everythin', lass. I saw everythin' clear at the river this morn. I've always known that ye and Ian shared a special bond. I hoped that someday there would be room for me." He took her firmly by the shoulders. "Promise me, Maven, ye'll na think on such a deed as this morn again. Promise me!"

Maven hung her head and nodded. "I'm so ashamed."

"'Tis Ian what should be ashamed. I should have guessed…were he here now, I'd wrap me hands around his neck."

"The fault is not all his. I thought…"

"I'll hear no more, lass. Marry me, Maven, and we'll ne'er speak of it again. If ye'll have me, I'll make ye a good life."

"It is na fair to ye, Tommy."

"It is na up to ye to decide what's fair for me. I love ye enough for the both of us, and maybe in time…" He looked at her with such love and hope, her heart ached.

His sturdy frame had grown in his adolescence, and he now topped her by a few inches. She reached up and took his broad, Irish face in her hands and kissed him with all the love she had left in her. She hoped in time it would be more.

CHAPTER 26

As they drove through the streets on their way home from the railroad station, Eleanor glanced out the carriage window at the soot-covered buildings and remnants of snow. After three months of visiting some of the world's most glamorous cities, Rossburg seemed small, dirty, and ugly. Funny how she had never noticed before.

"Eleanor, ye've been sulking since we left England," said Ian. "I think ye've carried this tantrum on long enough. 'Tis gettin' tiresome."

"I doubt I shall ever speak to you again. How could you cut short our trip without even a word to me? The season was just beginning. I don't see why you couldn't have allowed me to stay behind."

"Because, Eleanor, ye are my wife. We've debated this matter the length of the crossin'. I will nae debate it again," said Ian firmly.

She shifted her seat, putting a greater distance between them. "I shall never forgive you this."

In Europe she had enjoyed the admiration of men and, on the arm of her tall, handsome husband, the envy of every woman. Ian had been generous in his allowance, sending her to the best couturiers and never lecturing her on her spending. Much to her surprise, he had acquitted himself well, escorting her with surprising aplomb to the theatre, balls and the finest restaurants. For a time it had been easy to forget that she had married below her station and could even feel a modicum of pride in him. When he had finally refrained from inflicting further mortifying acts upon her person, she had guardedly allowed herself to enjoy his company, the feel of his arm beneath her fingers, the quiet strength of his protective hand on her back. For all too short a time, she had revelled in this perfect fairy tale. How could he so callously disregard her happiness, the only happiness she had known since her father had died?

As the carriage entered the gates of the Morgan estate—three months ahead of schedule—Ian, in his eagerness to be home, leaped out of the conveyance. He drank in the familiar sights, sounds, and smells of Rossburg. Eleanor was right about one thing, and he was damned proud of it. He never would be one of *them*, the idle rich. The one irony of the trip was that he hadn't had to pretend boredom. The aristocracy carefully cultivated an air of ennui that had come quite natural to him. Work drove him, nourished him, energized him. He loved the challenge, the unpredictability of the business, the company of unpretentious men, and he could hardly wait to get back to the mill. God it was good to be home!

Home. Ian looked up at the huge, stone mansion, and his enthusiasm suddenly dampened. Where *was* home? he wondered, suddenly feeling displaced. He didn't seem to belong anywhere these days—not in Europe, not in the Basin, not at the boarding house, certainly not in this house. The only place he felt any comfort was at the mill.

The problem was with the house, Ian decided, as he handed Eleanor out of the carriage and followed her into the great hall that had once so entranced him. The property belonged to Cyrus Morgan and always would. He needed a place that belonged to him, a place that carried his own unique stamp.

"I think, Eleanor, that we shall sell this property and build our own home," said Ian.

Eleanor looked at him as though he had lost his mind. "You must be joking. This is the grandest estate on the block, indeed in all of Rossburg."

"Then I shall build an even grander one."

"But it is worth…"

"Worth is determined only by another's desire for it," said Ian dispassionately. "Aye, we shall sell it and have our own."

Eleanor gave a short, mocking laugh. "Can you afford a million dollars?" Her derisive amusement faded under Ian's cold, narrow gaze.

"Yer father made the mistake of underestimatin' me, Eleanor. I would advise ye not to do the same."

"Welcome home, sir, madam," said the housekeeper, stepping forward from the staff that had lined up to greet them. "We hope your trip was enjoyable. We hadn't expected you back this early."

"Nor had I," said Eleanor in a clipped tone. "Please have Millie draw me a bath. I am indisposed and expect to remain so for quite some time." She glared at Ian and swept up the grand stairs.

Ian, recovering his good nature, explained that his wife was suffering from the rigors of the trip. He saw to the formalities and issued instructions in her absence. That done, he made his way to the study and poured himself a shot of Morgan's finest brandy.

He smelled the lingering aroma of the old man's cigar, and for a moment Ian actually fancied his presence. He shook off a sudden chill and turned to the portrait over the mantel. A stern Cyrus Morgan looked down at him. The corners of Ian's mouth slowly turned up in a triumphant smile, and he raised his glass in a toast.

"Over yer dead body," he said. He downed the drink quickly, anxious to check on matters at the mill. But first, he had another matter to attend.

*   *   *   *   *   *   *   *

Maven impatiently blew a damp strand of hair off her face as she moved the scissors along the lines of the pattern. Perspiration dotted her forehead and the bridge of her nose, despite the coolness of the weather. She paused for a moment, the muscles in her lower back making themselves felt as she bent over the worktable in the small, back room. She welcomed the long, tedious hours—it left her with little time to think.

The bell sounded at the opening of the door. Maven sighed. Another customer. It was the third one this afternoon. At this rate, she was never going to finish with this walking dress. Laying the scissors aside, she patted her hair in place and was straightening her dress when the customer stepped through the curtained doorway. Maven froze, her stomach doing a flip as she gazed up at Ian. She knew she would have to face this moment sooner or later, but today was not a good day.

A boyish smile lit up his face. "Maven, lass, how I've missed ye."

He looked so handsome, it made her heart ache. "What are ye doin' here?" she asked in a trembling voice. Hot, tired, and sick all morning, she didn't have it in her to do battle with her emotions yet.

"I could nae leave things as they were. All those weeks in Europe, all I could think about was ye." He reached out a hand to caress her cheek, but she turned away from him. If he touched her just once, she didn't know what she would do.

"Please leave, Ian."

"Nae until ye let me explain."

"Ye shared me bed and married another woman. There be nothin' to explain, Ian. 'Tis plain enough. I always knew ye were taken with Eleanor Morgan, but I thought when ye came to me that night it had meant ye had come to love me." She let out a bitter laugh and turned away to hide the tears in her eyes. "What a fool I was."

Ian gently took her by the shoulders, willing her to look at him. "Maven, I practiced no deceit with ye. My feelin's for ye have always been true. Ye're special to me in a way that nae woman e'er will be. Ye be a part of me, of my life that I can nae do without—like air and water. With ye I find peace."

"Then why did ye marry her?"

Ian winced. The hurt and pain in Maven's eyes were like a dagger to his heart, and he struggled to further explain himself. "Try to understand.

Morgan ridiculed me when I tried to tell him a better design for the boom. He said I should keep to my station in life. An' Eleanor once played me for a fool. I vowed then and there we would trade fortunes and pride. My only regret is that Morgan did nae live long enough to see the full measure of my revenge."

Maven broke away from him and stared at him in disbelief.

"Vengeance…ye destroyed the love we shared to marry another woman out of a sense of vengeance?"

"'Tis nae like that, exactly," said Ian with a hint of annoyance. "Eleanor strengthens my position in Rossburg, an' I pay her bills. 'Tis a fair exchange. Nothin' has changed between ye an' me."

"Everythin' has changed, Ian. God help ye if you can na see that."

Ian's temper flared. "Is it so wrong to want a better life? To have the things that only a few have?"

"'Tis a sin to want too much. It blackens the soul and goes against God's plan."

A muscle tightened in Ian's jaw. "God's plan! If God intended us to be content with our lot in life, he would nae give us brains to think, reasons to dream, or the need to achieve…. Think what I can do for ye, what I can give ye. I would see to it that ye ne'er needed to work again. Ye'd have only the finest—" Ian heard the resounding slap before he felt the sting of her hand across his cheek.

Maven's eyes flashed and red spots stained her cheeks. "Get out, Ian. Ye've robbed me of me love and trust. Ye'll not have me dignity, too. Leave now and do na be comin' back. I know ye not now. I do na wish to be knowin' ye anymore."

"Maven, ye can nae mean that."

"If ye could marry Eleanor for the reasons that ye did, it was ne'er love between us. I be seein' that now. Ye have no love in ye, Ian. Only anger and contempt for who ye are. No amount of money can help that."

*   *   *   *   *   *   *   *

The mill yards brought no relief. Ian paced the floor of his office, unable to keep his mind on his work. He was still feeling bruised and bloodied from his altercation with Maven. His first day back was not what he had expected. He didn't know what he had expected from Maven, but it wasn't what had occurred. He didn't know which stung more, her outright rejection of him or her attack on his integrity. There was something different about Maven that he couldn't put his finger on. It wasn't her anger. He had been on the receiving end of her temper many a time throughout the years. No, it was something else.

"Parker said ye were back. How was Europe?"

Ian looked up and smiled, happy to see a friendly face in the doorway. He waved Tommy into the office, eager for some normalcy.

"I returned three months early. That should tell ye somethin'," he said dryly. "I've been lookin' over the books. Ye've done a fine job of it. Should I be heartened or worried that ye managed this well without me?"

Tommy brushed aside the compliment. "Ye have good men out there. The mill practically runs itself. But 'tis glad we are ye're back if that answers yer question."

Ian's brow furrowed. There was something different about Tommy, too. The easy camaraderie that had always been so natural between them felt strained. "I stopped by to see Maven on the way."

"She told ye then."

"Told me what?"

"We married soon after ye left. She be expectin' a wee one."

Ian went still, and the blood drained from his face as he stared at Tommy in disbelief. Even if he had known what to say, he couldn't have gotten the words out. He was awash in feelings of anger, betrayal and jealously. Tommy stood with his legs apart, his hands hanging loose at his sides, his face devoid of expression. He appeared to be waiting, and Ian was aware of a quiet challenge in his friend's manner.

He was at a crossroads. At this moment, he hated Tommy, but he needed him.

He forced a smile and a steady voice and thrust out his hand. "Congratulations. I hope ye'll both be happy."

Tommy relaxed a bit and returned a firm handshake. "We will. Maven will have a good life."

Ian doubted it. Maven would end up like all the other women in the Basin, old before her years, birthing a baby a year, forever struggling to scratch out a substandard living.

"If ever ye need my help—"

"Thanks, but we stand on our own," said Tommy.

Ian felt a flash of anger at the quick rejection of his offer, but suppressed it. "Who was it who was always tellin' me stubborn pride gets in the way of good sense?"

"I guess 'tis only a few who practice what they preach."

Ian sensed a hidden meaning there, but didn't know what it might be. In the three months he had been away, Maven had changed, Tommy had changed. He sensed that the thread that bound them had broken. For the first time in his life, he felt totally alone.

Long after the mill had closed, Ian sat at his desk, an empty glass in his hand, a near empty bottle of whiskey in front of him. Questions bombarded him from every angle. Why hadn't Maven told him she had married Tommy? She didn't love him. Wasn't she just as guilty of the deceit she had accused him of? Had she done it for spite? As soon as the thought came to mind, he banished it. Maven wasn't spiteful. Tommy had been his lifelong friend. Together they had shared some tough times, and even now Ian would put his life on the line for him, but Tommy was not the right person for Maven. In fact, Ian couldn't name a man, in or out of the Basin, who was. In a flash of anger, he sent the glass crashing against the wall.

CHAPTER 27

Eleanor let out an impatient sigh. "I am growing quite weary. Aren't you finished yet?"

Maven kept her eyes lowered. She bit back a retort and continued to tack the hem. "'Tis a fine tea gown, ma'am. I should hate for it to be ruined by me haste."

"Well I do hope you'll finish before the season is out," said Eleanor with a touch of sarcasm. "It will do me little good in the spring. What a pity Mrs. Drury has fallen ill."

"'Tis both our misfortune, ma'am."

Eleanor glanced down sharply on the glossy auburn head. The seamstress's manner was not as subservient as she deemed proper, and she thought she detected a note of insolence in her tone. Eleanor made a mental note to register a complaint with Mrs. Drury. If the shop owner wished to have more of her business, she would take her protege in hand.

"I be finished tackin' now." Maven, rose heavily from her knees, somewhat encumbered by her thickening waistline. She had been able to cleverly conceal her pregnancy by altering the design of her dresses, but her rounding stomach was beginning to defy even her skillful hand. "If it be pleasin' ye to step out of the dress, I'll be on me way."

Maven unfastened the bodice and helped Eleanor out of the handsome, blue tea gown. She then threw her cape around her shoulders, gathered up her sewing box, and draped the garment across her arm.

"Good day, Mrs. Douglas."

God knew how she hated being here. She had been quite dismayed when Mrs. Drury had fallen too ill to keep the appointment. Thankfully her prayers had been answered. Ian had not been at home when she arrived. In spite of what Eleanor might have thought, and certainly with more eagerness than she could have suspected, Maven had dispatched her deed with as much haste as she dared, just as anxious to be on her way.

Her cape billowing behind her, she raced down the staircase and across the foyer.

"Maven, wait!"

Startled, Maven turned to see that Ian had emerged from a room and was rapidly approaching her. Her heart sank, and she ran to pull open the door, but Ian was too quick. He grabbed her arm and spun her around. She could tell by his grip alone that he was angry.

"Let go of me, Ian. I do na wish to be talkin' with ye."

"Well, I wish to talk with ye." He had been waiting days for this opportunity. When he returned home for the papers he had left behind, he couldn't believe she was in the house. "Why did ye nae tell me ye had married Tommy...among other things?" His eyes dropped to the thickened waist he hadn't noticed before, and she quickly drew the cape closed.

"What difference would it have been? Ye made yer choice, and I made mine."

"I told ye how it was between Eleanor and me. I thought ye were so high on honesty. How honest is it to marry someone ye do nae love, or are ye just foolin' yerself?"

Maven's eyes blazed, amber leaping from the angry green depths. "Ye dare to question *me* about honesty! At least I dinna marry for position or vengeance."

"Are ye so certain about that, Maven? Are ye so sure that ye did nae marry Tommy to spite me?"

"Ye overrate yerself, Ian."

Ian winced and switched to a new plan of attack. "What can Tommy give ye but a life of drudgery?"

"Something ye can na give me…a love that is honest….a love I can trust, and a life of laughter instead of tears."

"Ye've ne'er been one to hide yer feelin's, Maven. How long do ye think Tommy will be content to be second best?"

"It come to me while ye were away on yer honeymoon, Ian, that Tommy is not the one who be second best."

With that, Maven swept past him and out the door. He didn't try to stop her. He was still reeling from the last thrust of her sword.

"I hope Mrs. O'Brien wasn't giving you any trouble, darling. Some people don't know their place," said Eleanor smoothly, descending the stairs. "You seem to be well acquainted with her."

Ian glanced up at her, a deep scowl marring his features. "Maven and I grew up together. I had hoped she would have married better."

"Yes, I understand that sentiment all too well."

Ian's scowl darkened, and their eyes locked combatively. He started to say something, then changed his mind and abruptly left the house, slamming the door behind him.

Eleanor's haughty smile dissolved. She slumped down on the step and leaned her head against the balustrade, tears trickling down her cheeks. She had overheard the whole exchange. She knew that Ian had been enamored of her when they had first met. Most men were, and it gave her a certain sense of strength and power. But now to find out that he had married her only for vengeance and position and obviously had more regard for a seamstress was a huge blow to her self-esteem.

Eleanor suddenly let out a bitter laugh. Well, the joke was on him. If Ian thought that he could gain position by marrying her, he had a surprise coming. She may not know much about the real world, but she knew society, and what her poor, foolish husband had failed to take into account was that she was now an outcast herself.

Ian arrived home late that night and went straight to the study. He threw off his coat, loosened his tie and poured himself a finger of whiskey, downing the drink in a single gulp. All day long, he had been forced to suppress his frustration, his anger, his jealously every time he saw Tommy. The hardest pill to swallow was that Tommy now shared that special bond of intimacy with Maven that she had once shared only with him. And now she was carrying Tommy's baby. He discarded the glass for the decanter and flopped on the sofa, drinking freely and angrily. In the wee hours of the morning, he negotiated the stairs to his bed.

It was noon the next afternoon when Ian finally stirred. A hammer pounded in his head, and his stomach felt none too steady. Gingerly, he hauled himself out of bed and stumbled to the washstand. The cold water on his face and neck revived him somewhat.

He stirred shaving cream in the mug and began lathering his beard. With a critical eye, he appraised the gray, haggard reflection in the mirror and nearly dropped the shaving mug. Staring back at him were the vacant, bloodshot eyes of his father.

Eleanor entered the masculine, mahogany-panelled bedroom that had been her father's. It had been the ultimate usurpation the day Ian had installed himself in here and demanded that she occupy her mother's adjoining chamber. It continued to gall her to no end.

"I trust you had a good night," she said with heavy sarcasm.

"Do nae bait me, Eleanor. I'm not in the mood."

"I daresay I'm not surprised. Out every night this week at that disgusting bawdy house, doing God only knows what 'til all hours of the morning. 'Tis little wonder we've not have a single caller since our return."

Ian lathered his face. "I play cards, Eleanor, and that 'disgusting place' is host to many of Rossburg's fine, upstanding men, including Peter Jeffries. Now what is it ye be wantin'?"

"The regrets have been coming in all morning for our homecoming ball. I told you no one would attend. I suggest we cancel it and announce a postponement due to too many conflicting schedules while we still have a shred of dignity left."

Ian's hand tightened around the razor. It was a long moment before he brought the blade to his face. With studied deliberation, he slid it across one side of his jaw line and then along the other, careful not to nick his mustache.

"We will proceed with the ball as planned." He delivered his decision as a judge delivers a verdict, his voice low, firm and implacable. "I think ye will discover that our guests will suddenly find themselves free that night."

Eleanor doubted it, but she knew it was useless to argue with him.

Ian suddenly let out a curse as he nicked himself with the razor.

"Perhaps if you'd hired a valet, you wouldn't run the risk of bleeding to death," she said smartly.

"Yer concern is touchin', madam. We've been through this before, and I'll not discuss the matter again."

Eleanor glared at him. It was a great bone of contention that he had decreased their house staff to three—a housekeeper, a cook and a maid—since their return from Europe.

"We have the smallest staff of anyone on the Row now. Father would turn over in his grave."

"I won't abide a houseful of servants fussin' about and knowin' my business. It isn't necessary to hire someone to do for ye what ye can do for yerself."

Eleanor stamped her foot in frustration. "How can you expect people to forget your roots, when you cannot bury them yourself? Perhaps if you were to lose your accent…" Her voice trailed off as Ian turned an icy glare on her.

CHAPTER 28

For the first time since Morgan's death, the old estate was abuzz with activity on the cold, February eve of 1881. Bright, cheery lights poured through every window casting amber patches into the night, as broughams, landaus, and Clarences once again lined the circular drive to drop off their elegantly-clad passengers.

Inside, people climbed the rose-garlanded staircase to the ballroom on the second floor where a prominent New York orchestra played. On the other side of the double doors, Ian and Eleanor received stiff, unsmiling guests. When the last guest had arrived, Eleanor excused herself to seek a powder for her migraine.

No expense had been spared. Huge vases of mums, roses and carnations, as well as small trees, had been brought in from the hot house and arboretum and were placed around the room. Lace-covered tables lined the far end of the room, lavishly displaying culinary delicacies. And Waterford crystal chandeliers rained a fairyland of rainbows down upon the guests in stunning coloration.

It was an affair that would have done any host proud. But as Ian observed it from a distance, the mild disturbance on his face deepened to a dark frown. He signalled to the butler hired for the occasion.

"Tell the orchestra to play something livelier," he said. "This has more the feel of a funeral than a ball."

"You can lead a horse to water, but you can't make him drink," said Parker Stanton joining him.

"Meanin' what?"

"C'mon, Ian. You hold notes on half the people here. First you use them to force the members to give you a seat on the Board of Trade, and then you blackmail them to attend your party. Surely you don't expect them to show a good time."

"Every one of these people comes from immigrant stock, Parker. Their roots are as humble as mine, yet they dare to look down on me."

"Two differences, my friend. They're not just off the boat, as they say, and their humble beginnings began with the town's. Now they're the founding fathers of a thriving city…and a closed society. The iron gate was closed a long time ago, Ian. "

"Are ye tryin' to tell me now that money is nae important?"

"Not without the pedigree. That's how they preserve their power."

"What about Eleanor? Cyrus Morgan was one of the wealthiest and most powerful men in this town, yet they turned from her."

"She's a woman. She must have both pedigree and money. The Jeffries were looking to merge an empire. When she no longer had that to offer and good old Peter cast her off…" Stanton shrugged. "Such is the way of society. By forcing Eleanor to marry you, you made it impossible for her to ever regain her standing again. Don't look at me like that. I don't write the rules."

"I did nae force Eleanor to marry me," said Ian tightly.

"You didn't leave her any options either. In my book it's the same thing."

"We'll see how important their bloodlines are when they need somethin' I have."

Parker sighed in exasperation. "Haven't you heard anything I've said? There is nothing you can ever do to get these people to accept you. The best you can cultivate is resentment, perhaps some envy. You'll always be an outsider, Ian….I see that Franklin Jeffries and his son are conspicuously absent. My advice to you is to watch your back."

Ian's jaw tensed. The Jeffries' absence was indeed a slap in the face. "In time, every empire crumbles beneath the weight of arrogance…and Franklin Jeffries' has just begun to fall. I think, Parker, 'tis time for us to start our own society. But for now, let's make this a ball that it will kill these people to ignore."

"How are you going to do that?"

"Ye've heard of 'divide and conquer'. I'd be willing to bet these women would give their last dollar to dance. See how they tap their feet? Get a couple of them out on the floor."

"I'm only one man, Ian."

"Eleanor and I will join ye. I'll instruct the orchestra to break every few minutes, at which time everyone will seek a new partner. Women can be a persuasive force when the moment calls for it. I doubt few men will refuse their wives…if they hope to keep them safe from ye," added Ian with a slow grin.

He signalled for the butler again. "If the guests are reluctant to go to the tables," said Ian, "then we'll bring the food to them. Instruct the maids to move among the guests with trays."

The evening had been a strain, and after the guests had departed—en masse—Ian slipped into the study. The fire in the fireplace and the low light gave the room a warm, intimate feeling, full of solace and security. It was the one room in the house where he felt comfortable, despite the ghosts…or perhaps because of them. He pulled off his coat, loosened his tie and poured himself a brandy.

"You have nae won yet, old man," he said, lifting the glass to Morgan's portrait.

There was a rustle of petticoats at the door, and Ian turned in surprise to see Eleanor.

"May I come in?" she asked.

She looked exceptionally beautiful tonight in the claret velvet and pink satin gown. He felt a rush of pride and accomplishment that she was his. "Of course. This is yer house. A glass of sherry?"

Eleanor nodded, and Ian splashed a small amount in a goblet and handed it to her.

She surveyed the book-lined room. "I have never been comfortable in here, you know. It always seemed so forbidding. The truth is I've always hated this room." Her eyes glazed over and her voice dropped to a breathy whisper as she drifted in memory. "Perhaps 'resented' might be a better word. The little time that Father was home, he spent most of it in here. No one intruded unless invited. Not even Mother."

She walked to the desk, her father's desk, and ran her hand along the top. "I used to wonder what he did in here for so many hours. You're very much like him you know."

"Is that a compliment?"

She fixed a sober eye on him. "More like a curse, I think."

She continued to study him openly for a moment. He was undeniably handsome, and so elegantly attired, he looked every inch the gentleman. But he was an imposter and always would be. She had heard several women remark on his appeal as well this evening, only to follow up their admiration with, "What a pity he hails from the Basin." She felt a sudden stab of regret that it would always be the way of it.

An icy chill invaded then, refreezing the softening edges of her heart as she reminded herself that he had taken everything from her—her inheritance, her position in society, her dignity, her pride. She wouldn't easily forgive him that…if ever.

"The ball was rather a disaster, you know," she said in a crisper tone. "Garish was the word most often used, I believe."

A resigned smile tipped the corners of Ian's mouth. For a moment he had hoped…but the truce was clearly over. "I do nae agree," he said.

"You don't agree…how could you think otherwise?"

"I never saw people try so hard to be miserable. It had to be a success."

Eleanor stared at him incredulously. "The food was barely touched, and I don't think a near brawl between Caroline Conover's father and Parker Stanton over a dance qualifies an evening as a success. Neither does a mass exodus before midnight. I have never been so humiliated. We'll be the talk of the town for weeks!"

"Is that nae the idea?"

"To be envied, yes, but not laughed at behind our backs, regarded with pity and shunned."

"To be a force, one has to be noticed. Tonight, my dear, we were noticed. Give me time, and I promise ye Rossburg will be yers to command. Ye looked beautiful tonight. I daresay ye were more envied than pitied."

"Are you that blind? Do you not hear how everyone talks, see how they laugh and smirk behind our backs? People look at me with pity in their eyes. By forcing me to marry you, you've condemned me as well—" She broke off when she saw her husband's features darken.

"Ye had the option of refusin' my offer," said Ian tightly. "Face it, my dear, yer father condemned ye with his greed, and ye sold yer soul to recover what he lost. An' let's not forget that yer gallant, white knight turned out to be less than noble."

"Oh, you're impossible to talk with. I'm going to bed." She whirled on her heel to leave the room.

"Eleanor," Ian called out to her, "leave yer door open tonight."

The deep-timbred command settled over her like a mantle of stone. She turned back to him, her eyes wide and luminous. "The evening was not humiliating enough that you would seek to punish me further?" she asked, her voice trembling.

"Punish ye! Madam, there are women who would regard it a reward."

"Yes, I suppose so, but you weren't content to remain in the Basin." Eleanor swept from the room without waiting to see Ian's reaction.

She flew up the stairs, her heart pounding. Ever since their return from Europe, she had known that this night would come sooner or later, though she had prayed for never.

She entered her bedroom and pulled the bell cord. The maid appeared as she was taking the pins and comb out of her hair. Both were very tired and said nothing. Silently, the maid unhooked the gown and carefully lifted it over Eleanor's head. As she reached for the favored lace and silk nightgown, Eleanor shook her head.

"Bring me the linen one tonight."

The maid raised a questioning brow, but took out the plain gown as bidden. It was her mistress's least favorite and least flattering and was only kept in reserve.

"You may leave now," said Eleanor. "I can finish dressing myself."

The maid nodded and gratefully withdrew.

Fumbling with the corset, Eleanor wished she hadn't been so quick to dismiss the woman. Tears of frustration filled her eyes, and she nervously watched the door as she worked the knotted laces. Finally, the corset fell away, and she quickly slipped into the nightgown.

She stood in the center of the room, straining her ears for the sound of his footsteps, her eyes darting between the chamber door and the anteroom door. Finally, she heard him moving about his room, and her breath came in short, ragged gasps. As she traced his movement through the anteroom, her heart pounded in her chest and her mouth went dry. When he tried her door, she thought her lungs would cease working altogether.

The anteroom door slowly swung open, and Ian walked into the room. As Eleanor backed onto the bed, meeting his gaze with a gleam of defiance, he promised himself he would know her surrender this night.

In spite of his skilled touch, Eleanor willed herself to remain rigid and detached, and she continually reminded herself that it was a lady's place to quietly endure, not to enjoy. With a low growl of exasperation,

Ian finally gave up trying to arouse her. He was quick, impersonal, seeking, then, only his own release.

When he left her bed without a word, Eleanor uttered a small prayer that the ordeal was done. There was little of the pain of the first few times, and she was disturbed by some rather intense sensations she had experienced. But no matter his perverse attempts to elicit unholy responses from her, she had given nothing more than what was deemed proper for a lady. It would seem that his need for vengeance extended to the bedroom as well, and she was determined not to give him any satisfaction.

*   *   *   *   *   *   *   *

Ian smiled as he looked over the reports. "Production is up twenty percent over last month. Ye've done a fine job, Tommy."

"It's me job," said Tommy.

"Well, 'tis deservin' of a cigar, ay Parker?" Ian pulled out a box of cigars from the desk drawer. "Ye'll find none finer."

Stanton nodded. "Count me in."

"No thanks," said Tommy. "I'd best be gettin' back to me men."

Ian frowned as the door closed behind his foreman. "We were always as close as brothers. Since my return, there be a distance between us that seems only to grow wider."

Parker helped himself to a cigar. "There's been a shift of power. Tommy is an employee. You are the owner. It's as simple as that. Tommy understands it."

Ian wasn't so sure that it was as simple as that. He had the feeling there was something more.

CHAPTER 29

To all appearances, they were a storybook couple as they drove through the park in a new phaeton—Eleanor golden, petite and pretty; Ian fair, tall, and ruggedly handsome. The day was unseasonably warm—the early spring tease in mid-March. People from all walks of life had turned out in their Sunday best.

With great acting license, Eleanor sat proud and erect, defiantly meeting the eyes of her peers, ignoring their smirks and snickers and pretending not to notice their stiff greetings.

"Bloody hypocrites," she muttered, her teeth clenched in a fixed smile.

Ian cocked a brow in wry amusement. "Ye would know, madam."

She shot him a sharp glance. "I was never that bad. Harriet Brown has her nose so high in the air, I can't think how she can see where she's going."

"Ye do have the advantage there, madam. Yer nose be by far the shorter."

Eleanor gave a snort of exasperation. He seemed particularly light in spirit this afternoon, quite in command, and it irritated her, especially since she was in such a low mood and not of a particularly sound constitution these past few days.

The first time she had met Ian in her father's library, she had thought him an intense, young man, shy, awkward and lacking a certain amount of confidence—and she had had him in the palm of her hand. It had been easy to feel superior then. But somehow the tables had turned, and it was she who was feeling unsure and awkward now. How had that happened? she wondered.

As they drove along the path near the river, Ian's attention suddenly became focused on a group of picnickers on the bank, and he unconsciously slowed the buggy. Maven and Tommy were among them, and his gaze remained riveted on Maven as she left the picnickers to feed the ducks. Tommy joined her, and his jaw tensed as Tommy's arm went around her expanded waistline. He wanted to fancy an unhappiness between them, but his eyes refused to register his desire. They were laughing, and though he was out of earshot, he imagined he could hear the ring of her light, musical laughter in his ears. He had always loved her laugh.

He wished he could join them. He missed Tommy's jokes and good-natured jabs and the good times they had shared, but most of all he missed Maven's smile, her gentle understanding, her wise counsel, her unflagging belief in him. He yearned to stand next to her, hear her voice, hold her hand. But the thread was broken. With a heavy sigh, Ian dragged his gaze away and clicked the reins.

Eleanor twisted in her seat and looked back to see what had held his attention so raptly. Her eye immediately fell on Maven.

*   *   *   *   *   *   *   *

Eleanor alighted from the cab and paused uncertainly outside the dress shop. She wasn't in any need of a wardrobe, but she had to come. It had taken her three days to work up the courage, but she had to know what her husband found so fascinating about Maven O'Brien. A childhood friend, Ian had said of her that day. But the look on his face then and in the park told of a much deeper emotion. It was no consolation to her that the woman was married and quite pregnant.

Eleanor took a deep breath, stepped onto the boardwalk, and entered the shop. When Maven looked up and saw her, Eleanor could see the smile freeze on her lips.

There was one customer in the shop. Maven was showing the woman bolts of different cloths. Eleanor settled herself in a chair and picked up the latest copy of *The Young Lady's Journal* from the table, idly leafing through the pages. From under lowered lashes, she studied Maven. She had never taken much notice of her before. She was just a shop girl. But now Eleanor assessed her with a much more critical eye.

The girl couldn't be considered a classic beauty, but there was something striking about her that Eleanor supposed a man might find rather attractive. Her eyes were bright and intelligent, her smile infectious, and her voice was pleasant despite the annoying Irish accent. She was not petite and curvaceous as was desirable for the day, but she carried her tall, slender frame with a noticeable grace, despite her pregnancy. Eleanor had to concede that there was a certain charm about her. Her clear complexion and thick, auburn hair with its golden red highlights were worthy of envy. What surprised Eleanor most, however, given the woman's background, was her sense of style and poise. All in all, Harriet Brown possessed less class and taste than did Maven O'Brien.

The customer left, and Maven approached Eleanor. Her manner was courteous but businesslike. "How might I help ye, Mrs. Douglas?"

Eleanor looked up at Maven momentarily bereft of words. She didn't know how Maven O'Brien could help her. She really didn't know why she was here. "I…I've come to see your latest in satins," she said quickly recovering herself. "I may have need of an evening dress, and I haven't time to travel to New York."

"The satins are along that wall if ye be carin' to have a look," said Maven. "But I'm afraid I'll not be able to accommodate ye for at least a month."

"I beg your pardon."

"Our time is much taken with the Conover trousseau."

Eleanor's irritation dissolved into surprise. "Conover...Caroline Conover?"

"Aye."

Just then the door opened.

"Eleanor! What a surprise...how wonderful to see you."

Eleanor turned to see that Caroline Conover had entered the shop. She ran a cool eye over the pretty, young woman who used to be her closest friend. Like the others, Caroline's friendship had disappeared with Eleanor's inheritance, and it was her defection that had hurt Eleanor the most.

"Hello, Caroline," she said curtly. "You'll have to excuse me, I was just leaving."

Caroline timidly put out a hand to her. "Wait, Eleanor,...please. I-I want you to know that I am still your friend." At the dubious expression on Eleanor's face, she struggled to explain herself. "I-I know how things look. I'm so ashamed, and I'm sorry that I didn't have the strength and courage to stand up for you more against my parents and the others, but you know how they can be. Would you not have done the same thing in my place?"

Eleanor faltered. "I shouldn't like to think so...but I can't say 'no' with any certainty," she admitted with an honesty that surprised her. She looked at Caroline's stricken face. The girl didn't have a mean bone in her body, and she was finding it difficult to be nasty to her. "It's all right, Caroline. I suppose I shouldn't fault you."

Caroline gave a sigh of relief. "I've missed seeing you, Eleanor. We used to have such fun together. If it's any consolation to you, your ball was the talk of the town for days among the ladies. None of us really wanted to leave when we did."

Eleanor's stiff features dissolved into a tight smile. "Is that so?"

"Oh, yes. There's never been a ball quite like it. Mama said you even outdid your father. I daresay, there's no one among us quite likely to top it."

"You could have fooled me the way everyone stampeded to the door."

"Yes, well, appearances can be deceiving," said Caroline, somewhat chagrined.

"So I'm learning. I understand congratulations are in order. Who is the lucky man…Earl Brown?"

Caroline plucked nervously at the folds of her skirt. "No. It…it is Peter Jeffries."

The color faded from Eleanor's face. "Peter…Peter is marrying *you*?"

"It all happened so quickly. I don't know quite what to think. Eleanor, are you all right?" asked Caroline anxiously. "You look so pale. I know this must come as a shock to you. Everyone always thought that you and Peter would be the ones to marry."

"I'm fine, Caroline. 'Tis of no matter to me now. I have a husband. I wish you and Peter all the best. I really must be going now."

Eleanor wanted to run from the shop, but her dignity wouldn't allow it. Instead, she forced herself to move slowly, fluidly across the floor in the manner befitting her station—or what had once been her station. The shop had never seemed so large to her before.

She hurried down the boardwalk to the waiting cab, a cauldron of roiling emotions. Envy, hurt, and anger welled up inside of her until she thought she would burst. Caroline was going to occupy the place in society that should have been hers. It was a horrible day. She had been stabbed in the front and in the back.

When she arrived home, she charged into the entrance hall and up the stairs.

"Where is Mr. Douglas?" she asked the housekeeper, meeting the woman on the landing.

The housekeeper looked at Eleanor in surprise. She had never seen her mistress in such a state. "At the mill, ma'am."

Eleanor abruptly changed direction and stormed down the stairs and into the study. She threw her gloves, hat and cape carelessly on the sofa and went to the liquor cabinet. A crystal decanter of sherry rested on a silver tray. She hesitated, then decisively removed the stopper and filled a small goblet.

"A little early in the day for that, ay? What would Harrieta Oxnard Ward have to say about premature tippling in her book of etiquette?"

Eleanor jumped and glared at Ian as he entered the room, then defiantly picked up the glass and took a sip of the strong, Spanish wine. "Why aren't you at the mill?"

"I do occasionally come home, madam. I see I'm sorely missed." Ian eyed her closely. "What might the occasion be now?"

"A wedding…between my once dearest friend, Caroline Conover, and my once betrothed, Peter Jeffries." She raised the glass in salute and took another healthy swallow.

"I take it we'll nae be invited."

Eleanor let out a laugh bordering on hysteria. "'Twould be a cold day in hell."

"I shall see then to an invitation," said Ian. The announcement earned him a scornful glare.

"Didn't you learn anything from the ball? You can't force yourself on these people the way you…"

"The way I forced meself on ye?" Ian finished for her. She lowered her eyes, the gesture speaking volumes. "I do nae recall ye objectin' too loudly."

"It was either starve or marry you. What choice did I have?"

"Did yer father ask ye if ye wanted to marry Jeffries?"

"He didn't have to. Peter and I were destined."

"Oh, yes, I forgot. The joinin' of two empires. But did ye love him?"

Eleanor looked nonplussed for a moment. She had never thought about it before. She must have loved him; she wasn't repulsed by him. How else could she have agreed to marry him—social position aside?

"Well, of course I did," she said on a firmer note. "And what makes you think that it is in the past? A marriage ceremony doesn't change everything."

Ian sighed heavily. "Me poor, dear Eleanor. Ye still think your lot would be better cast with a fool like Peter Jeffries."

"He isn't a fool. And at least I wouldn't have to threaten people to attend my balls. Callers would call, invitations would be pouring in."

Ian's features clouded over. "One of these days, Eleanor, ye will learn just how much better yer life would have been with Peter Jeffries."

"What's that supposed to mean?"

Ian carefully weighed his words. "Just that a gentleman can nae always be determined by his blood."

"Bah! You're just jealous of Peter. You would say anything against him."

"Tell me, Eleanor, if Jeffries still wanted to marry ye and ye were in a position to accept, would it matter to ye that his character might nae be as ye thought?"

"Well, I'm not in a position to accept, am I?"

Ian let out a harsh laugh. "All my life I thought a man's worth was determined by his accomplishments."

"If you had thought that, you wouldn't have forced me to marry you."

The barb struck home.

As the days passed, Eleanor's comment weighed increasingly heavy on Ian. Each morning when he looked into the mirror, he liked less and less what he saw. If he possessed half the integrity he liked to think that he did, instead of putting her in a position where she was forced to marry him, he would have provided her with the dowry she had swallowed her pride to ask him for, so that she could marry her way back into society. And he wouldn't have cast off Maven as he did for the sake of revenge. Maven was wrong. He wasn't even second best. He was the same if not worse than Peter Jeffries. Eleanor's situation he could still remedy, but how could he ever make up for the hurt he had caused Maven?

When he arrived at the office, Parker Stanton was waiting for him, prepared to go over the books. Ian impatiently waved them aside. "I want ye to do somethin' for me, Parker."

"Sure. What is it?"

"Draw up annulment papers."

Stanton's jaw dropped. "Annulment papers! You're joking…aren't you? You can't be serious."

Ian turned to stare moodily out the window. "'Tis nae a joke. I mean to give Eleanor her freedom. What are the grounds for an annulment?"

"Well, a marriage can be deemed voidable if one or both principals are underaged or insane, if the marriage was secured by fraudulent means, or if a husband is unable to perform his-ah-duties. Eleanor would have to bring suit against you on one of these grounds."

"I suppose she could make a case for marriage by fraudulent means. She has made the charge enough times. Draw up the papers and take them to her."

"Ian, are you certain you want to do this? It could be messy."

"If I know Eleanor, money will dispatch the matter quietly and quickly."

"Divorce would be easier."

"It would hurt any chance she may have for regainin' her position in society. Tell her I'll see to it that she has a generous enough settlement."

"Ian, why are you doing this? You haven't been married long enough to give it a chance. Eleanor is a beautiful woman. You couldn't marry her fast enough. What has changed?"

"'Twas a mistake. Draw up the papers, Parker."

Stanton took out his tobacco pouch and began to fill his pipe. "Can't fight the ghost of Peter, ay?" When Ian answered him with a frosty glare, Stanton's lips curled up in a knowing smile. "Didn't you tell her the truth about her knight in shiny armor?"

"What good would it do? She as much as said that given the opportunity, she would marry him whatever his character."

"Ian, you fool, she doesn't give a tinker's damn about Peter Jeffries. She just needs to be back up on that damned pedestal, admired and envied. It is all she knows. It is her identity. In time, you will show her—"

"Damn it, Parker! I can nae hold a woman to marriage who cringes with disgust every time I touch her. I thought 'twould be enough to possess her..."

Stanton shook his head. "You want to be one of them, but you don't understand what it means to be part of the social elite."

"And ye do?"

"I used to be one of them until I understood what that meant. Then I abdicated. Look, Ian, it's not you. Eleanor would be repulsed by any man's hand—even Peter's. Look, admire, worship, but don't touch. From the moment they can read primers, young women have it drummed into their silly heads that proper ladies do not acknowledge their passion and desires. To do so puts them on an equal footing with low-bred women. If they cannot remain virgins in body, they are taught do so in mind. It makes for a rather difficult time for a man, I know, but that is the way it is. As a gentleman, you are expected to press your 'animal desires' no more than once a month. And of course never during pregnancy or the monthly cycle."

Ian stared at Parker in disbelief. "Affairs of the marriage bed are dictated as well?"

"Why do you think gentlemen have a need for places like the Crystal Palace? If you are going to play the game, you had better learn the rules."

Ian gave a contentious snort. "I play by my own rules. Draw up the papers. I'll not be treated like a leper by my own wife, sensibilities be damned."

CHAPTER 30

Eleanor wrung her hands and paced the floor of her bedroom, her face red and puffy from hours of crying. On her vanity lay the annulment papers. How could fate be so cruel? How could Ian be so cruel? She had no idea he could be this calculating and vengeful.

When she heard Ian moving about in his room, she picked up the papers and marched through the anteroom into the bedroom.

Ian had splashed water on his face and chest and was toweling himself dry when she came storming through the door.

"Is this some kind of a joke?" she demanded, throwing the papers at him.

Ian watched in astonishment as they fluttered to the floor. "Forgive my surprise, madam, but I had rather expected them to bring ye joy."

Eleanor's laugh was shrill. "Joy! It is a little late for that."

"I'm afraid I do nae follow ye. I thought I was doin' ye a favor. With the allowance I'm prepared to settle on ye, perhaps ye'll have another chance with Jeffries," he added on a snide note.

Eleanor glared back at him. "I doubt he would want to raise your child. "

His ears heard it, but his mind had trouble registering it, and he stared at her for a long moment before he spoke. "Ye're expectin' a bairn?"

"If you mean by that a baby, yes."

Ian burst into laughter. His whole damned life was a mix of irony.

Tears welled up in Eleanor's eyes. "I didn't know you hated me so much that you could be this cruel."

"Hate ye…" His confusion changed to incredulity with the sudden realization of what she meant. "My God, ye think I planned this…to impregnate ye and then serve ye with papers of an annulment?" He took her firmly by the shoulders. "Eleanor, I may have done ye an injustice, which I now tried to remedy, but I am not the heartless monster ye think me to be. As God is my witness, I did nae plan this."

He searched her eyes, but it was obvious she didn't believe him. In the next instant she dissolved into tears.

"I hate you," she said between sobs.

Ian sighed. "I fear 'twill always be the way of it. Get hold of yerself, Eleanor. 'Tisn't good for ye or the baby. Ye're just frightened. 'Tis natural for a woman to be fearful of havin' her first child. I'll see to it that ye have the best of care."

"I want Henney," said Eleanor, sniffing back tears.

"Who is Henney?"

"My old nanny, Julia Hennessey. She was like a mother to me."

"Very well. Send for her. Anythin' else?"

Eleanor wiped her eyes with the back of her hand in a childlike manner. "What I want you can never give me."

Ian's mouth twisted into a wry smile. Maven had said that very thing to him once, but he doubted that Eleanor was talking of love. Indeed, the woman measured it by a different yardstick.

*　　*　　*　　*　　*　　*　　*　　*

Ian studied the last page with the same diligence that he had examined the others before finally closing the ledger and leaning back in his chair. "Everythin' looks to be in order with the mill's finances. Ye've done a fine job, Parker."

"Don't thank me. I found a whiz with numbers to take over the accounting."

"Married or unmarried?" inquired Ian with the arch of a brow.

Parker groaned. "Oh ye of little faith. It's a man of whom I speak of course. Figures do not belong in a woman's head. Do you have the annulment papers with you? Might as well kill two birds with one stone."

Ian sighed heavily, running a hand along the back of his neck. "There is nae goin' to be an annulment."

Stanton blinked in surprise. "Say that again. I don't believe I heard you correctly."

"Ye heard me right."

"But, Ian, just a few weeks ago you were hell-bent on dissolving your marriage."

"A few weeks ago, I did nae know Eleanor was carryin' my child."

Stanton let out a low whistle. "Geez, Ian, you should have planned things a little better."

"Eleanor thinks I planned everythin' perfectly."

"Oh, I see."

"What have ye heard from the Opera House?"

"It has never fully recovered financially from the fire. Contributors were tapped out for repairs to the building. There isn't much left for operating costs. The owner doesn't know how he's going to pay for the season. Ticket sales won't cover it all."

"I read that Sarah Bernhardt will be tourin' New York City then. Can he get her for the first performance?"

Stanton shrugged. "With the right money, anyone can be gotten."

"Tell the manager I'll cover whatever cost it takes to get Miss Bernhardt to perform here in exchange for all the box seats, a percentage of the floor, and complete discretion."

"Why all the sudden interest in culture?"

"If Rossburg society will nae let me in the front door, I'll go in through the back."

"Which is?"

"Politics. When the time is right, I intend to run for mayor."

"Are you crazy? The position is bought and paid for by Jeffries, Brown, Conover and that bunch. You wouldn't stand a chance."

"Perhaps…but then again mill workers were ne'er encouraged to vote before. What are their biggest complaints?"

"You know as well as I do, wages and housing."

Ian leaned back in his chair. He smoothed the edges of his mustache and traced the line of his mouth with his thumb and forefinger in a gesture characteristic of him when he was deep in thought. "On the morrow," he said, leaning forward in his chair, "announce a ten-cent per hour wage increase…but call it a housin' allowance."

Parker shook his head. "I don't know about that, Ian. It is going to cut pretty deep into profits."

Ian smiled. "Nae if I form my own construction company. With the mill yard actin' as the supplier for materials, Douglas Construction ought to be able to build low cost houses quite profitably. What do ye think?"

Stanton considered the proposal for a long minute. "I think I like it."

Ian smiled. "Now for the best part…Douglas Construction will start off donatin' a parcel of land."

"You may be biting off more than you can chew. That will require quite an outlay of cash."

"Not necessarily. Ye know the land that Morgan deeded over to me on the corner of Evergreen and Locust Street?"

"Yeah. It's practically an entire block…you're not thinking of handing over *that* land. Ian, that's choice real estate. Besides, you'd be putting low cost housing in the back pocket of Millionaires' Row."

"Exactly."

A smile spread across Stanton's face as he suddenly caught Ian's intent. "I take it you want me to buy up as much of 'Grandview Place' as I can. Shouldn't be too difficult. It is mostly farm land. You ought to be able to get it for a reasonable price. Farmers have been having a bad year."

"Put Tommy in charge of hirin' for the construction company. He is a good judge of men," said Ian.

"Good jobs are hard to come by these days. You'll no doubt be the town savior to some. As to the powers that be…" Stanton shook his head. "You'll be lucky if you're not run out of town on a rail."

"I expect the grateful will outnumber the angered."

Ian pushed himself out of the chair and went to stand at the window. He looked down upon the lumber yard, the sawmill, and the planing mill. They may have once belonged to Cyrus Morgan, but they were the fruits of his genius and his labor. And this was just the start of his empire.

"You'll be stepping on the toes of some pretty powerful men," Stanton warned him.

"A piece of advice, Parker…never kick the man on the bottom. He may someday be on the top."

Chapter 31

Eleanor groaned, heaved into the chamber pot, and fell back against the velvet chaise. "Henney, I am going to die. I just know it."

Henney laid a cool cloth across her frightened mistress' forehead. "Tch, tch, dear, a little morning illness is natural in the first months."

"How could he do this to me? I look terrible. Even with a corset my waist is as thick as Harriet Brown's."

"Merely a temporary condition, I assure ye, madam. An' the doctor said to stay away from corsets," said Ian from the doorway. He sauntered into the room, looking rested and dapper. "Good morn, Mrs. Hennessey, how be my wife doin' on this glorious day?"

Henney favored him with a bright smile. "Good morning, sir. Miss Eleanor is doing just fine."

Eleanor made a face and rolled her eyes. Even Henney was a traitor. "I am not doing fine," she declared peevishly. "I am miserable...thanks to you. I'll probably die. Not that you would care."

"Nonsense. Ye're a healthy, young woman. Havin' a bairn is nothin' more than what nature intended. Women have them every day."

"Maybe in the Basin."

Ian stiffened and a coolness displaced his good nature. "Ye might feel better if ye had somethin' to think about besides yourself, Eleanor. Perhaps I should consider dismissin' the housekeeper to give ye somethin' to do."

"You wouldn't dare." The challenge in her eyes was undercut by alarm.

"Try me. I can make some allowances for yer condition, but if yer disposition does nae improve, consider the deed done. Mrs. Hennessey, I'll be at the mill if I'm needed."

As he exited the room, Eleanor stuck out her tongue at him.

"He treats me like a wayward child."

Henney picked up her knitting. "Perhaps you act like one."

Ian knew some satisfaction in having the last word, but as he climbed into the carriage and drove himself to the mill, he was hard pressed to throw off his dour mood. If Eleanor's mother had been anything like her, he thought sourly, it was no damned wonder Cyrus Morgan had locked himself up in his study for hours on end.

By the time he crossed the canal bridge and drove into the lumber yard, his spirit was beginning to lift. He sat in the buggy for a long moment, quietly surveying the sawmill, the planing mill, and the finishing mill, a little in awe of himself. Workers, many of whom he had sweated beside on the saws, waved and called out greetings to him. He smiled and waved back. He felt good. And it felt good to feel good.

After turning the phaeton and the horse over to the boy at the livery stable, he walked to his office. It was going to be a good day, he decided, taking the stairs two at a time.

Tommy followed him into the office, a broad smile stretching from ear to ear.

"Here, the first one be for ye." He flipped Ian a cigar. "'Tis not from Cuba, but it'll have to do."

Ian grinned as he sniffed the strong aroma of a cheap cigar. The moment held a flavor of the good, old days. "To what do I be owin' this reward and on a Monday morn no less?"

"Me son," said Tommy proudly. "Maven birthed him Friday night…a fine brawny lad he is, too."

The moment suddenly went flat for Ian. "Oh…congratulations. How is Maven?"

"She had a hard time of it. She be a bit feverish. Midwife says for her to stay in bed a few days, but ye know Maven."

"A midwife! For God's sake, Tommy, ye did nae fetch her a doctor?"

"Maven's been savin' up to buy the dress shop from Mrs. Drury. She will na let me touch a penny of the savin's. Besides, Rosie MacDonald's been deliverin' wee ones in the Basin since I can remember."

"We're nae talkin' about just any woman in the Basin. We be talkin' about Maven here. Why did ye nae come to me?" demanded Ian, hard pressed to control his anger.

Tommy looked Ian squarely in the eye. "We take care of our own." His tone was quiet, but the message was loud and clear. "I'll be gettin' back to me job now."

Ian had wanted to speak further with him about his ideas for the construction company, but the salt Tommy had just rubbed into his still raw wound hurt like hell.

"Aye. We'll discuss plans for an idea I have later."

The afternoon whistle had called the men back from lunch before Ian was of a temperament to approach Tommy again. They were in deep discussion in Tommy's office when Tommy's nine-year-old nephew rushed in. For a moment, Ian was transported back to another time. Years earlier, he had been summoned to his mother's bedside in just such a manner, and a chill gripped him before the boy got the words out of his mouth.

"Uncle Tommy, yer to come quick. Auntie Maven be real sick."

Ian was the first to react. "Tell O'Connor to take over for ye and go home, Tommy. I'll drive into town and get the doctor."

Tommy balked, but Ian's steely gaze allowed no room for argument. "This is Maven, Tommy. Pride be damned."

Tommy grabbed his coat and ran out the door.

Ian immediately shouted for his carriage. Inside of a half hour, hatless and coatless, he was whipping the horses through the crowded streets, cursing at obstacles in his path. He turned down a street of modest houses and stopped in front of one displaying a doctor's sign. He bounded out of the carriage and pounded on the door.

∗ ∗ ∗ ∗ ∗ ∗ ∗ ∗

Tommy paced the floor anxiously, while his mother and sister sat quietly waiting for word. All jumped, startled, when Ian burst through the door with the doctor in tow.

"Where is she?" Ian demanded to know.

"The back room," said Mrs. O'Brien. She watched in astonishment as Ian rushed the doctor to the back of the house.

Mrs. McInnis sat beside the bed, applying cool cloths to her daughter's feverish forehead. Ian's heart constricted at the sight of Maven. Her beautiful hair clung damp and matted around her flushed face. Her eyes that had sparked with a passionate fire stared vacant and lusterless in her delirium. When Ian's eyes connected with those of Mrs. McInnis, his worst fears were confirmed.

The doctor shoved Ian aside and made a cursory examination of the patient.

"When did she give birth?"

"Friday night," said Mrs. McInnis.

"How ill is she?" asked Ian anxiously.

The doctor set down his medical bag, threw off his coat, and rolled up his sleeves.

"I won't know until I make a more thorough exam." He looked at Mrs. McInnis. "You are her mother?" Mrs. McInnis nodded, and the doctor turned to Ian. "The sooner you leave, young man, the sooner I can get to the business of helping this young woman."

In the kitchen, Ian paced the floor, pausing every few minutes to stare down the hallway at the closed bedroom door. Tommy sat at the table staring into a cup of tea.

Ian's eyes shifted from the closed door to the cradle next to the stove before settling on Tommy. He felt a flash of anger, and he wrestled with the urge to send a fist crashing into Tommy's jaw. Tommy's mother pressed a cup of tea into his hands, disspelling the impulse.

The bedroom door creaked open an hour later, and all looked expectantly at the doctor when he walked into the kitchen. The frown on his face gave them little encouragement.

Ian set the chipped teacup on the table. "How is she?" he asked, his voice tense.

"Is she your wife?"

Tommy rose from the table and stepped in front of Ian. "I be Maven's husband. Will...will she live?"

"God willing," said the doctor. "She's young and strong. But I'll tell you straight, son, she should not have had this baby in the first place. Your wife's hips are too narrow. The birth tore up her insides pretty good. She may or may not be able to conceive again, but in any case, another birth like this will likely kill her." He took out a pen and pad and scrawled something across the paper, then handed it to Tommy. "She'll need this medicine. She should remain in bed at the very least a week. I've given her mother full instructions. I'll drop by in a few days to check on her. In the meantime, I would suggest a wet nurse for the baby."

Ian stepped forward again. "I'll be payin' all the expenses, Doctor."

Tommy looked at Ian, a hint of resentment in his eyes, but he said nothing. "May I see me wife, Doctor?" he asked.

The doctor nodded. "For a few minutes. She needs rest." He turned to Ian. "Now, sir, I presume you can return me to my home with more deliberation than you brought me here."

Ian hung back as the doctor started for the door. He wanted to stay longer to see for himself that Maven was going to be all right. He wanted to hold her, to comfort her. When Tommy went into her room and closed the door behind him, Ian felt a stab of jealously and anger that he was again being shut out of Maven's life. Reluctantly, he turned and followed the doctor out of the house.

*   *   *   *   *   *   *   *

It had been a long day, and Ian sat down at the dining room table that night, weary and short of temper. Maven still continued to haunt his thoughts, and underneath his concern for her was a simmering anger directed at Tommy. Damn him! How dare he put Maven's life at risk like that! he raged inwardly. He was unconscious of the fact that he had pounded his fist on the table until he heard a startled gasp and looked up to find Henney standing uncertainly in the doorway.

"Miss Eleanor asked me to inform you that she isn't feeling well and cannot leave her room, sir."

Ian ran a hand across bloodshot eyes. "An' what be the nature of madam's distress now, Mrs. Hennessey?"

"A headache, sir."

"A headache." His voice held a satirical edge. "I've seen the face of death today, Mrs. Hennessey, and I pray that it takes a holiday. Ye'll have to excuse me if I can nae elicit much sympathy for a headache. Tell madam nae to concern herself. I'll be at the Crystal Palace playin' cards if I'm needed. Tell the cook I'll nae be requirin' supper this evenin'."

"Yes, sir."

Henney carried the message back to her mistress.

"Cards my foot!" exclaimed Eleanor furiously. "I know what goes on in that place." She regarded her swelling stomach with disgust. "He ruins my figure and then seeks the company of one of those hussy's at the Palace. I lie here ill and disfigured because of him, and he spares me not a moment of consideration or sympathy." She began to sob. "Nobody cares about me."

"Hush, child, you mustn't upset yourself for the baby's sake."

"For the baby's sake," mimicked Eleanor through a veil of tears. "I am sick and tired of hearing that! All anyone cares about is the baby. How could he leave me in my condition and go to that place, Henney?"

"Some women might think it an act of consideration. Just imagine the indignities those poor women in the Basin must suffer from their menfolk who can afford no such diversion."

Eleanor sniffed back her tears and dotted her eyes with a lace-trimmed handkerchief. She knew what indignities the women of the Basin must endure, for she figured Ian to have subjected her to everyone of them the times he had come to her bed. And she knew she should be grateful for a place like the Crystal Palace. Without it, he might have come more often. But even more, she hated the thought of him plying his attentions elsewhere. She didn't want him in her bed, but neither did she want him in the bed of any other woman.

CHAPTER 32

Ian looked up in confusion as Tommy strode into his office and threw several bills on the desk.

"What's this?" he asked.

"'It's what we be owin' ye fer the doctor an' the medicine," said Tommy.

Ian frowned. "I do nae expect ye to repay me."

He pushed the money back to Tommy, but Tommy refused it.

"Maven wants it this way. She took the money from the savin's herself."

"Well put it back, dammit. Tell her ye got a bonus or somethin'."

Tommy put his hands on the desk and leaned forward, his steady, brown eyes commanding Ian's attention. "I want it this way, too."

After a long, tense, moment, Ian forced a laugh. "Maven must be fully recovered, ay. She's her own stubborn self again."

Tommy straightened to his full height. "Aye, she's feelin' well enough. I'll be gettin' back to me men now."

After Tommy left the office, a curse exploded from Ian's lips, and he angrily sent the money fluttering to the floor with the sweep of his arm.

*   *   *   *   *   *   *   *

Ian impatiently bided his time. For nearly a week he had furtively staked out the dress shop waiting for an opportunity to present itself. Now at last it had. Twilight had given way to darkness before the last customer left the store. Maven was pulling the blinds when he quickly and quietly slipped through the front door.

"'Tis sorry I am, but we be closin' now," said Maven, wearily drawing the last blind. "Can ye not come back tomorrow?"

"No, I can nae…. Hello, Maven."

Maven whirled about, her body thrilling at the sound of the familiar voice. "Ian, what be ye doin' here?"

Ian removed his hat, and Maven's heart twisted with an unwelcomed longing. "I wanted to know that ye were well again."

"Ye had only to ask Tommy."

"I had to see for meself." Ian's eyes slowly drank in every detail of her. In truth, he was alarmed. She looked tired, thin, and her features were drawn. She lacked the animation that was so much a part of her appeal, but he was relieved to see the rich, reddish sheen returning to her hair. And before she lowered her gaze, he saw that the fiery spark was back in her eyes.

"Ye must leave, Ian. I…I have to be lockin' up and be gettin' home now. The wee one be waitin' to be fed…. We be beholden to ye fer what ye done."

Ian took the bills from his coat pocket. "Then keep the money."

Maven's chin went up a notch and her reply was firm. "No. Someone I once knew taught me ne'er to take charity."

"'Tis not charity.

"What might it be then?"

Ian thought for a moment. "A company benefit. Will ye not take the money now?"

"How many other workers have ye given this benefit to?" she asked suspiciously.

"Well, none…yet. 'Tis somethin' new."

"I see. When others have been offered this benefit, then I shall accept it, too."

Ian's laugh was tinged with exasperation. "The union would do well to have ye in their midst."

"Please go now," said Maven.

Ian nodded. Giving her a wistful look, he set his hat. As he started to leave, she called out to him, and he turned back expectantly, full of hope.

"Ye must na try to see me again, Ian. It serves no one."

The gathering smile died on his lips and a sadness came into his eyes. "'Ever' is a long time, Maven. I can nae promise that. But I swear I'll not interfere in yer life if that's what be worryin' ye."

Ian opened the door then and disappeared into the night. As Maven quickly locked the door behind him, a single tear trickled down her cheek.

"No, Ian, 'tis not what be worryin' me," she whispered.

CHAPTER 33

In the secluded back room of the Rossburg Men's Club, several members of the inner circle were already gathered.

"Where's George?" demanded Franklin Jeffries, the self-appointed leader of the group.

"I don't think you had better count on him," said Ed Brown. "Douglas puts too much money in his bank. He's not going to kill the golden goose."

"George makes the fourth to break the circle," added Ben Thompson. "That's the trouble, Franklin, Douglas owns a piece of all of us. Even if he didn't still hold notes on the big mills, he owns the boom, and he owns the utility company."

"Yeah, and with the new construction company he's forming, he'll have most of the building industry under his thumb as well," said Jim Conover. "So far, it has been gentle persuasion, but if we don't start dancin' to his tune, things could get rough. Word has it that he has his eye on the mayor's seat."

"Good God, is the man out of his mind!" exploded Jeffries. "How can he think to win without our backing? I, for one, will not be strong-armed by him." He eyed each man meaningfully.

"He doesn't need us," said Brown. "He has the support of the workers."

Jeffries let out a derisive snort. "Since when do they vote? Besides, the Basin is outside the voting district."

"Douglas has promised them housing on Evergreen Street." Sam Springer, one of the more nervous members of the group, supplied this latest bombshell amid a flurry of twitches.

"Evergreen…why that's our backyard!" exclaimed an indignant Conover.

Murmurs of shock, anger, and fear reverberated around the room.

Ben Thompson, owner of the third largest mill in Rossburg, jumped to his feet, his face a mottled red. "I worked all my life to get to the Row. I'll be damned if I'll let Douglas turn it into another Basin slum! He's doing this to get back at us, Franklin. I told you we shouldn't have tried to keep him out. After all, his wife is Cyrus Morgan's daughter."

"He's right, Franklin," a chorus of voices shouted in agreement.

"Hell, Cyrus is the reason we're in this mess," Brown shouted, brandishing a beefy fist. "If he hadn't been such a greedy son of a bitch and backstabbed us to buy the boom, he wouldn't have lost everything to Douglas. He created this monster and left us to deal with it."

"How convenient for Cyrus to drop over dead when he did," said Jim Conover dryly.

"Gentlemen, gentlemen. We're not going to get anywhere fighting among ourselves." Jeffries turned and pounced on the bearer of bad news. "Now that you've gotten everyone so riled, Sam, show us what proof you have of Douglas' plans for Evergreen Street."

Sam blinked nervously behind his thick lenses. "My brother-in-law is new to town. I had him get a job at Douglas' Mills to keep track of what Douglas is up to. He told me Douglas is going to offer his workers a housing allowance."

"Now I know the man is crazy," said Jeffries with a complacent laugh. "He'll go broke before summer."

"Not if his construction company builds the houses. With his mills supplying the materials and labor…" Sam had no need to finish.

"My God!" exclaimed Thompson leaping to his feet again. "Do you know what this means? None of us will be able to keep workers without following suit."

"And any allowance we offer will go right back into Douglas' construction company," added Conover. "The bastard can't lose."

"That's not all," Springer went on. "According to my brother-in-law, Douglas is talking about picking up the costs for a doctor and medicine for not only ailing workers but their families as well."

Thompson sat down with a heavy "Ooof" as though someone had punched him in the stomach. "Pay a worker to be sick! I never heard such nonsense. I don't know of a man who would rather work when he can get paid for sitting at home. He'll have every worker in town waiting in line to work for his mill."

"I think we all agree then that Ian Douglas represents a very big threat to us...to this town," said Jeffries.

"What can we do to stop him...short of killing the bastard?" asked Brown.

"Why not kill him?" questioned one desperate member.

Jeffries raised his hands. "Gentlemen, listen to yourselves. You're losing all objectivity. The answer is simple. We knock out the cornerstone of his plans."

"And just how the hell do we do that?"

"We see to it that Mayor Bradley declares that section of Evergreen Street a park. Douglas will have to build his shantytown elsewhere...on land he'll have to buy. That should hurt his pocketbook plenty."

"He'll still have the workers' support. I say let's burn him out," said Brown.

"Be realistic. Even Douglas can't provide housing inside the voting district for all of them, especially if Bradley and the council should adopt some housing restrictions which add to the cost." Franklin Jeffries' proposal momentarily quieted the angry group. "Besides," he continued, "there will always be those creatures of habit. You would be surprised how many won't want to leave the familiarity of the Basin given the opportunity."

"What about him paying the doctor's costs for the workers and their families?" asked Conover.

"Douglas is letting the sympathies of his background get in the way of good business sense. We all know that if you give those people an inch, they'll take a foot. He'll either go bankrupt or wake up to reality and rescind the offer…in which case the workers will revolt. He can't win gentlemen. All we have to do is sit tight and let him hang himself."

"I don't know, Franklin. We underestimated Douglas once and look where we are. I say we try to reason with him," said Conover.

"You can't reason with a jackal."

"That's easy for you to say, Franklin. Y-you don't have Douglas squeezing one ball and your wife the other," stammered Springer.

Jeffries' nostrils quivered. He despised spinelessness. His own wife had poisoned herself rather than endure another pregnancy. "Just what do women have to do with this business?"

The men shifted uncomfortably in their chairs, and it was clear that Springer was wishing he had kept his mouth shut.

"Well," commanded Jeffries, "I'm waiting."

"The wives were pretty miffed at us over Douglas' ball last February because we wouldn't let them eat or dance," one of the men finally admitted. "I've never seen the likes of it before. An orchestra from New York, every food you could imagine. Not even Cyrus could have topped that—"

Jeffries impatiently cut the man off. "It was a pretentious and vulgar attempt by the man to buy his way into society. You would have been better advised to stay away as Peter and I did."

"It wasn't that easy. Douglas doesn't hold any notes on you," said another, growing irritated with Jeffries' pomposity. "Besides, Douglas now commands the attention of the press. Even you have to agree there is some advantage to that, Franklin. Especially if one is planning to run for mayor."

"The press will soon tire of his tricks."

"I don't think so," said Springer, growing uncomfortable in his capacity as official crepe hanger. "You know he has bought up all the box seats for the press and 'selected friends' for opening night at the Opera House. The word is he is responsible for Miss Bernhardt agreeing to perform here."

"The woman is a simple French actress, Sam…well past her prime."

"That so, then why are reporters coming from New York and Philadelphia," argued Springer. "Georgiana is prepared to throw her pride to the wind to get an invite."

"My wife, too," confessed Brown. "The only tickets left are on the floor, and I hear Douglas is subsidizing those to encourage people from the Basin to attend. I'll never hear the end of it if Harriet has to rub elbows with her washer woman. He has the whole town turned on its ear. Face it, Franklin, he's got us all by the ass in one way or another."

Jeffries snorted in disgust. "Who's in control of your households, you or your wives?"

"You're a widower, Franklin. Maybe you've forgotten that women have a way of making things damned uncomfortable for a man."

"Maybe you've forgotten, gentlemen, that you need my railroad to transport your timber from your inland tracts to the river to pay off your notes."

CHAPTER 34

With a forlorn sigh, Eleanor leaned her head against the windowpane. One by one phaetons, their occupants finely dressed, filed past the mansion and down the street to the Conover estate for the society wedding of the year.

"Look at them, Henney, so high and mighty. I can just imagine what they're saying as they pass by: 'Poor Eleanor, how far she has fallen.' She flounced on the sofa. "Oh, why can't it be miserable and stormy today? Why must it be so beautiful and glorious? Even the weather conspires against me."

"You mustn't carry on so, child," said Henney.

Ian strolled into the parlor. "Hello, ladies," he said cheerfully.

Henney looked up from her knitting and answered him with a bright smile, while Eleanor favored him with a doleful pout.

"Would you care for a cup of tea, Mr. Douglas?"

"No, thank ye, Mrs. Hennessee. Eleanor, I thought ye might accompany me on a drive. I have something to show ye, an' 'tis a fine day for a picnic."

"Or a wedding," she mumbled sourly.

Ian took a deep breath and struggled to hold onto his temper. "I'll take yer answer to be 'nae' then," he said curtly. He turned to Henney. "Good day, Mrs. Hennessey. If ye'll be so kind as to tell the cook I shall be home for supper."

"Yes, sir."

When Ian had left the room, Henney shook her head, the knitting needles continuing their steady click despite the handicap of arthritic fingers. "You should have gone with him, child."

Eleanor sniffed haughtily. "Why? If it hadn't been for him, Peter would be marrying me, and those carriages would be coming here. It isn't fair."

The click of the needles stopped, and Henney peered over her spectacles. "But they're not coming here, and might be you're the better off for it."

Eleanor turned sharply to her old nanny. "How you can say that!" Ian Douglas is ill-natured and completely indifferent to my feelings. Peter was completely devoted to me."

"Then why didn't Mr. Jeffries marry you when he had the chance?"

"It was all his father's doing."

"It appears to me that Mr. Douglas is the hero here. He's the one who stepped in to save you from a life of destitution."

"He made me an outcast."

"Were you not ostracized already by your father's doings?"

"Peter loves me. It would have been just a matter of time until he married me…. I know it," added Eleanor with less certainty.

"Young Mr. Jeffries does not strike me as a man who opposes his father on any matter. Child, child, don't make the same mistake your mother did."

Eleanor was growing annoyed at Henney's defense of Ian. "What mistake?"

"She mistook a sapling for a weed."

Eleanor looked at Henney in confusion. "What?"

"When your father met your mother," Henney explained, "he was a self-made man, rough around the edges, visiting from a young lumber town just finding its legs. Oh, he cut quite a figure in his day, and your mother fell head over heels for him, and he for her. Her family was an established Philadelphia banking family. They would have objected more to the marriage had your father not seen fit to invest much needed capital in your grandfather's bank."

Eleanor became pensive. "I can't picture Mother ever being happy."

"She was never content. No matter your father's success and wealth, she could never overlook his humble beginnings." Henney shot Eleanor a pointed look. "She couldn't let him forget them either. She wanted him to sell the mill, move them back to Philadelphia and work in her father's bank. When he refused, well, more's the pity she couldn't see all the important things he was for the few unimportant things he wasn't. Much misery might have been avoided. Mr. Douglas is much like your father I think."

"Yes, I've told him so, and I don't find the similarities flattering," said Eleanor.

"Perhaps because you are much like your mother." Henney gathered up her knitting and rose from the chair. "I'd think on that for a spell if I was you, missy. Take a closer look before you cut down that sapling for a weed."

Ian was about to climb into the buggy when Eleanor came hurrying out of the house.

"Wait!" she called. "I've decided to accompany you after all."

Ian threw her a quizzical look. "Suit yourself." He helped her into the buggy and climbed in beside her. Again, he stole a glance at her as he took up the reins. He had learned to be wary of her quicksilver moods, and he wondered what had changed her mind?

They drove down the quiet, tree-shaded streets to downtown, through Market Square, bustling with Saturday market stalls and merchant stands, and out to High Street. She had remained silent for the most part, fanning away dust with low murmurs of disgust as roads paved with Nicholson and stone soon gave way to dirt roads, and he braced himself for a steady patter of complaints. But there came none, and again he glanced at her guardedly.

He turned onto a narrow country lane lined with trees and farmers' fields and stopped before a cornfield on a gently sloping hill. Through the break in the trees, Eleanor could see a breathtaking view of the city below. Large maples dotted the property, and a larger hill crowned with a stand of oaks rose up from behind. A cool, fresh breeze stirred the fragrant scent of wildflowers.

"Well, there it is," he said proudly.

Eleanor looked around in confusion. "What?"

"The site of our new home. Remember, I told ye we would have our own house."

Eleanor turned to Ian, aghast. "You can't be serious. Leave Millionaires' Row for a farmer's field, in the middle of nowhere! You seek to degrade me even more. No, I won't have it."

The excitement faded from Ian's features. "I'm afraid, madam, that ye will. The matter is already decided. I've purchased two hundred acres on this road and have petitioned the city to rename it Grandview Place."

"Why…why must you do this? What have I done to deserve such treatment from you? Is it not enough that I'm bearing your child?"

"For godsake, Eleanor, this is not a punishment. Ye'll have the grandest house in all of Rossburg with all the latest conveniences."

"But it was always your dream to live on Millionaires' Row, to be accepted as a member of society. You married me hoping to achieve it, and now you would throw away every chance of it?"

"Millionaires' Row is the past," said Ian. "'Tis time to build a new future, a new society…one that ye and I will lead…. One that won't fear progress but will welcome and embrace it."

Eleanor scoffed. "From the middle of a farmer's field."

"These won't be farmers' fields for long. In time, this lane will be a wide boulevard lined with magnificent mansions, not like the gloomy mausoleums on the Row, but bright, shiny, and new. This…," he said, sweeping his arm across the landscape, "this is the future." He turned to

Eleanor, his eyes alight with his vision. "*We* are the future, Eleanor, and ye will again be the reigning queen of society."

Eleanor was doubtful, but as she looked at his face so full of confidence and determination as he continued to lay out his plans for her, she felt a stir of excitement, too. Maybe, just maybe, he was right.

＊　＊　＊　＊　＊　＊　＊　＊

July handed over its mantle to August and with it an uncomfortable wave of heat. It was a dry summer. Too dry. Ian stood on the veranda, tensely watching heat lightning zigzag across the evening sky, acutely alert to any smell of smoke in the air. Fire in the lumber tracts was a daily worry now. He couldn't forget how the fire of 1880 had crippled the large mill owners, affording him the opportunity to hold notes on them. He was stretched tight with the expansion of his business into construction and the added workers' benefits. If the fire of 1880 had put the lid on Morgan's coffin, a fire like that would most certainly nail Ian's shut.

Parker Stanton walked up the drive and headed for the front door when he saw Ian and joined him on the veranda. He took out a handkerchief and mopped his brow.

"Half past eight in the evening and still hotter'n hades," he said. "There was a fire up in Maston today."

"How bad?"

"Fifty acres, mostly pines."

Ian continued to stare stone-faced into the horizon. "Tell Tommy to keep the sawdust swept up. All it will take is one spark from a saw to level the whole damned millworks."

"I don't think he needs to be reminded of that." A heavy silence fell between them, and Parker took out his pipe and lit it. "I remember when you and Tommy arrived at the lumber camp that winter," he said off-handedly, taking a puff. "You were as close as brothers. He stood side by side with you when you took over the mill yards and those thugs tried to force you out. Now you talk only when matters at the mill necessitate it. I know this is none of my business, but I suspect this rift goes deeper than a change in roles."

Ian's jaw tightened. "Ye're right, Parker. 'Tis none of yer business."

Stanton continued undaunted. "Look, Ian. There are tough times ahead now that you've announced the housing allowance and medical benefits to the workers. You've made a lot of enemies, and you're going to need all the friends you can find. Whatever is between you and Tommy, you should know that he is a good man. He watches your back like none other at the mill."

"Thank ye, Parker. I needed to know that," said Ian.

CHAPTER 35

Eleanor's lips curved up in a smile of satisfaction as she examined her image in the cheval glass. Literally purring, she smoothed her hands over her flat stomach.

"Look, Henney. Almost perfect. No one would guess that I gave birth just six weeks ago." She made a face. "Such an experience I hope never to repeat."

"Come, now," said Henney, putting away one of the many dresses Eleanor had tried and discarded before finding one to finally suit her. "The doctor said it was one of the easiest births he attended. The first time can be frightening, but it gets easier with each child."

"It was the worst thing I've ever endured, and I have no intentions of ever repeating it," said Eleanor firmly.

"The way you carried on...poor Mr. Douglas thought you were dying. Such a state he was in."

Eleanor giggled. "Yes, he did look positively awful when he was allowed into the room. I think he was actually worried about me. He has been rather pleasant these last weeks, except for...well, there was that unpleasantness about the child's name."

"What's wrong with the name Mary Katherine?" asked Henney. "The child is named for his mother and sister. I think it is a lovely sentiment."

Eleanor gave an unladylike snort. "It sounds so...so lower east end. Half the female population in the Basin are named Mary this or Mary that. I suppose I should be grateful that he hadn't insisted upon the name Maven," she added smartly. "Then there was the argument about the wet nurse. I'm not a milk cow, for heaven's sake." Eleanor groaned. "I don't think he'll ever grasp the ways of the upper class."

A servant appeared in the doorway. "This came for you, madam."

Eleanor took the white envelope from the silver tray and dismissed the servant.

"Look, Henney, another invitation." She ripped it open with the excitement of a child. "They've been coming in two a day since Sarah Bernhardt's performance. Did you see the look on the faces of Harriet Brown and the others when they found their seats next to mill workers, while Ian and I sat up in the box seats with the likes of the mayor of Philadelphia, Senator Wilson, and Ambassador Stedtman? It was positively delicious."

She had to give Ian his due. He had promised her entree back into society, and he was delivering. For the first time since her father died, she had the upper hand. It felt good, and she wasn't going to easily surrender it. Miss Berhardt's performance had gone well at the newly renovated theatre, the private reception even better. Press from as far away as New York had descended upon Rossburg to cover the affair and report on the many theatre celebrities, politicians and dignitaries in attendance.

She hadn't been home to callers days before the event. She laughed aloud with delight, savoring again her victory. To see Georgiana Conover and Harriet Brown sitting elbow to elbow with the working class had been sweet revenge indeed. The ladies who had once shunned her now danced attention upon her, and she was relishing every moment of it.

Ian came to stand quietly in the doorway, a look of open admiration on his face. The afternoon tea gown of green velvet flowed alluringly over her body. A satin sash cinched her trim waist and accentuated provocative, rounded hips. Rays of sunlight streamed through the window, creating a shimmering aura around upswept blonde curls. Ian's heart wrenched. She was so beautiful. Desperately, he hoped that the birth of this child had mellowed her. Perhaps now they could make a marriage.

Henney saw him and quietly left through the anteroom.

"More invitations I see," said Ian.

Eleanor turned and favored him with a bright smile. "Yes, isn't it wonderful? Just like when Father was alive."

He looked down at her glowing face and was reminded of a child in a candy store. "Old fleas jumping on a new dog, ay?"

"Well, I wouldn't put it quite that way," she said with an infectious giggle.

"The nanny tells me ye haven't visited the nursery in two days."

"The child is in good hands with Mrs. Wilcox." Eleanor gave a slight pout. "I do wish Henney didn't have to leave tomorrow to nurse her ailing sister."

"Eleanor, babies need their mothers."

"Babies are no fun, Ian. All they can do is fuss, eat and sleep. Besides, between the fittings and teas and other obligations, I simply haven't had the time." She pinned her hat in place and drew on soft kid gloves. "I'm due at a tea at the Sinclair residence." She raised herself up on her toes and gave Ian a light kiss on the cheek, the reprimand dying on his lips. "I'll see you for supper and tell you all the delicious gossip."

He stared after her until she disappeared down the staircase, her perfume lingering in the air, her unexpected kiss still pressed against his cheek. Slowly, he crossed the hall to the nursery. The baby was not yet two months old, and he gazed down at his daughter in a mixture of awe and delight as he did twenty times a day. A blonde fuzz covered her perfectly round head and her wide, blue eyes were full of curiosity. She smiled and kicked and curled a tiny fist around his finger and his heart.

CHAPTER 36

Eleanor moved about the study, sliding her hand slowly across the top of the desk, across the spines of several books, across the back of the leather chair. Imagination or not, she could still smell her father's cigar now mingled with Ian's cologne. The fire in the fireplace banished most of the chill of the gray March day. The indulgence of sherry banished the rest.

She was sick and tired of reading about Mr. and Mrs. Peter Jeffries on the society page: MR. AND MRS. PETER JEFFRIES HOST CHARITY BALL...MR. AND MRS. PETER JEFFRIES TRAVEL ABROAD...MR. AND MRS. PETER JEFFRIES HOST RECEPTION...One would think *they* were the society! There had been no notice in the paper when she had married, no notice about her honeymoon trip or the birth of her daughter, thought Eleanor dismally. There was plenty of mention of Ian in the business section, but nothing about her...not since the Bernhardt performance and reception.

She wandered about the room, picking up objects and setting them down without really looking at them. With Henney gone, she was feeling a bit abandoned. She emptied her glass of the strong amber liquor, savoring the warmth of its afterglow. It served to fill the void that all her social engagements seemed unable to satisfy lately.

Her thoughts drifted to Ian, and she felt a stab of pain and anger. The consideration and attention that he had shown her upon the birth of their daughter had deteriorated into disdain, as he once again began coming to her bed. Ian had his child, why should she have to submit again to the revolting ways of men and endure yet another pregnancy? Why couldn't he just admire her, love her, worship her without the other things. She still had to wonder at what pleasure men found in an act that brought such humiliation to women.

"Mrs. Douglas?"

Eleanor whirled about. Parker Stanton stood in the doorway, a look of surprise on his face.

"I've come to see Ian on a business matter," he said apologetically. "The housekeeper said I could wait for him in the study."

"Come in, Mr. Stanton. I'm about to leave."

"I didn't mean to intrude. I hadn't expected to find you in here."

Eleanor gave a mirthless laugh. "It's rather amusing how things change. I always hated this room. Now that my husband will be forcing me out of my home soon, I find I shall miss it. It really is a lovely room, isn't it, Mr. Stanton?"

"Yes, madam, particularly with you in it."

Eleanor straightened her shoulders and patted an errant strand of hair into place, a pleased smile illuminating her features. She gave a girlish giggle. "Why, Mr. Stanton, how forward of you to say so."

"May I pour you another sherry?"

Eleanor considered the offer for a moment, then nodded and held out her glass. "Why not. I have nowhere to go this evening. For all of my husband's arm twisting, I fear we are still social outcasts. Did you know that? Oh, the invitations come, but they are for luncheons and teas with the ladies. Rarely to anything important...unless, of course, there is fund-raising involved. She gave a scornful snort. I'm tiring of their silly prattle anyway...never noticed before how boring they all are."

Stanton smiled and refilled her glass, then helped himself to a shot of Ian's best brandy. He had never seen her with her guard down before. There was something touchingly vulnerable about her. She reminded him of a wounded dove, set adrift in a sea of doubts and torments not entirely of her own making. He saw a motherless, lonely child brought up by servants and a father devoted to amassing wealth and power, whose sole parental responsibility extended to providing material possessions. It came as no surprise to Stanton that Eleanor had so little understanding of human emotions. Her hunger for acceptance and love, which she confused with worshipful admiration, left her no match for a man such as Ian, who was on his own ruthless quest for the same. What a pity they couldn't find it in each other.

She swayed slightly, and he put out a hand to steady her.

"Oh, yes, Mr. Stanton," she continued, taking no notice of his hand on her arm, "we're social outcasts. My husband has no breeding and my father left me no money...the two biggest sins according to Rossburg society. Tell me, Mr. Stanton, is it better to have breeding or money?"

Stanton shrugged. "Well, my feeling is that breeding doesn't put bread on the table or build the fanciest house in town."

"I'm afraid, Mr. Stanton, that is not enough."

"If I may ask, Mrs. Douglas, what is?"

Eleanor looked at him strangely, tears shimmering in her sky-blue eyes. "I don't know," she said in a tremulous voice. "I don't know." She put a hand to her head and set the glass on the table. "Please excuse me, Mr. Stanton. I suddenly seem to have developed a headache."

As she walked somewhat unsteadily from the room, Stanton stared after her. She was a thoroughbred and like all thoroughbreds required special handling. It was obvious Ian hadn't understood that yet. And if he didn't learn it soon, he was going to destroy her."

He had just poured himself another drink when Ian walked in look-ing haggard and preoccupied.

"You look as though you could use a brandy," said Parker.

Ian nodded and sank wearily into the leather chair behind Morgan's desk. "What are ye doin' here? It can nae be good news. Somethin' wrong with the books? Production down?"

"No, but you'd better drink this first," said Parker, shoving the drink at Ian.

Ian swigged the brandy carelessly. "What now? 'Tis been a long day, Parker. Two of the saws went down, half the mill workers are out with sickness, and the spring thaw is just a few weeks away."

"That's going to cost the company plenty. I told you to wait until spring to institute that damn health policy."

"Any other suggestions?"

"Hire new workers and fire the ones too sick to work."

Ian's brow shot up. "Do ye nae think that runs a bit contrary to our new policy?"

Parker shrugged. "You just tell them that it's nothing personal. You need to keep the saws in operation. You'll be paying their medical bills. That's already more than the other mill owners do. What more can they expect?"

"I promised Tommy that his men would have certain assurances."

"Hell, Ian, you've been making some pretty costly promises lately."

"'Tis called loyalty, Parker. Ye give it, ye get it back." Ian caught the skepticism that flashed across Stanton's face. "I know how you feel about this health program, but 'tis personal for me. My mum and sister might have lived if I had had the money for medical care."

"It was the influenza epidemic, Ian, rich people died. Are you sure Maven O'Brien isn't at the root of this?"

Ian's features darkened and his scowl left no room for misunder-standing or negotiation. "This is not a point for discussion, Parker. Now tell me what has brought ye here?"

"There's trouble with the housing project."

"What trouble?"

"Jeffries, Conover and that bunch have gotten an injunction against building on your property at Evergreen and Locust. They convinced the mayor to declare it a park."

Ian bolted upright, sloshing brandy on the polished, mahogany finish. "How the devil can they do that! I own the land."

"It's in the city's charter that a certain percentage of undeveloped land can be seized for recreational use when it is deemed more beneficial to the public. You will be compensated of course, but at a fraction of its worth."

Ian brought his fist down hard on the desk in a fit of anger and frustration. "I promised the workers decent housing that they could afford and by God they'll have it!"

"You can't possibly replace that land within the voting district without putting your cash flow in serious jeopardy, Ian."

"I will not go back on my word."

"The injunction is only half the problem."

"There's more? What else can there be!"

"The mayor has suddenly seen the need for certain housing construction codes to insure conformity, he says. These guidelines will add some fifty dollars to the cost of each new house we build."

Ian slumped back in the chair. The exhaustion ebbed from his body as his brain grappled with this latest attack. He wasn't beaten yet. He wouldn't be beaten. He'd be damned if he'd let Jeffries get the upper hand. He knew Parker was right. Cash flow was his Achilles' heel. Jeffries and the others knew that, too. Was he destined to make the same mistake Cyrus Morgan had made? he wondered. A slow smile suddenly spread across Ian's face.

"What are you thinking?" asked Parker warily.

"That I'm not down yet."

*   *   *   *   *   *   *   *

Franklin Jeffries regarded his visitor with ill-concealed contempt and complacent superiority.

"To what do I owe your visit to my office, Douglas? State your business quickly and leave. I'm a busy man."

Ian was not one to mince words either. "Call off Mayor Bradley on the housing project."

"Or what?"

"I do nae think yer investors would appreciate knowin' that the next leader of yer railroad empire is an opium addict."

Jeffries didn't flinch. "Blackmail, Douglas? That's something that only a desperate man stoops to. I hadn't thought it to be your style." His thin lips curled in disdain. "Truth is I've known of Peter's weakness for some months. He always was spineless...takes after his mother. I certainly would never risk putting him in charge of my empire. I intend to personally groom my grandson to take over the reins. All Peter is good for is begetting an heir."

"I guess someone should inform him of his duty then," said Ian. "But ye're right, Jeffries. Blackmail is nae my style. I much prefer cards."

"Too bad you used up your ace. Your time is up, Douglas. Close the door on the way out."

"Not yet, Jeffries. I still have a wild card." Ian took out the document and threw it on the desk.

"What's this?"

"Look at it."

Jeffries eyed Ian suspiciously as he picked up the deed. The temple in his vein throbbed and his scowl deepened as he looked over it. "Howard Townshend owns that land. What are you doing with it?"

"It was one of the pieces of property Morgan deeded over to me before his death."

"I have first option on that property. How did Cyrus come by it?"

"Same way I did...bad gamblin' debt. First options do nae cover that."

A slight tremor ran through Jeffries' fingers as he held the document. "What's your price?"

"Considerin' it be the key to the western expansion of yer railroad," said Ian, "I think we can come to an agreement."

CHAPTER 37

Parker Stanton carefully examined the document, reread it, and shook his head in disbelief.

"Holy Mother of God! The mayor has reversed his decision on the Evergreen property. I don't believe it! You're free to build. How did you do it?" He stared at Ian in awe.

Ian's complacent smile stretched into a roguish grin, as he turned to look down at the mill yard from his office window. "I had something Franklin Jeffries wanted."

"But how did he get Conover and Brown and the rest of them to agree?"

Ian shrugged and turned back to Stanton. "I do nae know, and I do nae care as long as he did it."

"*Why* would he do it?" asked Parker, growing a bit concerned.

"I sold him the West Meadow land for his western expansion...and the loan drafts that I held on the mills."

"Do you think selling the West Meadow land to him was wise?"

Ian gave a careless shrug. "It was useless to me."

"But not to Jeffries. Listen, my friend. Lesson number one...don't hand your enemy any ammunition lest he aim it straight back at you. You're helping him to strengthen his empire, for chrissake."

"I would nae worry about it, Parker. That land tends to flood with the ice floes in the spring. He'll be kept busy just repairin' washed out track."

"Yeah, okay, but why the loan drafts? Why would he want those? They're coming due in a few months."

"I had Tommy make some discreet inquiries among the mill hands down at Cozey's Saloon. Rumor has it that these poor bastards are all skatin' on thin ice. Brown had to replace some saws. They were becomin' dangerous to the point where the men were refusin' to work them. Springer can nae seem to stay away from the Johnstown horse races. And Whiting and Thompson are going to need an advance on next summer's profits just to set up camp this winter."

Stanton shook his head in wonder. "Funny thing about jackals...they'll turn on each other every time. No one will know it is Jeffries who holds the notes...except you, of course."

"Of course." Ian crossed over to the desk and sank back in his chair, his fingers laced behind his head. "I think in the future we're goin' to be seein' a good deal more cooperation from Jeffries."

"I wonder what the others will think of his sudden change of heart?"

"Whatever Jeffries wants them to think." Ian rummaged in the bottom of his desk drawer and produced a bottle of whiskey and two glasses. He splashed a generous measure in both, passed one to his friend, and raised his glass in salute.

"To success and more of the same," he said, and downed the liquor in one gulp.

"Hear, Hear," said Parker following suit. The fiery liquid momentarily extinguished the uneasy feeling gnawing at his insides.

*   *   *   *   *   *   *   *

Jeffries' hand closed tightly, possessively around the coveted deed. A sly smile tightened his lips. Ian Douglas was a bigger fool than he had credited him. Douglas had no idea to the lengths he would have gone to secure that property. The man in his youthful arrogance and greed had made it so easy, so cheap for him, going so far as to sell him the notes as well.

Cyrus Morgan had had something there with that dual ownership business, Jeffries decided. He should have thought of it himself years ago. It had been easy enough to convince Henry Bradley to revise the park zoning. The spineless twit knew which side his bread was buttered on. Now the Jeffries fortune was definitely made, the future secured for his grandson...provided that his worthless son ever provided him with an heir. Jeffries frowned, his elation momentarily ebbing. It was time to apply a little pressure in that direction, he decided.

The sight of the deed in his hand restored Jeffries' good humor, and he let out a chuckle of delight. Yes, Ian Douglas was a fool if he thought he had made the better deal. The brash, young man's finances were on shaky ground thanks to his ludicrous handouts to his workers, and the low cost housing would be the rope that hanged him. He would enjoy watching the man's slow strangulation. Too late, Douglas would learn that he can't give those ingrates anything. Too late, Douglas would learn that he was no match for Franklin Jeffries.

CHAPTER 38

The new residence of Mr. and Mrs. Ian Douglas on Grandview Place is now completed. Though located at the north end of town in a somewhat secluded area, the new house is spacious and elegant with sweeping verandas, a third-floor ballroom and balcony, marble and ceramic fireplaces, electric lights, electric bells, speaking tubes, a dumbwaiter and every other appointment of a residence of importance. Mr. and Mrs. Douglas will greet callers in their new home on the afternoon of October 6th, 1883.

Eleanor clutched the *Rossburg Gazette* to her chest and danced across the floor of her lovely new parlor, laughing with girlish delight. A riot of colors played upon the polished wood floor as the sun reflected off the magnificent stained glass inlaid in the top of the oversized windows.

Ian descended the stairs and started across the marble foyer when he heard Eleanor's laughter. He stopped in the doorway, his eyes widening in surprise as he watched her twirl happily about the room with uncustomary abandon. Her cheeks were flushed, and her eyes glowed with an inner excitement. A smile tipped the corners of his mouth as he leaned against the doorjamb, arms folded, to enjoy this rare moment.

When she saw him, he expected a swift change of mood, but her features remained bright.

"Did you see it, Ian? Did you see the notice in the paper?" She shoved the *Rossburg Gazette* at him. "See here," she said jabbing a finger at the paragraph. "It says our home has all the appointments of a residence of importance. That ought to put Harriet Brown in her place. Of course, I'm not too pleased with the inference that our property is located in the middle of nowhere..."

"I thought it sounded rather exclusive myself."

Eleanor's brow furrowed as she considered the line in question again. "I suppose it might."

Her cheery demeanor returned, and her eye swept the parlor, very pleased with what she saw. The magnificent plaster work with bas-relief moldings twelve inches deep, the handsome cherry and maple millwork, the marble and tile fireplace with its carved mantel, the unique bronze hardware, the rose covered wallpaper and hand-woven Chinese rug...this was all her doing. Ian had an eye for design, but she had the eye for detail. Balance was essential in a house like this or one was in danger of crossing over that fine line to garish. Showy was acceptable if done well; ostentation when done poorly was a serious breach of etiquette. Having been raised in the Basin, Ian's taste in such matters needed considerable guidance.

As the construction of the house progressed, she had found her interest in it increasing, especially when it became obvious to her that her touch was needed. If she had to live in the middle of a farmer's field, she was determined to do it in style. Ian had seemed to welcome and value her input, and she had soon become pleased to give it. Perhaps that was because she had never been asked her opinion on anything that mattered before. His only demand was that the house be bright and airy, and she had complied with lace curtains and panelled shutters rather than heavy draperies on the oversized windows. Pastel colors were mixed in to soften the brown, green and wine-red colors that were in vogue.

She and Ian had worked well together. The tension between them had eased, and in a spontaneous moment, she looped her arms around his neck and hugged him.

"It's a grand house, isn't it? The best in Rossburg."

Staring down into her upturned face, her lips so close to his, Ian felt a tightening in his loins. He started to tighten his arm around her waist, but stopped himself. He had twice made the mistake of responding to what he had taken to be a softening in her manner toward him, effectively putting an end to her seemingly giving nature. Since then he had come to understand that her generosity of affection was driven by the excitement of the moment—receipt of a valued invitation, an expensive piece of jewelry, a favorable notice in the paper. Not by any desire for him. Still, he found himself arranging such moments if only to feel her arms around him for the instant.

"Aye, the best house in all of Rossburg," he murmured.

"It's grander than Caroline's and Peter's, or any other house on the Row, isn't it?" Eleanor's laugh rang with amusement. "Caroline said that Grandview Place is becoming quite popular for Sunday rides these days. Oh, I shall enjoy seeing the color of green on their pinched faces."

"What makes ye think that any of them will attend the open house next Saturday? I no longer hold any of their notes," said Ian on a teasing note.

Eleanor smiled slyly. "Oh, they'll attend. The ladies will see to it. They're simply dying of curiosity."

"Pop-pa, Pop-pa!"

Ian turned at the childish squeal and held out his arms to an apple-cheeked toddler who needed no further urging. Eleanor watched his face transform into a picture of warmth and adoration as he scooped up the little girl and twirled her around. She couldn't help feeling a stab of envy.

"How's the prettiest lassie in all the world?" he asked, playfully tweaking a round cheek.

Mary Katherine giggled, scrunching large, blue eyes and flinging her blonde curls from side to side. Watching the loving interaction between father and daughter, Eleanor felt excluded.

"Mrs. Wilcox, I've told you before not to let the child intrude upon our conversation," she berated the nanny sharply.

"Sorry, Mrs. Douglas. We just come back from a walk."

"'Tis all right, Mrs. Wilcox," said Ian. "Mary Katherine is never an intrusion."

Eleanor turned a glaring eye on him. "If you continue to allow the child to do as she pleases, she'll never learn any manners or discipline."

"She's not yet two years old, Eleanor. She shall have my ear any time she needs or wants it. Is that clear, Mrs. Wilcox?"

The nanny looked uneasily at Eleanor and slowly nodded. "Yes, sir."

He shifted the toddler in his arms as she lay her head against his shoulder. "Let's see now. I wonder if I might be knowin' anyone who likes ice cream."

The little head immediately popped up. "Me, Pop-pa...I-cream."

"Ye!" The child nodded enthusiastically, sending her crown of curls into further disarray. "Well, I suppose we'll have to go into town and visit the ice cream parlor then."

"But it's time for her nap," protested Eleanor. "You'll upset her whole routine."

"Nonsense. I do nae think the world will come to an end if Mary Katherine misses a nap, ay, Mrs. Wilcox?"

The poor nanny looked helplessly from Ian to an increasingly irate Eleanor. "Well, a child does need to observe a strict regimen," she said weakly.

"And she will...as soon as we return," said Ian.

"What about the mill?" asked Eleanor. "I thought you had pressing business."

"It can wait. We will nae be long." He hoisted Mary Katherine on top of his shoulders and strode from the room.

The windows were open to catch the spring breeze, and Eleanor could hear their teasing laughter all the way down to the drive. She shut her eyes tight against tears trying to push their way to the fore. Again, she was abandoned, forgotten, and, in that moment, she wished she could be that little girl, the center of so much adoration and attention. It wasn't just Ian. Everyone who came into contact with Mary Katherine had come under her spell. In Mary Katherine's company, Eleanor had come to the conclusion that she might as well be invisible.

"I-ah-I have notes to write. I shall be in my sitting room, Mrs. Wilcox. When Mr. Douglas returns, put the child down for a nap."

"Yes, ma'am."

When she met the nanny's gaze, she could see the pity in the women's eyes. Eleanor swiftly vacated the parlor. She could abide a lot of things but not pity, never pity. It would seem that she had fallen a long way off that pedestal.

CHAPTER 39

The open house yielded much different results than did the post-honeymoon ball. The house was alive with exclamations of admiration, the ballroom with laughter, conversation and music.

The old guard stood glowering in the corners, but this time their wives and daughters weren't cooperating. Ian made certain the ladies found plenty of other willing dance partners on hand. This time, he had widened the sphere, extending invitations to promising, young newcomers to Rossburg. One had opened a new kind of a store, which he called a "departmental" store. One had just started a new Sunday newspaper. Another operated a highly successful tannery. All were bright entrepreneurs, quietly building their wealth and waiting to be recognized. These were the cornerstones of Ian's new society. He prided himself on never making the same mistake twice—at least in business—he amended with a sharp sigh as his eyes fell on Eleanor flitting about the room.

She looked radiant in the purple, ondine, silk gown. The black chenille network covering the bodice gave her cinched waist the illusion of an even smaller measurement. Her upswept hair, caught in a series of ringlets on top her head, shimmered in the afternoon sunlight that streamed through the windows.

Ian watched her work the room with wonder, smoothly integrating old society with new, subtly breaching the breastworks of the inflexible establishment through a younger more forgiving generation. He looked about him. Eleanor's hand was everywhere, her excellent taste understated where necessary and obvious on a grand scale where there was a point to be made. No one could find any amount of criticism this time.

He turned to Parker Stanton. "Do ye think they've gotten the word yet?"

"Who?"

"Brown, Springer, Thompson and the rest that they're no longer the center of the universe."

"I would say it's beginning to sink in. I'm told Conover and Whiting have made inquiries about buying property on Grandview Place. I don't think they were too happy to find that you own all the parcels or that a number of them have already been purchased by your new friends. Oh, oh, don't look now, but young Jeffries and his wife just arrived."

Peter Jeffries looked pale, thin, and drawn. Ian noticed that his hands trembled, but he felt that old flash of jealously at the pitiable sight of him just the same when Eleanor went immediately to him. The ever gracious hostess, thought Ian angrily. She greeted Caroline as well, but to Ian's mind she fussed over Jeffries more than her role should demand.

"Excuse me, Parker, I have guests to greet."

"Tread lightly, Ian, you're looking a bit green."

Ian ignored his friend and swiftly made his way to his wife's side. "Good afternoon, Mrs. Jeffries."

"Good afternoon, Mr. Douglas. Your home is quite lovely. Easily the most beautiful in Rossburg, I would say."

"Thank ye. But I believe my wife deserves most of the credit."

Eleanor glanced up at Ian, both surprised and pleased by his recognition.

"Yes. Eleanor always did have excellent taste," said Caroline graciously.

Ian turned to Peter. "I had thought to see yer father here today." He hadn't really, but he wondered what connivance the elder Jeffries might be up to.

"Father is reviewing the land you sold him," said Peter in his haughtiest Oxford accent. "I believe he is expecting to meet with the surveyors.

He is quite anxious to be about his plans for the western expansion you know."

"I'm sure he is. And how do ye figure in yer father's scheme?"

"Yes, Peter, do tell us," prompted Eleanor. "You must have a very important position."

Peter took out a handkerchief and dabbed at his forehead. "Ah, I haven't been well of late. Father feels I should put my resources into recovering my health…for the time being."

Eleanor's brow was knit in consternation. "You do look rather pale, Peter. I hope it's nothing serious."

"I believe it a malaise I picked up while traveling abroad."

Ian was hard pressed to stifle a snort. Peter's European malaise was nothing more than a fondness for the poppy flower.

"Eleanor, perhaps you will be so kind as to give me a tour before Peter becomes 'indisposed'," said Caroline.

There was a slight edge to her tone that only Ian seemed to catch. He had always liked Caroline, and he felt sorry for her.

As Eleanor walked Caroline through the house and over the grounds, they reminisced, chattered and giggled like schoolgirls, the years of estrangement falling away. Eleanor wiped tears of laughter from her eyes and impulsively hugged her old friend.

"Caroline, I haven't laughed like this for so long. How could we have drifted so far apart when once we were so close?"

Caroline's mouth twisted into a wry smile. "If I remember correctly, your father had the audacity to lose his money." She looked off into the distance and sighed. "Oh, Eleanor, how I envy you."

Eleanor stared at Caroline in wonder. "You envy *me*?"

Caroline sighed. "Life can be so weary when one must live it according to the expectations of others. In truth, it is no life at all. Society exacts a high toll. It robs you of your identity and often times your happiness. But you…you have managed to escaped all that."

Eleanor didn't know what to say. Escaped! She had regarded herself as an outcast. For the last three years, she had practically crawled on her hands and knees to regain admittance into a society that was supposed to be her birthright.

Eleanor laughed lightly. "I'm afraid we share a different view of the matter."

This time Caroline looked at Eleanor in wonder. "Don't you see? You can do as you please. You have a house full of new friends outside of the circle…interesting friends who judge and admire you for your accomplishments rather than for your parentage. You've shown Harriet, my mother, and all the others that you don't need them and their silly, boring society. You've dared to break all their rules and still acquired wealth and position in spite of them.

"Remember that day in the park when you introduced Ian to all of us girls? We weren't very charitable when you told us of his background. Actually, I think we were all a bit envious and then relieved that you couldn't have him either. But we were wrong about him, Eleanor. He's worth two Peter Jeffries." Tears welled up in her eyes, and she forced a smile. "The fantasies of foolish children…it is a pity we have to grow up and see what a lie everything is."

Eleanor was momentarily speechless. She laid a sympathetic hand on her friend's arm. "Aren't you and Peter happy?"

Caroline bit her lip to hold back further tears. "Peter is not the man you or I or anyone else thought we knew."

Just then Peter called out, and they looked up to see him walking across the veranda to them. Caroline hastily wiped her eyes and struggled to compose herself. She grabbed Eleanor's hands in a tight grip. "Eleanor, please think kindly of me no matter what happens…no matter what you may chance to hear."

Before Eleanor could question her further, Caroline hurried off to meet Peter.

After Caroline and Peter had left, Eleanor stood on the ballroom balcony looking out over the garden where she and Caroline had strolled. She was still surprised at her friend's confession. What did she mean that Peter was not the man that anyone thought? To think that all the time she had envied Caroline, Caroline was envying her. The introspection and evaluations that Caroline had shared with her prompted Eleanor to take a closer look at herself, at her life, at Ian. She returned to the ballroom in a pensive mood.

The Browns, the Conovers, the Springers and the rest of the stodgy, old guard had departed as well, but Eleanor was surprised to note that their absence wasn't felt. The room was still very much alive with laughter, conversation and music. Several couples tea-danced around the ballroom; the party was far from being over. Caroline was right. Her new friends were brighter and much more interesting.

Her gaze strayed to Ian, so tall, handsome, and commanding, and her mind once again drew a comparison between him and Peter as it had so often done over the years. Peter had always come out the winner, but this time...she wasn't so sure. After seeing Peter and Ian together today, she never realized before how physically lacking Peter was and how silly he sounded with that ridiculous Oxford accent. Lately, and especially after her talk with Caroline, she wasn't sure about a lot of things. But childhood fantasies were difficult to let go of. Resentment yet remained below the surface, and she still wasn't ready to hand Ian the victory she knew he sought.

CHAPTRE 40

Tommy opened the door and laughed as his son Patrick ran to greet him. He scooped him up in brawny arms, and tossed his son high in the air to shrieks of childish delight.

Maven stood at the old cook stove, the tantalizing aroma of stew and fresh-baked bread emanating throughout the house. This was what quickened Tommy's step from the mill every evening, what defined his life, what made him happy. With all of this to come home to, he reasoned, a man could want for nothing more.

With his son in one arm, Tommy wrapped the other around Maven's waist and kissed her on the cheek. She looked up at him, her gold-flecked eyes soft with merriment, and he kissed her soundly on the mouth.

Maven flushed prettily. "Tommy, whate'er will Paddy be thinkin' now?" she chided with mock severity.

"He'll be thinkin' his da loves his mum very much. And when he's abed, his da is going to show his mum just how much," he added with a smile and a wink.

The pale blush on Maven's cheeks deepened to a bright red, and she gently disengaged herself. "Ye're late, Mr. O'Brien. Now let Paddy to his play and take yerself to the table before everythin' turns cold." She placed a bowl of steaming stew on the table.

Tommy set the boy on his feet and gave Maven a playful pat on the behind before seating himself. His stomach growled in anticipation as he attacked the delicious, thick stew. "Ah, Maven, me luv, 'tis pure heaven," he said. He looked up, suddenly conscious of a stillness in the house. "Where is everyone?"

"Yer mum went to sit with Mrs. O'Donnell. She be feelin' poorly again. Yer da be down at the pub. And yer sister and her wee ones are down the street."

Maven set a stack of sliced bread, still warm from the oven, in front of him. "Tommy, we need to be thinkin' of gettin' a place of our own. Paddy be gettin' too big to share our room. He should have his own."

Tommy reached out and pulled Maven onto his lap, a mischievous grin splitting his broad, weathered features. "Might six months from now be soon enough?"

Maven smiled. Dear Tommy, he would give her the stars in the sky if he could, but one had to be practical. "'Twill mean settin' back our plans for buyin' the dress shop and perhaps runnin' the risk of losin' it. I do na know how much longer Mrs. Drury will be wantin' to continue before seekin' another buyer," she said, worrying aloud.

"Maven, me luv, 'tis a house *and* yer shop ye'll have."

"Tommy, just because ye wish it, does na mean it can happen."

"It already has. The mayor decided not to put a park on Evergreen and Locust. Ian has the go-ahead on the housing project. He's givin' us first choice."

"How much will the house cost?"

"Nary a penny."

"He's just givin' it to us?" Maven stood up angrily. "I do na want the house, Tommy. I'll not be takin' Ian's charity."

The excitement in Tommy's eyes dimmed. "Ye know me better than that, Maven. I take no charity. I work for everythin' I get. Ian has placed me in charge of hirin' for the construction company. What with bein' foreman of the mill, 'twill mean longer hours for awhile. In place of the extra money and a raise for two years, I requested the house."

Maven heard the hurt in his voice and felt ashamed. "'Tis sorry I am, Tommy. I should have realized. I know ye to be a good, proud man. I could na married ye otherwise."

"Ye ne'er complain, Maven, but ye deserve more than this." His hand swept the dreary, crowded room with cracked plaster walls and windows that seemed always smudged with soot, no matter how often Maven washed them.

"Ye should have nice things, and I mean to see ye have them. This house is goin' to be just the beginnin'. Ye'll see. I'll make ye proud, Maven."

Maven dashed a tear from her eye and put her arms around his neck. "I'm always proud of ye, Tommy. There now eat." She turned back to the sink, uncomfortable with the naked love on Tommy's face. A sadness welled up inside her, and she quickly busied herself with the dishes.

"Aye, 'tis just the beginnin'," Tommy repeated between mouthfuls. "One day ye'll have a place almost as fine as Ian's new house. I took him some papers there today. Ain't never seen anythin' that grand, not even on the Row. 'Course they won't be callin' it that for long. The mucky mucks are fleein' the Row like rats from a sinking ship. They think the likes of us is goin' to give the neighborhood a bad name. We'll most likely be turnin' them mansions into apartments like we're doin' with the old Morgan place. Ian's been pickin' 'em up real cheap."

"Where are all the people movin' to?"

"Out Ian's way. Heard tell he bought up all the land round there and is chargin' a pretty penny for a lot." Tommy chuckled. "The man may be Scottish, but he's got the luck of the Irish."

Later that evening, Tommy walked into the tiny bedroom. Maven sat perched on the edge of the bed, languidly brushing her hair. He glanced over at the far corner. "Be the lad asleep yet?"

She nodded and willed herself to be responsive to Tommy's touch as he laced his fingers through the thick, auburn locks. With a work-roughened hand, he gently tipped her chin and pressed a kiss on her lips. Open desire showed in his eyes. "How goes your cycle?" he asked huskily.

"'Tis all right, Tommy."

"Be ye sure now? Ye know what the doctor said. Another wee one could kill ye." He sat down on the bed beside her and pulled her close, burying his face in the soft nape of her neck. "I could na bear life without ye, Maven."

Maven closed her eyes against the heavy emotion. If only he didn't love her so much. Trembling, she untied the ribbons and let the nightgown fall. "'Tis all right, Tommy," she whispered, reaching out to him.

CHAPTER 41

"A lawn party for your mill workers...here? Ian, you must be mad! I'll not have those...those...*people* traipsing through my house!"

Ian stood before the mirror adjusting his cravat, deliberately avoiding the reflection of his wife's tightly drawn features as she stood beside him.

"They will nae be in the house, Eleanor, they'll be on the lawn."

"I don't care if you lock them up in the cellar. I don't want them on my property! The very idea of paying court to hired help is...well, it is degrading. Whatever will the Jeffries think? Whatever will the Springers, the Conovers, and the Browns think? They are still furious with you for extending those ridiculous benefits to your workers, and now you want to entertain them!" Eleanor folded her arms across her chest and tapped her toe, her temper one step above exasperation and rapidly climbing. "You go too far, Mr. Douglas. You certainly will not have my support."

Ian's patience was strained to the breaking point as well, and he turned a cold eye to her. "I'll not be requirin' yer support, Eleanor, only yer presence. And I will expect ye to be pleasant when the time comes. I intend to run for mayor when the time is right, and I'll need the support of the workers. A little good will goes a long way. Ye might do well to remember that," he added, directing a pointed look her way.

Eleanor bristled, but her angry retort was cut short by a loud crash, shattering glass, and a child's wail.

"What the devil—" Ian turned sharply and tore through the connecting dressing room into his wife's room, Eleanor close on his heels.

She let out a shriek when she spied the exquisite, venetian glass perfume bottle laying splintered on the floor, her favorite perfume from Paris soaking into the edge of the rug. Mary Katherine sat at Eleanor's vanity, her eyes round with fear.

"Nosey broke it, Mama. Nosey done it."

The mention of the imaginary pet skunk broke Eleanor's thin thread of control. "You little brat!" she screamed. She pulled a cringing Mary Katherine from the chair and shook the little girl. "You know no such thing. You did it, and you're going to be punished for it."

"Eleanor! That's enough!" A grim, white-lipped Ian caught her hand as she was poised to strike the whimpering child. "'Tis only a bottle of perfume for godsake."

Mrs. Wilcox came scurrying into the room, immediately taking in the scene. "I'm so sorry, Mrs. Douglas. I know Mary Katherine isn't allowed in your room. I just left her for a few minutes."

Eleanor rounded on the hapless nanny in full fury. "If you can't manage the simple task of watching a two and a half year-old, Mrs. Wilcox, I will find someone who can!"

"Yes, ma'am."

Mrs. Wilcox started to lead Mary Katherine from the room, but the sobbing. little girl broke free and ran to Ian.

He gathered her in his arms and carried her to the nursery. When he returned, Eleanor was kneeling dejectedly on the carpet, cradling the broken bottle in her hand.

"What's the matter with ye!" he demanded angrily.

"Nothing is the matter with me." She stood and faced Ian, her blue eyes snapping. "That child may have you wrapped around her finger, but she doesn't have me. She needs to be taken in hand, not coddled when she disobeys."

"Explorin' is part of growin' up."

"She's becoming more unruly every day."

"Maybe she needs a mother."

"What's that supposed to mean?"

"From the beginning, ye've ignored her."

"I gave birth to her, what do you want from me?"

Ian stared down at Eleanor with wintry silver-blue eyes, his voice twice as cold. "I want ye to be a mother, then maybe ye can be a wife. So far ye've been neither."

His words speared her soul. No other words he had ever said to her had cut so deeply. When the door slammed behind him, an anguished cry tore from her heart. She didn't know how to be a mother. She didn't know how to be a wife. She didn't know how to be a woman. She only knew how to be Eleanor Morgan, society debutante.

*   *   *   *   *   *   *

The clock on the mantel chimed midnight. Ian hadn't returned home since their early morning argument, not even for supper, and Eleanor had no trouble guessing where he might be.

She paced the floor of her bedroom and walked the hall, ending up in the nursery for some reason unknown to her. Mary Katherine lay fast asleep. The light from the hall wall sconce fell across her tiny face, framed by a crown of yellow curls. She looked angelic.

Eleanor peered down at her and sighed, lightly caressing a soft, round cheek. The child possessed her mother's fine features, the delicate coloring, the vivid blue eyes, and the honey blonde hair, but she was her father's daughter. He had determined her conception, her name, her spirit. Nothing of the child, thought Eleanor, with a painful tug on her heart, belonged to her.

The house was empty and eerily quiet. Ian allowed no live-in servants except for Mrs. Wilcox, who slept in the room adjoining the nursery. On edge, Eleanor made her way quietly down the curved staircase. The heels of her slippers clicked on the marble floor as she moved across the foyer to Ian's study. She turned on a light, noting for the first time how much the room resembled her father's study in the old house on Millionaires' Row.

She poured herself a glass of sherry, kicked off her slippers, and reclined on the sofa, rubbing a foot across the soft, smooth leather. Her thoughts drifted to Ian as they had so often done over the past several months. She hated him, she wanted him, she resented him, she needed him. At the thought of him, all manner of emotions tore at her as no such thoughts of Peter ever had. Peter had been a safe haven. His devotion had demanded nothing from her in return. But Ian was a different animal. He demanded everything. She drained the glass and was debating whether or not to refill it when she heard the front door open and close. She slid to her feet and padded over to the doorway. Ian strode across the foyer to a marble-top table and began sifting through the day's mail.

"Problem at the mill...or at the Crystal Palace?" she inquired with silky sarcasm.

Ian glanced up, startled at first to see her, then indifferent. "I'm not in the mood for a fight, Eleanor," he said, turning his attention back to the mail.

Buoyed by the alcohol, her inhibitions diminished, Eleanor glided fluidly across the floor to him, the marble cool beneath her bare feet. She untied the silk wrapping and slid it off her shoulders, allowing the garment to pool at her feet.

"Is this what you go to that whorehouse for, Ian? Is this what you seek?"

Ian looked up from the mail. His jaw dropped, and he gaped at her, speechless. The light cast a soft glow over flawless, creamy skin. Her breast were high and full, her stomach flat, her hips gently rounded. Her figure had matured, taking on more womanly curves. He clenched and unclenched his fists, and his mouth went dry. God how he ached to have her, but he knew what would happen the minute he touched her. She'd wither with disgust.

As she looped her arms around his neck, pressing against him, Ian shut his eyes, mentally struggling against the seduction. He uttered an oath, and his hands closed about her waist as his mouth hungrily sought hers, devouring its soft sweetness. He didn't know what game she was playing, but at the moment, he didn't care what it was.

Eleanor's head buzzed and something inside of her drove her forward with a force too strong to stop as the shackles dropped from heretofore tightly held emotions. She suddenly wanted more...needed more. Ian swept her up in his arms and crossed the foyer to the study in long, quick strides.

The next morning, Eleanor groggily awoke with a headache and stared at her surroundings in confusion for a moment before realizing that she was alone in Ian's bed. No clothes touched her beneath the covers. Heat suddenly spiralled from her toes to the top of her head, bathing her features in a bright, reddish hue as images of abandoned lovemaking flooded her memory. Her sensory perceptions were much more vivid than her mental recollections at the moment. She wasn't at all certain how she ended up in Ian's bed from the couch in the library, but she knew that every part of her body had been stimulated, some in ways she could never speak of.

She jumped from the large, masculine bed, scooped up her wrapper and ran through the dressing room to her bedroom. After locking the doors, she climbed into bed and pulled the covers over her head. She felt shamefully wicked, but the remembered pleasure of the night before of Ian's mouth on her lips, her neck, her breasts, his hand on her...If this is what the girls at the Crystal Palace endured, then God help her, she envied them. Unfortunately, she was Eleanor Morgan, and she wasn't permitted such pleasure.

That night at supper, Ian couldn't believe that the reserved woman who sat stiffly across the table from him was the same uninhibited temptress who had invited him to make love to her the night before. If it weren't for the nail rakes on his back, he might have thought he had dreamed the entire occurrence. Ian's sigh was heavy with anger, resentment and disappointment. He seemed always to take one step forward and two back with her, and he was no closer to understanding her now than he was when he married her. What the hell did she want from him!

CHAPTER 42

The grounds of the Douglas estate was a kaleidoscope of sights and sounds. Beneath the colorful tents dotting the spacious lawn, the ladies gathered to escape the sun and to indulge in the latest gossip. Brawny youths, lured by the aroma of fried chicken and roast pig, attacked the food laden tables. In the horseshoe pits, derisive hoots and groans accompanied the clink of horseshoes, and the excited laughter of children, as they engaged in a variety of games, further electrified this balmy June day of 1885.

Ian and Eleanor, with Mary Katherine between them, stood beneath a rose-covered trellis at the end of the walk to greet the workers of Douglas Mills Enterprises.

"Smile," he said to Eleanor between clenched teeth. "It will nae kill ye."

"It is enough that I've opened my grounds to these people. I don't have to like it."

Ian sighed. He had given up thinking she might change. Still a small part of him continued to hope. "'Tis because of 'these people' that ye are able live the way ye do, Eleanor."

Mary Katherine tugged impatiently on her father's hand, the excited cries of children beckoning her. "Can I play, Papa? Please."

Ian glanced down at his daughter and smiled, a mischievous twinkle in his eye. "I do nae know, Princess. Ye might eat all the ice cream before the others get to it."

The child danced around him excitedly. "I won't, Papa, I won't."

"What do ye think, Mother?"

"I think that she should not be mingling with the children of mill hands."

Ian's features turned to stone, and he felt his little daughter go limp with crushing disappointment. He gave her hand a reassuring squeeze. "Off with ye now an' have yer fun, Princess."

With a glance at her mother's disapproving face, Mary Katherine hesitated. She dearly wanted her mother's love and approval, but she so wanted to play with the other children. Perhaps if she were especially good tonight…

As she scampered off, Ian turned to his wife. "Ye forget, Eleanor, I was once one of those mill hands."

"How can I forget? You refuse to let me," she snapped. She closed her eyes, took a deep breath, and turned back to Ian, offering a timid smile. "I'm sorry. Please, let's not fight. I have something to tell you that should please you."

Ian glanced at her, unable to dispel that last trace of anger. "I'm afraid it will have to wait. We have guests now."

Eleanor's face fell. Tears burned her eyes and nose, and she quickly averted her gaze to hide her hurt. When she was able to look up again, she saw the tension suddenly ease from Ian's face and a pleased smile curve his lips. She followed his eye to the arrival of Maven O'Brien and her family.

Ian's heart lurched at the sight of Maven. He had been worried that she might not come. She was in high humor, and he watched her eyes crinkle with amusement as she smiled up at Tommy. Ian felt a keen pang of jealously. Once she had gazed at him like that, like no one else in the world mattered. Their eyes met and the smile froze on Maven's lips as Tommy steered his family toward the host and hostess.

"Looks to be a mighty fine day, Ian…Mrs. Douglas," said Tommy. "On behalf of the workers, I thank ye fer yer generosity."

"'Tis glad I am that ye and Maven could come. I hope ye will enjoy yourselves." His eyes remained on Maven a moment longer before he turned his attention to the copper-haired boy standing beside her. "And who might this fine, young man be?" he asked.

The little boy grinned and stepped boldly forward with an outstretched hand. "I be Patrick O'Brien, sir."

Ian scanned the bright, sunny face with the splatter of freckles, the hazel eyes, and the long, wiry body. He was undeniably Maven's son. He smiled and shook the little boy's hand, immediately feeling a liking for the lad.

"Pleased to meet ye, Patrick. This is Mrs. Douglas."

Eleanor sucked in her breath as she looked down at the little boy. Black dots danced before her eyes, and she fought back a rising nausea. She had to grasp Ian's arm for support. When she looked at Maven, she saw that the puzzlement on the seamstress' face had turned to alarm.

"Please excuse me, I'm not feeling well," said Eleanor. "The heat…" She turned and stumbled up the path toward the house. Ian caught up to her, but she waved him off. "See to your guests."

Tommy shook his head as he and Maven made their way to the food tent. "Wonder what be ailin' her. She got a mite peaked all of a sudden."

Maven forced a dazzling smile. "Let's forget them and have a good time, Tommy."

As the afternoon wore on, the day turned warmer. Tommy joined Patrick in a sack race, and Maven sought refuge in a secluded shady spot from which she could view the festivities.

"Mind if I join ye?"

Maven stiffened and looked up sharply at the sound of Ian's deep voice. She shrugged, feigning indifference, and trained her eyes straight ahead. "'Tis yer party."

Ian seated himself next to her on the stone bench, his eyes darkening with emotion. "It has been a long time, Maven. Ye look wonderful."

Maven continued to stare ahead. When she didn't respond, Ian reached out to take her hand. A sudden warmth surged through her body, and she quickly pulled her hand away.

"Tommy loves me, Ian, with his whole heart. He be a good man, a good father. He has given me a good life, and he has my deepest respect. I will na hurt him."

Ian sighed. "I know, but there's a bond between us, Maven, whether ye wish to acknowledge it or nae, that one day will no longer be denied."

Maven looked down at her hands in her lap, still unable to meet his eyes. "Ye have my heart," she said quietly. "To my ever-lastin' shame, I fear 'twill always be so. But as God is me witness, I will ne'er acknowledge it. We must na ever acknowledge it. Too many people would be hurt, and I'll not be havin' that on me conscience."

Ian wished she would look at him. "The only happiness I ever found after Mum, Da, and Katherine died was with ye. I was a fool to let ye go."

Maven raised her head and finally met his gaze. "Ye dinna let me go, Ian. Ye pushed me away, just like ye pushed away everyone who cared about ye in the Basin and everyone who cares about ye now."

There was a long pause as Ian finally faced a truth that he had been running from for the last eight years.

"After Mum and Katherine died," he said slowly, looking off to the horizon, "'twas too painful to care. Everyone I loved died. 'Twas easier not to love anyone."

"Ye can na live without love, Ian. Sometimes ye have to take that chance."

"And sometimes the price be too high. On the morn that Da died, he told me he loved me. I was so full of anger and disgust for him, I just walked out of the house." Ian shook his head. "I could nae tell me own da that I loved him anymore. The way he looked at me…the hurt and sadness in his eyes…I have ne'er been able to get it out of my mind. I might as well have pulled the trigger of that gun myself, Maven. The thought of it has haunted me all these years. Ye were right. Tommy is the better man. I seem only to destroy the people I care for." He turned to her, willing her eyes to meet his. "I've hurt ye in the past, Maven, but know this, if there ever be another time for us, I'll ne'er hurt ye again."

"There can ne'er be another time for us, Ian. Ye must promise me this."

Ian sighed heavily. "Are ye happy, Maven?"

"Happiness is a matter of degree. I'm...content."

He stood up, bent down, and kissed her on the cheek. "I do nae make promises I can nae keep."

Maven watched him walk away with relief...and fear in her heart.

CHAPTER 43

In the smoke-filled back room of the exclusive Rossburg Men's Club, members of the Board of Trade puffed away on cigars and pipes with very little pleasure and much agitation.

"This thing is getting out of hand, Franklin. Douglas is drumming up too much support among the workers. There's more of them than there are of us. Hell, if the election was held today, he'd be the next mayor," said Sam Springer, his eyes blinking rapidly from behind thick spectacles.

"He's right," spoke up Thompson. "It's not like you to take a 'wait and see attitude'. We may just wait and see what we don't want to see."

Franklin Jeffries sat back unconcerned, a smile hovering about his thin lips. "Gentlemen, gentlemen, the workers' housing and benefits and that monstrous home he has built have to be taking their toll on Douglas' funds. It won't be long until he can no longer meet his commitments. Then watch who jumps ship when it starts to sink."

Whiting shook his head doubtfully. "I wish I could share your optimism. He has a steady enough income from the boom and the Utility Company, not to mention the damned notes he still holds on some of us. They're coming due, and we've all been given notice the interest will increase again. We'll be in the poorhouse before he is."

"So pay off the notes."

"It isn't that easy," said Brown. "We're losing too many good employees to Douglas. We've all had to dig deep to buy new machinery and give better wages. Funds are short, and, according to the Farmer's Almanac, the spring thaw is going to be late."

Jeffries gave a cynical chuckle. "So Douglas has you on the run, hostage to your own mill hands."

Conover snorted angrily. "Hell, Franklin, haven't you been reading the papers? There have been strikes going on all over the country—Pennsylvania, Tennessee, Idaho. This thing spreads like wildfire. Our mills could be next…what's so damned funny about that!"

"Gentlemen, Cyrus Morgan sat in this very room and made the same speech six years ago. It was an empty worry then. It's an empty worry now."

"I wouldn't look so smug if I were you," warned Brown. "I hear tell your railroad workers aren't all that happy either, especially with the Chinamen you brought in to work. I hear Eugene Debs is trying to organize a railway union. He could be looking in your direction as we speak."

Jeffries' eyes took on a hard, ruthless glaze. "Let him look. Maybe it's you who haven't been reading the papers. There is rife unemployment in the country. We're sitting in the catbird seat. Workers are like fleas. For everyone you shake off, there are three to take his place. But getting back to Douglas…"

"He's too big to fight, Franklin. He's the single biggest employer in town."

"And that is going to be his downfall."

"Before or after the election?" questioned another wryly.

"I wouldn't hold my breath, gentlemen," said an unexpected voice.

All eyes swivelled to Ian standing in the doorway. Mouths fell open, and from one a cigar dropped to the table. The esteemed members of the Board of Trade were frozen in various degrees of surprise.

Ian strode nonchalantly to the front of the room.

"I'm sure it was an oversight, gentlemen, that I wasn't informed of the meeting. I'll remind ye again, in case ye've forgotten, that I am a member of this Board. I should think the finances of Rossburg to be a more fittin' topic than mine."

For once, Franklin Jeffries remained speechless. It was Brown who found his voice first.

"Rossburg's finances are our finances. The city's economic health rests on our economic health, Douglas, and when one of us gets too greedy, the balance is upset and the city placed at risk."

Ian calmly turned to the speaker. "To whom might ye be referrin', Mr. Brown?"

Brown's florid face flushed deeper. "Who do you think, Douglas? You're driving us into bankruptcy with those damned notes you're holding on us."

Ian's brow rose in surprise. "And how might I be doin' that, gentlemen?"

"You know damned well there are some of us who will be needing to extend the due date on the notes until the spring thaw," said Brown. "George won't do us any favors."

The bank president bristled. "Now Ed, I told you, money is in short supply. The nation's gold reserves are declining and the bank is in no position at the moment to—"

"What is yer point, Mr. Brown?" interrupted Ian.

"You keep hiking the interest rate on the notes is my point. How long are you going to continue to bleed us? Until you have control of all the mills?"

Ian turned a sharp eye on Jeffries. "'Tis an intriguing thought, Mr. Brown. However, I can assure ye that yer blame is misplaced."

"How do you figure that?"

"I no longer hold the notes."

A stunned silence followed this disclosure, and Ian commanded the close attention of all but one.

"Then who the hell does hold the notes!" demanded Whiting.

Ian held Jeffries' cold, steady eye. "I'm not at liberty to say. I'm afraid that's up to ye gentlemen to find out for yerselves. Now if ye'll excuse me, I must leave for another appointment. I'm declarin' my candidacy for mayor."

*   *   *   *   *   *   *   *

Stanton's brow was furrowed with concern. "What do you think Jeffries is up to?"

Ian twirled the cigar in his mouth, circles of smoke wreathing his head. "Ownership of the mills. Then it comes down to just him and me."

"Why didn't you tell those slick-backed hypocrites that the one jacking them up is one of their own?"

Ian gave a snort of derision. "By the time Jeffries was finished explainin', he'd have them believin' he had done it for their own good."

"All kidding aside, Ian, what are you going to do? Jeffries is an unconscionable son-of-a-bitch. He'd sell his mother down the river. When he decides that money is thicker than friendship and calls in the notes, he'll have controlling interest in all the other mills. They're still healthy mills with some good lumber tracts. He could run you out of business. You have to expose him."

"'Twill be more effective if they find out on their own."

"They're small time. Those fools aren't capable of finding their way past a sham corporation. They'll just think they're in hock to some out-of-town company, and despise you all the more for selling them out to an outsider."

"Then I guess we'll have to make certain they take the road all the way to the end, won't we now?"

As Ian's smile broadened into a grin, Parker's eyes twinkled with the promise of intrigue.

"What do you have in mind?" he asked.

Ian's thumb and forefinger played across his mustache as he considered the matter.

"Who has the most to lose?"

"Thompson I would say."

"He also has the worst temper. Have Tommy find out who his toady is. Then get someone ye can trust to stake out the mills and see who Jeffries sends as a collection boy."

"Jeffries isn't stupid. He'll hire an outsider."

"I do nae care what it takes. Just find out who it is. Tommy will take it from there."

"A bug in the right ear?"

Ian smiled. "The grapevine serves up more than wine at the tavern."

"So you succeed in discrediting Jeffries. He'll still have controlling interest in the mills."

"Only if Brown and the others can nae pay off their notes in the end."

"How are they going to do that? The bank isn't going to take them off the hook."

"Rossburg National Bank may not, but ours will."

"*Ours!* Ian have you lost your mind! We don't have the capital to start a bank. You heard George Steiner. With the diminishing gold supply, money is scarce."

"Parker, in a sense Douglas Construction *has* been acting as a bank for mill workers buying the Evergreen Street homes. The accountant came to me with the idea. Best move ye ever made hirin' that fellow. He has the structure already in place. All we have to do is come up with fifty thousand dollars and apply for a charter."

Stanton ran a hand through his hair and across his face as he paced in front of Ian's desk, his mind furiously working the numbers.

"It might work," he said, dropping onto a chair. "I could possibly come up with twenty-five thousand dollars as a stockholder."

Ian laughed. "Then I know 'twill work for ye to invest a penny."

"One other thing. Those notes are due soon. Getting a bank charter can take weeks, maybe months."

"That's why ye're goin' to hand-carry the application to Harrisburg yerself. I'm sure ye will nae have any trouble findin' a legislator or two who owe us a favor."

Parker's smile held a measure of appreciation and awe. "I should have known you would have it all arranged."

Ian took out the bottle of whiskey from his desk, poured two glasses, and handed one to Stanton. "To the Lumbermen's Bank of Rossburg," he said, raising his glass in a toast.

CHAPTER 44

Franklin Jeffries leaned back in his chair, relaxed and pleased with himself. It had been a good week. He had just returned from spending several days at the West Meadow land. The work was finished, the expansion of his railroad completed. There would be no stopping him now. His would be a boundless empire.

A sudden commotion in the outer office disturbed his musing. The door flew open and Brown, Springer, Whiting and Thompson stormed in.

"I-I'm sorry, sir. The gentlemen wouldn't give me a chance to announce them," stammered the clerk.

"Leave and close the door behind you, Smithers," Jeffries ordered the beleaguered employee. He calmly took out a box of cigars and set it on the desk. "Help yourselves, gentlemen, and have a seat. It's good you've come. I've been thinking on a plan to keep workers away from the voting polls."

"This is not a social call, Franklin."

Jeffries looked up at Brown. His eyes shifted to the others, noticing the dark scowls on their faces. "What's Douglas been up to now?"

"This isn't about Douglas," said Whiting. "By God, Franklin, I thought you were one of us. Douglas was an outsider, but you…"

"Gentlemen, I'm very busy. Do you mind telling me what you are talking about?"

Springer stepped forward, visibly shaking with anger. "We're talking about you buying our notes from Douglas."

Jeffries quickly covered his surprise behind a half-hearted laugh. "Gentlemen, I don't know what lies Douglas has told you, but I can assure you I had only your best interests at heart."

"Douglas didn't tell us anything. Me and the boys did a little investigating."

"It isn't what you think. I bought those notes to safeguard the mills from Douglas. None of you was able to pay off your notes in full, and Douglas would have foreclosed on the mills. How do you think he gained control of Cyrus Morgan's property? He'd own practically the whole city with your mills."

Thompson, the youngest of the group, pushed to the front. His deep set eyes narrowed warily. "Now you own it. Was that the plan, Franklin?"

"Of course not. I had hopes that George would reconsider and decide to lend you the necessary money."

"Why all the secrecy, and why did you keep raising the interest rate on us, then?" asked Brown with a certain hesitancy.

He sensed them wavering, and Franklin Jeffries gave them a placating smile. "I know you to be proud men. We're all social equals. I purchased your notes secretly because I didn't want you to feel uncomfortable. As for the increases in the interest rate, it was meant for your own good. Since you all seem to have difficulty in managing your funds, it had been my intention to place the extra percentage in an account. In the event of a strike you will need extra capital."

"Thought you didn't believe strikes to be a threat," Brown challenged him.

Jeffries shrugged. "That doesn't mean you shouldn't be prepared."

Thompson stepped forward and placed a wad of bills on the desk, a touch of sarcasm in his tone. "I thank you for your interest in my well-being and preservation, Franklin, but I would have my note now. You'll find the debt paid in full."

Jeffries wasn't quick enough to hide his astonishment when the others followed suit, slapping down bills in front of him and demanding their notes as well.

"I thought George wasn't lending."

"George isn't. Douglas is," said Brown. "He just opened a bank...the Lumbermen's Bank of Rossburg. As businessmen, we find his terms more to our liking."

Jeffries slowly stood, pressing his hands flat on the desk and leaning forward. "Gentlemen, don't get in the middle between Douglas and me, or I'll break you just like I am going to break him." His words sliced the air like a fine blade.

The men backed away, their bravado deserting them. They had made a serious enemy today. They hesitated, their gaze shifting from one to the other, then turned to quickly depart.

"Thompson!" said Jeffries sharply. "I want a further word with you."

When the door had closed on them, the two men faced off, a spark of loathing in Jeffries' eyes, an uneasy curiosity in Thompson's.

"Stay away from my son's wife, or as sure as I'm standing here, you'll live to regret it...if you live at all," said Jeffries. "Do you understand me?"

Thompson's rugged, square-cut features twisted in mock concern. "Those are mighty strong words, Franklin. You got anybody to back them up!"

"Listen good, Thompson. I know your kind. Always out for a good time no matter what the cost."

"Maybe I used to be..."

"A leopard doesn't change his spots. And I'm telling you now, if I hear that you come so much as within a mile of Caroline, you *will* regret it. I'll not have me or my son held up to ridicule by you or anyone else."

Thompson laughed. "You're son is already a joke, so don't threaten me. Do you think people don't know that he divides his time between the opium den in your Chinese shantytown and the gaming tables at the Crystal Palace? What do you think they'll say when they hear that he prefers other men to his own wife?"

Jeffries' face turned ashen, and his fingers gripped the edge of the desk. "You're lying."

"Caroline arrived home unexpectedly one day and walked in on, shall we say, a rather shocking scene. Peter and his 'friend' were too engaged to notice her."

"You're lying! Who's going to believe you over me? By the time I get through with you, your word won't be worth a tinker's damn."

"Maybe. But there will always be the whispering and the wondering, won't there?"

*   *   *   *   *   *   *   *

Jeffries was beside himself with rage when he collared Peter outside the opium den later that night. He pulled his son into the cover of darkness away from any lights and slammed him up against the side of the building. Peter stared back at him wild-eyed and slack-jawed.

"I've turned a blind eye to your addiction and your gambling," Jeffries hissed, "but by God I'll not have a pervert for a son."

Peter went limp and began crying. Jeffries' stomach turned. It was bad enough he had a spineless twit for a son, but it was inconceivable and totally unacceptable to him that his flesh and blood was a "Nancy".

"I'm fifty years old and, at the moment, my only heir is you," he spat contemptuously. "If you don't present me with a grandson in twelve months, I'll no longer be responsible for your income or your gambling debts. I'll be watching you, Peter. The only bed I had better find you in is that of your wife. Am I clear?"

At a vicious shake from his father, Peter nodded, choking back sobs. Jeffries threw his son to the ground with disgust. "One year, Peter. See if you can grow a spine for that long."

*   *   *   *   *   *   *   *

Eleanor was about to enter the departmental store when she was waylaid by Harriet Brown, Belva Whiting, and Amanda Springer.

"Did you hear the news?" asked Amanda, clutching a hand to her ample bosom in shock.

"Caroline Jeffries has run off with Ben Thompson," interjected Harriet Brown, scooping her.

Amanda threw her friend a look of disgust and quickly picked up the narrative. "Just imagine the scandal. Why, her poor parents are beside themselves. They say that Franklin is absolutely livid, and I'm afraid Peter isn't doing well either."

Eleanor was speechless. Of all people, she would never have suspected Caroline to do such a thing. She knew her friend to have been unhappy, but to run away with another man…what must Caroline have been thinking? Poor Peter. How could she do this to him?

It was the talk of the town. Everywhere Eleanor went that day, it was the topic of choice. Scandal had never been this good. And while the pillars of society happily crucified Caroline, Eleanor was surprised to find the shopkeepers much more sympathetic.

"I think the poor girl done the right thing runnin' away with Ben Thompson," the milliner said to Eleanor. The sentiment was the same at the bakery, the general store, and at the draper. The only shopkeeper who refused to render an opinion, it seemed, was Maven O'Brien. She was too busy, she said, to engage in idle gossip.

"How can you defend what Caroline Jeffries has done, especially with her husband being so ill?" Eleanor demanded of the draper's wife.

"Ill!" The woman laughed heartily. "He's been an opium addict for years. Rose's husband is a handyman at Mr. Peter's house, and the stories that man has to tell…" She rolled her eyes. "Why if it weren't for his father, Peter Jeffries would be out on the street, begging alms. Gambled away all his money, he did, and his wife's, too. But that ain't the straw what broke the camel's back." She leaned close to Eleanor and said in a low voice, "The housekeeper told me that Mrs. Jeffries caught her husband in bed with

another man. If ye ask me, the poor woman done the right thing runnin'
off with a real man."

Eleanor reeled with shock from the news. Not Peter…it couldn't be.
It just couldn't be! She remembered, then, Caroline's comment that
Peter wasn't the man that they thought they knew, and her friend's last,
desperate appeal that Eleanor not think poorly of her no matter what
she heard rang clearly in her head. Eleanor staggered to a chair in the
shop. She suddenly felt very foolish. She had fancied Peter's unrequited
love for her to be at the root of Caroline's unhappy marriage. The few
times their paths had crossed socially, Peter hadn't paid her any special
attention, she recalled, but she had imagined that he watched and worshipped her from afar. Had Ian known about Peter? she suddenly wondered. God, she felt like such a fool!

*   *   *   *   *   *   *   *

Parker tapped out his pipe ashes into the ashtray. I don't like it, Ian.
Ben Thompson suddenly decides to sell his mill to Jeffries and leave
town…he hates Jeffries."

"The fact that he had been carrying on an affair with Jeffries' daughter-in-law might have had something to with it," said Ian dryly. "That
and the fact that Jeffries offered him nearly three times what the mill
was worth."

"You think it was a payoff…to get Thompson out of town and away
from Caroline Jeffries? Only Jeffries didn't expect his daughter-in-law to
go running off with the man." Parker shook his head. "I don't know, Ian,
a payoff is just not Jeffries' style. He would have preferred ruining
Thompson, grinding him into the dust, instead of paying him all that
money. No, there's more to this…"

"Like blackmail?" suggested Ian.

"Yeah, but what in the hell could Thompson possibly have on Jeffries
that could be so damaging? Jeffries doesn't part with his money easily.

Maybe Jeffries just figured to kill two birds with one stone. Get rid of Thompson and hit you at the same time."

"How do ye figure that?"

"Divide and conquer. You pulled the loans out from under him, and he fights back by buying out the mill owners one by one. Then it all comes down to just you and him."

"Not if he's payin' three times what the mills are worth. He might win the battle, but he can nae possibly win the war. He would be too weak financially."

"Men bent on revenge aren't always rational," said Parker. "God knows you haven't always been." Catching Ian's glare, Stanton muttered a perfunctory apology.

Ian lit up a cigar and leaned back in his chair. Whatever the case, the matter demanded further scrutiny. Unknowns where Franklin Jeffries was concerned were dangerous.

"Tell Tommy to keep his ear to the ground," he said.

Both men looked up in surprise as Eleanor strode into the mill office.

"Mr. Stanton, I'd like a word with my husband, if you please—alone."

Ian and Parker exchanged curious glances. The firm set of her chin and mouth and the intensity of her gaze gave evidence to a tightly coiled anger, and Parker quickly gathered up his papers. "Of course, Mrs. Douglas." He left, quietly closing the door behind him.

Ian stubbed out his cigar and got to his feet. He was reminded of that long ago day when she happened into the mill looking for her father. She had found him instead. She looked just as beautiful, but instead of appearing lost this time, she was a woman with something on her mind. He pulled up a chair for her, but she refused it.

"You've heard the news about Caroline Jeffries and Ben Thompson?"

"Aye, that I have."

"I'm going to ask you something, and I want the truth."

"I've always given ye the truth, Eleanor."

"Perhaps, but there have been times when you've conveniently omitted it as well. You knew about Peter being an opium addict, about him gambling away all of his money?"

"Aye."

She closed her eyes and took a deep breath. "Did you know that…that he preferred men to women?"

Ian wanted to shout *Hallelujah!* but he answered with a simple nod of his head instead.

"How long? How long have you known all of this?" She grilled him like an inquisitor.

"Since before we were married."

"Why didn't you tell me?"

"Would ye have believed me? 'Twas better for ye to find out on yer own. I had hoped it would nae take these many years though," he added wryly.

Eleanor trembled with anger. "I must have given you quite a good laugh, throwing up a destitute, opium-addicted fop in your face. I hope you enjoyed it because it is the last laugh you will get at my expense."

As she turned on her heel and stormed out of the room, confusion rippled across Ian's features. He had expected redemption not condemnation. He was still trying to absorb this new twist, when he heard her scream. He raced outside just in time to see her go tumbling down the stairs.

$$* \quad * \quad * \quad * \quad * \quad * \quad * \quad *$$

Ian paced the doctor's office, his features drawn. Parker and Tommy sat quietly in the corner. Stanton had been in Tommy's office when they heard the scream. He would never forget the look on Ian's face as he flew down the stairs to Eleanor's crumpled form. It was Tommy who had the presence of mind to fetch the carriage from the livery. They had all breathed a sigh of relief when Eleanor moaned as Ian gently lifted her in his arms.

The door to the examining room finally opened, and they all jumped to attention as the grim-faced doctor appeared.

"I'm having her transferred to the hospital for a few days. She suffered a concussion and some nasty bruises, but no broken bones." He took Ian aside. "I'm sorry, Mr. Douglas, but your wife lost the baby..." The doctor's voice trailed off as Ian stared at him in shocked disbelief. "I take it she didn't tell you. She was nearly four months along."

Ian shook his head, his face a stone mask. "I want to see her."

"In a few hours. I've given her a powder to make her sleep. Perhaps I ought to give you something."

"I'm fine." But he didn't look or feel fine. He turned to the others. "Tommy, ye and Parker take the carriage back to the mill. I'll walk."

"Ian, that's nearly three miles—" Parker shut up when Tommy nudged him.

"He knows how far it is. Come along, Mr. Stanton, I'll drop ye at your office. I think we've finished with our business," said Tommy.

Eleanor gazed numbly at the dim, green walls of the hospital room. Her last recollection was of her tumble down the stairs of the mill office. She seemed to fall forever. She hadn't remembered the stairs being so long. Everything else was a haze. But she had clearly heard every word the doctor had said. She knew they had moved her from the doctor's office to the hospital while she slept to minimize the pain...and she knew she had lost the baby. Tears swam in her eyes.

She turned her head at the sound of the door opening. Ian entered the room. He looked haggard, but this time she drew no satisfaction from it.

"Why did ye nae tell me about the bairn?" he asked, his voice ragged and hoarse. There was no accusation in his tone, just pain and an obvious struggle to understand.

"I tried...that day of the lawn party. You said you had guests to see to," she replied quietly. She didn't have the energy to fight.

Ian winced, recalling the moment. He started to raise his hands, but let them drop helplessly to his side. He wanted to gather her in his arms, but past history revealed more than once, she had no need or desire for him. And his emotions were pretty bruised at the moment. God, he must be a beast! His own wife couldn't tell him she was expecting their child.

"I'm sorry," he said simply, not knowing what else to say or do. There was a long pause as he continued to struggle with his guilt. If only he had told her about Peter in the beginning this might not have happened. She couldn't have hated him then anymore than she probably did now. "The doctor said not too stay long, that ye need yer rest. I'll drop by to see ye tomorrow."

Eleanor's heart dropped. He blamed her for the loss. She knew he did, and what's more she couldn't fault him for it. She had been foolish for so many years; she was tired of being foolish.

1886

CHAPTER 45

Ian stood on the gazebo draped with red, white and blue bunting. His voice rang clear and steady across the gathering crowd in the park.

"Douglas Mills and Construction has been a leader in this town. Since I became a member of the Lumbermen's Exchange, yer wages have increased, the mills have become safer, ye've been given the opportunity to build new homes, to build a better future for yer children. As a member of the Board of Trade, I have seen to it that a measure of Rossburg's wealth, which yer sweat has provided, has touched ye as well. The Gas and Water Works have expanded services to include yer neighborhoods. As mayor of Rossburg, I will pledge to work for the continued improvement of Rossburg for all its people…"

Maven watched Ian, entranced by the power of his voice, the power of his speech, the power of his presence. The immigrant lad from the wrong side of the tracks had made good. The only person from the Basin who had the determination to do what everyone else only dreamed of doing. But at what price? she wondered. He looked out over the people, seeming to catch sight of her, and smiled—a smile meant for her. A ridiculous notion to be sure, but Maven claimed it for her own, pressing it close to her heart. She wondered if this ache and longing inside of her would ever leave her.

Hecklers strategically placed on all sides of the group suddenly interrupted the passionate flow of Ian's speech. Several of the mill workers exchanged heated words with the disorderly men, and fists seemed certain to follow when several burly men materialized to take up positions directly next to the hecklers. One look from them, the hecklers fell silent, and the rally ended without further incident.

Ian stepped off the platform and immediately became lost in the throng of people that surrounded him. Maven smiled. There was a time when Ian was that "trouble-maker who stepped too high". Now they proudly claimed him as their own.

She turned and walked quickly out of the park. She took the trolley to Fourth Street and began to walk in the direction of her house, changed her mind, and turned back to the square. She had no desire to go home. Though it was Sunday, Tommy had gone to the mill to finish some paper work and had taken Patrick along with him, allowing Maven time to herself.

She was looking tired, working too hard at the shop and at home, he had told her. It was true. Mrs. Drury was turning over more and more of the work to her, but she never thought of the shop as work—more of a respite from thought. Here her mind became too full with the business of fittings and cutting and sewing to think of anything else.

Maven unlocked the door to the shop. The usual transformation she experienced when she stepped over the threshold was missing. The merry tinkling of the bell that welcomed all comers failed to lift the heaviness from her heart, and she wished now that she hadn't gone to the rally. Listlessly, she removed her hat, patting her hair in place more out of habit than necessity.

A shadow fell across the sun-spattered floor, and Maven stiffened as Ian appeared in the doorway. He stared at her for a long moment, then slowly closed the door behind him.

"I saw ye at the rally," he said, his voice low and husky. "By the time I was able to break free of the crowd, ye were gone. I hoped ye might come here."

Maven moved to the cutting table, picked up a bolt of cloth and began to rewind it.

"I should na have gone to the rally," she said.

"But ye did."

"Ian, ye should na be here."

"I told ye, I do nae make promises I can nae keep."

Ian crossed the distance between them and seized Maven by the shoulders. The bolt of material slipped to the floor, and a sob escaped her as Ian's mouth closed on hers. She threw her arms around his neck, responding to his hungry kisses with a love she had labored so long and hard to repress. Ian pulled her tighter to him and pressed fiery kisses along the soft column of her throat. His fingers began to work the small buttons of her bodice when she drew back. The effort it took her was clearly marked in the agonizing twist of her features.

"Ye'll have no need to force me to yer will, Ian. God help me, 'tis me own desire as well," she said in a trembling voice. "I pray ye do na ask it of me, for I could ne'er live with meself if we did this act."

Ian stared at her as tears slowly slid down her face. He had never seen Maven cry. In that moment, he realized just how much he was hurting the woman he had promised never to hurt again. He hadn't meant for this to happen. He had just wanted to talk with her, to hear her voice, to see her smile, but the moment he saw her, he knew he couldn't stop there. He ached down to his soul these days. He needed a healing touch. He needed love, the kind of love only she seemed capable of giving.

Slowly, he dropped his hands. "I'm sorry," he said. His voice was a hoarse whisper, his own face a mask of suffering and guilt. "I...I promise, I will nae try to see ye again." He turned and left the shop.

Maven pressed her face against the wall, her tears staining the white plaster. She feared that Ian might be right, that the bond between them was stronger than either of them.

CHAPTER 46

Ian jumped out of the carriage before it had come to a full stop in front of the firehouse, his features tightly drawn in a thunderous scowl. Parker came running to meet him.

"How did this happen!" demanded Ian.

Parker fell in beside Ian's brisk stride. "Jeffries has to be behind it. He's the only one underhanded enough and with enough clout. Tommy was the first to notice it and came to me when he couldn't find you."

"How many have voted?"

"Too many. The polls have been open for two hours."

"Get someone out to every voting station to alert the voters."

"I already have."

"Just make damned sure that everyone who passes through the voting lines from hereon knows that Mayor Bradley's name and mine have been reversed on the ballot. That damned Jeffries."

"He's counting on a lot of men not being able to read," said Parker.

"He won't be far wrong," said Ian, grimly appraising the situation that threatened to dissolve his political career.

"I don't know what the hell difference it makes. The voting polls don't open until the mill hands are at work, and they close before the work day ends. You're the only mill owner who gave employees time off to vote."

Ian abruptly spun on his heel and headed back to the carriage.

"Hey, where are you going?" Parker called after him.

"To show Brown and the others that I make a much better friend than foe."

"Hold on. Maybe you don't have to." Parker pointed to a wagonload of men pulling up to the firehouse.

Ian and Parker grinned as they recognized the mill hands from Brown's mill. Close behind was another wagonload of workers from Springer's and Whiting's mills.

"I'll be damned," murmured Ian.

It was a long day. Ian impatiently awaited the final count of the election at home. His eyes periodically darted from his pocketwatch to the clock on the mantel, the brandy decanter within easy reach. He heard the front door open. It had to be Parker. The footsteps weren't hurried or excited or jubilant as they crossed the marble foyer, and Ian's confidence dropped a notch.

He looked up from his desk, his eyes narrowing with concern as Parker slowly walked into the study devoid of his usual jauntiness.

"Well?"

Parker poured himself a drink and collapsed into a chair, his handsome face unnaturally drawn and gray. "The ballots are three-fourths counted. It's close, Ian. The election is just too damned close to call yet. We may have to demand a recount."

"Have ye posted men at the polls?"

"One at each elbow of the vote counters. I don't know…Jeffries may have won this round."

The two men sought to alleviate the tension with more snifters of brandy while they silently watched the hours tick by. By midnight there was still no word.

Ian finally stood, massaging the tight muscles in his neck. "Go home and get some rest, Parker. We'll know soon enough in the mornin'."

＊　　＊　　＊　　＊　　＊　　＊　　＊　　＊

Franklin Jeffries attacked his breakfast in unusually high spirits. Further enhancing his culinary favorites—ham, eggs, and biscuits—was his anticipation of favorable election returns. He took out the morning paper and eagerly scanned the front page. He dropped his fork and promptly acquired acute indigestion as the headline screamed out at him: DOUGLAS WINS BY NARROW MARGIN.

He felt the heat spread up his neck and into his face. Veins stood out on his temples like throbbing ropes. When he finally exploded, he vented his fury in a string of burning epithets as he ripped the paper to shreds.

Jeffries stormed over to the window. Across the river, smoke from the mills mingled silently with the morning mist. So! Whiting, Springer, Brown and the others had decided to align themselves with Douglas. His lips lifted in a sneer, and his laugh was decidedly unpleasant as his hands tightened into fists. He would crush them. He would crush them right along with Douglas. He would take his time, let them wait and wonder. Then he would strike when they least expected it.

CHAPTR 47

Eleanor gazed at the reflection in the mirror. A beautiful woman gazed back. She no longer possessed the fresh, youthful beauty of an ingenue, but a more breathtaking beauty of a mature woman of twenty-eight. Eleanor smiled. She liked what she saw. Instead of a corroding anger and desperation, she saw serenity and a quiet strength, if not a bit of resignation, in calm blue eyes. Even more, she liked the spark that suddenly came into them.

She was a recognized member of society, one might even say a leader, once again. Her husband was the mayor. He was rich and powerful and that made her rich and powerful—her life's goal. It had been a circuitous, most unexpected route and not one without a great deal of pain, but she was there. The problem was that none of it mattered to her anymore.

During her convalescence, she had done a good deal of thinking. She had thought about what Henney had told of her parents' unhappy life together, of the parallels of their life and hers with Ian. She had thought about Caroline and Peter. She had started to re-examine her life once before, after her conversation with Caroline, but this time, Eleanor really took stock of herself. The end analysis was difficult and sobering. It wasn't easy for her to admit that her life had been based on meaningless values and empty goals and that she had failed miserably as a mother and a wife.

"Eleanor, we must be leavin' now, or I'll be late for my own inauguration."

Eleanor turned to see Ian, attired in a gray top hat, dark blue coat and gray striped trousers, standing in the doorway. A very properly dressed Mary Katherine held his hand. Eleanor had begun to notice that they adopted a wary, subdued manner in her presence.

Mary Katherine whispered shyly to her father. "Mama looks pretty, doesn't she, Papa?"

Ian gazed at Eleanor for a long moment. She looked stunning in the gray crepe dress trimmed in dark blue velvet bands. "Yes, your mama looks very pretty," he murmured.

Eleanor thought she saw a spark in his steel-blue eyes, but when she looked again, his features were inscrutable, and she desperately hoped it wasn't too late to reach him.

She flashed a tentative smile. "You look very pretty yourself, Mary Katherine, and your papa is quite handsome."

She fastened her hat and threw a cape around her shoulders. Ian held out his arm and she readily took it.

Standing by Ian's side as he was sworn in as the next mayor of Rossburg, Eleanor felt something for him she hadn't been conscious of before—respect and pride. It had been a long time since Rossburg had a mayor who was his own man.

Though the day was gray and cold this January day of 1887, it was anything but somber as well-wishers thronged the podium at the conclusion of the ceremony. A reception followed at the Carleton House. Douglas Mills was closed for the day and most of the mill hands and their families were in attendance. Eleanor stood uncomplaining in the reception line for over two hours, her smile slipping just twice—once when she came face to face with Maven, and once when she caught sight of Mary Katherine happily playing with Patrick O'Brien.

*　　*　　*　　*　　*　　*　　*　　*

Franklin Jeffries stomped into the house in a black mood. He had been held hostage for the better part of the afternoon in a traffic jam of wagons, coaches, and carriages bearing people into the city for the inaugural activities.

Jeffries cursed and grabbed the readied tumbler of whiskey from the perceptive butler, downing the drink in a single gulp. He signalled for a refill, and the butler quickly obliged.

No other newly elected mayor had put on such a spectacle and certainly not for mill workers. The man hadn't been elected President for chrissakes! Jeffries took his second glass of whiskey and headed for the drawing room. He had to think. Whatever it took, he was going to force that bastard out of office and out of Rossburg.

He ordered his supper to be brought to him. Hours later, his plan was laid. The staff had long since left and the butler, the only live-in servant, had retired for the evening. As the grandfather clock at the bottom of the stairs chimed the tenth hour, Jeffries rose and stretched. A sly smile of satisfaction spread across his face. It was time now to seek his bed, and he'd have no trouble sleeping this night.

*   *   *   *   *   *   *   *

Ian finished dictating the letter and dismissed his administrative clerk for the day. He lounged back in his chair, feeling a bit smug as mayor. Parker Stanton closed the door on the employee and slouched low in a chair, his mood pensive.

"Somethin' has been botherin' ye all day, Parker. What is it? The transition went smoothly. Bradley yielded graciously."

"I guess that's what's bothering me. Everything has gone too well. You've been mayor for six months now, and Jeffries hasn't thrown one cog into the wheel. What do you think the man is up to?"

Ian shrugged. "Could be Jeffries sees more advantage in workin' with us than against us."

Parker shot Ian a dubious look. "You don't believe that any more than I do."

Ian chuckled. "You see conspiracy everywhere, Parker, ever since Cyrus Morgan pulled that angry husband trick on ye."

Parker glared at him. "Go ahead and laugh. But mark my words, Jeffries isn't done with you yet. He's a snake lying in some pretty tall grass. Just because we can't see him, doesn't mean he isn't there ready to strike."

"Ye worry too much." Ian pulled out his watch and marked the hour. 'Tis time to go home. We'll talk of this another day."

*　*　*　*　*　*　*　*

When Ian walked into the house, he was surprised to find that Eleanor was waiting supper for him in the dining room.

"Mary Katherine tells me that you plan to take her to the mills tomorrow," she broached casually when the maid had served the meal and departed.

Ian bit off a piece of roll. "I take her every Saturday."

"Yes, I know, but I'm not sure that it is a good idea. The mills are no place for a child."

"The mills are Mary Katherine's heritage."

"She is not yet six years old."

"'Tis not too young to be learnin' about the business and to be knowin' the people. They'll be workin' for her one day. Besides, she enjoys playin' with Patrick O'Brien."

Eleanor hesitated. "That's what I mean. Mary Katherine is an impressionable child. She should be associating with children of her own…type. There is a private boarding school in Philadelphia that would better suit her."

Ian looked at his wife in disbelief. "Send Mary Katherine away…no I will nae hear of it."

"She is becoming wild and unruly. The way you and the nanny dote on her, the child knows no discipline. She possesses no social graces. Good heavens, she is beginning to sound and act like those people at the mill." The minute the words were out of her mouth she knew she had made a mistake.

Ian stiffened. "Might I remind ye," he said with cool disdain, "'twas those people who made you first lady of Rossburg. Besides 'tis about time that Mary Katherine knew her roots."

"What doors will roots from the Basin open for her?" demanded Eleanor, losing her temper. "What good will it do her to know how common her father's stock is."

Ian's eyes glinted like polished steel and were just as hard. "I wasn't referrin' to just my roots, madam, but to yer father's, which, I believe, make them yers as well. The only difference separatin' ye from them is money. And I can remember a time when ye had none." He stood up and walked to the doorway. "I'll take my supper in town."

As the front door slammed on his departure from the house, Eleanor sighed wearily. She had thought she was making some progress in mending their relationship. Why did she always seem to make the same mistakes?

*   *   *   *   *   *   *   *

It was Saturday, and Ian always looked forward to Saturdays at the mills, especially with Mary Katherine. He picked up a cigar, clipped the end, and lit it, wreaths of smoke encircling his head. At the sound of childish laughter, he walked to the window and looked out. Mary Katherine and Patrick were playing tag. He smiled, delighting in her fun, taking devilish pleasure in her rumpled appearance. He knew Eleanor would have a fit. She continually complained that the child was becoming a hoyden. Mary Katherine is a child. She will grow out of it, he always argued back. Beneath the dishevelled curls and dirty face, he could see the makings of a beauty. Her hair was the color of spring wheat and her eyes as blue as cornflowers. And though she possessed the fine, delicate features of her mother, she had the stubborn will of her father. Ian's smile broadened. One day she would be a match for any man.

His gaze shifted to Patrick. He was a fine, handsome boy, smart, strong, dependable...perhaps a bit too serious for his age. He had Maven's stamp all over him. Again, Ian felt that knife twist in his stomach.

"Thought you would be here," said Parker, striding into the office. He walked to the window and watched the children play for a few minutes. "They're great kids."

"Someday Patrick will make a fine foreman of these mills," said Ian.

"What if he wants more?"

Ian looked at Parker in surprise. "What more is there?"

"What you have."

Ian's eyes narrowed. "What are ye tryin' to say, Parker?"

"What if he wants to marry Mary Katherine? What if she wants to marry him?"

The silence was deafening. Ian turned away and stubbed out his cigar. The aroma suddenly soured. If he spoke his heart, he would be guilty of the snobbery he so often accused Eleanor of. The revelation stunned him.

"Ian," said Parker soberly, "Eleanor came to see me. I've been your partner for years, and you've trusted me with all aspects of your business. Trust me now when I say that Eleanor is right. It is in Mary Katherine's best interest that she attend the school in Philadelphia, be with children of her own background."

"And what is my background, Parker?"

"You're a wealthy industrialist, Ian. Mary Katherine is the daughter of a wealthy industrialist. It's as simple as that."

"I have to ask myself, would Mary Katherine be better off with the likes of Peter Jeffries?"

"No, but she might be with the likes of Joseph Benway's son. That departmental store has been a real gold mine for Benway. They're a good family."

It was a long moment before Ian spoke. "I'll have to think on the matter."

Tommy strode quickly into the office, a worried frown creasing his forehead. "I may be wrong, but I think there might be some trouble brewin', Ian."

"What kind of trouble?"

"A stranger by the name of Pittman has been tryin' to stir up the men at the tavern with some nonsense about an eight-hour work day. Looks to me like he's been catchin' the ear of more than a few."

"Charlie Pittman?"

"Aye. Ye've heard of him?"

"He used to be Gomper's right-hand man until they had a fallin' out. Heard he had a part in the strikes in Chicago last year."

"What's he doing here?" asked Parker.

"My guess is he's a rover."

Tommy gave an indignant snort. "Well, he won't be findin' any business here at this mill. The men are well-paid, they get their medicine and doctors paid for, they got nice homes. What more can they ask for?"

"Do nae underestimate Pittman."

Ian immediately called for a meeting of the Lumbermen's Exchange.

"What's so damned important, Douglas?" demanded Brown, taking his seat at the table with the other mill owners. He didn't take kindly to having his poker night interrupted.

"Charlie Pittman is in town," said Ian. An audible gasp and sudden stillness answered him.

Whiting was the first to find his voice. "What's he want?"

Brown cursed loudly. "To make trouble, what else. That's what guys like him are all about. They don't give a damn about the workers. They just want to keep the pot stirred up. Thanks to you, Douglas," he said snidely, "the damn mill workers here live better than any other laborer in the country. What's left to give them?"

Ian sat lost in thought for a moment, running a forefinger across his mustache. "I think we would be wise to keep an eye on the matter for now," he said. "That, and make certain the machines are kept in safe working order." At this, he shot Brown an uncompromising look before continuing on in a dry tone. "A little respect and recognition on occasion from you or your foremen might not hurt either, gentlemen."

CHAPTER 48

Tommy sat in the corner of Cozey's Saloon and watched the tall, thin man with the sharp features and pockmarked face continue to try to stir discontent. For nearly a week now, Tommy had observed Charlie Pittman at work, collecting only a handful of disgruntled workers despite his skillful manipulation.

Pittman was not a happy man. He stood at the bar and glowered over the crowded room. This was his most difficult job to date. Frustrated, he ran a hand across the back of his neck. How the hell was he supposed to fan a fire where there weren't any hot coals!

Pittman glanced down at the end of the bar where a sullen man sat drinking alone and casually sidled up to him.

"Buy you a drink, friend?"

The man looked up, the scowl on his weathered face unchanged. "I ain't yer friend."

"Maybe not, but I could be the best one you ever had."

The man gave a disbelieving grunt. "Not unless you got a job fer me. I got eight mouths to feed."

"What's yer trade?"

"Mill hand. I work the saws."

"Doesn't 'pear to be a shortage of mill jobs around these parts."

"Might as well be. I punched out the foreman at Brown's today. The son-of-a-bitch has been ridin' my back fer days."

"So get a job at another mill."

"Those bastards all stick together. The word's probably out on me now."

Pittman grinned inwardly. He had his pigeon. "Don't seem fair to me. Ye've probably worked damned hard for years."

"Nigh on twenty...since I was fifteen. Ain't as young as I used to be. Been playin' out afore the end of the day."

"Twelve hours is a long work day. Ain't much time to spend with the family. Seems to me you men should be demandin' a eight hour day."

The man looked at Pittman as though he were crazy and laughed. "Ain't ever likely."

"Why not? The miners in Idaho got a eight hour day. It's the truth, so help me God," said Pittman catching the man's dubious look.

"How'd they get it?"

"With the backing of the union, they went on strike. The Labor Reform Union can help you mill workers do the same here. You find me a couple more interested mill hands, and I'll have representatives of the union in town within forty-eight hours to help you organize."

"I don't know..."

"Look, you already lost your job. What have you got to lose? Did you ever see any mill owners workin' a twelve hour day?"

"No."

"That's cause they got you poor fools to do it for them. You get old afore your time, and they just get richer. I'm stayin' at the City Hotel, room fourteen. Bring some of your friends by tomorrow night, and we'll talk some more." As the man started to hedge once more, Pittman added, "It's to your interest, friend."

"How's that?"

"None of you realize the power you have. What would you say if I told you that, together, you mill hands have more power than the owners have?"

"I'd say you was nuts."

A wide smile split Pittman's scarred face. "What gives 'em power is money. What do you think would happen if you workers all refused to work and the mills had to close. They'd be ruined. The real power, friend, is in your hands."

"Yeah. I ain't never thought of it that way. But ye ain't gonna get the men to strike. Most of 'em live pretty good. How they gonna put food on the table if the mills can't pay?"

"The Labor Reform Union will provide assistance to any man who strikes. "You could be a hero, a leader in labor reform, friend, instead of just a man out of a job."

*   *   *   *   *   *   *   *

Parker passed a hand wearily across his face. He wasn't getting much sleep these nights.

"I don't know, Ian. This business is getting out of hand with the union."

"It'll blow over if Brown and the others do nae overreact."

Parker shook his head. "Pittman and that damned Labor Reform Union are playing up the high rate of accidents, which they say are caused by too long a work day. I'm telling you, the situation is a powder keg waiting to blow. It's just a matter of someone lighting the fuse."

"Come now, Parker. Ye always tend to be overcautious."

"I believe you were the one who said not to underestimate Charlie Pittman. You sit here playing politics all day. You don't know what it's like in the mills now. The tension is so thick, you can cut it with a knife. The foremen are losing control. They're afraid to say or do anything for fear of sparking a riot. Tommy is at his wit's end. Just one incident is all it's going to take, Ian."

Ian frowned as he started to grasp the seriousness of the matter. "How the hell did everythin' get so out of hand? A few weeks ago, Pittman could nae raise any interest, and now it has come to this?"

"Pittman has been building up the mill hands' importance. He tells them that together they have more power than the rich mill owners, that they have the capacity to cripple the mills if they so choose. That's pretty heady stuff for a laborer when all his life he has been made to feel powerless."

Ian understood the feeling well. "Tell Tommy to shut down the mills for a few days with pay and advise Brown and the others to do the same. Maybe it will take the wind out of Pittman's sails."

"And if it doesn't?"

"We'll deal with that when the time comes."

     *   *   *   *   *   *   *   *

Pittman looked furtively over his shoulder as he made his way down the dark alley to a side street. The electric street light cast elongated fingers of illumination across the deserted road. The carriage waited for him in deep shadows out of view of the light, and he had to stare hard to see it. He fought off a feeling of uneasiness. He wasn't liking this business much at the moment. Things weren't going the way he had envisioned and now he had to explain why to the "man".

Pittman considered his employer. He didn't know who he was, but he didn't like him either. Their meetings were always the same—late at night on some, little traveled side street. The man sat in the darkness of a plain, black carriage, and they conversed through a small, curtained window.

This didn't have the feel of his other jobs. The miners and the railroad workers had a legitimate complaint, but the mill hands of Rossburg...the union agitator shook his head. No, there was more behind this than met the eye. He made a hesitant approach.

"You're not earning your money, Mr. Pittman," a disembodied voice hissed from inside the carriage.

Pittman bristled. "It's difficult to fan discontent where there ain't any. I'm doin' the best I can."

"Your best doesn't seem to be good enough."

"Look, I was startin' to get things stirred up when the mills suddenly decided to give everyone a little holiday." Pittman's voice took on a sarcastic edge. "It ain't easy to get men to bite the hand what feeds 'em that good. I been all over. I know the labor market, and I'm tellin' ye the mill hands here have it better than any laborer in the country."

"I'm not paying you top dollar to whine and make excuses, Pittman. Do something and do it fast!"

Pittman cursed under his breath as the carriage suddenly lurched forward and bowled off into the night. He returned to the tavern. It was more crowded than usual, and he carefully scanned the faces. When he finally found the disgruntled mill worker who had been fired from Brown's mill, a gleam came into his eyes.

CHAPTER 49

Ian looked down from the window of his mayoral office with growing uneasiness. The crowd continued to swell in the square across the street, and he estimated there to be about two hundred people.

Charlie Pittman stood on a bench, flanked by representatives of the Labor Reform Union.

"How many of you mill workers have suffered the loss of fingers, the loss of use of hands or legs? To add insult to injury, how many of you were blamed for the accident? Yes, blamed for costing the mill owner money…never mind the loss to you, to your family, the fact that you are crippled for life. Chances are you was told the accident wouldn't have happened if you hadn't been lazy or careless. Am I right?"

A loud chorus of cries assured him he was, and Pittman continued on righteously. "The fact of the matter, friends, 'tain't yer fault. And it wasn't the fault of those four men injured at Brown's mill this week. They was jest plum tuckered out after twelve hours of backbreaking work. I'd like to see a mill owner who can match anyone of ye hour fer hour without losin' a finger. Join in this fight against tyranny. As an individual standing alone you will lose. As a group standing together you can win."

A frightening clamor rose in rousing response, and a chant went up demanding an eight-hour day or strike. Crudely lettered banners displayed the slogans: WORKERS UNITE, LABORING MEN SHOULD

RULE and MEN STAND UP FOR THEIR RIGHTS; COWARDS DO
NOT. Suddenly the crowd turned and began to move en masse down the
street. The chanting rose to ear-splitting shouts. Ian ordered his carriage
to be brought around and was bounding for the stairs when he nearly collided with Parker running through the door. Before Stanton could get a
word out of his mouth, Ian grabbed him and pulled him along.

"Come with me, unless I am mistakin', they're headin' for the mills."

Parker Stanton raced after him down the stairs. As they leaped into
the carriage, Ian shouted to the driver, "To the mills, Henry, and be
quick about it! Take the canal bridge."

The driver nodded and cracked the whip. Immediately, the carriage
sped off, throwing the men back against the seat.

Parker took out a handkerchief and wiped his brow, still breathless
from the exertion and high excitement. "I just left Brown. According to
his foreman, the saws were sabotaged…if you can believe him. We all
know Brown pinched pennies when it came to improvements in his mill."

Ian's jaw was set in a hard, tight line. "If the mills are shut down,
there'll be a run on the banks."

Parker looked at him in alarm. "My god, I never thought about that."

Acutely conscious of their slowing pace, Ian stuck his head out the
window and uttered an oath. "The street is jammed. Ye take the carriage
and fetch the police. I'll get to the mills faster on foot."

"Ian, you can't go out there. People know you. The mood they're in,
they'll tear you apart."

"I'll be all right. I'll take the back streets."

"But Ian—"

"I do nae have time to argue, Parker. Just get the police." Ian opened
the door and jumped out, quickly disappearing down a side street.

The crowd had become a mob, picking up more people as it went,
surging down Mill Street to the canal. In a race against time, Ian skirted
the throng as long as he could, but now he could no longer avoid being
in the thick of it. He would have to take his chances at being recognized.

He had long ago shed his coat and vest, and his clothes were rumpled, his face streaked with perspiration and dirt as he elbowed his way across the canal.

An acrid smell filled the air, and a cheer roared from the incensed crowd. As black smoke billowed from Douglas Mill Yards, Ian stepped up his efforts and finally broke through the mob.

"There he is. There's Douglas!" someone shouted.

Hands grabbed at him, tearing at his clothes and hair. Ian tried to fend them off, but he was exhausted from the run across town and was fast losing ground. Suddenly, strong hands pulled him from their midst. He looked up to see Tommy beside him. Together they fought their way to the hastily constructed barricade where loyal employees pulled them to safety.

"Fire!" someone shouted.

Angry clouds of smoke and the crackle of burning lumber filled the air.

"'Tis the planing mill," yelled Tommy.

He and Ian shouted orders to the workers to pump water from the holding pond. Men scurried frantically about the yard, struggling with the hoses, trying to put out the fire before it spread to other buildings.

Hours later, the air was heavy with smoke for miles around as the mills smoldered. Ian kicked at a charred board on the ground and moodily surveyed the destruction. A muscle twitched angrily in his jaw. For several long minutes, he just stared, saying nothing.

Tommy cleared his throat, uncomfortable with the silence. "Luck be with us, Ian. We only lost some lumber, the planin' mill and yer office. And there's some roof damage on the saw mill. 'Tis easy enough to rebuild."

"Always the silver lining, ay, Tommy. Ye sound like Maven." Ian laughed but it sounded hollow.

"Tommy is right," said Parker. "We saved most of the papers. Brown's, Whiting's and several of the other mills were burned to the ground before the police could stop that crazy mob. Count your blessings...and thank Tommy. If he hadn't gotten that barricade across the entrance when he did, your saw mill could be gone too."

Ian turned to Tommy. "Ye saved more than my mills today, Tommy. Ye saved my life as well. I will nae forget it."

He extended his hand. Tommy shook it, and their eyes locked. All that had passed between them fell away, and for the moment, they were just those boys from the Basin...the Pine Street Warriors. When Tommy turned away, Ian suddenly felt alone and adrift again.

"Tommy, take yerself home and get some rest," he said. "I have a feelin' we're not done with this business yet. Parker, close the mill for the rest of the week, and post a twenty-four hour guard."

As Ian's eyes followed Tommy out of the yard, he felt a twist of envy. Tommy would go home to Maven, and she would soothe and reassure him as only Maven could.

"Are you going home?" Parker asked, interrupting Ian's thoughts.

Home. Ian let out a harsh laugh. "No, Parker, I'm not going home. I'm going to my house."

*   *   *   *   *   *   *   *

Freshly bathed and clothed, Ian dragged himself into the drawing room. He grabbed the decanter of whiskey and a glass and collapsed wearily into a leather chair. His body was sorely bruised, and he felt far older than his twenty-eight years.

He poured himself a drink and took a healthy swig. At the rustle of taffeta, he sighed and threw back the rest of the liquor. "I do nae have the energy to argue now, Eleanor."

"Was the fire bad?" Her voice held an anxious note.

"Bad enough, but ye do nae need to worry, yer wealth is intact and yer social position secure."

Eleanor winced at the sarcastic bite in his tone. "I'm not here to fight, Ian. Amanda said it was a pretty ugly crowd. I-I was worried you might be hurt."

Ian let out a harsh laugh and refilled his glass. "Ye'll be left well taken care of."

Eleanor swept across the room to him and furiously swatted the glass out of his hand. The fine crystal shattered against the hearth, splattering whiskey across the floor and staining the fine oriental rug. Astonished, Ian looked up into flashing violet eyes.

"You clod! I'm trying to tell you I'm sorry for your trouble at the mill...that...that I want things to be different between us. I'm tired, Ian...tired of this rancor," she ended on a lower, more hesitant note.

Her courage fading, color flooded her features, and she turned to run from the room. Ian jumped to his feet and grabbed hold of her arm. She was so beautiful, and, at this moment, he needed her more than he could ever remember. His mouth closed on hers. Encouraged by a faint response, an intense longing surged through him and with a certain desperation, he pulled her close against him. His kiss became more demanding. When she didn't pull away, Ian pressed her onto the sofa, lifting her skirt.

Eleanor frantically recalled the parameters of her duty. She tried not to show the distaste the etiquette books deemed proper, for she had come to realize that it angered Ian. Yet, she could not appear overzealous in her passion for fear of disgusting him, as the etiquette books also strongly suggested. More than anything else, it was important to her to be considered a lady. She thought she had struck a careful balance when Ian suddenly went still.

He sighed heavily and rose. "Even after seven years, ye still can nae bear the touch of a common mill hand, can ye?"

Eleanor looked up at him dazed and hurt by his sharp, almost jeering tone. "No...I don't understand...Where are you going?"

"Out! Where a woman welcomes my touch."

As the front door slammed behind him, Eleanor's eyes filled with tears. She thought she had done everything right this time.

*   *   *   *   *   *   *   *

In his office at City Hall, Ian stared out the window, troubled and weary. It hadn't been an easy three weeks.

"Ian, did you hear me? I have some bad news," said Parker soberly.

Ian slowly turned. He laughed harshly. "The town has gone mad. The mills that escaped burnin' have been closed for twenty-two days because men tryin' to return to work have been beaten and threatened by the strikers. Women and children are starvin', and the economy of Rossburg is in shambles. The Labor Reform Union hasn't come through with its promised assistance, yet the strikers are continually persuaded to refuse the proposal of the Lumbermen's Exchange of an eleven-hour workday, ten hours on Saturday, and a twenty-five cent per day advance. Ye be mistaken, Parker, there could nae be any more bad news left to report."

"It's Tommy, Ian. He's been beaten. He was found down near the canal."

For the first time, Ian took note of the lack of color in Parker's face and the gravity of his tone. His chest constricted, and he caught his breath sharply. "How bad?"

"I sent someone to bring his wife...and the priest. He's over at the hospital. Your carriage is waiting downstairs." Parker barely had the words out of his mouth before Ian flew past him and down the stairs.

*   *   *   *   *   *   *   *

When Ian was ushered into the hospital room, he was stunned. Tommy lay writhing and moaning, his battered face barely recognizable.

The doctor pulled Ian side. "He's pretty broken up inside. There's a lot of internal bleeding and organ damage. This wasn't the work of just fists. I'm sorry, Mr. Douglas. There is nothing I can do for him except to give him something to ease the pain." He shook his head in defeat. "The rest is in God's hands."

Ian stared at the doctor, unwilling, unable to accept the diagnosis when Maven rushed in, followed by the priest. She swooned at the sight of her husband, and Ian reached out a hand to steady her. As the priest began to administer the last rites, Ian was forced to accept the inevitable. He helped Maven to a chair at the bedside and slipped out into the hall. He never had dealt well with death.

Three long, agonizing hours elapsed before Maven emerged from the room. "Tommy is conscious. He wants to see ye," she said in a voice devoid of emotion.

Pale and worn, she held herself erect. Ian suspected her spirit must be as crushed as Tommy's body, but she exuded an aura of strength that amazed him. He longed to take her in his arms, to comfort her, to gather some of her strength to himself. Instead, he nodded and entered the room, taking the chair she had vacated.

"I'm here, Tommy."

Tommy turned his head, and stared at Ian through swollen, purple slits. His jaw was broken, and it was difficult for him to speak. "Patrick…son…Maven." He grew agitated, driven by the need to tell Ian something.

"'Tis all right, Tommy, you do nae have to worry. I'll take care of them."

Tommy struggled to say more, but the effort proved too great, and with a final shudder, his body went limp. Ian stared in numb disbelief, a tear rolling down his cheek. From a distance, his mind registered the sound of Maven's soft weeping.

CHAPTER 50

At the gravesite on the bleak hillside cemetery, deja vu gripped Ian. Twice before, he had stood here—first for his mother and sister and then for his father. Now he stood here for Tommy, and this time it lay to him to comfort Maven. He cursed God silently and pledged his wealth to find the culprit and extract retribution.

Most of the town had turned out for the funeral. Ian could almost feel envious. Tommy had been well-liked and respected. Ian wondered briefly how many would have turned out if it had been his funeral instead. He looked out over the crowd. It came to him in a flash of introspection that while he had money and power, it was perhaps Tommy who had possessed the real wealth.

When the last person had paid his respects, Ian helped Maven and a stoic Patrick into the carriage. Maven placed her hand on his arm as he started to hoist himself in beside her.

"We'll be all right from here, Ian. I'd like to be alone for awhile now. Thank ye for everythin' ye've done for us."

Ian hesitated, reluctant to comply with her wishes, but the amber-flecked green eyes she fixed on him were unyielding.

"Very well, Maven, if that is your wish. If ye be needin' anythin'..."

"There is somethin' I do need. Do na let Tommy's death be for nothin'. Stop this strike, Ian, before anyone else gets hurt."

* * * * * * * *

Charlie Pittman clumsily put the key in the lock, wavering drunkenly from side to side. The damned thing seemed to have a mind of its own, and he cursed it loud and long. After several attempts, he finally succeeded in unlocking the door and lurched into the room, kicking the door shut behind him. He fumbled with the gas light until it flickered to life, then staggered to his bed. For the first time since coming to town, Charlie Pittman didn't give a damn that it was empty this night. Come morning, he was going to put this town behind him.

The death of Tommy O'Brien had a sobering effect on the strikers, and, ignoring his counsel, they had voted to accept the original proposal of the Lumbermen's Exchange.

"If the 'old man' don't like it, he can go to hell," he grumbled.

It was a testament to his, Charlie Pittman's, skills that he had been able to string along the strikers as long as he had without the benefit of the financial aid the Labor Reform Union had promised but hadn't produced. He had done enough, and he was going to get out while the getting was good.

Pittman stared dumbly at a footstool which suddenly came to life, sliding across the floor and stopping at his feet. He peered about the room and started in terror as his befuddled mind beheld a great hulking aberration hovering in the shadows.

"W-w-what-who-are you?" His voice quivered and perspiration beaded his forehead.

As Ian walked into the light, Pittman recovered some of his cockiness and grinned. "Well, well, if it ain't his Honor, the Mayor, payin' ol' Charlie a visit."

"I'm not here as the mayor tonight, Pittman."

Pittman's lips curled. "Then why are you here?"

"To avenge the death of my friend."

"Them things happen during a strike. Can't tell ye no more'n that."

As Pittman turned away, Ian's large hand shot out and steel-like fingers wrapped around the man's scrawny neck.

"Oh, I think ye can tell me a great deal, Mr. Pittman." The man gasped and clawed at his throat, but Ian only tightened his grasp. "Who sent for ye in the first place?"

"No one," said Pittman in a strangled voice. "I just heard there was some worker unrest in the mills here." His eyes bulged as Ian's thumb pressed against his Adam's apple.

"I do nea like that answer. Try again."

Fear of death produced a sobering effect on Pittman. "All right, all right. He ain't worth losin' my life over. Ain't paid me but half what he owes me anyways. I don't know his name. That's the truth…I swear it," he hastened to add as Ian's hand tightened again. "We always meet on some dark side street late at night. He stays inside his carriage. I ain't never seen him."

"Tell me about the carriage."

"It's just a carriage…black…one of them expensive kinds."

Ian threw the hapless creature to the floor in disgust where he collapsed in a heap, wheezing and gasping for air.

"That description could fit a hundred carriages in Rossburg. Who's responsible for the beatin' of Tommy O'Brien?"

Pittman massaged his neck, cowering as Ian took a menacing step toward him. "They was thugs the 'old man' brought in from out of town. They wasn't supposed to kill O'Brien. Just rough him up a bit as a warnin'. The strikers was makin' noises 'bout returnin' to work. The 'old man' didn't want that to happen."

"I want names."

"Don't know any. They skedaddled as soon as they heard that O'Brien died. I swear, that's all I know."

"Take yer union and be out of town before noon tomorrow, or I'll see ye charged for murder as an accessory. An' ye might not make it to trial. Do ye understand me?"

Pittman nodded vigorously and scrambled out of Ian's path as he moved toward the door.

*   *   *   *   *   *   *   *

Ian kicked open the leaded, glass-paneled door and bowled past the astonished butler.

"Where's Franklin Jeffries?"

The look on his face precluded any argument, and the butler mutely indicated a partially closed door down the hall.

Jeffries sat contentedly in his favorite chair in the drawing room enjoying a cigar and an after-dinner brandy. He nearly choked on his drink when Ian burst into the room. He stared up at Ian looming menacingly over him, and a stunned second lapsed before he regained the use of his sharp tongue.

"How dare you force your way into my house! Get out, or I'll have you arrested. Now won't that be a scandal for the town…'Mayor breaks into prominent citizen's home'—"

Jeffries' words ended abruptly as he was grabbed by the lapels of his smoking jacket and lifted free of his chair, his face brought to within inches of Ian's.

"Save your pretense for someone else, Jeffries. Because of some sick vendetta ye have against me, I know ye hired Pittman to come to Rossburg to stir things up in the mills. An' I know ye're responsible for Tommy O'Brien' death. I can nae prove it yet, but by God I will if I have to turn over every rock in Rossburg. When I do get the proof I need, not even God will be able to help ye. Ye're going' to regret tryin' to get to me through people I care about." He released Jeffries and shoved him roughly into the chair.

Jeffries' eyes shone like red-hot coals, and his mouth twisted into a savage smile. "Try all you want. You'll never pin anything on me, Douglas. But perhaps someone did you a favor. With O'Brien out of the way now, you can finally have his wife. Of course, Eleanor may have something to say on the matter…"

Ian lunged for him, once again dragging him to his feet, but the older man, now on guard, proved to be a strong adversary.

"You lean too hard on the O'Brien business, and you may find yourself a prime suspect," he said with a snarl. "A certain detective who happens to be in my employ has witnessed several of your visits to Mrs. O'Brien's dress shop. Perhaps the two of you took advantage of the union trouble to be rid of her husband."

Ian recoiled sharply, the impact no less than if Jeffries had dealt him a physical blow. He knew he should walk away, but the nasty, superior smile on Jeffries' face drew his fist like a high-powered magnet.

Jeffries dropped to the floor, a stunned look replacing the arrogant smile. Ian stepped over him and met the horrified butler in the doorway.

"I suggest ye take out the garbage," he said. "'Tis leaving a foul odor in the room."

Behind him, Jeffries let out a furious shriek. "I'll get you for this Douglas! You've not heard the last from me!"

CHAPTER 51

Eleanor straightened her skirts, patted some color into her cheeks, and critically viewed the figure in the floor-length mirror. Childbearing and the accumulative years had left few marks on the trim body. The full breasts remained firm and high, the waist, small and enviable, and the hips narrow. An abundance of still radiant, blonde hair framed a yet flawless complexion. The blue eyes deepened to the color of violet as her thoughts turned inward, away from the vision in the mirror.

Mary Katherine had been sent off to the school in Philadelphia. Parker Stanton, presented with Eleanor's view of the matter, had proved to be a good friend and a strong ally in convincing Ian to send Mary Katherine away. When the trouble started, Ian was much more in agreement with the decision, fearing that his family might become a target. Mary Katherine, though not happy about the idea at first, became more enthusiastic about the adventure when she stepped onto the train. Eleanor smiled wistfully. The child reminded her much of herself on the day she had been sent away to school. It had been just after her mother had died. She had been so scared and had tried so hard not to show it.

Eleanor gazed about the room. She hadn't expected the house to feel so quiet and empty. She deeply regretted that she hadn't been able to be the loving, compassionate mother that Mary Katherine needed and deserved. She hoped that some day she could find it within herself to make amends to the poor child. Perhaps if her own mother had been a happier, more loving person; if her father had been less indulgent and more attentive; if she and Ian had gotten off on a better foot; or maybe if she had been better prepared to assume the role of a wife…When she looked into the mirror again, dear Henney was looking back at her.

"Look close, child," she could hear the old nanny saying to her as she had so often done over the years. "That little word 'if' takes up half the space in 'life.' Don't spend time fretting about things that might have been. Get on with fixing what you can."

Eleanor wished that she had taken that bit of advice to heart years ago. She prayed that it wasn't too late now. She was tired of this bitterness, the angry resentment between Ian and her. She was tired of the empty feeling inside of her. It made her feel old and weary. She laughed softly at a subtle irony. There was a time when she was unrivalled in her prowess for flirting, and now she had no idea how to court her own husband.

The death of Tommy O'Brien had profoundly affected Ian. In his grief, it seemed to Eleanor that he had turned to her in a way he never had before. Last night, he had been most attentive at the theatre. Upon returning home, he had kissed her cheek and, for a moment, she thought he might ask to come into her bedroom. For a moment, she had thought of inviting him in. But he hadn't asked, and her courage had failed her.

This evening she had taken more care than usual with her toilette, choosing a dinner gown of pale mauve, duchess satin with a lace fall over the large puffed sleeves and low-cut bodice. Her golden hair was caught in a coil on top of her head with wispy curls arranged over her forehead. She gave herself a last cursory glance and nodded in approval.

She felt like a schoolgirl on her first date, as she skipped down the stairs to meet Ian in the dining room. If they could just start over, she knew she could do better. It wouldn't be easy, but she was determined to try.

Eleanor stopped on the last step when the sound of Ian's agitated voice reached her from the drawing room through the partially open door. Silently, she crossed the foyer, a vague feeling of disquiet gripping her.

"The bastard thinks he can turn the tables on me!" shouted Ian, pounding his fist on the table.

"Is there any evidence to support his charge of an affair?" It was Parker, and he sounded worried.

"Nae. What kind of a fool do ye take me for?"

"A big enough one. Jeffries' detective caught you leaving Mrs. O'Brien's shop, didn't he? He must have seen something."

Eleanor stood frozen at the door, the spark fading from her eyes.

"He has nothin'."

"Because there is nothing to tell or because you think you've been cleverly circumspect?"

"I'll not answer to ye or to anyone, Parker."

"Ian, for godsake, man. We're talking about a possible murder charge here, if Jeffries decides to plant the idea in Chief Tenley's head that you engineered Tommy O'Brien's death so you could have his wife. Even if nothing comes of it, the scandal could cost you dearly. You should never have confronted Jeffries tonight. He's coiled and ready to strike now."

"What do ye suggest we do?"

"Nothing until I can make some inquiries and find out what kind of ammunition he has."

Anxious to be about his mission, Parker flung open the door and nearly ran into Eleanor.

"Mrs. Douglas...my apologies," he said, startled to see her. "I-I didn't know you were there."

Ian quickly appeared in the doorway, and he and Parker exchanged looks, both wondering how much she had heard. When neither could find the words to dispel the awkwardness of the moment, Eleanor summoned a tremulous smile.

"Dinner is served. I didn't mean to intrude. Perhaps Mr. Stanton will join you, Ian. As it turns out, I don't feel up to dining this evening."

She turned and, with great dignity, retraced her steps across the hall, her back straight, her head held high.

Ian called after her. "Eleanor, wait."

But she continued up the stairs without a backward glance.

Parker angrily turned on Ian. "You're a damned fool, my friend. You had to have a thoroughbred, but you made no damned effort to learn how to care for one. Yesterday is gone, Ian. If you use your head, you might save tomorrow." He strode across the foyer and out into the night.

Ian returned to the drawing room and poured a stiff drink…then a second…and a third, downing them in quick succession. There was an ache deep in his soul that he had never been able to banish or satisfy. With Tommy's death, it seemed only to intensify. He looked around at the opulence of the room, taking stock of the expensive furnishings, of his many possessions. He was a long way from the Basin. He had everything. He had nothing. He felt as bankrupt as Cyrus Morgan was the day he died.

His eye fell on the life-size portrait of Eleanor. She had sat for it a year ago. The artist had captured the small, perfect features, the sheen of the honey blonde hair, the brilliant blue eyes, and the luscious curves of her small-waisted figure so well, Ian half expected her to walk off the canvas. But she was no more accessible to him in the flesh than she was on canvas. He turned away flushed with drink and an indulgent sense of pride, certain he had detected a hint of derision on the lovely face, a mocking smile on the slightly parted lips. He could take scorn. He could take indifference and rejection. But by God, he would never suffer derision or pity. He called for his hat and coat.

Eleanor stood at the top of the shadowed stairs and watched the front door slam behind her husband as he departed the house. A single tear slid down her cheek, as her heart splintered into a thousand pieces, each bearing its own tragic imprint.

CHAPTER 52

Maven opened the door to find Ian standing on her doorstep. He looked older in the few weeks since she had last seen him. The shock and emotion of Tommy's death had carved deep lines into his handsome features. She wasn't surprised to see him, but she felt a flash of anger that he hadn't allowed her more time to gather her strength.

"I...may I come in, Maven?"

"Ian, 'tis late."

"I know. I've been walkin' for hours. I tried not to come, but I could nae help myself."

Her heart responded to the suffering in his voice, and she motioned him into the parlor.

He laughed. It was a cynical laugh, heavy with confusion and hurt. "I went down to Cozey's Saloon tonight. Tommy and I used to drink there every Saturday night in the old days, shoot pool, throw darts, complain about Hawkins, the foreman at the mill. My God, Maven, I grew up with those men, worked side by side with them for years, and they looked at me as though I was a stranger to them."

"Ian, that was in the past. Ye stopped bein' one of them when ye became their employer and moved to the Row," Maven said gently. "You can nae have it both ways."

She offered him a chair, but he declined, too restless to sit. He obviously had something weighing on his mind, and Maven waited patiently for him to find the words.

He threw his hat and coat on the sofa and turned to her. "Maven, I can nae lose ye again. I'm goin' to offer Eleanor anythin' she wants if she'll grant me a divorce. I want to marry ye." He gathered her in his arms. "I need ye, Maven," he murmured. "I've needed ye all my life. I can nae go on without ye."

Maven shut her eyes against the tears that threatened to spill down her cheeks, and there was a sad, little smile of resignation on her lips. Just when she thought she could feel no greater pain, she was proven wrong. She pulled away from him for the last time.

"Go home, Ian. Go home to yer wife," she said, choking back tears.

The look on his face was one of stunned bewilderment. "I do nae understand. Ye love me. Ye said that ye do."

"Aye, Ian, I love ye, but ye do na love me."

"Of course I do."

Maven shook her head. "No, Ian. I've tried to deny it for too many years. Ye've only spoken of yer need for me, never once of yer love. There be a difference. Did ye not hear yerself just now? Even now ye can na say the words."

"They're hard words for any man to say."

"Not when he truly feels them."

"Maven, ye know ye've always been special to me."

Maven took a deep breath and composed herself as best she could. "I know, Ian, but ye do na love me in the way that I need to be loved. I'm yer refuge when ye're in need of comfort, when ye need what Eleanor can na give ye." Her voice broke with the painful revelation. "More's the shame I denied me heart and soul to the love that was always there for the love that never was. Go home, Ian. Go home to Eleanor and find what ye seek."

"Without ye, I have no home."

"Home is where yer heart is. And I know it isn't here with me. It lies with Eleanor. It always has."

Ian turned away angrily. "What is this, a conspiracy? First Parker, now ye. Well, I'm sorry to contradict ye both, but Eleanor has despised and resented me since the day I married her. It would make little difference if my heart was there or nae."

"Can ye blame her now? Ye forced her into a marriage based upon vengeance and gain. Did ye ever court her? Did ye ever make her feel loved or special or appreciated? Did ye ever try to look at things from her point of view? In Eleanor's eyes, ye robbed her of everythin' that was important to her—her wealth, her position, her respect, her pride. Of course she resents ye."

"Then we must be even," he said, his voice laced with bitterness, "for neither has Eleanor let me forget that she was forced to marry a mill hand."

Maven was far from feeling like the all-wise saint, but there were words that needed saying, words she should have said years ago.

"Ye forced yerself into a world ye knew nothin' about, Ian, and made no attempts to understand or respect it. Can ye deny that ye have feelin's for Eleanor?"

"What does it matter? She has none for me."

"Ye're wrong, Ian. I saw it in her eyes at the inauguration when she looked at ye. Ye just haven't been able to see it for all the anger in ye."

"Ye're the one who is wrong. She cringes every time I come near her."

"Have ye ever asked? She's as much afraid as ye are. Love is like a fragile flower. It needs to be cultivated, Ian. It takes patience, understandin', respect, and bein' able to entrust one's self to another. Give her a chance, and she'll give ye one."

The words hung heavy between them, until a banging on the door shattered the silence. Maven went quickly to answer it, grateful for the interruption. If Ian so much as touched her hand, she didn't know if she could stand her ground.

With a curt nod to Maven, Parker rushed in. He went directly to Ian, seemingly not surprised and a little disgusted to find him there.

A scowl darkened Ian's features. "What are ye doin' here, Parker? I told ye before, my personal life is none of yer business."

"This has nothing to do with you and Mrs. O'Brien, though heaven knows you being here does nothing to help you and everything to help the police."

"The police…what are ye talkin' about?"

"Franklin Jeffries was found murdered at his home an hour ago. He was shot."

Ian stared at Parker, momentarily stunned. "What's that have to do with me?"

"You're the number one suspect."

"Me! Why me?"

"Why not? Everyone knows there's been bad blood between the two of you for years. You were at his house earlier this evening and left him laid out on the floor after a heated argument. You have motive. Jeffries had threatened to expose your…relationship with Mrs. O'Brien. Come, man, the police can't find you here."

The color drained from Maven's face. "He's right, Ian. Ye must leave now."

Parker scooped up Ian's hat and coat, pressed them into Ian's hands, and shoved him to the door. "I have a carriage waiting around the corner."

"Wait…Maven—"

"Goodbye, Ian," she said firmly and closed the door on him.

Parker hustled Ian down the street to the closed carriage. To avoid notice, he instructed the driver to drive slowly through the neighborhood, and for several blocks, they rode in tense silence.

"How did ye know I was there?" asked Ian.

Parker continued to stare out the window. "Eleanor suggested you might be there."

"Eleanor! How the devil…"

"She's not a stupid woman, Ian. I should think you could have some regard for her feelings. Can't you see how hard she's trying...oh, what's the use. I hope you have sense enough to wait until this all blows over before filing for a divorce."

"'Tis not the way ye think."

Ian closed his eyes to quell the dull ache behind them. God, what a mess he had made of everything. He tried to sort things out and found himself tightly bound by Maven's words. Now he was suspected of murdering Jeffries. Once again, all the familiar moorings had been severed, and he was cast adrift without safe harbor...without Maven.

CHAPTER 53

Police Chief Chester Tenley hurried to the mansion on Grandview Place. When first informed of Franklin Jeffries' murder, Tenley saw a window of opportunity. Here was his chance to prove that he wasn't the political flunky his predecessors were, but a man of integrity, merit and sound police practices. Upon learning that the prime suspect was Ian Douglas, however, he had experienced a few misgivings. On one level, Tenley figured that he owed his job to Ian. Since becoming mayor, Ian had successfully challenged the political wind and broken the machine, giving Tenley the chance he had been waiting for to advance his cause. But Tenley was not one to let loyalty or sentimentality cloud the issue for long, particularly when the possibility existed for him to make a name for himself. This case was going to attract national attention, and Tenley was determined to get his share of it. The public outcry over lack of action during the mill riots and after Tommy O'Brien's death had forced his predecessor to resign. He would not make the same mistake. Tenley was determined that Ian Douglas' wealth, power, and connections would buy the mayor no favors.

The Douglas housekeeper opened the door to him and showed him into the parlor. Tenley was properly awe-struck in spite of himself. Though he secretly dreamed of being in the ranks of the elite one day, he dutifully reminded himself to be critical of their excesses, their privileges and eccentricities. He surveyed the attractive parlor, struggling to dismiss the richness of the room—indeed the grandness of the entire Douglas mansion—with an indifferent eye.

At that moment, Eleanor swept into the room, and he jumped to his feet like a schoolboy caught in a misdeed. A bewitching smile played upon her lovely face, and with measured innocence, eyes the color of a clear, summer sky fixed upon Rossburg's newly elected police chief.

An avowed bachelor, Tenley, nevertheless, was one in the legion of men who had always admired Eleanor Douglas from afar. At arm's length, she was even more beautiful. He had heard the rumors of Ian's affair with a seamstress. What on earth could the man be thinking? he wondered as he continued to gaze at Eleanor.

"Chief Tenley...Chief Tenley, how may I help you?" she asked in a soft, breathy voice.

It was a moment before Tenley realized that she was speaking to him, and he struggled to pull himself together. At the sight of her, all thought seemed to have fled his mind.

He cleared his throat. "Ah, Mrs. Douglas, I'm sorry for the lateness of the hour, but I...that is..."

"Chief Tenley, I am happy to have you visit whatever the hour," she said warmly.

She glided across the room and extended a small, soft hand. It lay in his huge paw like a captured butterfly that he was reluctant to release.

"Thank you, madam, but I have come to see your husband. "

Eleanor gently disengaged her hand from his. "I'm afraid Mr. Douglas isn't at home, sir. However, I do expect him shortly. Perhaps you will join me for tea?"

The chief nodded, intoxicated by the light scent of her perfume as she guided him to a chair. He watched her every move as she gracefully seated herself on the sofa opposite him. He cleared his throat again and, with a beefy hand, absently pulled on the over-large mustache that was reminiscent of another era. Though he might not be the first to adopt it, be it fashion or idea, once embraced, Tenley was slower yet to discard it.

"Mrs. Douglas, do you know where your husband might be now?" he asked, more in command of himself.

"Why, yes. He is at Mrs. O'Brien's house, I do believe," she said, smoothing her skirts and smiling demurely. "Excuse me while I ring for tea."

Tenley blinked at her naiveté or stupidity, he was undecided which. This case was falling together easier than he had dared to hope. "Mrs. Douglas, I don't wish to distress you, but I am here on a very serious matter."

"Oh…I cannot imagine anything that could be that serious."

After several false starts, Tenley launched into an account of the murder of Franklin Jeffries, of the rumored affair between Ian and Maven, and of Jeffries' threat to ruin Ian with the information. It was with a tweak of conscience that he disclosed the more intimate details to one of such a delicate nature, but he hoped that she might be shocked or angered into letting something slip that would nail down his case even tighter.

Eleanor was very much aware of the whole mess. Parker Stanton had blurted out the news of the murder when he had come tearing into the house looking for Ian earlier. She had quickly deduced the serious ramifications it held for Ian. Now Eleanor turned eyes wide with surprise and shock upon the chief and expressed her great hurt and disappointment that a man of his intellect could possibly give credence to such lies or suspect her husband of such perfidious acts.

A shiver of apprehension ran through Tenley, and perspiration trickled down between his shoulder blades. He suddenly realized that in his determination not to repeat the mistakes of his predecessor, he might have acted a bit prematurely. What if Ian wasn't the murderer? If Tenley were to arrest him, and he was innocent…Ian was a powerful man. He could sue him and the whole damn city for false arrest. Add to that the fact he had just told the mayor's wife that her husband might be having an affair. Tenley groaned inwardly. His tenure as Chief of Police of Rossburg could be very short, indeed.

The housekeeper entered with the tea service and set it on the table. At that moment, Ian stormed into the parlor and was stopped dead in his tracks. Parker, right on his heels, pulled up short behind him. Before their eyes sat the beautiful Eleanor doing what she did best—entertaining. It was her guest that evoked trepidation in their hearts.

"Ian...Mr. Parker. How nice. I am about to pour tea. Come join us. I was just telling Chief Tenley that you were most likely at the O'Brien house," she drawled sweetly.

Parker's jaw dropped, and Ian paled.

"That right, Mayor Douglas?" The police chief eyed Ian suspiciously.

Eleanor smoothly intercepted her stunned husband. "Of course it is. Mr. and Mrs. O'Brien and my husband were childhood friends. Aside from that, Mr. O'Brien was a very valued employee. Mrs. O'Brien is my dressmaker. My husband would never think of abandoning the family in such a deeply distressing time. In fact, I had insisted that he go to see if there was anything we could do to help the family."

Eleanor deftly poured tea in china as fragile as egg shells and served the burly policeman. He swallowed nervously, and she smiled her very perfect smile, pretending to be unaware of his discomfort but endeavoring very hard to add to it.

"You are an honorable man, sir. Would you abandon such a long friendship in time of need?" she asked serving Parker without missing a beat. "I think not, sir."

The chief blushed as the sparkling, blue eyes looked deeply into his. "Ah, yes, well, of course not," he stammered. "But that's beside the point."

Ian accepted a cup from her small, white hands and set it aside without touching the tea. He opened his mouth to speak, but Parker gave him a quick jab in the ribs and circumspectly maneuvered him to the perimeter of the room. Parker ignored the bewildered look Ian shot him and relaxed against the marble mantelpiece. An appreciative grin slid across his face. This was Eleanor's scene, and she was carrying it off beautifully.

"So you see, Chief Tenley," continued Eleanor in a low, honeyed voice with just the right amount of righteous indignation, "the very idea of an affair between Mrs. O'Brien and my husband is absolutely ridiculous. I have every confidence in your expertise and intelligence that you will consider the source and recognize the rumor for what it is, the dirty work of an avowed enemy of my husband."

If Ian was speechless before, he was now totally dumbstruck. She glanced over at him and her smile was sweet, her eyes devoid of the usual sharp recrimination. There was a radiance about her that jogged his memory back to that day in the park when he had first seen her. Every article of her dress, from the rose bedecked hat to the pink, high top shoes was still vivid in his mind. He felt the old familiar aching in his soul. Maven was right. His heart was with Eleanor.

Chief Tenley nodded his head, his attention riveted on the lovely lady before him. "Yes, Mrs. Douglas, I can see now how a rumor of this sort could be groundless. Franklin Jeffries was known to be a malicious man. But we can't ignore the fact that Mr. Jeffries' plan to launch such an attack on Mayor Douglas' reputation does gives the Mayor motive enough. And your husband did raise fists against the man earlier this evening."

Parker grinned as he lifted the cup of tea to his lips. Apparently, it did not occur to the Police Chief to direct his attention and inquiry to the suspect. Indeed, Ian might as well have not been in the room.

"Do you have any proof that links my husband to Mr. Jeffries's murder?" Eleanor pressed him.

Tenley shifted uncomfortably on the dainty parlor chair. "Well…ah…no. It is all circumstantial at this point."

Eleanor sighed, her voice assuming a somber tone of reasoning. "Chief Tenley, I can assure you that if I thought for one minute that my husband could be capable of the acts of which you speak, I would not stand so staunchly beside him. I do have my honor, my pride, and my child to consider."

Tenley looked down at the floor. He had the feeling that he had lost control of the situation.

"Chief Tenley," continued Eleanor smoothly, "if my defense of my husband is not reason enough to convince you he is innocent, I ask you to consider the crisis you would throw this city into if you wrongly arrest its mayor. Franklin Jeffries had many enemies. I think it would be to your best *personal* interest to investigate further."

The cup rattled on its saucer, and Tenley hastily deposited them on the tea table in front of him. He heard the threat very clearly. He feared he might be on shaky ground before; he knew it now. She was not the naive woman he had at first taken her to be.

He cleared his throat and stood up. "Yes, I think further investigation is warranted in this case. Thank you for your time and hospitality, Mrs. Douglas." He turned to Ian as though suddenly remembering he was present. "I'll need a statement from you tonight...preferably at the station."

Chief Tenley quickly exited the Douglas mansion and was instantly besieged by reporters. He groaned inwardly. He had forgotten he had announced his intentions to arrest Mayor Ian Douglas for the murder of Franklin Jeffries. To the clamoring reporters he gruffly stated that no arrest had been made at this time. He guardedly explained that although Mayor Douglas may have been the last person to see Franklin Jeffries alive and even though fisticuffs had been employed, other evidence suggested further investigation was in order.

"What other evidence, Chief?" questioned one reporter.

"I am not prepared to say at this time. Mr. Jeffries had made many enemies in business. And should Mayor Douglas be wrongly accused, the government of the city could be plunged into crisis."

Standing inside the foyer, Parker and Ian struggled to contain their laughter.

"What's next, Parker?"

Stanton turned to Ian, immediately sobering. "Now you thank your wife for the best damned performance of her life—and yours. If it weren't for her, you would be in jail now on a murder charge. I'll accompany you to the station to give a statement." He inclined his head toward the reporters outside. "Hopefully, those vultures will leave with the Chief. I'll wait for you in the kitchen."

Ian stood alone in the foyer for several minutes. He ran a hand wearily across his face, feeling very worn by life. Slowly, he walked into the parlor. He had no idea what to say to his wife. In the past, much of their conversation had been fueled by anger and cynicism, fanned by feelings of resentment and betrayal. Eleanor stood regally in the center of the room, and he realized with sudden clarity that he didn't really know this woman at all.

The unfamiliar words caught in his throat. "Thank ye, Eleanor. Thank ye for yer defense. I must confess it was a bit unexpected."

"We've spent a lifetime resenting each other, Ian. It takes a lot of energy, and I don't have it anymore."

"Does this mean ye believe in my innocence?"

"I know you to be a hard and, at times, ruthless man, but you are no murderer. And I owe it to Mary Katherine. I haven't been much of a mother. She needs her father."

"I've hurt ye much, haven't I?"

"We've hurt each other."

"Has our life together been so terrible for ye?"

Eleanor thought long on the question. All her life she had been accustomed to taking or, as she had justified it, receiving. Ian was the first person in her life who refused to give unconditionally. She thought he hadn't understood the ways of her class and had scorned his actions as barbaric and ignorant. Now she suspected it was she who had been all wrong.

She took a deep breath and blinked back tears. "I think our life together might have been quite lovely had we allowed it to be." She looked up at him with a tremulous smile. "I believe Mr. Stanton is waiting for you."

"Eleanor…"

"Please go. I would like be alone for awhile." She turned away from him.

So much hurt, so much pain. Ian wanted to take her in his arms, but the old fear of rejection still plagued him. Quietly, he left the room in search of Parker.

Investigation over the next few weeks turned up no new evidence, and the finger of guilt crept ever closer to Ian. The sly insinuations that continued to appear in the newspapers were tempered only by Eleanor's striking and dignified defense of her husband. The notoriety involving such prominent figures caught the fascination of neighboring communities and cities from as far away as Philadelphia, New York, and Chicago. Each day saw an influx of new reporters. Tension was at its height when the district attorney forced an indictment of the mayor.

CHAPTER 54

Maven jammed the bolt of cloth back on the shelf. It was obvious that her customer had been more interested in gleaning information than in selecting material for a dress, and, with uncharacteristic rudeness, Maven suggested that the woman consider the selection at the departmental store instead. She was the owner of the shop. She could do that now, and it gave her a large measure of satisfaction. This was the one place where she still had some control.

This was not an isolated incident. Ever since the story had broken, there had been a steady stream of curiosity seekers trooping to her shop to see Mayor Douglas' mistress and hoping to hear some juicy tidbit. The dress shop had become well known, with her name now practically a household word.

Featured almost daily in the papers, her relationship with Ian was maligned, pondered over, examined and exaggerated, the truth blithely glossed over for the most part. Her husband had been dead for six months now, but the public's insatiable desire for sensationalism had allowed her no time to mourn.

The side door to the alley opened and closed. Maven hastily wiped away tears as Patrick entered the shop loaded down with a delivery of cloth. Nearly seven, he was tall, sturdy for his age, a handsome boy with blue-green eyes and thick, reddish-blond hair.

"Where do you want these bolts, Mum?" he asked.

Maven pointed to the empty shelf on the far wall. "Over there."

Her eyes welled with tears again. She wondered if her heart could possibly break anymore. Tommy's death had been hard enough for her son to deal with, but the ugly storm swirling around them was more than he could handle. From an outgoing, friendly little boy, he had turned into a resentful, angry and confused youngster, his childhood robbed of its innocence. Fiercely protective of his mother, he blamed Ian, the only other man he had admired as much as his father, for his mother's public humiliation.

He turned, catching her off guard and his features settled into a dark scowl. "You've been crying again."

Maven forced a smile. "Of course not. Did ye not learn anythin', Patrick O'Brien? An Irishman never cries. We're a tough lot, we are."

She reached out a hand to tousle his hair, but he sidestepped her. Maven's smile faded. The suffering was plain in his eyes. He had never been very good at masking his feelings.

"It'll all be over soon, Patrick, and the truth will come out," she said softly.

The boy stared solemnly into her eyes. "Aye, but which truth."

Maven squared her shoulders, drawing herself up to the challenge. "The truth that says Ian Douglas is no murderer and nothin' less than an honorable man, well deservin' of yer trust and admiration, Patrick."

In the face of such firm conviction, her son wavered, wanting desperately to believe her.

The bell tinkled as the door opened, and Maven turned to greet what was bound to be yet another curiosity seeker. She stiffened and her chin rose a defensive notch as Eleanor stepped into the shop.

"May I help ye, Mrs. Douglas?" she asked with cordial reserve.

Eleanor opened her mouth to speak, then drew in a sharp breath as her attention was drawn to the boy. The resemblance to his mother was unquestionable, but, at this moment, with his brow creased in question and eyes narrowed in wary suspicion, Patrick was very much his father's son.

Maven's own breath caught in her chest as she saw it, too. "Patrick, yer grandmum be waitin' for those supplies." She spoke harshly, her tone drawing a quizzical look from him. "Ye'd best be goin'," she said more quietly, curbing the desperation welling up inside her.

Patrick hesitated, looking from Eleanor's stricken face to Maven's ashen features, reluctant to leave his mother. The presence of Mrs. Douglas had obviously upset her.

"Off with ye, lad," said Maven.

The firmness of her tone and steady gaze of her eye finally prodded him to action. Patrick grabbed up the parcels she had prepared and walked out.

An unnatural stillness hung over the room. The two women remained motionless, frozen in a difficult situation both could no longer deny. Eleanor's careful composure was dangerously close to dissolving, but she was the first to speak.

"I guessed that he was Ian's son when I saw him at the lawn party three years ago. I didn't want to believe it, but..." She shrugged, her smile sad and resigned. "A woman knows these things, doesn't she? I take it that Ian doesn't know."

Maven shook her head.

"He's bound to suspect sooner or later. Why haven't you told him?"

"Ian doesn't need to know. My husband was my son's father in every way that was important. Tommy was a good and honorable man, and Patrick loved him very much. I'll not have that destroyed. He has lost so much already. Is there somethin' ye be wantin', Mrs. Douglas?"

"I've come to tell you that the police have found Franklin Jeffries' killer. It was that man, Charlie Pittman, who had instigated the strike. Evidently, Franklin had hired him to disrupt the mills and neglected to pay the man his due. Pittman followed Ian to Franklin's home that night. When Ian left, he sneaked in. He threatened to expose Franklin's part in the strike if he didn't get the money that Franklin owed him plus a good deal more. Franklin drew a gun on the man. There was a struggle, and the gun went off."

Maven gave a sigh of relief. "Then 'tis done?"

"Yes, Ian has been exonerated of all blame."

"How did the police find out about this man Pittman?"

"He got drunk and bragged to some woman with whom he had spent the night about what he had done. She went to the police. It seems that she is an admirer of Ian," Eleanor added dryly. "I've also come to tell you that you win, Mrs. O'Brien."

"Win?"

"I'm giving Ian a divorce. I know he will be happier with you. God knows we…well, never mind. Maybe now you can tell him about his son."

Maven looked up at the ceiling, willing back tears. She had had this conversation before, and it didn't get any less painful.

"Ye're wrong about Ian and me, Mrs. Douglas."

"Please don't deny it. Grant me that I'm not a stupid woman. I've tried to tell myself that it didn't matter…" Eleanor's own eyes filled with tears, but she attempted a half-hearted smile. "I bear you no ill feelings, Mrs. O'Brien. I suppose I deserve no better than I got. I'm just not very good at being second best." With such an admission of defeat, Eleanor's defenses completely crumbled.

Maven's heart softened. They both had suffered. "'Tis true," she said, "I've loved Ian since we were children. 'Twas always the four of us…Tommy, Ian, Katherine, and me." She gave a soft, wistful laugh. "We called ourselves the Pine Street Warriors. And we vowed always to be there for one another. Then Katherine died. Tommy and I helped Ian bury his sister, his mother, and his father in less than a year's time. He had a terrible hurt inside of him, then. I was the only one who could bring him any measure of comfort. I thought he had come to love me the way I loved him, but I was mistaken. He married ye."

"We both know the reason why," said Eleanor with a bitter laugh.

"I do na believe ye do. I was with Ian the first time he saw ye that day in the park. 'Twas the Independence Day celebration. I'll ne'er forget the look on his face. He could na take his eyes off ye. I think I knew then that he loved ye, but I chose to fool meself for a very long while."

Eleanor looked at Maven in confusion. "You must be mistaken. I've seen him look at you the way I wished he would look at me."

"There are different kinds of love, Mrs. Douglas. Yes, Ian loves me. We shared a childhood and experiences that will forever be a part of our lives, but he does not love me in the way that he loves ye. 'Tis yer love and yer acceptance he needs and wants most. Ian is a proud man. He has proven himself to everyone but himself. To do that, he needs ye."

"He never told me."

"Perhaps if ye had shown him something more than contempt. Did ye ever tell him how much ye needed him or wanted him or loved him?"

Startled, Eleanor drew back from the woman whom she had regarded as her rival all these years. "I…well…no. I thought he had married me just for spite and to humiliate me. I couldn't tell him those things."

"Ye do love him, do ye na?"

Eleanor skirted the question. "I-I don't know. I'm not sure I know what that means. I have certain feelings for him…but there has been so much hurt, so much anger between us." Her blue eyes teared over. "I think it is too late for love."

"'Tis ne'er too late for love if it is there to begin with. Go home, Mrs. Douglas. If ye meet Ian halfway, I think ye will find the life ye both want."

"Thank you, Mrs. O'Brien. I…I'm very sorry."

"For what?"

"I have misjudged you. I know how difficult this must be for you."

"We've misjudged each other, Mrs. Douglas."

The two women looked at each other and smiled. In that moment, there was a new understanding between them. They would never be friends, but they would be allies. They would share a love for the same man and a secret that would bind them together for the rest of their lives.

CHAPTER 55

Ian arrived home, gray with exhaustion. All charges against him had been dropped. He was free now to get on with his life, but the ordeal had taken its toll.

He knew he should have taken care of that bastard Pittman when he had had the chance and saved everybody a lot of trouble. He couldn't say he was sorry about Jeffries, but he hated what all the publicity had done to Eleanor and Maven...and to Patrick.

Yes, he was free to resume his life, but what life? He walked into the drawing room and poured himself a drink, pausing to stare up at the portrait that always so haunted him. This time, gentle, blue eyes gazed down on him with no hint of mockery upon the soft, pink lips. Or was it wishful thinking...his imagination working overtime again? She had stood by him throughout this mess, and it was a different Eleanor he was seeing, a mature Eleanor of unexpected strength, charm, mastery, and intelligence.

The knot in his stomach gave a hard twist as Parker's harsh criticism and Maven's hard words rained down upon him. He downed the drink and strode into the foyer, eager to escape his jury of peers. He knew they were right.

A grandfather clock boomed the hour, bouncing echoes off the ten-foot-high ceiling. In its wake, a suffocating quiet seeped through the house, a quiet without definition. To Ian, it seemed a reflection of his life. He plodded wearily up the stairs and down the hall. As he passed Eleanor's room, he noticed that the door was ajar. He pushed it open. She wasn't there, and an uneasy feeling beset him. The house seemed empty...emptier than it should be.

The maid appeared from the dressing room with an armload of towels, stopping short at the sight of Ian.

"Mr. Douglas, I did na know ye was home," she said.

Ian noticed her uneasiness, and alarm now gnawed at him.

"Where is Mrs. Douglas?"

"Madam is gone, sir," the maid said in a soft, hesitant voice. She took an envelope from her pocket. "She left this for ye. I was about to put it in yer room."

Ian ripped open the envelope and read the note, the knot twisting ever tighter in his stomach. He hadn't finished it before he tore out of the room, ran down the stairs, and out of the house.

"Henry!" he shouted, racing into the barn. "Hook up the carriage, and be quick about it!"

"Yes, sir."

The groom pulled the harness off the wall and began the task of hooking up the carriage, but Ian, impatient to be off, stepped in to finish the job.

"Henry, did ye take Mrs. Douglas to the railway station?"

"No, sir. She asked me to drop her in town. She said she had some business to see to first. Said for me to drop off her trunks, and she'd take a cab to the station."

"Did she say which train she was takin'?"

Henry scratched his head and thought for a moment. "I believe she was taking the 2:10 to Philadelphia. Said something about needing to learn how to be a mother."

Ian jumped in the carriage and grabbed the reins from him. Traffic was heavy in town and, in frustration, he abandoned the conveyance a block from the station and ran the remaining distance. He heard the train whistle blow and pushed his way to the platform. His heart dropped when he saw that the train had pulled away and was a half-mile down the track.

* * * * * * * *

Parker looked up in surprise as Ian stumbled through the front door of his office. "What happened to you!" he exclaimed. "You look like hell."

Ian fell heavily onto a chair, the life knocked out of him. "Eleanor left me, Parker. I went after her, but the train had already departed the station. She left a note saying ye were drawin' up the divorce papers. I need to know where she's stayin.'"

Parker replaced the file and closed the file drawer. "Why?"

"Ye were right. I've been a fool. I can nae let her walk out of my life...not now."

Parker inclined his head toward the door to his inner office. "Why don't you tell her that yourself."

Ian turned. Eleanor stood in the doorway, and he nearly overturned the chair in his haste to reach her.

"Eleanor, thank God...they told me ye were on the train."

"It was my intention to leave, Ian..."

"Eleanor, I know I've hurt ye too many times, and I know I do nae deserve another chance, but I'm askin' ye to trust me with one." He hesitated, then cautiously took her hand. When she didn't cringe or pull away, he was encouraged. "I-I love ye," he said haltingly. He was amazed how easily the words came out. They felt right. They were right, and the rest flowed out of him. "I've loved ye since the first time I saw ye in the park. I still remember what ye were wearin' that day. I did nae marry ye for vengeance or position. That was my pride an' my anger talkin'. I want ye to...I need ye to be a part of my life. Nothin' that I have means anythin' without ye to share it. I know that now."

Eleanor's eyes shimmered with tears. "Oh, Ian, we both have much to make up for and so much to learn. It was so easy for us to misjudge, hurt, and condemn one another. I wonder if it's possible for us to learn how love each other."

"Wounds can heal, Eleanor, if we allow them to. I want us to try. I want us to begin anew." He looked searchingly into her eyes and held his breath.

After a moment's hesitation, she raised a hand to his cheek. "Yes, Ian, I want that, too."

He caught her hand and kissed it, then bent his head and pressed his mouth to hers in a gentle caress. Her lips quivered beneath his. Slowly, shyly, her arms went around his neck, and she hesitantly responded.

Parker smiled and tore the divorce papers in half.

* * * * * * * *

Maven locked the door of the shop and stepped out into a clear, cool spring evening, the smell of lilacs heavy in the air. She took a deep breath and smiled. After so many years of inner turmoil, she was finally at peace with herself. Her heart still ached, but it was no longer the soul-wrenching ache of a vulnerable youth. At twenty-seven, it would seem that she had come of age at last.

"Good evening, Mrs. O'Brien."

Maven turned. "Why good evenin' to ye, Mr. Stanton. What brings ye to this side of town?"

"I was hoping you would do me the honor of accompanying me to the Carleton House for supper," he said.

Maven tilted her head and considered him for a long moment, surprised by his presence and even more astonished by his invitation.

"Mr. Stanton, I've felt yer disapproval of me on more than one occasion. Why would ye want to invite me to supper?"

Parker chuckled. "Ian said you were a tough one. It comes to me, madam, that I have judged you unfairly. If you'll permit me the chance,

I should like to know you better, for I have come to realize that you are quite an admirable woman."

Maven's finely drawn brow shot up. The large green eyes glowed with intelligence and humor. "Do ye now. Well, Mr. Stanton, in truth I've been quite the foolish woman. As to yer kind invitation, I thank ye, but no. Good evenin' to ye, sir." Her refusal was blunt but polite.

Parker watched the tall, willowy figure stroll gracefully past the storefronts. She had not Eleanor's classic beauty, but she possessed a striking beauty of her own. He was very sorry that she had turned him down. It was in his mind to chase after her, but he understood that one didn't chase after a woman like Maven O'Brien.

Maven suddenly stopped at the end of the walk, and turned. "Mr. Stanton, would ye care to see me home?"

Parker smiled. He did indeed.

ABOUT THE AUTHOR

Alice Billman is a resident of Spring Hill, Florida and has taught creative writing for several years. She is a published, award-winning author of short stories and is currently working on a series of children's books.

Kathy Keller is a resident of Ormond Beach, Florida and a published author of two award-winning historical romances. She has a degree in journalism from The American University, Washington, D.C.

Both authors grew up in the Williamsport area.